PENGUIN BOOKS

Wish You Were Here

Wish You Were Here

CATHERINE ALLIOTT

PENGUIN BOOKS

PENGUIN BOOKS

UK | USA | Canada | Ireland | Australia
India | New Zealand | South Africa

Penguin Books is part of the Penguin Random House group of companies
whose addresses can be found at global.penguinrandomhouse.com.

First published by Michael Joseph 2015
Published in Penguin Books 2015

001

Copyright © Catherine Alliott, 2015

The moral right of the author has been asserted

Set in 12.55/14.86 pt Garamond MT Std
Typeset by Jouve (UK), Milton Keynes
Printed in Great Britain by Clays Ltd, Elcograf S.p.A.

A CIP catalogue record for this book is available from the British Library

ISBN: 978–1–405–95982–7

www.greenpenguin.co.uk

Penguin Random House is committed to a
sustainable future for our business, our readers
and our planet. This book is made from Forest
Stewardship Council® certified paper.

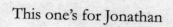
This one's for Jonathan

Chapter One

Somewhere over the English Channel travelling north, closer to the white cliffs than to Cherbourg and whilst cruising at an altitude of thirty thousand feet, a voice came over the tannoy. I'd heard this chap before, when he'd filled us in on our flying speed and the appalling weather in London, and he'd struck me then as being a cut above the usual easyJet Laconic. His clipped, slightly pre-war tones and well-modulated vowels had a reassuring ring to them. A good man to have in a crisis.

'Ladies and gentlemen, I wonder if I could have your attention for a moment, please. Is there by any chance a doctor on board? If so, would they be kind enough to make themselves known to a member of the cabin crew. Many thanks.'

I glanced up from *Country Living*, dragging myself away from the scatter cushions in faded Cabbages and Roses linen I fully intended to make but probably never would, to toss attractively around the Lloyd Loom chairs in the long grass of the orchard I would one day possess, complete with old-fashioned beehive and donkey. I turned to my husband. Raised enquiring eyebrows.

He pretended he'd neither heard the announcement nor sensed my eloquent brows: he certainly didn't look at them. He remained stolidly immobile, staring resolutely down at the Dan Brown he'd bought at Heathrow and had taken back and forth to Paris, but had yet to get beyond page twenty-seven. I pursed my lips, exhaled loudly and meaningfully through my nostrils and returned to my orchard.

Two minutes later, the clipped tones were back. Still calm, still measured, but just a little more insistent.

'Ladies and gentlemen, I'm sorry, but if there is a doctor or a nurse on board, we would be most grateful if they would come forward. We really do need some assistance.'

I nudged my husband. 'James.'

'Hm?'

His shoulders hunched in a telltale manner, chin disappearing right into his neck and his blue-and-white checked shirt.

'You heard.'

'They mean a *doctor* doctor,' he murmured uncomfortably. 'A GP, not a chiropodist.'

'Oh, don't be ridiculous, you're a foot surgeon! Go on.'

'There'll be someone else,' he muttered, pale-grey eyes glancing around nervously above his glasses, a trifle rattled I could tell.

'Well, obviously, there isn't, because they've asked twice. There could be someone dying. Just go.'

'You know I hate this sort of thing, Flora. There's bound to be someone with more general expertise, more –'

'I really think, young man,' said the elderly woman in the window seat beside him, a well-upholstered, imperious-looking matron who'd removed her spectacles to regard him pointedly and reprovingly over her tapestry, 'that if you do have medical experience, you should go.'

She made him sound like a conscientious objector.

'Right. Yes. Yes, of course. *All right*, Flora, you don't need to advertise me, thank you.'

But I was already on my feet in the aisle to let him out, gesticulating wildly to a stewardess. 'Here — over here. Make way, please.' This to the queue of people waiting patiently beside us for the loo. We were quite close to the front as it was. 'He's a doctor.'

'Make way?' James repeated incredulously under his breath, shooting me an appalled look as the entire front section of the plane turned to look at the tall, lean, sandy-haired, middle-aged man who'd unfolded himself with effort from his seat and was now shuffling forwards, past the queue to the bog, mumbling apologies and looking, in his creased chinos and rumpled holiday shirt, more like a harassed librarian than a paramedic in a hurry.

I sat back down again, feeling rather important, though I didn't really sit: instead I perched on the arm of my aisle seat to get a better view. Luckily, a steward had redirected the queue to the loo at the back and I could now see that a little crowd of uniformed cabin crew had gathered around a young girl of about nine who was sitting on the floor, clearly in distress. In even more distress was the very beautiful woman in tight white jeans and a floral shirt standing over her, her hands over her mouth. She was pencil thin with a luxuriant mane of blonde hair, and her heavily accented voice rose in anguish.

'Oh, *mon dieu*, I can't do it again — I can't!'

I saw James approach and address her and she gabbled back gratefully in French, clutching his arm. I'm reasonably fluent, but at that range I couldn't make it out, but then she switched back to English, saying, 'And I have only one left – please – help!'

She thrust something into my husband's hand, at which point I was tapped on the shoulder from behind.

'Excuse me, madam, would you mind taking your seat? We're experiencing a spot of turbulence.'

The glossy, lipsticked smile on the expertly made-up face of the stewardess meant business. The plane was indeed bumping around a bit. Reluctantly, I lowered my bottom, which obviously meant I missed the crucial moment, because when I craned my neck around the stewardess's ample behind as she passed, the crowd at the front were on the floor and James was crouching with his back to me, clearly administering something. They'd tried to move the girl to a more secluded position and shield her with bodies, but a plane doesn't yield much privacy. The blonde, clearly the mother, was the only one standing now, pushing frantic hands through her hair, clutching her mouth, unable to watch, but unable to turn away. My heart lurched for her. I remembered the time when Amelia shut her finger in the door and almost sliced the top off and I'd run away as James held it in place with a pack of frozen peas, and also when Tara coughed up blood in the sitting room and I'd raced upstairs, screaming for her father. You knew you had to help, but you loved them so much you couldn't bear to watch. There was a muffled collective murmuring from the crew and then, without looking indecently ghoulish, I really couldn't see any more, as the mother had dared to crouch down, obscuring James as well.

I went back to my magazine. An interview with a woman

from Colefax and Fowler informed me that, on the paint-effects front, Elephant's Breath was all over. Everyone was coming into her Brooke Street showroom asking for chintzes and borders now. Borders. Blimey. I had rolls of the stuff in the attic. Did Laura Ashley circa 1980 count? Probably not. My mind wasn't really on it, though, and I narrowed my eyes over my reading glasses. James had straightened up and was answering a series of quick-fire questions from the mother, whose relief was palpable, even though strain still showed in her eyes. My husband, typically, made light of it, brushing away what were clearly effusive thanks, and came back down the aisle, perhaps less hunched and beleaguered than when he'd gone up it, as quite a few passengers now regarded him with interest. I got up quickly to let him slide in and sit down. The ordeal was over and relief was on his face.

'Well?' I asked. The matron beside him was also agog, needlework abandoned in her lap.

'Nut allergy,' he reported. 'She'd taken a crisp from the girl beside her and it must have been cooked in peanut oil. The mother realized what had happened but had never had to administer the EpiPen before, and she cocked it up the first time. She had a spare one but was too scared to do it in case she got it wrong again. The stewardess was about to have a stab.'

'So you did it?'

He nodded. Picked up Dan Brown.

'Did it go all right?'

'Seemed to. She's not dead.'

'Oh, James, well done you!'

'Flora, I have given the odd injection.'

'Yes, but still.'

'I say, well done, young man,' purred his beady-eyed neighbour approvingly. 'I couldn't help overhearing. I gather you're a surgeon?'

'Consultant surgeon,' I told her proudly.

'Ingrowing toenails, mostly,' said James, shifting uncomfortably in his seat. 'The odd stubborn verruca.'

'Nonsense, he trained as an orthopaedic. He's done hips, knees, everything, but he gets a lot of referrals from chiropodists these days, when it's out of their sphere of expertise.' I turned to James. 'Will she be all right? The little girl?'

'She'll be fine. It just takes a few moments to kick in.'

'Anaphylactic shock,' I explained to my new friend across his lap. Like most doctors' wives I considered myself to be highly qualified, a little knowledge often being a dangerous thing.

'Ah,' she agreed sagely, regarding James with enormous respect now, her pale, rheumy eyes wide. 'Well, that's extremely serious, isn't it? I say, you saved her life.'

James grunted modestly but didn't raise his head from his book. His cheeks were slightly flushed, though, and I was pleased. Morale could not be said to be stratospheric in the Murray-Brown household at the moment, what with NHS cuts and his private practice dwindling. When he'd first decided to specialize, years ago, he'd chosen sports injuries, having been an avid cricketer in his youth, but that had become a very crowded field. He'd seen younger, more ambitious men overtake him, so he'd concentrated on cosmetic foot surgery instead. A mistake in retrospect, for whilst in a recession people would still pay to have a crucial knee operation, they might decide to live with their unsightly bunions and just buy wider shoes. He'd even joked with the children about getting a van, like Amelia's boyfriend, who was a DJ, adding wheels to his trade, morphing into a mobile chiropodist, perhaps with a little butterfly logo on the side. 'A website, too!' Amelia had laughed, 'I'll design it for you.' But I'd sensed a ghastly seriousness beneath his banter. He spent too much time in what we loosely called 'the office' at the top of our house in Clapham, aka the spare room, pretending to write articles for the *Lancet* but in fact doing the *Telegraph* crossword in record time, then rolling up the paper and waging war on the wasp nest outside the window. Not really what he'd spent seven years training at St Thomas's for. This then, whilst not the Nobel Prize for Medicine, was a morale boost.

I peered down the aisle. I could see the young mother standing at the front of the plane now, facing the passengers, her face a picture of relief, casting about, searching for him. I gave her a broad smile and pointed over my head extravagantly.

'He's here!' I mouthed.

She'd swept down the aisle in moments. Leaned right over me into James's lap, blonde hair flowing. 'Oh, I want to thank you so very much,' she breathed gustily in broken English. 'You saved my daughter's life.'

'No no,' muttered James uncomfortably, but going quite pink nevertheless. He tried to get to his feet, his manners, even on an aircraft, impeccable.

'No, don't get up,' she insisted, fluttering her pretty, bejewelled hands. 'I will see you later. I just wanted to say how grateful I am, how grateful we all are. My Agathe — you saved her!'

'Well, I administered an EpiPen, but not at all, not at all,' James murmured, gazing and blinking a bit. She really was astonishingly beautiful. I marvelled at the yards of silky hair which hung over me, the tiny frame, the vast bust, the enormous blue eyes. Was she a film star, I wondered? She looked vaguely familiar. A French one, perhaps – well, obviously a French one – in one of those civilizing arty movies I went to with Lizzie occasionally at the Curzon when James was watching *The Bourne Identity* for the umpteenth time. I didn't think this was the moment to ask and watched as her tiny, white-denimed bottom undulated back to its seat.

Once off the plane at Stanstead, on the way to Baggage Reclaim, I saw a father point James out to his son, perhaps as someone to emulate in later life: where all his GCSE biology studies could lead, and the reason he, the father, enforced the homework. The boy stared openly as he passed, as did his younger sister, and I surreptitiously got my lippy out of my handbag and gave a quick slick in case anyone should want his autograph. By the time we got to the carousel, however, most people seemed intent on getting out of the place and had forgotten the heroics. Including the mother and child, who hadn't yet materialized, I realized, glancing around. Perhaps they were hand luggage only? Had swept on through already? Hard to imagine what they were doing on easyJet at all. But then, just as James returned from the fray with our battered old suitcase, I saw them enter the baggage hall. The little girl seemed fine now and was skipping along in front, holding a man's hand. He couldn't be the father, I thought; too thuggish and thickset. Indeed, there seemed to be a couple of similar heavies in tow, whilst the mother strode along in their midst, in sunglasses. Were they staff? Certainly the small, dumpy woman carrying all the Louis Vuitton hand luggage must surely be an employee, and the swarthy man with the cap couldn't be the husband either.

The blonde seemed about to sweep on through, but then, just as she neared the exit she spotted us. She whipped off her sunglasses and came striding across, beaming.

'*Alors*, there you are! *Regard* – look at my *petite* Agathe. As right as what you English bizarrely call rain, and all thanks to you, *monsieur*. My name is Camille de Bouvoir and I am eternally grateful.'

James took her tanned, extended hand. 'James Murray-Brown.'

'Orthopaedic surgeon,' I purred. 'And I'm his wife, Flora.'

She briefly touched the fingers of the hand I'd enthusiastically offered but turned straight back to James.

'I knew you were a surgeon. I could tell by those hands. So sensitive, yet so capable.'

'Aren't they just?' I agreed, although no one seemed to be listening to me.

'And I would like to repay your skill and kindness.'

'Oh, there's really no need,' demurred James, embarrassed.

'May I take your email address? I somehow imagine you would be too modest to get in touch if I gave you mine.'

'He would,' I confirmed, scrabbling around in my bag for a pen and withdrawing a distressed tampon instead, but Madame de Bouvoir had already produced her iPhone. She handed it to me wordlessly and I tapped away dutifully, very much the secretary to the great man. Very much peripheral to proceedings.

9

'I will be contacting you,' she promised, pocketing it as I handed it back to her. 'And now, Agathe wants to say something.' She gently shepherded her daughter forward. '*Cherie?*' The child was as slim as a reed, with widely spaced almond eyes in a heart-shaped face. Although not yet on the cusp of puberty she was very much in the Lolita mould: destined for great beauty.

She took a deep breath. 'Thank you so very much, *monsieur*, for saving my life. I will be for ever grateful to you and thank you from the bottom of my 'eart.'

She'd clearly practised this small, foreign speech on the plane with a little help from her mother, and it was delivered charmingly. An elderly couple beside us turned to smile. James took the hand she offered, bowing his head slightly and smiling, for who could not be enchanted?

'*Mon plaisir*,' he told her.

Courtesies having been observed, Mme de Bouvoir then kissed James lightly on both cheeks three times. She briefly air-kissed me – only once, I noticed, as I lunged for the second – and then, as a socking great pile of Louis Vuitton suitcases were wheeled towards her by one of her chunky attendants, she sashayed out of the concourse ahead of the trolley, bestowing one last lovely smile and a flutter of her sparkling hand.

James and I gave her a moment to get through customs, where no doubt she'd be met by a man in a uniform, before we waddled out with our bags.

'Great. You know exactly what that will be, don't you?' muttered James.

'What?' I said, knowing already: even now regretting it.

'Some poncy restaurant we've been to a million times

already. We'll have to sit there pretending we never go any-where smart and endure a lengthy, excruciating meal, which we're force fed anyway on a regular basis.'

'Not necessarily,' I said, with a sinking feeling. I grabbed my old blue bag as it threatened to slide off the trolley.

'We're probably going there tonight!' he yelped.

I avoided looking at him, stopping instead to look in my handbag for my passport. James froze beside me.

'Dear God, I was joking. Please tell me we're not out tonight, Flora. I'm knackered.'

'We have to, James. I've got to get the review in by tomorrow.'

'You're not serious.'

'I am.'

'Jesus.'

'How else d'you think we're going to pay for that bloody holiday? Shit. Where's my passport?' I delved in my bag.

'I've got it.' He produced it from his breast pocket. 'Where are we going?'

'Somewhere in Soho, I think. Oh yes, Fellino's. I have a feeling Gordon Ramsay's trying to take it over and he's resisting.'

'Hasn't he got enough bloody restaurants? Have you texted Amelia?'

'Yes, and she's outside whingeing about us being late. Apparently, we should have let her know the plane was ten minutes delayed. As if I haven't sat for enough hours in that wretched car park waiting for her.'

'Can't you ask Maria to put it in next week's edition? Say you'll go tomorrow?'

'I've tried, but apparently Colin's already let her down.

11

He was supposed to do the new Marco Pierre but he's got a sore throat, so someone's got to do one.'

'Oh great, so Colin's got his excuse in first, as usual.'

I ignored him. We were both very tired.

'You could google the menu on the web? Write the review from that? Say how delicious the tiddled-up turbot was?'

'Oh, good idea. Like I did at Le Caprice, only, unfortunately, the turbot was off that night, and the scallops, both of which I'd waxed lyrical about. I'd rather keep what remains of my job, if it's all the same to you.'

'But you know Fellino. Can't you ring him and ask what the special is? See what he recommends for tonight?'

'It's fine, I'll go on my own.'

'No, no, I'll come,' he grumbled. 'Blinking heck. Who goes out for dinner the night they get back from holiday?'

'We do, if we're going to go on holiday at all,' I said with a flash of venom. There was the briefest of pauses. James's voice, when it came, was light, but it had the timbre of metal.

'Ah yes, forgive me. For a moment there I thought I was the successful alpha male in this partnership. The high-earning surgeon with a career on a meteoric rise to the stars, providing for his family.'

Heroically, I held my tongue as, tight-lipped, we followed the other weary travellers down the corridor to the escalator. We climbed aboard wordlessly, passed through Passport Control, then trundled out through Nothing to Declare.

Chapter Two

We ran from the terminal building in the pouring rain, not an umbrella between us, the trolley skidding around in front of us on the wet pavement, heading for the drop-off zone, where two pounds secured ten minutes.

'There!' I shouted, pointing as I spotted Amelia in the battered old red Clio she shared with Tara. The trolley span out of control as we tried to escape the hail which lashed our faces and we lunged off at a tangent to retrieve it. The car, when we reached it, was vibrating to ear-splitting music whilst our daughter sat boot-faced within, smoking, engine running, exhaust fumes billowing.

'Where have you been?' she shrieked as I flung open the boot. 'I've been here ages, it's cost me ten quid already. I've had to go round five times!'

'Why didn't you park properly?' I asked breathlessly as James tossed the case in.

'Because I thought that would be even more expensive, and the car park's miles away, and it's raining, in case you hadn't noticed. Why didn't you text me to say it had been delayed?'

'Why didn't you track it, Amelia?' asked James. 'With all that expensive technological equipment at your fingertips that surely would have been the sensible option. "Hello, Mummy and Daddy, did you have a lovely time in Paris?"'

I slammed the boot shut, thinking of the countless times

I'd waited for her in Arrivals, excited as she came back from school trips, skiing holidays, her gap-year travels.

'And some bastard keeps moving me on when I'm literally a second or two over time. Quick, get in.' She was revving up now, glancing fearfully in her rear-view mirror as, sure enough, a uniformed jobsworth bore down. 'Dickhead,' she muttered, giving him the finger, but only once his back was turned.

Soaked to the skin, James and I eased ourselves gingerly into the hideous melee of crisp packets, water bottles, Styrofoam cups, empty beer cans, cigarette cartons, articles of clothing, sleeping bags, fancy-dress paraphernalia, make-up and even a pair of underpants that decorated her car. *Our* car, James would seethe, periodically. As I limbo-danced into the back, my husband in the front dared to turn the music down. Not off, but down.

'It's really cut into my allowance,' she told him grimly as she shifted into first. We pulled away with a lurch. 'And I got stuck in horrendous traffic on the way so, basically, it's cost me a fortune in petrol.'

'Well, it's lucky you got stuck, isn't it, since the plane was delayed,' remarked James. 'Otherwise, it would have cost you even more.'

'It's very kind of you, darling,' I said smoothly from behind, knowing which battles to pick. 'Everything OK at home?'

'Yes, except I had to buy way more food. You didn't leave nearly enough, so that's totally cleaned me out.'

'I left masses! A lasagne in the freezer, two pizzas, and the fridge was bursting with cold meat and salad. We've only been gone three days!'

'Tara had some friends round on Saturday night. They pretty much saw it off.'

'All of it?'

'Well, no, because, as I say, I bought some more. Spent about forty quid, I suppose,' she said wearily, as if exhausted by the responsibility of running a household. She raked a hand through her hair. 'But I'll tot it all up at home and add on the petrol. Let you know the damage. How was it, anyway?'

'Very refreshing, darling,' I said buoyantly, slapping on a smile, determined not to fight quite so soon.

'After all, water is refreshing,' James observed as the windscreen wipers swept away litres of the stuff.

'Oh, shit, you had this? All weekend, like we did?'

'Pretty much. There was a glimmer of hope on Saturday between eleven and twelve and we managed a quick canter through the Tuileries and a twirl round the Place de la Concorde but other than that, it was bars and restaurants.'

'Which you spend your life in,' she said, with a hint of genuine sympathy. 'That sucks.'

'Particularly since yet more sucking ensues tonight, with a visit to one of the West End's premier eateries. Would you like to accompany your mother, Amelia? Endure a slap-up meal?'

'No, thanks,' she said quickly. She was an old hand at these lengthy marathon events. 'Unless Toby and I can go?' she hazarded, for effect only, knowing I was vociferous on the subject of her and Toby the Troglodyte, as James called him, impersonating her father and me. I subjected this to the silence it deserved.

'Still,' she smiled, 'you kids had fun? Hotel not too scabby?'

'Not too scabby, darling.' I returned her grin in the rear-view mirror. Approaching sixty pounds now clinking assuredly into her pocket, she was prepared to be cheerful.

'And did it all come back to you? Paris?'

'Well, I was only eight when I left, but yes, it did. I saw my old school, went to Montmartre, where our apartment was, visited the café we had lunch in, which was still there, that kind of thing. Took a trip down memory lane.'

'Cool. You know what Granny said when I first found out you'd lived there? I said, "Gosh, Granny, you must know Paris really well," and she puffed away on her ciggie and said, "Not really, darling. I only ever saw the ceiling of the Hôtel de Crillon."'

She hooted with laughter as I grimaced. My mother's reminiscences about the wilder side of her youth were, in equal proportion, a source of fascination for her granddaughters and horror for me.

'Well, that's a fat lie, because Philippe bought us an apartment.'

'She was joking, Mother. Do pipe down.'

I breathed deeply. Counted to ten.

'She came round, by the way,' Amelia went on, swerving suddenly to avoid a cyclist. I clutched my handbag nervously. 'Granny, I mean. To check out Tara's new boyfriend. We agreed, obviously.'

'Obviously,' I said testily. 'But you forget, I've met him, too. And I think he's quite delightful.'

She smirked. 'Because he's going to Durham to do history. Did you spot the ironed creases in his chinos?'

16

'At least he's got chinos,' commented James, trying to retune the radio into the Test match. 'Unlike the Trog.'

'Ah, but the Trog's got soul, Dad. Try long wave, it's better for Radio 5.' She expertly switched it across for him. 'We were wondering when we were going on holiday, by the way. Is it still the first week in August?'

I stiffened. 'Who was wondering?'

'Well, me and Toby, obviously. I imagine it's OK if I bring him to Scotland? To Grandpa's?'

I tried frantically to catch James's eye in the rear-view mirror, but failed; he was still fiddling with the radio dial – a heroic feat on this white-knuckle ride. The Trog and the Brigadier, James's father? On his Highland estate? Plus James's two sisters?

'Yes, fine, darling,' said her father, who never saw any complication until it reared up and bonked him hard on the nose. 'The more the merrier.'

'Great. I'll tell him. We might bring Will and Jess along, too, they can come in the van. Oh, and they've got a dog, they found it in Streatham, but Grandpa won't mind.'

I shut my eyes and rested my head. This was so like my elder daughter. Spot a small gap and push home the advantage. Within a twinkling there'd be an army of drop-outs dripping around the glen, trailing long skirts, greasy hair, cigarette ash and stray dogs. Exhausting. *Quite* exhausting. And who was going to be cooking for all these people?

'Can we just pause a moment, please, Amelia? Talk about it when I've got over one holiday and got my head round the next? I've only just got off the plane!'

'Yeah, yeah, sure, we can pause,' she said in feigned astonishment, eyes widening in disingenuous wonder at me in the mirror as if I were completely overreacting. Unhinged even. 'I've mentioned it to Jess, obviously, but only, like, briefly. I'll tell them I'll let them know. When you've calmed down a bit.'

I clenched my teeth. What was the point in going away? In having a so-called 'mini-break' when it disappeared so quickly and assuredly down the plughole the moment I returned? I wasn't up to Amelia's strength of purpose, her sheer doggedness, I decided. She should be a shop steward, a trade union official. She campaigned for things and, once she'd got them, beaten her opponent, she popped up again like a mole with something else, waving it like a crusade flag. Had I spoiled her, I wondered? Indulged her? Yes, because all children of this generation were indulged, possibly because we'd had them later and had more money to spend on them. 'They're so lucky!' we mothers would shriek to one another in our designer kitchens over our glasses of Chardonnay. 'Our parents didn't even know which O levels we were taking they took so little interest, and we had to work in shops, Mars bar factories, weren't given bungee allowances!' But our parents had had us in their early twenties – or, in my mother's case, when she was just nineteen – so they were still young and involved in their own lives, not scrutinizing their children's. There was a lot to be said for being a young parent. Except that Tara, who was eighteen months younger than her sister, and therefore had an even older mother, disproved this theory. She was less . . . grasping. Less sharp-eyed. But then, life was easier for her. If you were pretty and clever, life tended to plop into your lap more, didn't it? There was less cause to be opportunistic.

As we neared home, lurching heave-makingly around the corners in our grid of Clapham streets, I wondered nervously if that purple thing I could see poking out of the back of Amelia's T-shirt was another tattoo. Or just a label? I leaned forward to peer, but she braked suddenly at a junction and I nosedived hard into her neck.

'Shit – Mum!' she squealed.

'Sorry, darling – sorry! Just wanted to – to see what speed you were doing.'

'Thirty, obviously, in a built-up area, and that really hurt. I've just had Toby's initials put there in Sanskrit.'

You had to admire her candour. Her carapace. No shame. No guilt. She was eighteen years old and she'd jolly well do as she liked, thank you very much. No doubt always would.

'Your father saved someone's life on the plane,' I said quickly, to change the subject. Needles full of purple dye piercing my darling daughter's neck, the back of which, as a baby, I'd cradled as I'd lowered her into the bathtub, or, later, divided two plaits between as she went off to school, loomed heart-wrenchingly to mind.

'Really? What – mouth to mouth?' She turned to her father.

'No, an EpiPen to the leg. Your mother's exaggerating, as usual. Well, if you're frittering away your allowance on a tattoo, I'm clearly giving you too much. You can foot the grocery bill *and* the petrol. Thank you, Amelia. We can walk to the kerb from here, in the words of Woody Allen.'

Amelia had stopped outside the house and was about to reverse into a space, but her father was already out, slamming the door and walking up the path to our front door, his back rigid.

'What's his problem?'

I sighed. 'He's old-fashioned enough to imagine you at some glittering ball in a few years' time, your hair piled on your head, a silk gown slipping off your shoulders, diamonds in your ears, Toby's initials trailing down your back.'

She gave it some thought. 'Yeah, sounds good. Hasn't hurt Angelina Jolie, has it?'

Angelina Jolie's looks and my daughter's were similar to the extent that they both had long, dark hair.

'No, it hasn't,' I muttered meekly.

'And anyway, Tobes paid, so I didn't use Dad's precious allowance.'

I was too weary to say that her boyfriend paying to have his mark branded on her neck for posterity would probably incur her father's wrath only further, and left the conversation where it was. It was done, and that was the end of it. Apart from a skin graft, of course. Hideously painful and expensive, but always possible and, naturally, where my mind had already fled. Come two in the morning, I'd be creeping downstairs in my dressing gown having not slept a wink, googling it. And ringing Clare in the morning. Clare's twenty-three-year-old son had recently had a dagger removed from inside his wrist before embarking on his new job at Goldman Sachs and, as a neat, cautionary tale Clare had made his fifteen-year-old brother watch from the gallery, to illustrate the lunacy of gap-year indiscretions.

And of course this was Amelia's gap year, she was

bound to spread her wings, make a few mistakes, even. But surely a gap had to be between something? Her A-level results from one of Berkshire's premier boarding schools had precluded university, but photography at art college had seemed a possibility, until Amelia had poured scorn, claiming that all art-school photography looked the same and she'd be better off doing it herself. She'd tossed her dark curls dismissively. 'I'd rather find my own voice, thank you.' I hadn't dared glance at James at this but, to my surprise, he'd jumped at it.

'Right, well, she can jolly well find her voice while she's working,' he'd said hotly as we'd got into bed later that night. 'She can get a job. A proper one. Get off the frigging pay roll.'

Knowing this would go down like a cup of cold sick, I'd suggested the gap year first, as a balm, unaware that Amelia considered it mandatory anyway. Like a polio vaccination.

'Well, of course I'm having a gap year,' she'd said scornfully when I'd offered it up to her magnanimously, beaming delightedly as I did so. 'Everyone does.'

'And then, your father thinks . . . a job?'

'Well, obviously I'll do something short term, everyone does that, too. To pay for my travels. In a shop, maybe. Or a bar.'

No. Long term. For ever, James was thinking. A career. Working from the bottom up, as an apprentice. Whereas I still harboured dreams of further education of some sort, because I didn't care if all her photos turned out like everyone else's, or even if she arranged flowers for three years, I just wanted her to meet someone other than Toby Sullivan, with his ponytail and his van with the mattress

21

inside and his decks – I'd learned not to call them turntables – which she wouldn't do working in a bar and living at home. This, though, I couldn't share with James, whose focus was to stop paying through the bloody nose for his bloody layabout children, not to steer their emotional lives. Well, except Tara, perhaps. Tara had embraced her A levels and was keen to be a vet, and I could see James being very willing to accommodate the expense of her ambition.

I sighed as I got out of the car and retrieved our case from the boot, lugging it up the path to the terraced house in a row of identical Victorian terraced houses. Identical lives, mostly, too. Stockbrokers and their wives, who'd once worked in advertising or publishing, bankers and doctors, hard-working professional people, many of whom I knew and who'd had children growing up with mine, all of whom were battling identical problems. Many far worse than the ones I had with Amelia. Some of their offspring sampled drugs on an epic scale: thank the Lord, Amelia was vociferous in her opposition to them, after a friend had died tragically in horrible circumstances at a festival the previous summer, reshaping my elder daughter's world for ever. I wasn't sure about the Trog, though, and when I'd asked Amelia she'd regarded me sternly and said everyone had to be their own person and what business was it of mine? Only that I cleared up her bedroom and, those funny little papers I found littering her carpet . . . were they really just for his roll-ups? And didn't he smell quite strange? Or was that joss sticks? I'd tried to buy some to remember what they smelled like, but the Indian woman in the gift shop on Lavender Hill had looked at me pity-ingly, saying there wasn't much call for them these days.

Heaving another great sigh up from the bottom of my recently purchased Parisian boots which, less than an hour ago, I'd been enjoying enormously but were now begin-ning to pinch, I trudged after Amelia to the front door, secretly admiring her trailing gypsy skirt scattered with tiny mirrors glinting amidst the embroidery, topped by a vintage matador jacket. If nothing else, Amelia had style. She turned to me on the step, twirling the car keys on her finger.

'Oh, just to give you the heads up, Granny's given every-thing the Swedish look. I said you wouldn't mind.'

I frowned. 'Granny's . . .' I crossed the threshold to the smell of fresh paint and the sound of James spluttering within. My heart lurched as I walked down the hall. I col-lided with him as he emerged from the sitting room with a face like thunder, pushing past me, hissing, *'Your bloody mother!'* before storming upstairs to his office at the top of the house. The attic door slammed hard.

'Mum . . . ?'

I rounded the corner in gypsy girl's wake to see my mother on her hands and knees, paintbrush in hand, at the far end of the knocked-through sitting room, newspaper thankfully covering the carpet. She was just putting the finishing touches to a heavy sideboard which sat opposite the dining table and which, historically, had been dark oak but was now a streaky shade of pale grey.

She sat back happily on her heels, popped the brush in some turps in a cup and beamed with pleasure. Then she pushed her blonde hair from her eyes, stretched out her slim brown arms and gave me some jazz hands. 'Ta-daa!' My mother is far more beautiful than I will ever be and, when animated, as she was now, could still dazzle.

'Good *God* . . .' I gaped. But not at her beauty.

'Surprise! Don't you love it, darling? You know how you said you hated all that heavy brown furniture? Well, look! The girls and I have transformed it! Given it all a makeover.'

'All . . . ?'

'*Regard!*'

She waved an armful of jangling bracelets to indicate yonder, through the kitchen to the garden, where, sure enough, under cover from the rain on the veranda stood a large chest of drawers, a tallboy, a knee-hole desk, the hall table, all now distressed – in every sense of the word – to a stripy pale grey, which, as far as the naked eye could tell, had been achieved simply by dragging a paintbrush full of white paint across them.

'The girls . . .' I faltered, staring.

'Oh yes, they helped. They were marvellous. Well, Amelia did. It's fab, isn't it?'

My mother still relied heavily on her sixties vocabulary.

'But it's James's stuff, Mum. His family's. Who knows how much it's worth?'

'Oh, very little. I had the local auction house come and look at it first and they said it would fetch barely anything. Said people are chopping it up for firewood these days and they simply can't shift it in the sales. This has transformed it!'

It certainly had. And, in a way, it was quite nice, and I

24

did hate the heavy brown oak which seemed to loom oppressively and almost consume me sometimes, particularly on gloomy winter afternoons, but . . .

'But you can't just barge in and do it!' I stormed. 'It's got sentimental value, for James at least!'

'I didn't barge in, darling. I told you, I did it as a present. Like a surprise party. I've been planning it for ages. Didn't for one moment think you'd prefer it as it was.'

Her china-blue eyes widened in alarm and she became childlike in her consternation and confusion. She got up from the floor.

'You are *so* mean, Mum.' Amelia rounded on me furiously. 'Granny's spent ages doing this!'

'And did Tara help?'

'Well, she put the paper down and washed the brushes, yes!'

Damage limitation, clearly, on the part of my younger child. I was aware of Tara moving silently around in the kitchen, out of sight, keeping a low profile. I was pretty sure she'd have tried to put the brakes on these two. She appeared in the archway now: petite, pretty and blonde like her grandmother, barefoot in jeans and a white T-shirt. She came across and we hugged silently. Amelia glared at her, daring her to show her true colours.

'It *was* a bit depressing, Mum, all that dark wood,' she said.

'Yes, but it was your father's dark wood!'

'I know.'

It was all in those two little words. *I know . . . but what could I do?* Against the steamroller of momentum that was my mother and elder daughter, what on earth was my

25

level-headed younger child to do except suggest they keep the paint off the carpet and clean up afterwards?

'Well, darling, I can take it off,' said Mum, lighting a cigarette and looking around speculatively, completely undaunted by the magnitude of her actions, at transforming someone's home without a by-your-leave. Oh God, she'd even done the *grandfather* clock! She pursed her lips doubtfully. 'But I honestly think you'll be making a mistake.'

'Mistake? Mistake?' I heard James yelp from halfway up the stairs, clearly thundering his way back down from the office. 'It was a mistake to imagine we could escape this madhouse for one weekend, to have the temerity to claim precisely thirty-six hours to ourselves, to leave the cares and worries of our poxy little lives behind for one single, solitary –'

In one fluid movement I'd stepped across and shut the sitting-room door firmly on his diatribe. I can move when I have to.

'D'you know, I think he's right,' remarked my mother quietly after a moment. 'I'm not sure this break *has* done him much good, Flora. He looked terribly pale and strained when he came in, and he barely said hello to me.'

'Yes, but that's because he was looking forward to coming home to the house he'd left behind!'

'What about taking up sailing again? Getting him out in a boat?' She puffed away on her ciggie and perched on a sofa arm. 'D'you think that might help? He enjoyed that weekend in the Isle of Wight, when you went with the Milligans. And Philippe always loved a sail in Antibes.'

How to explain to this free-spirited, flower-powered

mother of mine that if one took seriously the responsibilities of a house and family, they weighed heavily on one's mind. She came from a different planet to that of my husband: one that had accommodated her getting pregnant when she was nineteen, not even knowing who the father was, and dancing on through life in a glamorous yet highly irresponsible manner, and yet I loved them both equally. How to explain to one that bobbing around in a boat was not going to transform this Englishman's view of his castle, or to the other that she was only trying to be kind? Personally, I didn't care about the grey streaks, just about keeping the peace, and what I wanted more than anything right now was a cup of tea and to take these sodding boots off.

I disappeared, limping, into the kitchen, where Tara was already putting the kettle on.

'What were they thinking!' I seethed, perching on a stool at the island and kicking my expensive footwear off with gusto.

'I couldn't stop them, Mum. You know what they're like when they're in the grip of a good idea.'

I did. And not for the first time it occurred to me how strange it was to have two so different daughters: one who so obviously not only looked like me but behaved like me, too – oh, I knew where Amelia's dark looks and combative streak came from – and another who looked like her granny and behaved more like her father. What would the next one have been like, and the next? I'd often wondered. Right now, though, I wondered if I could gratuitously exploit this one's good nature even further. I kneaded my sore toes with my fingers and sighed.

'I've got to go to this bloody Italian restaurant in Charlotte Street tonight, Tara. Maria wants some copy by the morning. I'm not sure I can sit opposite your father in his condition for three hours. He'll be breathing more fire than the flaming sambucas.'

She paused, but only for a second. Then she nodded. 'Yeah, OK, I'll come. I want to ask you something anyway.'

'Oh?' My ears pricked up. 'Ask away.'

Tara looked a bit furtive. She picked at her blue nail varnish. 'No, it's OK. It'll wait. I'll go and change.'

I was about to say no, tell me now, as I hate having to wait for news of any sort, good or bad, but my phone rang in my bag, and by the time I'd plunged my hand in, rooted around and found it, then assured Fellino that, yes, we were definitely coming, he wasn't to worry – Tara had disappeared.

Chapter Three

It takes experience to canter through a three-course *à la carte* menu complete with *amuse-bouches*, not to mention petit fours, but Tara and I had had years of it. We therefore had certain things down to a fine art. Don't, for example, choose courses that involve lengthy preparation in the kitchen, like slow-roasted, hand-trapped pigeon (you'd be forgiven for thinking they were still trapping it); go instead for the goat's cheese salad or the soup. Never have an aperitif or a coffee, and glance at the menu on the iPad en route. Obviously, I'd ruined my children's haute-cuisine restaurant experiences for life, since they'd been accompanying me on such lightning gourmet missions for as long as I'd been able to pass them off as adults, but needs must. I couldn't sit there on my own, looking so palpably like a restaurant critic, even though, it has to be said, I nearly always warned a chef before I came in, feeling it was unfair to spring it on them.

'It totally defeats the object,' Amelia would say scornfully as we'd sweep into a sea of bowing waiters. 'You're supposed to be the average punter, not have the red-carpet treatment because they know you work for *Haute Cuisine*.'

She was right, of course, but I'd tried it the other way many times and, for some reason, it always seemed to be when the kitchen was having an off day. Too many times

I'd had grudgingly to write a bad review and have my favourite chef ring me in panic:

'Oh, Flora – I can't believe you came in on Thursday! My fish supplier literally let me down at the last minute, which was why the Dover sole was off. I had no idea the muppet in the kitchen would unfreeze a lemon sole instead!'

Once or twice, they'd been tears. 'Oh God, Flora, is there any way you'd come in for a free meal next week? The owner is absolutely going to kill me when he reads I overcooked the rabbit and, if we lose a star, I'll be fired.'

How could I possibly be responsible for the livelihoods of people I liked and admired as chefs? Watch them lose their jobs as I wielded the hatchet? We all had our off days – my copy didn't always bear forensic scrutiny – but my head didn't roll as a result. On the other hand, I couldn't lie, either, say the rabbit had been cooked to perfection, even though, nine times out of ten, I knew it was. This way, I gave them fair warning and, if they got it wrong, they couldn't say I hadn't warned them. They rarely did. I'd write a glowing review and everyone was happy, except my daughter.

'Pathetic. And you're deceiving your readers, you know that, don't you?'

'I do now, Amelia.'

She was derisive, too, of my survival kit. The Rennies she reluctantly accepted, speed-eating being an occupational hazard, but the napkin I brought from home to spit revolting morsels into and spare the kitchens' blushes, she did not. Neither the plastic bag for entire meals 'employed only once, Amelia, when that sweet young guy at Mason's put salt instead of sugar in the meringue.'

'Twice,' she'd retorted. 'Remember when you had those dodgy langoustines you should have reported but instead put them in your bag and forgot about them until people started moving away from you on the Tube?'

I sighed as Tara and I approached the entrance to the Italian restaurant on Charlotte Street.

Fellino, stout and with his waistcoat stretched over his ample stomach, hastened to meet us at the door, hand outstretched.

'Don't have the fillet steak,' he whispered confidentially as he hurried us to a corner table, knowing I liked to get a wiggle on. 'I couldn't get the Aberdeen Angus, so it's a bit tough, but the calf's liver is *magnifico*.' He kissed his thumb and forefinger.

'Thanks, Fellino,' I said, settling down as he flicked pristine white napkins over our laps and in record time had our glasses filled with the wine Tara had ordered by text from the car. Shame. Fillet took two minutes, but never mind; the calf's liver should be equally quick, and Tara sensibly opted for flash-fried prawns.

'And thank you so much for coming. I know you just got back from Paris, I speak to James to check you on your way, we haven't been reviewed for so long, and you know, opposite . . .'

He jerked his grizzled head meaningfully, shrugged and spread his hands despairingly.

'I know, Fellino.'

Rodrigo's new venture had opened across the road last week, to glowing reviews, one of which had been mine.

'He steal our march,' he said sadly, smiling at Tara, who'd taken a bread roll he'd offered her. 'Take a poppy-seed one, *bambino*. Ees better.' She obeyed and replaced the brown.

'Nonsense, you've been here for ever,' I said, 'and your food's just as good. It's only because he's the new boy on the block, that's all. You got our text about starters?'

'I did, and ees coming out right now in two shakes of a lion's tail. I go to see.'

He did, scurrying off, while Tara tucked into bread and wine and I resisted manfully. The temptation, of course, was to eat everything (it was so delicious) and to become the size of a house – oh, and get completely plastered, too – but after a year in my late twenties when I'd been well on the way to looking like the 'Before' photograph in a Weight Watchers ad, I'd imposed my own rules, which I'd pretty much stuck to ever since. No bread, no more than a glass of wine and just taste the carbs, don't eat the lot. This would be sacrilege if I were only doing it once a month, but I wasn't. These days, with the internet and blogging and a bit of freelance on the side, I could be out every other night. Lizzie, my best friend and partner in gourmet crime for ten years, was lyrical on the subject. 'One mouthful of each course is all you need to know about an establishment.'

'But, Lizzie, that's quite rude. And it's supposed to be fun, what we do. Eating for a living.'

'But because you insist on doing it properly, you've come to dread it. You should have widened your net, like I did.'

Lizzie still wrote for *Haute Cuisine*, but not as a restaurant critic: she'd defected to the other side, to editorial, to write their weekly column, and did it with aplomb. In fact, she did it so well she could pretty much write about anything she fancied. She plundered her own life for copy, her friend's, her ex-husband's, mine, she was ruthless in her rummaging and pillaging, but ever since she'd written about 'the crab that twitched', which she swears happened when I took her to Le Gavroche, I'd cut her off my list.

'Please take me. You know I love a good pig-out, and Jackson can't afford it.'

Jackson was her latest beau. Young – very young – black and gorgeous: a jazz singer with nothing to his name besides a second-hand Armani suit.

'No. You lie. You lied about the crab and you lied about the man dying next to us after one mouthful of soup.'

'He did die!'

'Yes, but not because of the soup. Poor Henri Dupont had to instruct lawyers in the end. It cost him a fortune.'

'I won't do it again.'

'I don't believe you. Any woman who tells the world her best friend has piles on her perineum and has to take a cushion along to restaurants is going to invent some fiction about a winking octopus in the seafood salad.'

'The world doesn't read *Haute Cuisine* – according to Maria, we've got a readership of five at the moment – and, to be fair, I didn't invent the piles and there was a cushion. Anyway, no one knew it was you.'

'Everyone who knew me knew it was me, which is everyone who matters.'

She'd sighed. 'Oh, well. Forget the feasting. Can I still come on holiday with you?'

'What d'you mean, *still*? I haven't asked you yet.'

'No, but you did last year.'

'That was last year. Yes, of course you can come. How can I survive it without you?'

'And can Jackson come, too?' she'd asked.

'Of course. He's much nicer than you.'

'But won't James's father mind?'

'Why would he? You brought Neighing Nigel last year.'

'Yes, but he was my age and . . .'

'White? The Brig's got a broader mind than you have, Lizzie.'

'Courtesy of Pentonville.'

'It was Dartmoor, actually, and I'd say Eton and the army did most of the work.'

She'd hugged me then, pleased to get her August plans under her belt, just as I knew my daughter, sitting opposite me now, was about to do.

'*Buon appetito*,' murmured Fellino, having deposited our starters before gliding noiselessly away, as if on skates, back to the kitchen.

'Looks good,' I hazarded, admiring the sheen on my scallops and Tara's pretty beetroot salad.

'Mm,' she agreed, before plunging in. Conversationally, that is. 'Um, Mum, apparently Amelia's bringing Toby on holiday. And of course you've asked Lizzie, which is lovely, so I was thinking . . .' She picked up her fork and toyed with her salad, wondering how to approach this.

'You'd like to bring a girlfriend? Of course, darling. Ask Charlotte. Why not? She loved it last time.'

'Well, no, it isn't that . . .'

I knew it wasn't. Had already worked it out in the

car. What I hadn't quite worked out was what I thought about it.

'I thought I could bring Rory.'

I sighed. Sometimes I wished I'd married the sort of man about whom I could say, *Ask your father*, but he'd just say, *Yes, sure*, so I had to work this out for myself.

'Where's he going to sleep?' Let's cut to the chase.

'In the spare room, obviously.'

Obviously. Except that wouldn't happen. He'd end up in Tara's room, or she in his, and she was only just seventeen, and how did I feel about that? Weary, was how I felt. Weary of having to shoulder the responsibility of making the decisions whilst James took a more liberal view.

'It's going to happen anyway, so why fight it?' I could hear him saying. 'Not if I patrol the corridors after dark with a rolling pin.'

'No, not if you do that. Quite tiring, though.'

I regarded my daughter now.

'Well, I don't know what Grandpa would think.'

'Grandpa won't mind. You know what he's like.'

Unpredictable. As rigid as you like about some things – the way his lawns were manicured, or his ancestral portraits cleaned, for example – but surprisingly unbuttoned about others, as I well knew. I was playing for time.

'I'll think about,' I said, playing for more.

'What's there to think about? We've been going out for ages now –'

'Six weeks.'

'Seven, and you like him, and Daddy likes him, and he gets on with Amelia and Toby. It'll be fun.'

Fun. The annual holiday at James's father's pile in Kincardine: it was never fun. Oh, it might start out that way – in my head, at the planning stage – but it always evolved into a rather tense, tight-lipped affair. It didn't help that I had to bite those lips so hard around James's sisters – well, not Rachel but Sally, who, try as I might to make a new start every year and get off on the right foot, inexplicably found my nerve endings the moment I set foot in the house, the house which they both, as unmarried spinsters, regarded as their domain. And quite right, too, because they lived there, but . . . wasn't it a tiny bit James's, too? The Brig was his father as well. And he the only son. Perhaps we went for too long, I pondered, as I speared a slippery scallop. Perhaps three weeks was too ambitious. But the children had loved it so when they were young: the freedom to roam over all that land after the confines of London, the gloriously scented pine woods to hide in, the picnics by the stream, damming the burn, swimming in the loch. The little boat we'd patched up and rowed about in, catching trout, diving off the side into the freezing, clear water. There'd even been an old pony to ride as it clambered up the steep, rocky path amongst the purple heather behind the house, one girl on its back, the other leading.

These days, of course, they barely strayed from the television in the basement, or the terrace where they sunbathed, should that glorious, pure Scottish sun deign to shine, but still, it was a proper break and, more to the point, it was cheap. Yes, all right, free. And our finances were stretched to the brink these days – disastrous subsidence in our house which had been staggeringly expensive to repair had seen to that – so there was no point looking a gift house in the mouth. Also, if I'm honest, ticking off the whole of James's family in one big flourish, particularly when we saw so much of my own mother in London, gave me a warm glow inside and made me think I'd done my bit on the in-law front for the rest of the year. I chewed briefly on the slippery mollusc in my mouth. How would my daughters' love lives go down with their maiden aunts? Neither had had boyfriends in tow last year. Again, reactions could be unpredictable. Rachel, fine probably – distant, but fine. Sally, sententious and disapproving or keen to be part of the bright-young-thing gang? And then hurt when she felt left out? My heart began to pound.

'I've already rung Sally, just to check,' said Tara, helping herself to some water. She had the grace to blush. 'She's cool about it.'

'You've already . . .' I blinked.

'Just so you'd have one less thing to stress about. I wasn't going round you or anything.'

Well, she was, but at least she'd done it. So I didn't have to. You had to hand it to my daughter, she'd be our girl in Africa one day.

'What did she say?'

'Well, she was thrilled I'd rung, obviously –'

'Obviously!' I could well imagine Sally's delight. She was at her most natural with Amelia and Tara, finding security, I personally thought, in reverting to her youth.

'And then we had a lovely girly chat about which room I could put him in – the blue one, she thought – and how we might be able to drag out the rowing boat, oh, and check out the new Chinese in Kincardine. She thought you'd like it.'

Tara grinned. Sally was a cook by profession, for Scottish house parties mostly, and was frighteningly competitive with me on the culinary front – not just that front either: don't get me on the identical shoes and handbags. She couldn't understand why I wrote chiefly about London restaurants when there were so many good country ones I ignored. 'We do have restaurants around here, you know, Flora,' she'd say, frosty and offended. It didn't matter how many times I told her I simply followed orders and did what Maria, my editor, told me, she felt snubbed, and my current ruse of sampling the eateries and then pretending Maria had vetoed the review was wearing thin.

'Also, she had news, too. She's got a boyfriend.'

'*Sally* has?' I put my fork down.

'Yeah, I know, I nearly dropped the phone. She met him at a house party, apparently. Where she was cooking.' Tara grinned at me. 'The mind boggles.'

'Doesn't it just!'

Sally was mid-forties, pretty – once very pretty – but my heavens she was huge. If you know your P. G. Wodehouse, she looked like that girl who'd been poured into her clothes and had forgotten to say 'when'. To my knowledge, she hadn't been with a man for about twenty years. I gawped, gripped by this information. I picked up my fork. 'Good God. How long? Have Grandpa and Rachel met him?'

'No idea, that was all I got. Except that she's potty about him.'

'Oh, *good*!'

'I know, isn't it?'

It was. It really was. If Sally had a life of her own, it took the heat off me. And my daughters. Who were my life, obviously, since, as Amelia had told me the other day – I believe in all seriousness – mine was pretty much over and I was clearly living vicariously through them.

I sighed, but there was relief in it as well as fatigue.

'Well, it looks like you and Sally have got it all sewn up, Tara. Do I have any choice?'

'Of course you do. I just thought it would help if I did the spadework for you. What's this sauce, by the way?'

'Ginger. Is it not nice?'

'No, it's fine, just a bit . . . no, it's lovely actually.'

Tara was fond of Fellino, too: his family had owned this restaurant for two generations.

'What about yours?'

'Good,' I said, making a quick note on the pad on my lap that the addition of cumin had been masterful, even if I privately thought the infusion could have been done with a slightly lighter touch. The Jerusalem artichokes, however, I noted, had been a lovely and unusual accompaniment to the liver, which had arrived pronto, together with another anxious smile from Fellino. I watched him hasten back to the kitchen. How would he feel about his seventeen-year-old daughter bringing her boyfriend on holiday, I wondered? Well, it wouldn't happen, would it? The lad would be sent packing with a clip round his ear. But then we weren't a patriarchal Sicilian family steeped in Catholic traditions.

'Yes, fine, darling,' I said, taking the path of least resistance. 'But at either ends of the house, OK? The blue room for him and you in your usual.'

'Cool – thanks, Mum.' She whipped out her phone and texted away happily, one hand forking beetroot salad into her mouth, her eyes on the reply.

'Oh, Mum, just one tiny thing.' She coloured slightly. 'Would you mind ringing Rory's mum?'

'Why?'

'Just so she knows the arrangements and everything.'

'Why can't she ring me?'

'She wants to know he's – you know. Been properly invited. And what the arrangements are,' she said again.

'What arrangements?'

'You know, the . . .'

'Sleeping.'

'Yes.'

I crunched hard on my artichoke. So I was to look like the super-keen mother dragging her son to Scotland, and she was to need reassurance that her darling boy wasn't the innocent victim of some sort of honey-trap. No, don't be silly, Flora, I told myself; she just wanted to know the invitation was official, that's all, and that they weren't sharing a bed.

'OK,' I said shortly. 'I'll do it when we get home.'

'You couldn't do it now?'

I gave Tara a level look over our supper. 'No. I couldn't do it now.'

When we got home, Fellino's reputation and Michelin star intact, plus a good review in the bag, or at least in next week's edition, I promised, as he pressed both my hands in his at the door, it was to an uncharacteristic greeting. As I went down the hall to the kitchen to kick off my shoes, put the dishwasher on, swallow a couple of paracetamol and stagger up to bed after what had been a very long day, I heard, 'Hi, Mum!' from the sitting room.

I froze mid-stride. No one ever greeted me without reason. Just ignored me. 'The Thing in the Kitchen', as they'd once jokingly referred to me – I'd stupidly laughed so, naturally, the title had stuck. Without enough irony, to my mind. Suspicious, I retraced my steps, but they were already breaking out, coming to meet me. At least Amelia and Toby were. So the Trog had clearly crawled out of his own bed at home and come across to occupy one of ours, light his strange cigarettes. Oddly, Mum and James were not far behind, their faces animated and excited.

'Have you checked your phone?' demanded Amelia, steering me back in the direction of the basement kitchen, keeping step with me all the way.

'No, I turned it off. It kept buzzing with some strange number. Why?'

'That was easyJet. They rang us on the landline in the end. Kept trying you because you booked the tickets.'

'Tickets?'

'To Paris.'

'Oh. Problem?'

'No, quite the contrary.' Amelia's eyes were shining as I bent down to start the dishwasher. I straightened up. 'You know the girl Dad saved on the plane?'

'Well . . . yes.' I glanced at my husband, who'd slid around the other side of the island to face me. He shrugged modestly but was looking very pleased with himself, blinking behind his glasses. My mother, too, was very bright-eyed, puffing eagerly on a cigarette.

'It was Camille de Bouvoir's daughter. You know, the opera singer? Does glam rock, too?'

'The . . . opera singer?'

'Didn't you recognize her on the plane?'

'No!' I scrolled my mind back to the flaxen-haired beauty. Tiny, but big-chested – of course, big lungs and therefore voice. And, now I came to think of it, perhaps with more make-up, and her hair up, making a guest appearance on *Strictly* ... in a long, pink, sparkly gown, singing whilst the dancers performed their routine in front of her ...

'Oh! Was that her?'

'The very same. And she's grateful, Mum. *Really* grateful. Oh God!' Amelia clasped her hands with glee and gave a little involuntary jump. 'This is good. This is *such* good news I can't tell you!'

Chapter Four

I looked at the row of shining, animated faces around me: Amelia, Toby and Mum didn't try to hide their excitement and even the famously composed James was having trouble.

'How much?' I breathed, before I could stop myself.

'Oh no,' said Amelia, looking shocked. 'It's not money, Mum.'

'We couldn't possibly accept that,' added James, with a disapproving frown.

'No, no,' I agreed, secretly thinking, Yes, yes. I'd like to see anyone in this room turn it down.

'But what she *has* got, right,' went on Amelia, 'is this amazing place in the south of France. Which she's not using at the moment – not using at all this summer, in fact, because she's touring – and she's asked if we'd like to borrow it!'

'Oh!' I sat down heavily on a kitchen stool.

Tara whooped. 'Where is it?' she shrieked. 'On the coast?'

'No, about an hour inland. Provence. Up in the hills. Sleeps eighteen, stunning infinity pool' – Amelia ticked off the amenities on her fingers, sounding like an estate agent – 'tennis court, party barn, cinema room – all the toys. You name it, we've got it.' She leaped up to embrace her sister, and they danced wildly around the kitchen together, carolling loudly, already lying by a turquoise pool in their bikinis, paperbacks in hand, pina coladas beside them.

I gazed at James, bug-eyed. 'Seriously?'

'Seriously.' He grinned. 'She was so nice.'

'You spoke to her?'

'Yes, you'd written down my email wrong, which was why she had to contact us through the airline. She is so amazingly grateful. The girl is the apple of her eye apparently, an only child. And, to be fair, it's not like she's really *giving* us anything. I felt we could accept the loan of a house, don't you think?'

'Of course you can flaming well accept!' I said with feeling. 'Oh my God – how amazing!' I shot my hands through my hair.

Already, Brechallis House in Kincardine, with its forbidding grey stone walls and black-framed windows flanked on all sides by dark, pine woods and, invariably, cloud and rain, was being replaced – courtesy of a wavy film dissolve – by a white stucco villa complete with vast terrace and pool, surrounded by sun-drenched olive groves and swathes of sage and lavender, not a damp gorse bush or a plague of midges in sight. Oh, the *midges*! I unconsciously scratched my neck just thinking about them.

'When can we have it?' I breathed, snatching up one of Mum's cigarettes from a packet on the island, which I only do in moments of extreme stress or extreme euphoria. I lit it and inhaled greedily. France: my favourite country in the world; the south, this time. Already I was in a sundress – or capri pants perhaps – and a straw hat, off to market under an azure sky to buy *saucisson* and salad to prepare for lunch.

Not to Kincardine under a slate sky in the bone-shaking Land Rover to buy mackerel whose slimy bodies I'd have to gut before cooking.

'Any time we want – it's just sitting there. So we thought – well, same as usual, pretty much the whole of August, just as if we were going to Scotland.'

'And it's got these amazing views, Mum, which you'll *love*,' Amelia told me, eyes alight. 'You can see the sea in the distance, this dear little bay, just like a Cézanne painting, with tiny red rooftops and sweet little fishing boats. Look!'

She was busy on her laptop, flicking up photos.

'Oh! How did you . . .' I moved across to peer over her shoulder.

'She sent us the link,' explained James, looking pretty pleased with himself, I have to say. And why not? For creating such joy in his family, such delight: the girls were flushed with pleasure. *Why not?* I put my arms around him and he squeezed me back as Amelia explained that this was the front, OK, an unbelievable-looking palace, with turrets – towers even. More like a castle than a villa.

'It's like a chateau!' I exclaimed.

'It is,' she said. 'Chateau de la Sauge. Look, it says.' She flipped to a picture of an ornate sign on a wrought-iron gate. 'And this is the terrace . . . and the walled garden with the pool inside . . . and the tennis court . . . and the badminton and boules courts . . . and some of the bedrooms – this is the master one, yours, I imagine. With a four-poster. And the galleried kitchen and the dining room . . . drawing room . . . table-tennis room . . .' And so it went on.

James and I stood, our arms around each other, gazing in disbelief at this slide show, Tara shrieking with delight at

45

every new picture. Toby punctuated proceedings with approving grunts: 'Oh man.' 'Get in.' 'Epic.'

'This would cost a fortune to rent,' I observed.

'Wouldn't it just,' agreed James.

'Megabucks,' confirmed Tara.

'And it comes with a housekeeper, too,' James told us.

'You are *joking*.' I dropped my arms and turned to look at him properly.

'No, she lives in the lodge cottage with her husband, who gardens.' He took a deep breath. 'She does all the cooking.'

James knew he'd delivered the lottery win. The *pièce de résistance*. He'd been saving it. Perhaps even sworn the girls to secrecy. Because, forget the pool. Forget the court and the table-tennis room. Forget the snooker room. We had a cook? Blinking heck. I wouldn't be buying cold meat in the market, I'd be buying floaty dresses and espadrilles!

'Pretty nice to have someone to look after us, don't you think?'

'It's more than nice — it's bloody marvellous. And you, my darling, are a complete star.' I reached up and kissed him squarely on the lips, a rare display of public affection in this house. The girls cheered and clapped.

Bottle it, I thought later, as I went to bed, having said goodbye to Mum as she trotted out to her little red Polo, yet another fag on the go, and thence to her cottage in Fulham: these moments should be preserved, to uncork at a later date when they were most needed. When things were back to normal again, turgid even, to remind us of how we could be, how life should be. That's what I'd like to do. Even Toby had looked almost attractive – what you could see of him amongst the facial hair – brown eyes shining, socks and shoes on for a change, hiding his great hairy toes, as he told us about the time he'd spent in Aix, as a waiter, the previous summer. Picking grapes, too. What a great place Provence was.

As I slapped night cream on my face in the bathroom, my reflection smiled back at me. We'd had some pretty gritty times recently, James and me. I'd had to work that much harder since his private practice had dwindled, forcing us to rely almost exclusively on his NHS salary, and, consequently, I'd been that much grumpier and bad-tempered. The stress of Amelia's exams had taken its toll, plus her disappointing grades, and there'd been a general feeling of battling on amid the strife. To jet off to the sun, to switch off and forget all our petty troubles, to soak up a completely different way of life for a few weeks was surely just what we needed?

We even made love that night, which, let's face it, we were too knackered to do much these days. Well, I was. Despite having just been to Paris for the weekend, that side of things hadn't been an unqualified success, what with both of us being too tired the first night, James too pissed the second, and us having a flaming row about Amelia and what James called 'her spectacularly selfish streak' the third. But tonight, in our own bed, in the house we'd lived in for nineteen years, ever since we got married, tonight it was good.

Afterwards, we lay on our backs, if not still entwined, as we would have been nineteen years ago, at least holding hands. Next door we could hear Amelia and Toby talking.

I hoped no more, but there was nothing I could do about it so I shut my mind to it. Refused to let it spoil things.

'I'll have to explain to Dad, of course,' James murmured.

I turned my head towards him on the pillow. 'I know. I was just thinking that. But he'll understand, surely?'

'Oh, yes. Might be a bit disappointed, though.'

'Mm. We could go up in September?'

'We could.'

We both knew we wouldn't. Couldn't afford the time.

'And the girls . . .' Not ours this time but James's sisters, who, I told him repeatedly, he couldn't be responsible for, not for ever – but I wasn't going to get into that argument tonight.

'Sally will be pleased not to have to help cook for us all?' I hazarded. 'And, you never know, she might even be relieved to conduct her new relationship in private. Not to have to expose her beau to the entire family immediately.'

James grunted non-committally. He'd been as floored as I had about the man's very existence when I'd told him earlier, but he hadn't wanted to sound disloyal.

'I'll probably have to invite Lizzie,' I said cautiously, something I'd already thought about when I was brushing my teeth. 'After all, she was coming to Scotland.'

'But not for the whole time.'

He'd clearly considered it, too, brushing his.

'No, not for the whole time,' I said quickly. 'Just a week or two.'

'A week.'

'Well . . .'

Silence.

'Who's she boring the pants off at the moment?'

'That nice chap, Jackson, the jazz pianist. You liked him.'

'Oh, yes. Well, that's something, I suppose. Although, knowing Lizzie, it'll be all change by August and she'll saddle us with some God-awful toyboy again.'

Lizzie's taste in men got younger as she got older. Jackson was no exception, but it had been dark in the jazz club when James met him. Plus, I'd lied a bit. Told him he was a metrosexual – which I'd then had to explain meant he was pampered and well-preserved, not gay.

'And then there's the age-old question of what to do about your mother,' he said.

'We'll have to ask her, too.'

'I know.'

He did. We'd both seen the light in her blue eyes, although she'd sweetly said nothing. She'd spent her younger, even more beautiful, years jetting around the bays of Juan-les-Pins in speedboats whilst *en vacances* from Paris. She hadn't been back for years. Her lover at the time, my stepfather in all but marriage, had been the wealthy politician Philippe de Saint-Germain, and he'd run my mother blatantly alongside his wife. At his funeral in Paris, both women had been at the graveside, in tears, just as two women had at Mitterrand's. It was the French way. Where had I been, I'd wondered? I don't mean at the funeral – I'd been there beside Mum, just across from his two sons – but in the Juan-les-Pins days? Bouncing around in a Moses basket in the back of the speedboat? I'd asked, one day. Mum had looked vague. Drawn vacantly on her cigarette and her past, and said, 'D'you know, darling, I've absolutely no idea.'

'With a nanny? Back at the hotel?' I'd suggested sarcastically.

'Yes, that'd be it,' she'd agreed, possibly believing it. There was no guile with Mum. Just forgetfulness.

'But that's it on the hangers-on front.' James turned away from me on to his side. He bunched up his pillow and punched it hard. 'We don't want hordes of freeloading friends of Amelia and Tara, or any appendages of your mother. You know what she's like.'

I did. I also thought it probably wasn't the moment to mention Rory, who would no doubt be swapping Scotland for France in the blink of an eye, and, since it was further away, would likely be with us for longer. I'd already decided to veto Will and Jess, but who knew how long Toby would stay? He practically lived with us as it was.

'I'm going to see Camille tomorrow. Tell her our plans.'

I blinked. Sat up. 'Oh?' I gazed down at his immobile form in the darkness. 'Is she coming here?' I went hot at the thought of the frayed stair carpet, the Ikea throws covering the tired sofas, the damp on the sitting-room wall. Wondered, wildly, if I had time to paint it? Who was it who'd said that the smell of fresh paint followed her everywhere? Oh, yes. The Queen.

'No, she's at the Albert Hall this week and rehearsing during the day, so she's invited me to lunch at her hotel.'

'Oh! How lovely!' I was stunned for a moment. Not me, of course. No, of course not me. But why couldn't we both go? 'Are you free?' I demanded. I certainly was. 'Don't you have clinic tomorrow? Private patients?'

He rolled over enough to peer at me over his shoulder in the gloom. 'Free to have lunch with a famous opera singer at the Hyde Park Hotel? Who's lending us a ten grand a week house for the entire summer? I think so, Flora. Peter Hurst is covering my list for a couple of hours; I've emailed him.' He rolled back.

'Oh. Right.' I lay down again. I couldn't help thinking he'd been to enough smart restaurants with me not to get excited about the Hyde Park Hotel, but I forced myself to be the bigger person. 'Do tell her we're completely thrilled, won't you? That we're enormously grateful.'

He grunted. Reached out a backward hand to give me a reassuring pat.

I went to sleep happy, barely needing the eye mask, the socks, the earplugs, the drops of sleep-inducing lavender water on the pillow, the Rennies, or even the swig of Night Nurse – although, naturally, I employed them all anyway, just in case.

The following morning I lay in bed until nine o'clock, luxuriating in my family's absence. Tara had taken a bus to her school across the river; James, after much discussion about which tie to wear, the Tube to St Thomas's Hospital; and Amelia and Toby had walked – or bounced, in Toby's case; he had a funny walk – to their crammer, where they were both doing retakes. About this, James and I had been practically on saucepan-throwing terms earlier in the year. There'd been tears and shrieks from all quarters, mostly from Amelia, who'd baulked at the inconvenience it posed to her gap year, but also from James, who'd baulked at the cost, since he'd already shelled out thousands for private school. Thousands we didn't have. I'd prevailed, though, as I knew I would, but it had been the bloodiest of family battles. At the crammer, she'd met the

Trog, so in some respects I'd scored an own goal, but I was pleased she was having another go, even if it was only at one A-level, sport science. The telephone rang beside me. I lunged in the dark for the receiver, removing an earplug.

'Eau, helleau, it's Penelope Friar-Gordon here.'

I didn't know anyone by that name. I propped myself up on my elbow. Pushed up my eye mask to let the light flood in, and removed the other earplug.

'Sorry, I –'

'Rory's mother.'

'Oh, right.' I struggled to sit up.

'I gather you've kindly invited Rory on holiday with you this summer?'

I came to. The 'kindly' had been crowbarred in somehow. Overall, the voice was distinctly frosty.

'Yes – yes. I was going to ring you, actually, but we've only just got back from Paris, and last night was a bit hectic. To be honest, I only recently learned that Tara's invited him. You know what they're like!'

If I'd been hoping for a spot of mothers-with-teenagers camaraderie, I was disappointed.

'I see. I got the distinct impression from Rory that Tara had invited him a while ago?'

Realizing I was about to drop Tara in it, I became vague. 'Oh, well, I can't quite remember when it was decided. But the thing is, it's France now. Our plans have changed. Provence,' I added happily, thinking that even Mrs Icecold in Gloucestershire would thaw.

'Eau. I thought he'd be doing some stalking?'

For a moment I visualized Rory, in pressed chinos,

perving round Kincardine after the local talent, which was generously sized and, generally, underdressed. Then it dawned.

'Oh, no, my father-in-law doesn't ... he no longer shoots. Just a bit of fishing.'

'Right.' She sounded incredibly disappointed. 'I was distinctly told . . .'

What *had* Tara said? That she was from some wealthy Scottish aristo family whose land marched with Balmoral, and with whom we shared lavish shooting parties? Whereas, in fact, the Brig, albeit landed and creaking gentry, had acres of scrubby gorse and masses of mangy sheep?

'Well, as I say, it's immaterial,' I said crisply, disliking this woman intensely, ' because we're going to Provence this year.'

She caught my tone. 'Ah, yes, I see. How lovely. And that's yours, is it?'

'No, it's very kindly being lent to us.'

It occurred to me that it would be simpler to send this woman my bank statements. Spectacularly overdrawn, no Scottish pile, no French one either, just a four-bed semi in Clapham with a mortgage.

'And Rory is very welcome to join us.'

'Obviously, they'll have separate bedrooms?'

'Obviously!' I seethed. Blimey, I was the *girl's* mother; she was the *boy's*. Was her precious son at the mercy of my siren?

'Only they are very young. Rory is still only sixteen.'

I shut my eyes. 'They are.' I said quietly. 'Very young.' I got out of bed and clenched my fist hard. I wanted to say,

D'you know what? He's no longer invited, but knew, for Tara, I couldn't.

'I think I need another word with Henry,' said Mrs Friar-Gordon doubtfully.

Presumably, the husband. 'It's my pleasure,' I said, as if she'd thanked me profusely instead of insulted me, which, happily, wrong-footed her. She remembered her manners.

'Oh, er, yes. Thank you.'

'You're welcome. Goodbye.'

I didn't exactly put the phone down, but neither did I wait for her to reply.

Instead, I peeled off my T-shirt and ran into the shower, emerging a few minutes later, wet and steaming. I was just running naked down the corridor to the airing cupboard at the far end of the empty house for clean pants when the phone rang again.

'Bloody woman!' I shrieked, turning back, just as the door to Amelia's bedroom opened. Toby emerged, his huge, hairy body squeezed into my daughter's Cath Kidston dressing gown.

There was a ghastly freeze-frame moment. Our eyes locked briefly, then my hands flew – one up, one down – but not before his eyes had beaten my hands to it. He disappeared quickly back into Amelia's room.

Shit. Bloody *hell.* I ran on, going as hot as the sun. What was he *doing* here? Well, lying in, clearly, whilst Amelia went to college, which, frankly, *was not on.* Toby staying here at all had slipped under the radar after a supper party six months ago, when we'd had some lovely friends from Wiltshire staying with all four of their children. Naturally, we'd all got roaring drunk, and Toby had been too pissed to drive home. He obviously couldn't go in the spare room, as usual, due to the guests, and Amelia had said, 'Why doesn't he just kip on the floor in my room?' I'd been too tired and drunk to argue. This, then, had set a precedent. Wedged a thin end. And now he'd seen me *naked*. Back in the bedroom, still lacking pants, or any clothes at all, the phone was still ringing. I dived back under the covers.

'Hel*lo!*' I barked, furious.

'What's up?' It was Lizzie.

'Oh. Lizzie.' I groaned. Covered my eyes. 'Toby's just seen me with no clothes on.'

She paused, startled. An excited note crept into her voice. 'Gosh, I didn't know you two . . . does Amelia . . . ?'

'Oh, not like that, Lizzie,' I said, irritated. 'This isn't some torrid Alan Clark mother-and-daughter *ménage à trois*, this isn't an episode out of your life. I ran into him on the landing.'

'Oh.' She was clearly disappointed. 'Oh, well, do him good. See what's in store for him twenty years down the track.'

'Put him off for life, you mean.'

'Nonsense, there's nothing wrong with your figure. If he'd seen mine, he'd be far more devastated. Anyway, France,' she said excitedly.

I narrowed my eyes. Sat up a bit. 'How do you know?'

'Amelia popped round to borrow my tent. She's going to some music festival.'

'Leeds – I know – but not for ages. You have a tent?'

'Remember I went to Glastonbury? With Neighing Nigel? Anyway, isn't it fab? A whole month! For free!'

'Yes, well,' I hedged nervously. 'But we've literally only

55

just heard ourselves. So, obviously, I'll have to talk to James about exactly who he wants to come and how long –'

'Oh, we *definitely* don't want the Harrisons,' she interrupted. 'Remember they came to Scotland that year and he banged on and on about his bonus and how all his children had got into Cambridge? And she kept passing wet wipes round the Land Rover in case anyone had touched a dead rabbit?'

'No, not the Harrisons,' I said weakly. 'But Lizzie, a month is a long time. I was thinking –'

'Oh, *don't* be so wet, Flora. It'll fly by, you'll love it! You are absolutely not to ring and say we'll have it for less. Think how brown we'll be!'

'Yes, well – oh. Hang on, Lizzie.'

Amelia had put her head around the door. 'Why are you still in bed?'

'Because I am *trying* to get up, but the phone keeps ringing. Why aren't you at college?'

'No classes. It's an Ofsted day. Tobes and I are going to Reading. Is there any petrol?'

'How would I know if there's any petrol in your car?'

'Oh, OK, there isn't. Can I borrow your card? I've got, literally, no money. I'll only put a bit in.'

'No, you cannot borrow my debit card. It is not some magic wand to wave around willy-nill—' Toby had stuck his head above Amelia's in the doorway. He grinned.

'It's in my bag downstairs,' I whispered, mortified.

'Thanks, Mum. Can I give it back to you when we get back? It's just –'

'Yes, just *go*.' Toby was still grinning at me. The door shut on their faces. I waited, horrified.

'I don't think he's told her,' I hissed, aghast, to Lizzie. 'He's just been in. Don't you think that's weird?'

'Who?'

'Toby. I don't think he's told Amelia. And he was *grinning* at me!'

'What, so you think he fancies you?'

'*No*. It's just . . . I mean, surely you'd say – Oh, help, I've just seen your mother with no clothes on? It's just odd!'

'I don't know, Flora. I wouldn't get too hung up on it if I were you. I doubt you're the first older woman he's seen in the buff. That boy's given me the eye before.'

'*Has* he?' I was horrified. 'God, that's *terrible*. You should have *said*. I must tell Amelia.'

'Don't be silly. He's a flirt, that's all. Nothing wrong with that. Anyway, I can't spend all morning on the phone to you, I've got a meeting with Maria at eleven about the summer hols. I want one of the interns to cover for me. And you'd better get up.'

'I've been trying to get up for –' I said, but she'd gone. To see our editor, and no doubt angle for an extra week off in order to come to *my house in France* – in my head, I already owned it, was very definitely the chatelaine – which was what *I* had intended to do, so that I could be free to swan off for longer myself. I shut my eyes and breathed deeply, in . . . out . . . in . . . out. The air exiting my teeth made a strange whistling sound, more like an old woman in the last rattling throes than a much younger, more glamorous one on the brink of her own personal belle époque.

Chapter Five

James returned that evening looking, if possible, even more flushed and thrilled with himself. He was bouncing a bit, too – bounding, almost – and it seemed to me his chest had expanded. He strode masterfully across the kitchen to where I was changing a fuse on the iron, removed the instrument of domestic drudgery from my hands and replaced it with a box of chocolates.

'What are these for? I asked, gazing at the little green box in disbelief.

'Well, you know,' he smirked, hopping about a bit more. 'I just thought I haven't bought you anything for ages.'

'You haven't, and buying After Eights indicates just how long. I think you'll find chocolates have moved on and it's all Green & Black's, these days, but thank you, darling. How sweet.'

He frowned at the box. 'It *is* green and black. What's wrong with you?'

'Not the packet, you fool – oh, never mind. How was lunch?'

'Good, really good.' His eyes shone like a little boy's. He thrust his hands into his pockets and jangled his loose change around, rocking back on his heels. 'God, she's nice, Flora, you'd really like her.'

'I'm sure I would, if I met her properly.' Ridiculously, I was struggling to keep an edge from my voice. When I'd glanced at the clock at lunchtime over my cheese-and-pickle sandwich, I'd felt slightly peeved, but had consoled myself by reaching for my iPad and re-counting the bedrooms at the villa. Ten, including the one in the attic. I'd decided to talk to James about asking the Carmichaels. They'd love it, and I adored Kate and Harry. I was looking forward to ringing and saying, *Kate, we've got this villa in the south of France . . . yes, of course the children, too.* Hear her shriek with pleasure. And, of course, James was busy securing the deal, so I shouldn't be miffed, I'd thought as I'd closed my laptop, put my plate in the dishwasher, flicked the kettle on again, but . . . surely we came as a couple? After all, I was the one who needed to know where the spare linen was kept, where the pool towels were . . .

'She needed to tell me about the keys to the pool house, where the barbecue is. That kind of thing,' James said importantly.

'Right. Yes, well, I can see that might be beyond me.' I picked up the iron again. 'Did you get the keys?'

'No need. They're with the housekeeper, who's her sister, by the way. Her brother-in-law's the gardener.'

'Really?' I made a face. 'Must be a bit galling, surely? Scrubbing floors for your sister?'

'I think it's really nice, actually. A way of looking after a sibling who hasn't done so well. Giving her a job, a free cottage. Her husband, too.'

'I suppose.' I was surprised. James sounded quite strident. And his chin was jutting out in a horribly familiar fashion. Were we taking up positions here? About a family we didn't know? How had that happened?

'And, speaking of siblings who haven't done so well,' he

went on in a rush, 'I rang Dad and Sally. They're really upset.'

'Oh!' Suddenly, I knew what was coming. Why he was a bit punchy and bullish. The chocolates. I put the iron down and sat warily on a stool. 'Oh, James – you *haven't*.'

'I had to, Flora. I couldn't say – Sorry, we can't come this year, we're swanning off to the south of France – without asking them, could I?'

I was speechless. 'But your father! In Provence? He doesn't go out of Kincardine, for God's sake, and Sally!'

'Oh, for heaven's sake, we're not that parochial. Have been beyond the end of the glen.'

'When? When has Rachel ever been beyond the end of the glen? Name me one time.'

He scratched his chin. 'The odd funeral.'

'At the church. In the glen.'

'That's uncalled for, Flora.'

'But we agreed! This morning, before you left! A holiday on our own terms for once, without the extended family.'

'Yes, I know, but it didn't feel right. I felt shabby. Camille completely understood. That's why she helped her sister.'

Camille. He'd discussed it with her before discussing it with me. With a complete stranger. I breathed deeply, teeth clenched.

'I tried to ring, but you were on the phone all morning. In bed, Amelia said.'

'Amelia?'

'I rang her mobile to get her to give you a nudge, but she was driving. On her way to some festival.'

'What festival?'

'Gets back Monday, she said.'

Oh my God, *Reading*. Not the high street, shopping – the *festival*. And I'd thought Leeds, later in the summer. *With my debit card*. I went hot. I simply couldn't tell James. My mind scrolled back to more pressing problems.

'But Sally –'

'Is much calmer now she has a boyfriend, Rachel said.'

'Is *he* coming?'

'Of course. They're a couple.'

'And Rachel?'

'Of course Rachel. I can't have one without the other.'

'Why do we bloody well have to have either!'

James and I had by now squared up to one another across the kitchen island, eyes blazing. I knew he was taking a stand and that I'd have to be very firm if I was going to win this one.

'Why not ask some friends for a change, like normal people do? The Carmichaels – they asked us to Cornwall. I'd love to have them!'

'We still can.'

'Of course we can't! Not with –' I broke off.

Not with Sally and Rachel. They were unusual. Sally, enormous, as we know (absolutely nothing wrong with that), and both unmarried, as we also know (nothing wrong with that either), but both, in their own ways, utterly heartbreaking and awkward.

Rachel, by far the easier of the two, was very religious and extremely quiet. Pious in the true sense of the word. I never quite knew if she approved of me, but I dare say others would say the same. She made a lot of people nervous; Kate Carmichael would be terrified of her. And no doubt get disastrously pissed to hide her nerves. Rachel's standards were hard to live up to and, although she probably didn't mean to, she had a disapproving demeanour. She would, in another era, I think, have become a nun. She was the eldest and had sheltered James and Sally to an extent when their mother had died. Or been shot. Murdered. Except no one ever said that word.

Naturally, that terrible trauma had taken its toll. In that big, draughty house at the head of the glen, when Vicky Murray-Brown had come back that night from Aberdeen – or Dundee, perhaps, I couldn't remember (James had told me very quickly, so many years ago, I'd had to fill in the gaps with my imagination) – and had let herself in quietly at the back door at two in the morning, but of course, not so quietly, being very drunk. And then, after that shot had rung out – and how it must have done so in that huge, echoing house – the dreadful silence that had fallen remained, in a sense, to this day, thirty-odd years later. A ghostly emptiness prevailed at Brechallis. Always had done. Where once a garrulous, headstrong girl, too glamorous for her own good, certainly to be tucked away in an isolated glen with an aging brigadier, had resided as a young wife and mother, now, an old man, a silent daughter and one who talked constantly but whose words were empty, remained. Where once arguing and shouting had filled the air – but at least she'd been a presence, clattering around the kitchen, singing, drinking too much, crying, banging down pans, hollering at her husband and children, desperately unhappy and desperate for love – now, only the wind whistled in her place, through the shabby rooms, the dark corridors. She'd found some comfort in her children, but not enough, and finally, desperately, she'd taken her love to town, with – had it been Fergus? Who did the fencing? Or, no, Darren, a local builder, that had been it. And, actually, now I thought about it, it hadn't been in the faraway clubs of Aberdeen or Dundee but in dour little Kincardine, the small town at the entrance to the glen, with its rows of faceless houses and billowing litter. Teenagers with needles in their arms, and unemployed fathers. Where poverty and despair overwhelmed, but which, from where Vicky sat, staring out at the gorse bushes and the sheep, was the nearest thing to life.

In some stark little pebble-dashed pub Vicky had drunk with Darren and the other regulars one Saturday night. She must have made quite an entrance, flouncing in defiantly in her fur coat, her heart pounding, taking a solitary stool at the bar. After that, she was there every Saturday night. And she made friends. Many were drinking to forget their tough, gritty lives, the monotony of their day-to-day lot, but Vicky was drinking to forget the horrendous mistake she'd made in marrying her much older husband – and in doing so, of course, she made a mockery of him to all his neighbours. In that part of the world, twenty miles made you a neighbour. And geography notwithstanding, he was the laird at the big house. Everyone knew Drummond Murray-Brown.

Home she'd weave in her car in the early hours, along dark, narrow lanes where she wouldn't meet a living soul, let alone a police car, her face sagging with make-up, drink and sorrow, her clothes reeking of cigarettes and her body of Darren's bed. In she'd stagger, feeling her way upstairs in the dark to the spare room, laughing, yes laughing, if the

Brig blundered out of their bedroom to howl in pain and anger, knowing he'd never lay a finger on her.

Not a finger, no. But one night, after she'd gone to town, and come back drunk and sated, he'd lain in wait. Or sat in wait, alone, at the kitchen table, with only a candle and a bottle of whisky. And when she'd returned in the dark, in the middle of the night, there'd been a fearful row. She'd already told him months ago she wanted a divorce. Had informed him one evening, before she'd gone to Kincardine, wearing a silk dress, earrings jangling, slipping into her fur coat, before running down the gravel drive to the car, that she would file for one: take the children to Edinburgh and, more to the point, take half the house and land, as was her right. The house and land that had been in Drummond's family for two hundred and fifty years. Handed down from one generation to another, from father to son. It was to be sold. Divided up, and half the proceeds given to Drummond, half to Vicky. For there was no money to speak of, nothing for Vicky to be paid off with; it was all in the land. Four thousand acres of scrub, peppered with sandstone boulders and bracken and gorse, where nothing of any consequence grew and only sheep scratched a living. Where a large, preposterously ugly, grey stone house presided forbiddingly, its dark windows daring anyone to question its hideousness. He couldn't even afford to let rich bankers come and shoot his pheasant, couldn't afford the infrastructure to facilitate that: the gamekeeper, the beaters. Couldn't get a loan from the bank.

Letters flew from solicitor to solicitor and then back to Drummond. He'd read them at the kitchen table with shaking hands. Half the house and half the land, that was what she wanted. That was fair with three children under thirteen, that was what she needed to release herself. She'd married a man twice her age, it had been a mistake. Hers, she realized. She'd pushed for the marriage, to this confirmed bachelor whom she'd met at a Highland wedding and who had looked rather splendid in his kilt, certainly to a young girl from Godalming, Surrey. Yes, she had pushed him into it. He'd been unsure. But now she needed out. It wasn't going to happen, Drummond said again and again to himself as he read those letters with a horrified, clenched anger. It simply wasn't going to happen. Over his dead body. Or, as it turned out, over hers.

Of course, he hadn't intended to shoot her, or even threaten her, not with a gun — with words, perhaps. But when she'd opened the back door, still giggling, tripping over the step, filling the kitchen with fumes from her painted lips, and when he confronted her and she'd shouted right back in his face, about his sexual prowess, or lack of it, and Darren's overwhelming competence in that department, he'd reached behind the door in a blind rage and, the next thing he knew, she was dead.

Life imprisonment, obviously, for shooting your wife. Nine years, in those days. And some say he'd weighed it up. Some cynical old neighbours on another crag, in another pile, who'd been there for centuries, applied their own warped logic and said, *Yes, reckon Drummond gave it some thought and decided, Well, I'll be out in nine years and the house and land will still be mine. And then my son's.* No one who truly knew Drummond's heart believed that, though, they knew it had been a tragic accident, and anyway, James didn't want the house. And we never, ever talked about it.

When I met him, he told me about it, obviously. I remember it must have been as early as our second date: 'By the way,' he'd said, 'there's something you need to know about me. My father killed my mother.' It was a sort of 'Take me or leave me now' statement. Warts and all. I took him. Loved him for thinking it needed to be out there so soon, wanting no deception, no misunderstandings. No difficult decisions a few months down the track, by which time I might have fallen in love with him. In fact, he pretty much told me, defiantly, 'My father's an ex-con.' Although I was very shocked, I remember liking his defiance, in that wine bar off the Fulham Road. I'd just come out of a long relationship with someone who'd been much more economical with the truth. Truth was what I needed. What I liked.

We were engaged within ten months and, naturally, during that time I went to Scotland and met the Brig and James's two sisters, not spinsters then, just two girls at home with their dad. And Drummond, who'd been out for a good few years by then, seemed just like any boyfriend's father: a little older and crustier, perhaps, because he was, and quite grand and scary in his big Scottish house, but certainly not like anyone who'd spent nine years in Dartmoor.

Just like Eton, Sally told me later Drummond had said, because of course, although James wouldn't talk and I respected that, girls do. And Sally, being the more verbose and vocal of the two sisters, had prattled away in the morning room at Brechallis, on the worn, gold Dralon sofa, hugging a cushion. Up to a point. No one ever discussed

66

that night, when three sleeping children had awoken to a single blasting shot ringing out. A hideous scream. A father in pieces. But Sally told me about the court case. Swift and conclusive due to a guilty plea, but with lots of old friends giving mitigating evidence, supporting and swearing allegiance to an old friend who'd married the wrong girl. Not a wrong-un – different class and generation that these neighbours were, they could see there was nothing bad about Vicky Murray-Brown. It was just that she was not right for Drummond. And Sally told me about Dartmoor, where they visited him and where their father had been so resilient, so cheerful. Saying they weren't to worry. That he had a splendid view of the moor, the smell of heather, just like home. And that the food was better than he'd had in the army, and he was reading loads, making his way through the classics, which was marvellous. He was in charge of the prison garden, too, eating the vegetables from it, and really making the whole experience out to be so much better than it must have been.

And, meanwhile, the three children were sent to boarding school, and stayed with an aunt – Aunt Sarah, Drummond's sister – in the holidays and kind friends at weekends. And whilst nine years didn't exactly fly by, when it became seven – because, of course, he was a model prisoner, Sally said – suddenly, it did. They'd all assumed he would serve the full term, and no one had told them any differently for fear of getting their hopes up. But then, all at once, Daddy was coming home.

'And how did you feel about him?' I'd wanted to ask Sally, but didn't. How did you feel about your father robbing you of your mother with a single shot, which, when I found an old newspaper clipping in a drawer at Brechallis years later, was what had happened. But Sally knew what I wanted to know.

'The same,' she'd told me frankly, looking at me from the other end of the sofa with those wide grey Murray-Brown eyes, bright in her pretty if increasingly moonlike face. 'He was still our father. And, yes, we'd lost our mother, but it had been an accident, a terrible mistake. We could either decide to lose both parents, or keep one. Keep Daddy, which we did.'

They all did. All stood, and have stuck by him, which says a lot for Drummond Murray-Brown, and perhaps not a great deal for Vicky, although they never blackened her name either. Whatever she'd done, she didn't deserve what befell her. An invisible veil of intractable silence regarding their mother descended on the family, and what remained of them was tight, for obvious reasons. Almost twenty years into a marriage with one of the siblings, I sometimes wondered if two out of the three had ever got over it. I suspected they hadn't. James was fine, I knew that. I'm even conceited enough to believe that the girls and I had made him so, but Sally and Rachel were not fine, and I think James felt guilty about that. That he'd survived. Escaped, if you like. And they hadn't. Remained trapped in a house full of ghosts and regrets.

As I faced him now in our Clapham kitchen, I knew. Knew that their lives were entangled more inexorably than those of any other family. Knew, too, that just as we had always, throughout our married life, spent almost a month – a long time in anyone's calendar, my friends were always staggered – with the Brig and Sally and Rachel, so we would now, even in the south of France. It couldn't be avoided. And it had been foolish – selfish of me, even – to imagine it could. To believe that this summer would be any different.

Chapter Six

The ferry crossed the Channel on a rough and churning sea. It felt like a force ten to me, but James assured me it was only a moderate swell, not even a proper gale. You could have fooled me. I'm not one of nature's travellers, though; in fact, on our honeymoon I notched up motion sickness three times in one day: once on the aeroplane to Athens, once on the boat to Zante and, lastly, in the taxi across the island whilst James supplied me with sturdy paper bags and surreptitiously read *The Times*. This time, however, I was not the only one in trouble. Rory was up on deck beside me, clinging to the rail as the others played Perudo in the bar below, no doubt knocking back the rosé, lurching hilariously this way and that as the boat plunged and soared, roaring with laughter as the dice and the cups rolled off the table. Rory and I couldn't look at one another, let alone speak. So intense was our mutual concentration that our knuckles were white with the effort of clinging to the rail, our faces dizzying shades of eau de Nil. It wasn't so much the rise and fall of the great boat in the swell that I had trouble with, it was the uncertain length of the pause in between. The prow would keep rearing up on the crest of a huge wave, hesitating . . . oh God, the *tension* . . . and then swooping down again, like a roller coaster at a so-called funfair. The fact that the pause wasn't always followed by a swoop but sometimes by a dead drop, like a lift plunging from top to bottom, was my undoing. It was this last motion that caused havoc with my stomach and, eventually, despite me gulping desperately into the gale, caused me to vomit over the side. Unfortunately, the wind blew it straight back into Rory's face.

He was terribly good about it. Wiped his face and his pink Ralph Lauren shirt down with a 'Couldn't matter less, Mrs Murray-Brown', even though I'd ceaselessly told him to call me Flora. But it wasn't my finest hour. Naturally, I was horribly embarrassed, but Tara was mortified.

'Mum – how could you!' She flew into the Ladies to find me as I mopped myself down, clutching the basin in an effort not to be thrown across the room, as the boat continued to lurch hideously.

'Well, obviously I didn't intend to throw up in your boyfriend's face, Tara,' I said through my teeth, gritted in case there was more; in case I needed the basin for more than just support.

'Yes, but it's so gross! I am *so* embarrassed.'

Amelia materialized beside us, pale and tight-lipped, but not from the swell.

'Toby's just told me something awful. Apparently, you skipped past him on the landing with no clothes on, is that right?'

'I *ran* to the airing cupboard, Amelia.'

'*Naked?*'

'I didn't know he was in the house!'

'Oh, like you run around the house with no clothes on a lot! You're not doing a Mrs Robinson, are you?' She narrowed her eyes suspiciously at me. 'Trying to seduce him?'

'Don't be ridiculous!'

71

'Well, you're not making a very good impression, Mum. Try harder, OK? I am not impressed.'

Two pairs of appalled eyes bored into mine and then the sisters stalked off, united in their disgust, flashing me horrified backward glances over their shoulders as they went and murmuring mutinously.

Frankly, I was beyond caring, so sick did I feel. I only felt remotely human again when we got to Calais and I was able to change in the loo in a bar and put my dress and Rory's shirt in a plastic bag in the boot of the car. Even then, I have to admit, the smell still wasn't great and, to be honest, whatever they say in the adverts, having six people in one people carrier is not ideal. We certainly got to know one another pretty well during that ten-hour drive down to the south of France.

Rory's manners were impeccable, really exemplary. But much as I hoped they'd rub off on the rest of us, it was rather exhausting to hear once again how extraordinarily comfortable he was, and did everyone else have enough room? I hoped he'd relax when we got there. Toby and Amelia, at the back, couldn't have been more relaxed, slumped against each other, plugged silently into their music, Toby, whenever I glanced in the rear-view mirror, foraging furiously up his nose with his finger. Tara was engrossed in a book on Virginia Woolf, so it was rather left to Rory to keep the conversational gambits going. He gave us a valiant running commentary on the flat, northern countryside, explaining how the landscape had disadvantaged the Allied troops during the war – did I mention he was reading history? – and how Montgomery had intended to march his men in strict formation over these fields with

a view to accessing the beaches below, but the lack of natural topographical camouflage had hindered him. He told
us about pincer movements, back-up plans, resources. It
really was all extremely interesting, but there was a limit to
how many times I could say, 'Really?', or 'That's so fascinating, Rory,' and since it was my turn to drive and James,
who'd normally be a willing participant in this sort of conversation, had nodded off, I was rather left flying the flag.

Finally, my mouth dry from chat about the Axis and
the Allied powers and eyes glazed from miles and miles of
boring French countryside, the vista gave way to more
exciting, hilly terrain as we twisted and turned our way
across the Alps. James had taken the wheel now and Rory
had gone very quiet behind me. I knew why, and truly felt
for him – really, I did – but I certainly wasn't relinquishing
my front seat. After a while – and quite abruptly – a brightly
coloured landscape materialized, as if a roller blind had
suddenly been let to fly up. The sky in Normandy had
been low and grey – much the same as at home – but now
the hefty clouds rolled back to reveal a deep azure blue,
uninterrupted by even a wisp of white. As we thankfully
opened the windows to greet the warm, still air, heavy with
mingled scents of sage and lavender, rows of vineyards
and vast fields of sunflowers interspersed with dusty village after dusty village assured us we were indeed in the
south of France.

'Nice was once part of Italy, you know,' said Rory, who'd
clearly recovered his equilibrium. We passed a rococo-style
villa at the side of an olive grove. 'Hence the pastel-coloured
stucco you see around here, like in Turin. It was called
Piedmont until 1860.'

At least he wasn't reading mechanical engineering, I thought. Or physics.

'I think I knew that,' said James, with genuine interest. 'Although, of course, we're not going as far as Nice.'

'No, but you still see the effects, even this far inland. What are we, about an hour away?'

'From the coast, yes, but by my calculations we're only about five minutes from the villa.'

Even Toby and Amelia unplugged at this. Sat up. Funny how selective their hearing could be.

'Five minutes?' Amelia demanded.

'Just at the top of this hill, according to Camille's directions.' He could have said, 'according to the directions', but he said her name a lot these days. Also, we'd listened to quite a lot of opera in the car, instead of the usual Lighthouse Family. 'We should see the villa any minute,' he went on.

'Chateau,' corrected Amelia as, at that moment, we took a sharp right turn between the endless rows of regimented vines.

At the end of the lane was an elaborate iron gate which gave on to a long, straight drive lined with gently swaying poplar trees. The house rose up before us. Both had been right. It was a villa in the classical Roman sense, flanked by cypress trees and with faded grey shutters, but a chateau in breadth and magnitude. Long, pale and elegant, with a flight of steps leading up to the double front door, which was partly obscured by an extravagant fountain cascading into a round pond in the foreground, it was breathtaking.

'Beautiful,' I breathed, on the edge of my seat now, the horrific journey forgotten.

This was what we Murray-Browns needed, I thought as I gripped the dashboard. This was what we had come for. In the distance, beyond the house, the vale spread out palely below: parched grass shimmered lemon in the bright sunshine and was studded with small farms and the odd charming cluster of tiny houses, their red roofs pierced by slender church spires. Further into the distance, the horizon stretched away to the glittering blue Mediterranean, where little boats bobbed and white sails flapped.

We tumbled out of the car into the intense heat almost before James had stopped, so desperate were we to escape the metal box that had encased, and not necessarily enhanced, our jarring personalities: keen to escape, swim and explore.

'Except we haven't got a key,' I thought out loud, as James and I heaved a couple of cases out of the boot. The children headed off eagerly around the fountain, empty-handed.

'No need, remember? Camille said her sister – ah. Here they are.'

As if on cue, the front door opened and a youngish couple emerged at the top of the flight of steps. The man was very handsome, with dark, flashing eyes in a narrow, tanned face and wearing a pale-blue shirt and tight jeans. His wife, slight and pretty with auburn curls, was in a white broderie anglaise sundress.

'You must be the Murray-Browns.' She smiled broadly, a slight lisp combining charmingly with her heavy French accent as she came down to greet us. The man glided quickly to relieve James of his case, just as servants would in one's dreams. Indeed, it felt like a dream as they introduced themselves as Thérèse and Michel Fragonard, here to look after us during our stay. As he took my bag, Michel looked deep into my eyes. Thérèse, meanwhile, was exclaiming how lovely it was to have us here, shaking our hands as we gushed our enthusiastic responses – both James and I speak French – saying what a fabulous place they lived in and how lucky they were. Introductions to the children were then achieved and the couple led us up the steps and through the front door. In we went, into a huge, double-storeyed hall. It was a tower, in actual fact, or a turret; you could see right up to the ancient wooden rafters. The centuries-old, thick, white walls were plastered all the way to the top with heraldic masonry and crossed swords and there was even a suit of armour in the corner.

'Oh – it's like a castle!' Tara exclaimed, spinning round like a child.

'It was once. Well, a chateau,' smiled Thérèse. 'But a tiny one, *bien sûr.*'

'Looks pretty big to me,' muttered Toby. I could see that Rory was pink with pleasure, and already going across to examine the shields.

Through double doors, we eagerly followed the petite and delicate Thérèse into an inner hall, and then along a corridor into a thoroughly modern and vast kitchen, complete with a highly polished slate island big enough for us all to sleep on and with enough stainless-steel equipment to baffle me for weeks. I circled around, gazing up at the gallery above. I wasn't sure how it would work vis-à-vis smells drifting up, but it was certainly very dramatic. The kitchen in turn led to a comfy sitting room with an enormous television, and then, again via double doors, into the more formal rooms, which were of such size and stature that everything in them seemed lost. They were all furnished in the most terrific French taste, with tapestries hanging from the walls and spindly Louis Quinze furniture dotted about, but very much designed for *petites* French *mesdemoiselles*, not hulking great Englishmen.

'I hope we don't break anything,' I murmured nervously, stroking a tightly upholstered chaise longue and considering Toby's bulk.

'Oh, it would not matter, it is all *brocante* finds,' Thérèse assured me. She seemed to do all the talking, I noticed, while Michel was more watchful. 'Camille, she is so clever, and everything she has found is for really very little in the markets. It is not good.'

She meant in the valuable sense, but the whole effect was very good indeed, and it struck me that Camille was surely a woman of many parts to be able to sing like a nightingale and furnish houses effortlessly, when it took me weeks to decide on a rug for the hall.

'And the bedrooms?' asked Amelia, keen to get to the nub of the matter. We'd been admiring the view over the grand piano in the drawing room down to the olive grove, but Amelia had seen enough olive groves on our drive. Michel, meanwhile, was opening a connecting door to a study, and I saw him glance at James for approval, but my husband was still distracted by the vista.

'*C'est très jolie!*' I assured Michel quickly, moving across to admire the pretty toile-papered room which housed the computer.

Michel nodded and gave me the smallest of smiles back, but his eyes were still on James as he closed the door. He had a dark, brooding intensity that was terribly attractive. Lizzie would be all over him, I thought.

'Yes, yes,' Thérèse was saying smilingly in answer to Amelia. 'Come, I show you.'

We followed as she turned on her elegant, tanned ankles and led us back through the interconnecting rooms to the front hall, then on up the curling stone staircase. The galleried landing which hovered above the drawing room and kitchen had a long corridor peeling off it which revealed one bedroom after another, all beautifully decorated and at our disposal, apart from a locked one – presumably Camille's – at the far end. With so many to choose from, even I couldn't foresee a fight, although I would definitely make sure I was in charge of allocating them, I thought, as my daughters' eyes glinted with intent.

Finally, we reached what was clearly the master bedroom, with a four-poster canopied bed, complete with a little crown at the head of a sweep of heavy red damask. Open French windows issued on to a balcony with a tiny iron table and chairs. Bougainvillea trailed off the balcony rail.

'Oh!' I gasped.

'You like it?' Thérèse smiled.

'I love it!' I assured her, but then realized she was not addressing me. Thérèse was gazing intently at James.

'We do so 'ope you will be 'appy here, Jaimes,' she said earnestly, pronouncing it with a soft 'J', 'and enjoy very much your stay. We are so very grateful.'

'Very grateful,' Michel echoed. It was almost the first time he'd spoken. He had an unusually deep voice. 'My niece, she is so special and precious to us all. The only child in the family, you see. We are indebted. You saved her life. You are a great man.'

In all his years as a doctor, I don't suppose James had ever been paid such a compliment. He went the colour of the damask draped over the bed. The rest of us gawped as Thérèse and Michel stepped forward solemnly and ceremonially to kiss him three times on each cheek.

'Oh, well, no, really, it was nothing. Anyone could have done it,' James blustered, scratching his pink cheek.

'Not anyone. Only a very eminent physician, such as yourself,' Thérèse told him, her amber eyes shining up into his. 'I 'ave looked you up on the internet, and you 'ide your light. You are famous in your field.'

'Good heavens, no. Hardly.'

'Books published.'

'Well, a paper, in the *Lancet*. I wouldn't call it a book. Pamphlet, perhaps. OK, a small book.' James ran his hand delightedly through his hair. Hopped about a bit.

'I should like to read it, Jaimes.'

I bit my lip to stifle a laugh. Knew, if she called him Jaimes again, I was in trouble. I couldn't look at the children. But Thérèse hadn't finished. She tripped prettily out to the balcony and plucked a sprig of bougainvillea which she then proceeded to tuck into the buttonhole of James's shabby, ancient linen jacket. She stroked the lapel reverently. 'There,' she murmured. Was she going to kiss that, too? 'And now' – she glanced around at the rest of us, as if emerging from a reverie – '*à bientôt*. We leave you.'

With a last charming smile, she and her husband departed, the latter, as he shut the door behind them, casting me another of his dark looks, as if confused by the wife of such a great man. Why so scruffy? So smelly? So . . . English?

The moment they'd gone, Thérèse having assured us that supper would be ready in an hour, the children mobbed their father up. 'Oh, so totally heroic, Dad, like, an EpiPen to the leg, so hard,' before disappearing off to argue over bedrooms.

To say that James had a spring in his step would be putting it mildly. He positively bounded around the room, taking off his jacket, but being careful with the buttonhole, emptying his suitcase, humming all the while, pausing occasionally to glance in the mirror and smooth back what remained of his fair hair from his high forehead.

'Lovely girl, that.'

'Very,' I agreed. 'Lovely couple, actually.'

'She had such a charming way about her, didn't she? Very like her sister, in fact.'

'Really?' I said lightly, forcing myself not to say darkly, *I wouldn't know.*

'Yes. They've both got this endearing way of being terrifically sincere and making one feel really . . .' He searched for the word.

'God-like?' I hazarded.

He grinned. 'I'll take that.'

Still humming merrily and refusing to be deflated, he placed his battered old sunhat on a chest of drawers, hung his shirts in the wardrobe, removed the flower from his jacket and popped it in the vase out on the balcony, and then broke out, dear God, into the aria from *The Pearl Fishers.*

Later, when I'd reallocated the children's rooms, telling

them they couldn't possibly take the best ones and must leave the nicest for Sally and her boyfriend – the very idea of Sally sleeping with anyone made my eyes pop – which was next door to ours, and no, not the second best either, that was for Grandpa, and generally shuffling them off to the far end, making sure Tara stayed firmly up here opposite us, I had a shower and changed into something cooler. It was still incredibly hot at seven in the evening and, as I put on a flimsy dress, I was pleased to see that the fake tan appeared to have worked its magic. The wobbly bits seemed marginally less off-putting and, if I walked slowly in my swimming costume to the pool, I decided, so as not to jiggle the cellulite, I might not frighten the natives. I smiled to myself in the mirror as I added a slick of lipstick and a dash of scent, then headed downstairs for a much-needed drink.

Supper was already underway, judging by the delicious smells wafting from the kitchen. As I passed through, out of habit I offered to help, but was told firmly 'Non, merci!' by a smiling Thérèse as she chopped garlic efficiently, gold bangles jangling. Redundant, I stepped outside on to the vast crenellated terrace. I stopped, momentarily, to let the low sun bathe my face, feeling its warmth, then helped myself to the most sumptuous basket-weave armchair with creamy calico cushions, still in the sun's rays. As I settled back happily, closing my eyes, Michel appeared, as if by magic, to ask huskily what I would like to drink. James had gone for a prowl around the grounds after his shower and I dithered now, held by those mesmerizing dark eyes, wondering what was on offer.

'The champagne is delicious,' he purred.

'Well, that sounds perfect, Michel,' I said, trying not to behave like a sixteen-year-old ingénue and to get a grip. I had actually been on holiday before. Stayed in nice hotels. 'Let's open that, shall we?'

He disappeared with an enigmatic little smile, and I couldn't quite decide if it was a smirk or a smoulder. Was he laughing at me, or flirting? The former, probably, as he no doubt spotted that I was way out of my depth. I determined to be a bit more assertive and, when he came back with a bottle and some glasses on a tray and slowly poured the champagne, handing it to me, I sipped it speculatively as if determining how good it was.

'Lovely,' I declared eventually. I put my head on one side, giving him an appraising look. 'I imagine we've rather ruined your quiet summer, Michel. Just what you need, a crowd of unexpected guests to cater for!'

'Not at all. We depend on people passing through for company.' His eyes didn't leave mine for one moment. 'It can be very quiet, just the two of us, in such a large house. Lonely. Particularly at night.' He meant the evenings, of course, his English not being up to the finer nuances of the language.

'Yes, I can imagine. Although I gather you have your own cottage?'

'The lodge, yes. You passed it at the top of the drive.'

'Ah, yes. Of course.' There was a pause. It went on for longer than was entirely comfortable. 'Won't you sit down?'

He was still standing over me: not hovering uncertainly, more from a position of strength, making me feel uneasy.

'Thank you, but I must help Thérèse in the kitchen.' He inclined his head with a little bow but, again, there was something mocking in the gesture, and the eyes were definitely amused. I wondered if he was goading me on to make amused eyes back, twinkle knowingly, so I deliberately didn't, knowing it was the sort of thing Lizzie would do. Also, I remembered Mum telling me that all Frenchmen were scallywags and I made up my mind not to make a fool of myself.

'Oh, good – is this for us?'

The teenagers were upon me, wrapped in towels, fresh from the pool, hair dripping, faces still damp. I made them take the cushions off the chairs before they sat in wet costumes but enjoyed seeing them lounge delightedly about, then leap up again and line up for champagne as I filled their glasses. Rory sweetly remembered, before he sat down, to ask if I needed a top-up, but was much more relaxed, I thought, in swimming trunks and a T-shirt, laughing with Toby. And since our life had so little jam on it, I was delighted to see them all revelling in the lap of luxury for once, realizing that the exquisite canapés were actually for them too, reaching for them eagerly, telling me excitedly about the amazing pool, which I'd seen from my window.

'Infinity, Mum, so the water literally laps at the edge and seems like it's going to spill out. You feel like you're falling into the valley.'

'It's constantly topped up, automatically,' Toby told us, his huge frame in a large armchair somehow looking better here than it did in London, in our semi. More space for it, perhaps. And, of course, they'd all be brown soon, had caught some colour on their faces already. Suddenly I warmed to these boyfriends of these daughters of mine.

They were just young lads, someone's precious boys, as mine were my precious girls, and I determined not to be judgemental, not to live my daughters' lives for them. Just because I'd made mistakes, it didn't follow that they would, and anyway, it was unlikely either of these boys would break their hearts as mine had been broken at their age, I thought, watching Rory gaze adoringly at Tara. If anything, it would be the other way round. I must stop being so vigilant, so constantly on the lookout for a bastard. These two had far more of James about them in terms of temperament than the man I'd been supposed to marry, the man I'd been engaged to, which was a very good thing.

And much as I'd wanted to invite friends, now that we were here on our own, it was nice to be just us, I thought, as I listened to them chattering away about a bar they'd found, made from logs, down on a terrace below in the olive grove. Yes, to be a family, and to expand into a house and a sun that wasn't usually ours: to eat and swim and tan and laugh together – I wanted that. As James came up the sloping lawn towards us, eyes as alight as his children's at what he'd found while patrolling the boundaries, exploring the gardens, I was so pleased for him, too. If anyone needed a little ego massage it was James, and I resolved to tell him tonight that what Thérèse and Michel had said was true. That he was the cleverest man – after all, hadn't he graduated at the top of his class at St Thomas's when he was twenty-four, then watched, as less able but more obsequious men, adept at oiling the management wheels, had swept past him? I resolved not to make fun.

As he approached the brow of the hill and the terrace, he stopped. Turned around, back to a sound in the distance behind him, and shaded his eyes. I followed his line of sight. Below us, on the valley floor, a dusty white lane snaked its way between the vineyards, the same one that had brought us here. It clearly carried barely any traffic but navigating it now was a small red Polo with a bulging suitcase on its roof. You could almost hear the music blaring from here: almost smell the cigarette smoke from the pair of them, hear the gales of laughter. I smiled. Mum and Lizzie. Who got on like a house on fire and always had done – Lizzie being the daughter my mother should have had – and who had come out a couple of days before us, to stop, sensibly, for a night or two on the way down, but had been told in no uncertain terms not to arrive at the chateau before us. They'd done quite well, I thought: shown unusual restraint, leaving a respectable hour or so for us to meet Michel and Thérèse and settle in. I smiled. Probably been in a bar around the corner all the time.

I guessed Mum was behind the wheel, as the car was shifting and she only had one speed: ninety. That went for her life, too. Throttle out, foot down. Full on. Of course Lizzie admired her, who wouldn't? But she hadn't been brought up by her. We were always moving apartments, moving schools, I was constantly walking into strange classrooms, sitting down at a desk beside yet another slightly guarded child, no brothers or sisters to share the experience with, to moan with later over tea. Mum's boyfriends coming and going. But why hadn't I forgiven her? Why hadn't I grown up about all that? I'd had an awful lot of love, too. Watching Mum and Lizzie make their no doubt hilarious way towards us, I determined I would, this holiday. Make a new start. Try to see her as Lizzie and my girls – and even James, to an extent – did. As a free spirit, someone to be admired and cherished, not as an irresponsible irritant, an extra child.

The car disappeared from view for a bit but then reappeared as it came round the corner. Down the poplar-lined drive it bounced, before sweeping into the gravel around the fountain. I put my drink down and prepared to go and greet them. As I got to my feet, smoothing down my dress, Lizzie, surprisingly, emerged from the driver's side. My mother, in a bizarre pair of mauve dungaree shorts, got out of the back. Then the passenger door opened and a strange man got out from beside Lizzie. This was not Jackson. He was tall and rangy and very suntanned. He wore a pink shirt and bright-blue linen trousers and was attractive but probably older than he looked, despite the leather bracelets dangling from his wrist. He gazed around appreciatively, as they all did, not yet spotting us at the side of the house on the terrace.

Mum's hand shot up when she saw me. 'Darling!' she called. 'This is just totally and utterly divine!'

As she came tripping across the gravel towards us in pretty gold sandals, Lizzie turned and took a bag out of the boot. The stranger helped her with it and they exchanged smiles.

The children glanced round at me enquiringly. I shrugged, lips tightening. Amelia's mouth twitched.

Slowly, I went to meet them. Lizzie was laughing up at the man now, and pointing at the conical towers in delight. Then she spotted me coming towards her and waved, leaning in to her new companion, obviously telling him who I was. Oh, she was the limit, I seethed to myself. The absolute limit. Jackson couldn't come, so she'd brought someone else – not even told me! Knew I'd say no, probably. Lord knows what James would say. As they came closer, though, I stopped. My mother had paused to let them catch up, and suddenly it was she who was linking arms with the pink-shirted one. She who was gazing adoringly up into the leather-braceleted one's eyes as they came across to the terrace.

Lizzie reached me first. Embraced me warmly. 'Nothing to do with me, Flora,' she said firmly in my ear. 'Absolutely all her own work.'

Chapter Seven

'Darling! How gorgeous! What a pad!' My mother was tripping across the gravel towards me, beaming widely. In another moment, she was embracing me warmly. 'This is Jean-Claude by the way, isn't he heaven? I found him just outside Valence.'

What could I do but shake the hand of the tall, attractive man who was advancing, murmuring, '*Enchanté*,' his smile reaching right up to his sleepy sea-green eyes, which crinkled at the edges.

My smile was a great deal tighter than his and, although I managed to say something in response, it certainly wasn't '*Enchanté*'. Luckily, Lizzie was alive to the situation and appeared like magic to move him swiftly on to meet the others. Mum was oblivious, naturally, cigarette already alight, eyes, too, as they followed Jean-Claude's lean silhouette on its way.

'We stopped off at his antique shop,' she went on in a low, excited voice. 'Such a dear little place, we spotted it because it had the prettiest things for sale outside. Darling little bistro chairs, birdcages, baskets – just the sort of shabby-chic things I like – and inside, we found poor Jean-Claude slumped behind his desk. He'd got a terrible attack of the glums because he needed to get to the *brocante* fair in Aix for more stock – he'd practically run out – but his van had broken down. So I said we'd take him. Wasn't that lucky?'

'Very. So he's off to Aix, is he?' I kept the bright smile going, admittedly slightly encouraged by this news.

'Oh, yes. Eventually.'

'Right. So how long is he staying?'

'Just a few days. You know how it is.'

I did. Just a few days could turn into months with my mother, and in the case of one particular character called Neville, years. 'Is he your stepfather?' the children at school would ask. 'Yes. No. I don't know.' I didn't. What constituted a stepfather? Someone who took you to ballet and swimming (he never did that) or someone who slept with your mother (he certainly did that) before sliding off to some dodgy record company he ran just off the King's Road. Neville, Charles, Tommy, Casper . . . all pleasant men, none violent or unkind to me – my mother picked well – but just not what I wanted. Not what I'd read about in Enid Blyton. I wanted a mother who made jam, a father who came home in a suit, a brother called Tim and a dog called Rufus.

'He's the most terrific cook. He's been telling us about how to marinate hams and smoke fish properly. And he does all sorts of fascinating things with pickles.'

'We have a cook. And you know all about pickles, you're forever getting yourself into one.'

'Oh, darling, don't be a bore, he's terribly amusing. And the children will love him.'

'Is he a boyfriend, Mum?'

'Oh, boyfriend, shmoyfriend . . .' She waved her

cigarette airily. Saw my face. 'No, of course not,' she said quickly. 'But he is frightfully attractive, don't you think?'

He'd gone to help Lizzie with more luggage from the car and was well out of earshot now.

'Mum, you promised!' I hissed.

'I promised no more unsuitable younger men. But he's older than he looks, darling. At least fifty.'

'But what will the Brig and the others think?'

'Oh, the Brig won't mind, you know what he's like. He's on cracking form, incidentally. Looks divine in his summer gear, very tropical.'

'You've seen him?'

'We bumped into him and Rachel on the boat. They were staying at hotels on the way down, too – in fact, we thought they'd beat us here. Sally and her new man are making their way separately.' Her face puckered a moment and she looked worried. 'Flora, speaking of Sally's new man, Lizzie told me something rather disturbing in the car. She had a chat with Rachel on the boat, and it seems Sally has hooked up with someone ... well, someone rather surprising. It appears she's lost a bit of weight and she ran into him while she was cooking at a rather grand house party in Fife. Flora –'

'Granny!'

'Darlings!' She broke off suddenly, her face wreathed in smiles as her granddaughters came running across the lawn towards her. Having met Jean-Claude, they were keen to get the lowdown, and looked thrilled to bits. Nothing their grandmother did could ever shock them. They ran into her arms and whatever my mother was about to say about Sally's new beau was lost in a flurry of greetings and exclamations. They immediately went into a huddle to whisper about Jean-Claude.

James had made it up the hill by now and was viewing the scene with dismay. I couldn't meet his eye.

'Lizzie, what were you thinking?' I hissed when she came back with her case.

'I couldn't stop her,' she muttered. 'You know what she's like, batting her eyelids: bat, bat, bat. He was in the seat beside her before I could say, "*Comment s'apelle?*"'

'Oh, I *knew* I should have brought her with us. She's not to be trusted.'

'Well, never mind, he's here now, and it won't be for long. He's actually terribly nice. Come on, show me around. And I need to talk to you.'

I linked her arm in mine and took her off, aware that James was tailing me. He caught up with us upstairs, despite me having taken the stairs at a canter, and cornered us halfway down the corridor. He was breathing rather heavily as he bore down on us.

'Who, pray, is that man?'

'He's an antique dealer on his way to Aix. Lizzie gave him a lift.'

Lizzie glanced at me in alarm.

'He's clearly your mother's latest lover.'

'No, no, of course he's not. He's about fifteen years younger than her.'

'Exactly. Where's he going to sleep?'

'Down the far end.' I waved my hand to indicate a long way away. 'Next to Rory. And Mum can go next door to us.'

'What, and you'll stay up all night patrolling the corridors on account of our daughter *and* your mother? Well, I hope she creeps in his direction rather than ours. I really don't want to lie awake listening to that all night.'

'Well, imagine how I feel!' I said heatedly.

'I can't think what Camille will say.'

'What's it got to do with Camille?' I snapped.

'Well, she's bound to hear about it, isn't she? It's her house. It doesn't look great, does it?' He shot me a venomous look before stalking off pompously.

He was usually quite sympathetic towards my mother: the one telling me to relax about her attraction to increasingly younger men and to go with the flow, that it was no reflection on me. Under the opera singer's roof, however, it was clearly a different matter.

'Unlike James to take the moral high ground,' commented Lizzie as I showed her into her room.

'I think he's got a crush on our hostess and he wants us to all match up. I wouldn't mind, but when the Brig arrives he'll launch into "When I was at Dartmoor . . ." as if it's Sandy Lane, Barbados, but that's all right, apparently. As long as it's *his* family,' I said petulantly, which wasn't like me. I loved the Brig.

'Crikey, I've even got a bell pull!' Lizzie was exploring excitedly.

'It doesn't work. Amelia's already tried it with Tara listening to the row of bells in the kitchen, but they still have to revert to texting me when they want something.' I sat down miserably on the bed. 'I'm so glad you're here, Lizzie. I've a feeling I've bitten off more than I can chew by having both sets of parents here. And now bloody Jean-Claude.'

'Or JC, as your mother calls him – totally without irony, incidentally. It'll be fine, don't worry. Um, listen,

Flora, talking of James's family, we met the Brig and Rachel on the boat coming over.'

'Yes, I know. Mum said. With the Brig looking like something out of a Brian Rix farce and Rachel telling her that Sally has met someone even my *mother* thinks is unsuitable.'

'Exactly. And the thing is . . .' Lizzie scratched her leg awkwardly. 'Well, the thing is, you know how you always say Sally is so competitive with you. So keen to outdo you . . .'

'Oh, *don't* get me started on that. Remember that Christmas when James gave me some pearl earrings, and the next time we saw her she was wearing some which she told me were *much* bigger than mine!'

'I know, and –'

'That Joseph coat I bought, exactly. Which I'd saved up for ages to buy, and then she went straight on the internet and bought the exact same one. Albeit several sizes larger.'

'Well, that's the other thing, Flora. She's lost some weight, apparently.'

'So Mum said.'

'Which means she's much more marketable, if you see what I mean.'

'Well, that's no bad thing, although, knowing Sally, it'll be a couple of pounds at the most and it'll all be back on by the end of the holiday. Oh God.' I glanced at my watch. Got hastily to my feet. 'We must go down to supper, Lizzie. Thérèse said eight o'clock, and I don't want to be late on the first night. James will kill me. He wants us all on parade.'

'Yes, OK, but hang on a moment, going back to this

competitive thing.' Lizzie looked strangely nervous. 'The reason this guy she's with is unsuitable –'

'Is because he's one of Mum's ex-boyfriends. I'm already there, Lizzie.'

'No, not one of hers . . .'

'Shit – one of yours? Please don't tell me it's that chiselled-faced moron you met last time we were in Scotland? The druggy-looking one?'

'No, no, nothing like that. It's –'

'Well, thank the Lord, because, frankly, I sometimes think that despite Amelia being so opposed to it all at the moment it wouldn't take much to skew her in the opposite direction. She is so mercurial, and the last thing I want is some good-looking dude peddling wacky bacc –'

'Oh, *wouldn't* it take much!'

Suddenly, Amelia flew through the open door and was amongst us. I froze, horrified.

'Oh! Darling. I was just saying –'

'Just saying you think I'm so fickle that if some sad boyfriend of Sally's or Granny's turned up with an ounce of grass in his pocket I'd be like – ooh, how exciting, can Tobes and I have a spliff, you experienced old hippies, you? Thanks for that, Mum. No, really. Thanks. I came to tell you supper's ready, by the way.'

She turned on her heel and stalked off towards the staircase, furious. I raced after her, appalled. Flew down the stairs after her.

'No! Amelia, I did *not* mean that! All I meant was that, delighted though I am that you *don't* indulge, I certainly don't want the older generation to think that just because they're with the young, you won't be shocked. Have carte blanche to roll up wherever they want. You know how Mum likes to be part of the cool gang, and –'

Amelia turned on her heel at the bottom of the stairs. I nearly banged into her. 'No, Mum, she *is* cool. Just because she doesn't act as everyone expects an older woman to act, *you* think she's embarrassing. Well, she's not. She's true to herself. And that is so refreshing.'

'Refreshing! To you it might be, because you're a generation removed, but let me tell you, young lady, it wasn't much fun having no example to follow when I was growing up, and I am determined –'

'To revert to the 1950s? Call me young lady?'

'No, I'm just saying –'

'What, Mum? Think about it.' We were glaring at each other in the hall; the colour was high in her cheeks. 'You didn't turn out like Granny, did you? If anything, you're prim and proper, so how does it follow that setting a *good* example is going to create a good child? You should probably go in for a bit of free love and dope-smoking if you really want to take your responsibilities to me and Tara seriously. If you really want us to end up exactly like *you*.'

Her dark eyes blazed right into mine before she turned and marched off. Through the double doors she swept, in her long patchwork skirt, to the inner hall, then out through the open French windows to the terrace, where supper was laid on a pretty Provençal cloth, and where everyone was sitting waiting, ready to eat. Amelia, now on the other side of the table, facing back towards the house, glared at me when I came into view.

Oh, splendid. Splendid. What a terrific start to the holiday, I thought, heart pounding, as Lizzie, who'd clearly been waiting for the coast to clear, slipped past me to the terrace. She shot me a sympathetic look. I walked unsteadily after her and took the only remaining place at the table, which was between Rory and Jean-Claude, and, unfortunately, opposite Amelia.

I shook out my napkin, feeling wretched. I hated rowing with her. Would feel low for days now, worrying as she made me suffer: scowling and sulking and shooting me black looks at every conceivable opportunity, as she was now, across the table. And it couldn't be a more beautiful setting, I thought sadly, as I managed to smile at Thérèse who was setting enormous bowls of daube provençale on the table in front of us. This elevated terrace with its vast urns of pink bougainvillea, its limbs twisting right up to the balcony above, cicadas calling to one another in the soft, balmy air, the heavenly view over the valley and the sea in the distance, surrounded by my nearest and dearest. Let's face it, it was my dream. Why, then, did it suddenly taste so sour? I helped myself to a few pieces of beef and onion and felt it turn to dust and ashes in my mouth.

My phone vibrated in my pocket. Although I always told the children not to look at their phones during meals, I did, surreptitiously. It was a text from Sally: 'On our way. Had a puncture in Rouen but be with you at about midnight. Save us some food.'

Despite my mood, I gave a small smile. Sally never forgot her stomach.

'What?' demanded Amelia opposite me, not about to let me off the hook.

'It's Sally. They're on their way. They had a puncture.' I glanced at my husband to make sure he'd heard.

James nodded, more kindly now that he sensed I was getting it in the neck from our daughter. 'We'll save them some food.'

'That's what she was asking.'

We exchanged a knowing smile, at peace again, as James and I could be in moments. One sulker was enough in a family.

'Not a secret lover, then?'

I turned to Amelia. 'No. I have no life of my own, Amelia. You know that.'

'More fool you.'

The meal continued. Toby looked awkward as Amelia looked mutinous, and I wondered how he dealt with her temper: it must have come his way by now. Mum, rather bucked now the pressure was off her, chattered away gaily. Tara sensed drama and looked nervous for Rory's sake, but she needn't have worried. He smiled gamely and even bravely tried to engage Amelia in conversation. Such was his heroism, it forced me to smile at JC beside me.

'How long have you had your antique shop, Jean-Claude?' I asked.

'Not long. One year, almost. I want for more.'

Don't we all, I thought. 'I'm sure you'll have many more years to expand,' I said encouragingly. 'It's always hard starting a business.'

'Yes, because too many people want to sell crap like me.'

'Oh.' I was startled. 'I'm sure it's not crap.'

'Is that not what you call it?' He frowned, perplexed. 'Your friend Lizzie, she come in and say, "What a load of old crap."'

'She meant bric-a-brac,' I said quickly. 'That's what we call it. Or antiques, of course.'

My mother was sitting beside him and I realized he had his hand on her knee. He saw me look. Smiled. 'You are protective of your mother. But you need not worry. We understand one another.'

'Of course you do, because age is no barrier to anything, is it? We should all just be free spirits and leap into cars with any old passing trade.'

I'd said exactly what had come into my head, employing no filter whatsoever. I was slightly out of control and knocked my wine back boisterously, missing my mouth, so some went down my chin. Amelia was watching me again. Jean-Claude removed his hand from my mother's knee.

'Your mother is a very beautiful woman,' he told me seriously. 'Photographed by Donovan, dressed by Dior, Lizzie told me in the car. A flower of her generation. That sort of appeal never fades.'

'I know,' I said, tears unaccountably springing to my eyes. 'I know, and she's like that inside and out. Which is rare.' I swallowed.

'Your father is dead?' he asked, changing the subject.

'No idea.' I said brightly, blinking hard. 'Mum got a bit confused in the seventies. A bit . . . flowery.'

'Bitch,' muttered Amelia.

'No, darling, Granny would say the same.'

'What would I say?' enquired Mum.

'That you got a bit muddled about my father.'

'Oh, yes, I did. Sometimes I think it might have been Cat Stevens but, in my heart, I know it was probably that frightfully good-looking photographer who keeled over in the nineties.'

'Didn't you think it might be Leonard Cohen?' asked Amelia, brightening to this, her favourite subject. Rory was looking stunned, and I saw Tara make frantic eye contact with me to call a halt to proceedings, but it was too late. Amelia was showing off, enjoying herself. 'After all, Mum's got a similar personality,' she went on.

'Oh, thanks. Depressive? Gloomy?'

'Exactly. And there was that song about Suzanne –'

'Oh, no, that wasn't me,' interjected Mum. 'He'd got the hots for Suzanne Verdal by then, Armand Vaillancourt's wife.'

'But . . . you mean you honestly don't know . . .' Rory asked quietly.

I turned. 'Who my father was? No. And was never tempted to find out. As my mother says, in all likelihood, he's dead and, if not, he'll be married, and who wants that sort of bombshell turning up on their doorstep?'

'I suppose,' said Rory doubtfully. 'But when you were younger . . . ?'

'Oh sure, I wondered,' I said lightly. *Wondered?* I'd been consumed by it. Even stalked a few other possible suspects with my then boyfriend, who was as intrigued as I was. I recalled the two of us gazing down into a Kensington basement kitchen, watching an older man in cords and a jumper eat Sunday lunch with his family. Reading about another in a fashion magazine. But I never did anything about it.

'Mum hasn't got the nerve,' Amelia said. 'You'd think she has, but she hasn't. God, if it was me, I'd have been snipping bits of their hair off, testing for DNA.'

'Yes, you would,' I admitted, knowing she was still furious with me or she wouldn't be so unkind, but also knowing Amelia envied me my exotic parentage. She was at that age when she didn't want middle-class, middle-brow parents, would have loved to have been able to say, 'Mick Jagger might be my father . . .'

'Do you think you ever will? Find him?' Rory clearly didn't like loose ends.

'No. I'll leave it to Amelia to discover on *Who Do You Think You Are?* when she's famous.'

I smiled, meaning it. Wanting her to know I meant it. To my surprise, she smiled back, this sparky, combative, argumentative daughter of mine, whom I loved, along with her sister, more than life itself. And who I truly believed could do something great one day, if she put her mind to it. 'Mum thinks I'm going to be the next David Bailey because I can take a few pictures.'

'Why not?' I told her warmly, sensing an olive branch, knowing we were fine suddenly. Almost fine. Almost agreeing a truce on this balmy, delightful, Provençal evening: almost agreeing it was too beautiful to spoil, no matter how upset or hurt we were. 'Amelia won this terrific *National Geographic* prize —'

'When I was about fifteen.'

'Sixteen.'

'And went on to win another one run by *Countryfile* on TV. A national competition.' It was Toby who'd spoken up this time.

I turned down the table to smile at him, prepared to love anyone who loved my children. I'd often wondered if Mum loved me like that. She didn't seem to. Not in that fiercely protective, perhaps obsessive, way. She just did her own thing and let me get on with mine. I sighed. Knocked back some more rosé. There was no prescription for mothering, of course. Sometimes it was best not to be too analytical, as I was disposed to be. Just let it all wash over you.

The evening wore on in a far more convivial manner than it had begun although, of course, nine bottles of rosé helped enormously. We'd all succumbed to first-night excitement and our relief to be here and, hopefully, the first rows were over and done with. We were settling down now under the soft, navy-blue sky to get seriously pissed.

James had nipped inside to ask Thérèse and Michel to join us after pudding, and Michel had arrived with a tray of tiny glasses, full of something evil-looking, which we all regarded in mock-horror but gulped down heartily. I watched as James, arms extended over the backs of the chairs beside him, expanded happily on his work to Thérèse when she asked him about it, enjoying her interest. Michel sat quietly by, listening, leaning in, picking up tips from the great man. Very occasionally, he'd glance in my direction as I pretended to listen to Mum's prattle and, again, his dark gaze would linger for a few moments longer than was absolutely necessary. Flirting. Definitely flirting, I thought with a sudden rush of excitement and neat alcohol to the head. But why me? I sucked my tummy in and sat up a bit straighter. No one had flirted with me for years, and Lizzie was younger and far more chic, with her snappy little haircut, Agnès B shirt and pedal-pushers. I wondered if she'd noticed? But she was engaged in a heated debate with Tara and Toby at the other end of the table about whether or not feminism was dead, if it had all been sorted out in the sixties. Cigarette stuck to her lower lip, eyes drooping, mouth lurching off to the side; she was clearly spectacularly drunk, unlike the young, who were far more used to shots than us, the white-wine-guzzling generation. Why did we drink the filthy stuff when there were gorgeous liqueurs like this around? I knocked back another thimbleful when Michel slid one across the table to me, together with one of those sizzling stares.

This, along with the laughter, chatter and general state of inebriation, meant that we – or certainly I – completely forgot we were expecting other guests, so when Rachel's car drew up, only James heard it. But then, it was his family, so perhaps he'd been a little more alive to their imminent arrival. At any rate, he set off across the well-sprinkled lawn, and it was only when I heard car doors slamming and voices raised in greeting that I realized they were here.

James materialized from the darkness around the side of the house with his father, who looked older and smaller, as the elderly often do when you haven't seen them for some time. And of course he'd just endured a long car journey; quite shattering for any eighty-one-year-old. Under the twinkling lights hanging in the trees he came across the lawn with his stick, shuffling fast, blinking delightedly. I was already on my way to meet him and when I did I reached for both his hands, which were papery and bony in mine, like birds in rough silk.

'Drummond. You made it.' I kissed him fondly. 'How lovely to see you.'

It was. His delight was childlike, as I knew it would be.

'My dear! What a place! What a *palace*, in fact!' He waved his stick about demonstratively, mouth and eyes gaping.

'I know! Aren't we lucky?'

'*Aren't* we? I say, frightfully good of you to have us, Flora. You didn't have to, you know. Could have had a year on your own for a change, without the blasted outlaws. Or asked friends. But we are *so* thrilled.'

As so often happens, when one does the right thing against one's baser instincts and someone appreciates it, it felt good. I felt warm and happy and so pleased we'd asked them. There would be irritations, of course, but I loved the Brig and revelled in his pleasure.

'And I'm thrilled you're here. I'd show you around, but it's best when it's light. Right now, what I'm sure you'd like most in the world is a drink.'

'Would I!' he roared, squeezing my hands again but releasing them to wave his stick in greeting towards his granddaughters, who were hastening across. 'Darlings! Get the beers in!'

'Got more than beer, Grandpa!' They embraced him fondly. They adored their grandfather, long ago accepting the circumstances of the family tragedy.

Rachel was standing beside me now under the tree lights, her presence quiet and enigmatic as always. She'd probably been there all the time whilst the Brig and I had been talking, without me being aware.

'Really decent of you, Flora,' she said, in her clipped, slightly detached fashion. She was small and squat with a sharp beak of a nose and a no-nonsense haircut streaked with grey. Not a shred of make-up. She rearranged her mauve cardigan around her shoulders. 'I wouldn't have bothered if I'd been you. Would have given us a miss this year.'

'Nonsense, it's lovely to have you.'

It was now. And Rachel was never any trouble. Just a bit socially awkward. She never really initiated a conversation and found it unnecessary to keep one going for the sake of it, so one ended up making all the running, which was a bit exhausting. But then, she'd had a difficult life. Had never moved out of home, and probably never would now. She was the Brig's carer and was happy enough in that role, I think. It was the other one who was trickier. The other one, who, when her car arrived, would bound out of the semi-darkness towards me like some enormous puppy, all breathy and sweaty, ready with some incredibly chippy remark about how this place was lovely, but, my gosh, you should have seen the castle she'd cooked in the previous summer. That really *was* something. I hadn't seen Sally since Christmas, when she'd told me the Christmas pudding I'd brought was too dry and the cashmere shawl I'd given her would be perfect for Barney, her dachshund's, basket.

'Where are the others?'

'About ten minutes away, apparently. They would have been here before us, but they had a puncture. Flora, before they get here, can I just have a word?'

'Of course. In fact, I was going to show you your room first anyway. I had a feeling you'd rather settle in and get your bearings than launch straight into the drinks.'

'I wouldn't mind. I'll just say hello to the girls.'

She went across and greeted her nieces and my mother, and I waited for her by the French windows that led into the kitchen. Her face seemed strained, but then Rachel was hard to read and I knew the best way was to give her time, not to prattle on and fill the silence but wait for her to formulate what she wanted to say. I wondered, as we went silently through the vast house to the front hall and stairs, if this would all be a bit overwhelming for her. Brechallis was a big house, to be sure, but this was on a different scale, and so opulent and richly furnished – over the top, even. She'd need time to adjust. I was glad I'd given her the small, slightly old-fashioned green room with a paisley print on the walls, shelves of paperback books and low lamps. It was somewhat apart from the others and it had its own little bathroom, so she could be private. I showed her inside. She gazed around as I leaned down to turn on the bedside lamp.

'It's lovely, Flora. Thank you.'

I could tell she meant it and was pleased I'd got it right. I crossed the room and opened the French windows on to the tiny balcony.

'I thought you could sit out here and have breakfast if you didn't want to join the throng downstairs. Not everyone does.' Rachel, I knew, liked the morning to herself, usually to sketch in her room or go and paint on the hill behind the house.

She joined me outside, and we gazed down on to the drive below. 'Oh, I'll manage a croissant with the gang. Don't worry about me, Flora.'

'Well, we certainly will be a gang,' I warned. 'When Sally and her boyfriend arrive we'll be thirteen – imagine – for every meal!'

She turned to me and moistened her lips. Looked

worried for a moment. 'Yes, and that's what I want to talk to you about. Sally's boyfriend.'

'Who is he, Rachel? Lizzie and Mum keep hinting darkly that he's entirely unsuitable and that, apparently, we know him. Sally doesn't know anyone that I know, not that I'm aware of.'

'No. She didn't.' She groped for the words. 'But you know how she looks up to you, Flora. Copies you, even.'

I blanched. 'She copies me, but I don't think it's because she looks *up* to me. Quite the opposite, in fact.'

'Oh, she does,' she said quickly. 'She admires absolutely everything you do. Your recipes, your articles, reads every-thing you write –'

'Yes, but we're both cooks.'

'It's not just that. There's a very obvious hero worship going on.'

I made a face. Not from where I was sitting. More of a gleeful needling. I stared at her, wishing she was slightly more forthcoming. 'What are you saying, Rachel?'

'I'm saying that you mustn't blame her, really.' She looked truly concerned now. 'Of course, it seems extraor-dinary in the cold light of day but, in the scheme of things, taking everything I've said into account, it also seems quite natural. That if she ran into him, and if the timing was right –'

'Ran into who?' I interrupted, bewildered, wishing Rachel could just spit things out. At that moment, a car swept down the drive, headlights blazing, no doubt illuminating us on the balcony. It swung around the fountain and came to a halt right below us, just proud of the chateau steps.

The automatic outside lights had already sprung into action, so the interior of the sleek convertible clearly showed Sally's blonde head. She was in the passenger seat. Behind the driver's wheel was a dark, male one. For a moment, just a crazy, stupid moment, my heart stopped beating. I gripped the balcony rail. But then it carried on. My heart. *Don't be mad. Don't be idiotic. Not in a million years.*

Sally's door opened and she got out, except — she'd changed. Enormously. She was much, much smaller. Slimmer. In fact . . . she must have lost about five stone. I gawped as she glanced up to us on the balcony. She waved and smiled triumphantly, her usually chubby face chiselled and heart-shaped.

'We're here!' she cried.

I stared down in wonder. Her generally unruly mop of blonde hair, which hitherto had hung down her back in a messy heap, was cut in soft layers, ending around her chin — just the one chin, where there used to be many. My eyes travelled in disbelief down her figure. She was still statuesque, but totally devoid of fat, and not wallowing in a billowing smock but wearing trim white trousers and a smart blue blazer. She looked incredible.

Her companion got out of the car, a lean figure in a creased linen jacket and jeans, but Sally's eyes didn't leave my face for a moment. She would have seen me step back in horror. Would have seen my hand go to my mouth. Because, even before he looked up, I knew who it was. Before that head topped by floppy auburn hair, only faintly flecked with grey, turned, and that intelligent face looked up, blue eyes twinkling, I knew. That the man Sally had met whilst cooking at a house party in Fife and had brought down to the south of France to plunge amongst my family was none other than my ex-boyfriend – my ex-fiancé, in fact. None other than the man I'd spent my formative years with and been very much in love with. His merry eyes met mine in the bright lights, and everything flashed. It was Max.

Chapter Eight

I don't even remember when I met Max. He was just one of the crowd all those years ago, part of the scenery, and although he was incredibly good-looking, there were more interesting boys around. His sort of looks were too obvious, too conspicuous. I liked a bit more subtlety. A touch more light and shade. Six foot four – too tall for me, really; I'm five three – so I remember not considering him at all as we sat around the wine bars and pubs of Clapham and Fulham, me, Lucy, Gus, Fiz, Mimi, Parrot, the rest of the gang. Someone that handsome clearly knew it and he was exuberant and noisy too, with that braying, self-confident laugh. My girlfriends, particularly Mimi, were all over him. It made my lip curl. Everything about him was a cliché, from his floppy nut-brown hair and tawny, ski-tanned complexion to his huge smile, long legs and broad shoulders. The way he drank too much and partied too hard – he was an unusually good dancer, which annoyed me. Who wants a man who can dance? And he drove too fast in his predictable, red MG convertible. Ghastly.

And so I ignored him. And watched as Mimi's skirts got ever shorter, her tops lower as she crossed off the days until she'd see him at the next party, meanwhile, dragging me off to Oxford Street to find the perfect little top to go with her latest mini. We believed, in those days, as my daughters do now, that the perfect top could snare the perfect man, and all day Saturday was spent in the pursuit of it, so that, even if you didn't have a boyfriend, it felt as if you did as you engaged in the ritual of whether he'd like it or not, whilst the boys played cricket, or rugby, never giving us a thought until the evening. We were just one part of their lives, whilst they, I'm ashamed to say, were all of ours. Time not spent shopping was spent discussing them, to a degree they'd have been amazed at. Oh, to an extent, we were involved in our fledgling careers – or degree, in my case – but it was very much secondary to the main event: the snaring, bagging and keeping of a boy-friend. Look, I'm sorry, I'm just being honest.

So I ignored Max, and he, it seemed, ignored me. Until one evening, at a particularly noxious and drunken party in Onslow Gardens, he pounced. As I was emerging from the kitchen, a glass of punch in each hand, one for me and one for Mimi, he put his hand above the door frame, blocking my way into the sitting room. I couldn't go for-wards, and couldn't go backwards into the melee I'd just squeezed from. He smiled down from his great height.

'Drinking for two? Not pregnant, are you?'

'Yes, I am, actually. It's due next month.'

'Have you given Charlie the good news?'

Charlie was the boy I was sort of seeing. An interest-ing, slightly dull but terribly intelligent cove reading bio-chemistry at Imperial.

'I was politely toying with your witty opening gambit, Max. Didn't expect you to run with it. No, I haven't given Charlie the good news because, obviously, I'm not preg-nant. We're not that stupid.'

'No, no. Charlie's very clever, isn't he?'

It was true, I did have a weakness for intellectual boys. Perhaps word had got about. I handed him one of the drinks and brushed his shoulder. 'Is that a chip I see before me, Max?'

He grinned. 'Yes, that's it, I'm insanely jealous of Charlie's gigantic Bunsen burner. Is this for me?' He took a swig. 'How kind. Didn't know you were chasing me, Flora?'

'I'm not, it's for Mimi. Deliver it, would you? I'm going to the loo.'

I ducked under his arm and headed for the stairs, and thence the bog. When I came out, having queued for ages, I was pleased to see he had at least given Mimi the drink and that her eyes were shining as he flirted madly with her. We shared a flat, and she was full of him that night in the taxi on the way home, then as we clattered up four flights of stairs in our heels to our pokey top-floor flat in Mendora Gardens.

'Honestly, Flora, he got me a drink without me even asking, and then chatted me up for ages. It's the furthest I've ever got with him.'

'Except he left with Coco Harrington,' I pointed out. I'd seen him lurch into a taxi with her, pinching her bottom as she got in before him.

'Coco's his cousin,' Mimi said quickly. 'There's nothing in that.'

'Second cousin. And posh families don't take any notice of that sort of thing. They're all inbred.'

'You just don't like him because he doesn't flirt with you,' she said petulantly. I thought of his wicked blue eyes twinkling down into mine from under that floppy fringe, then roving up and down the admittedly rather tiny dress I was wearing, which was backless and therefore bra-less, in an attempt to try to rev Charlie up a bit. He was more experimental with the mice in his laboratory than he was with me.

'You're right, he doesn't,' I lied. 'But he does with everyone else, Mimi. He's what another generation would call a rake.'

'I know, but every rake has to gather a few leaves along the way and, one day, when he's mine and we're living in that flat in Chelsea his grandfather left him and I'm pregnant with our second child, gazing adoringly at our first in his cot, I'll be glad he got it all out of his system early and isn't cheating on me. I'm playing the long game, Flora. I've got all the time in the world.'

And off she went, singing drunkenly, to her bedroom, stopping en route for the Nutella and a spoon, then, remembering the long game, putting it back.

The next time he tried it on was at Charlie's birthday party. Charlie lived in now deeply fashionable but then extremely suspect Brixton. His particular dive was a dingy basement flat he shared with two other scruffy scientists. On this particular night it was throbbing with flashing lights and loud boy music – Hawkwind, or something hideous. Max arrived with Coco and some other exotics in his peacock-blue shirt and tight jeans, looking alarmed. He clutched his throat theatrically.

'Where am I? I can't breathe. Have I died and gone somewhere penitentiary? Will the crumpet-catcher survive outside, or will I emerge to find its tyres slashed? So many questions. It's a mark of how much I fancy you,

Flora, that I follow you literally to the end of the earth, if not the Victoria line.'

'Oh, shut up, Max,' I muttered, for more reasons than one. Mimi was in earshot, and a pointed glance told me she'd overheard. 'You fancy everyone, so please don't believe I'm remotely flattered by that.'

'Except that it's you I love!' he roared, grinning delightedly as I stalked off.

Mimi caught up with me. 'You didn't tell me he flirted with you, too.'

'He didn't, until last week. And he only does it to get a reaction.'

'And because you don't fall for him,' she said slowly. She stared at me. 'It's fine,' she added more coldly. 'I won't stand in your way. If you want him, don't hold back for my sake.'

'Oh, don't be ridiculous, Mimi. I don't even fancy him, and neither should you! I'm going out with Charlie, anyway.'

'Only because you feel you should. Because he might invent the cure for cancer one day or something. And because you're too up yourself to go out with fun men.' She stalked off crossly.

'Who are these people, darling?' Max was in my ear. 'Are they all experiments of your boyfriend? Why are they doing that flappy chicken routine with their elbows?' Status Quo were playing to exuberant reaction. 'Some don't seem to wash their hair.' He put his peacock-blue collar up for protection.

'Are you gay?' I asked.

'I am tonight.' He shuddered.

I had to admit, even by Charlie's standards, this lot were

geeky: skinny, lank-haired, hollow-chested, bespectacled. And the boys weren't much better.

'Is that a boy troll or a girl troll?' Max asked in a mock-horrified whisper as a couple took to the dance floor, achingly uncoordinated, glasses clashing. My mouth twitched despite myself. He took my arm. 'Come on. Let's show them how it's done.'

Before I could stop him he'd dragged me on to what passed for the dance floor – a patch of sticky carpet – at which point the music unfortunately changed from Quo to Al Green.

'No!' I gasped as he clasped me delightedly in a tight clinch.

'It's a dance,' he cooed in my ear, 'not a sex act. You don't shout "No!" if a boy asks you to dance, it undermines their confidence. I could be crushed.'

'Nothing short of a runaway truck could do that,' I retorted, wishing he couldn't dance so expertly and move me around the floor in a way Charlie couldn't, wishing I could stop my body moving with his, natural rhythm being about the only thing I'd inherited from my mother.

'You're enjoying your-self . . .' he sang in my ear.

'I'm no-t,' I sang back.

'You're ly-ing. You lo-ve me.'

'I don't even li-ke you.'

He threw his head back and laughed, and I saw Mimi, in a corner of the room, snogging a friend of Charlie's called Derek. You'd have to be really desperate to snog Derek. Before the song ended, I was away, to the garden this time, to join fellow smokers and, hopefully, crowds of people Max didn't know and would hate. I was longing for Mimi to disentangle herself and appear. But she didn't. In fact, Lucy told me she was under a pile of coats with Derek in one of the bedrooms, and since I couldn't leave without at least consulting Mimi – we'd shared a taxi here – and probably should stay because I was at Charlie's, that left me rather stuck. When Max finally left with the cohort of friends he'd brought with him – 'What are we *doing* here, Max?' from the glamorous Coco as they all headed out to the MG – I was at least able to crash in Charlie's bedroom, taking any coats off the bed and depositing them in the hall, knowing, as host, it'd be a lot longer before he came to bed. Knowing I could curl up and go to sleep.

Charlie came in sometime later and I roused myself dozily.

'Hi,' I said sleepily. 'Has everyone gone?'

He grunted something, and I wondered if he was annoyed I hadn't been with him much. He'd either been drinking home brew in the kitchen, which I hated, or having long, intense talks with his lab buddies, and although I liked the intellectual stuff, doing journalism at college was very different to reading chemistry down the road at the real thing. Having bagged my Oxbridge type, I'd begun to wonder if he was for me.

'Get into bed,' I said softly, knowing this wasn't the night to make any decisions or have a drunken row, and hoping he didn't want anything else. Unlikely. Charlie had quite a low sex drive. As he crept in naked beside me, a hand snaked over my tummy. Damn. I held it, hoping a little hand-holding might suffice, but as he moved in for a cuddle I froze. Scuttled to the edge of the bed and switched on the light.

'Shit!'

In bed beside me, naked and grinning hugely, was Max.

'What the fuck are you doing here?'

'You told me to get into bed.'

'I thought you were Charlie!' I could hardly speak. Squeaked instead. 'Where's Charlie?'

'In the bath, asleep. He climbed in, having puked in the loo first; he seemed to think it was the next obvious step. I put him in the recovery position, rather considerately putting a cushion under his head. I did ask if he might be more comfortable elsewhere, but he said he was very happy there and, heavens, it's his house. Who am I to argue?'

I stared in horrified disbelief, clutching the duvet with both hands around my chin. 'Are you naked?' I whispered.

He threw back the duvet to reveal a brown torso and pink boxer shorts. 'Kept my shreddies on. Ever the gentleman.'

'*Never* the gentleman! You must go,' I went on in a low, angry voice. 'Go now! This is outrageous. Get out!'

'But, darling, I can't. Coco took the car. So I have no suitable means of transportation, since the Tubes have long since terminated and I imagine taxis are an endangered species round here. And Mimi and a man who looks like a door are in the other bedroom and, what with your boyfriend in the bath and two pituitary cases coupling on the sofa . . .' He smiled winningly, clasped his hands behind his head and crossed his ankles neatly ' . . . what's a boy to do?'

'I'll sleep on the floor,' I told him. 'Turn your back. I want to put some clothes on.'

He frowned. 'Seems foolish, with an entire double bed

at our disposal. I won't ravish you, you know. Or don't you trust yourself with me?'

I'd already reached down to the floor for my pants and a T-shirt of Charlie's, and wriggled into them under the duvet. I sat up in bed, arms crossed, furious.

'I am *not* sleeping with you, Max.'

'I can see that,' he laughed. 'But what about sharing a bed? Surely there's no harm in that?'

There was a lot of harm, but since it was four in the morning and I was too tired to argue, we did, after I'd tossed him Charlie's dressing gown and ordered him to put it on, which he did, but only after having insisted on modelling it first, in the manner of a mad scientist, finding some test tubes on Charlie's desk, pretending to brew a potion, back hunched, scratching his head naughtily in the way that Charlie had, until even I laughed. It was at that moment that Mimi came in. She looked from one of us to the other and her face said it all.

'I was wondering if we should share a taxi home, but clearly not.'

'Mimi! Wait – no!'

Too late. The door had slammed. I stared, horrified, at the paintwork. Sank back on the pillows and groaned. 'Great. In one evening, you've cost me my best friend – and probably my flat, since her father owns it.'

'Nonsense, you'll patch it up with her, darling. And Lucy's your best friend, not Mimi. I've done my research. And if she does turf you out, you can always come and live with me. I've got a nice little place in Draycott Terrace.'

'Oh, don't be ridiculous.'

'I'm not, I think we'd be good together. But, frankly,

Flora, if you don't put it to the test, we'll never know, will we?' He leaned right over me, an elbow propped either side of my head. I tried to look cross but, God, he was attractive. And when those wicked, glittering blue eyes softened, as they were doing now, he was terribly hard to resist. I'm not proud of myself, but a bit of me felt I had at least resisted for ages and, of course, once I'd let him kiss me I was in too deep, and then, naturally, it was sensational. Sometime later, I lay in his arms, staring at the dawn as it came up behind the thin bedroom curtain.

'Darling,' Max murmured, 'promise me, if you ever run away from me again and I have to chase you round London, don't let it be south of the river.'

I smiled, thinking I hadn't actually thought about running away, and then I fell asleep.

In the morning, of course, there was a bit of a scene. Charlie had staggered in while we were fast asleep. He wasn't best pleased. In fact, he could hardly speak he was so incandescent with rage, and Max and I took advantage of that, wriggling into clothes, finding shoes, keys, money, Max saying in a loud voice what a terrific party it had been and how kind it was of Charlie to have invited him as we hurtled past him standing bug-eyed and spluttering in the doorway. I was puce with shame and stopped to mutter, 'Oh God, I'm so sorry, Charlie, you see –' before Max dragged me down the hall and out of the front door.

'Never complain, never explain,' he told me as we clattered up the uncarpeted basement stairs.

Outside, the crumpet-catcher stood prettily at the kerb, all in one piece. I turned, astonished. 'I thought you said –'

'I lied!' he cried, arms outstretched, smiling broadly.

In an instant he'd concertinaed down the roof and we'd jumped in. We shot out of Branksome Road, around the dustbins and the scruffy-looking cars, the cats returning from a night out, into the crisp air, which clashed violently with our hangovers, and a sunny, bright-blue morn. Off we sped. I'm sorry. But after four months with a very clever chap, having deep conversations in gloomy pubs where everyone drank beer – even the girls – the novelty had worn off. Here I was, flying across Battersea Bridge, wind in my hair, the Thames shimmering beneath me, in a bright-red sports car, beside an incredibly handsome man in a peacock-blue shirt, with nut-brown hair, similarly coloured forearms . . . what could I do?

We had breakfast at the brasserie at Brompton Cross: fresh orange juice and croissants slipped down a treat and there were gleeful grins and more jokes from him whilst I tried not to smile and assumed an ashamed expression, and then I refused to have any more to do with him. I refused to go back to Draycott Terrace and spend the rest of the day in bed, as he suggested, and I refused to walk in Kew Gardens and 'get steamed up in the hothouse'. I also refused to laugh any more than I could absolutely help. It was what I'd missed, though, I realized wistfully. Laughing. Instead, I made him drop me back at my flat – at the end of the road, in case Mimi was at the window glowering – and walked, with fear and trembling, down to number 42.

From the doorstep I gazed up at our top-floor windows, to the eaves where the pigeons roosted, dry-mouthed. Mimi was good fun, but she had a temper. She was also very good-looking and used to getting the boys. Although a bit of me thought that it wasn't as if she was going out with him I knew the sisterhood rules: knew I was in the wrong. I was pleased to see my belongings were not stacked up in the hallway as I opened the front door, and was also pleased to find her in the kitchen, making an apple pie, radio on, window open to the sunshine. Food was our big bond. We'd met on a cookery course in Paris during the summer holiday the previous year, where we'd both agreed, as we sat in pavement cafés drinking espressos and wearing short skirts and feeling very grown up, that in times of crisis and emotional stress there was nothing that couldn't be solved by making a batch of profiteroles. I thought back to that summer – exciting days when you meet a new friend, swap confidences, thumbnail sketch your life up to now and then fill in the details more thoroughly as time went by – and felt sad.

'I'm so sorry, Mimi,' I began humbly, realizing I didn't even know what I was going to say. Was it 'I won't see him again' or 'I'm going to see him again, you'll have to deal with it'? That it depended on her?

She turned. Her face was strained, but she managed a brave smile. She looked me in the eye.

'It's not as if I was going out with him.'

'No, but still. I knew you liked him.'

'And you didn't?'

'I didn't think I did, because everyone else did,' I said truthfully. 'But then, yesterday, I realized that wasn't a good enough reason.'

'So now you do?'

I struggled, wondering how to put it.

'It's fine,' she said quickly, knowing immediately. 'I'm

not going to make a scene over a blatant mutual attraction. Go for it, Flora.'

I felt everything inside me relax. I could have hugged her, but knew from her rigid back as she turned back to roll out the pastry that it would be a step too far, so didn't.

'Thanks, Mimi,' I breathed. I wanted to add – And we won't be obvious. Won't flaunt it in your face in the room next to yours, we'll be at his place, not here; but I knew this wasn't the moment for the geography of the coupling. For the details. Surprisingly, though, she did want to know how it had happened, and I was relieved that I hadn't sought him out: that he'd ambushed me. I wanted to clear that side of our friendship, and she even had the grace to laugh.

'You must have got the shock of your life when you realized it wasn't Charlie. God, the audacity!'

'He's got balls,' I agreed, before realizing that wasn't the most tactful thing I could have said.

I withdrew hastily from the kitchen and scuttled to my bedroom, leaving her to her baking. There, I drew my curtains on the day and went to bed, even though it was barely the afternoon, the sun was still shining, and the pigeons outside my window were still cooing to one another on the crumbling ledge. I needed, though, if I was going to live here with Mimi, for it to be tomorrow. I shut my eyes and snuggled down. For it not to be the day I'd cheated on my flatmate and let a man lead me, uncharacteristically, into temptation.

Chapter Nine

I didn't worry that he wouldn't call the next day, I knew he would, and he did. Luckily, Mimi was out, and I sank happily into the sofa, chatting for a whole indulgent hour, picking stuffing out of the exploding arms, before he went to his parents for lunch, promising he'd meet me tomorrow. The next day, he was waiting outside the London College of Printing, where I was trying to become a journalist in an already shrinking column-inch world, and we went for a drink in Holborn. As we sat on stools at the bar, I thought how easy it was to misjudge someone. He was just a boy. With a very nice face. Who'd driven to see his parents in the country on a Sunday, because he was worried about his sister, who'd fallen off her pony. He was as lovely as someone who was poor with an unfortunate face. It made no difference where people came from, or what they looked like.

There was also the added dimension that I'd gone all the way from hating him to liking him, so that, even then, so early on, the distance between the two made it seem dizzyingly close to love. After a few drinks, we went to the Spaghetti Opera in Fleet Street, which he'd heard about through his contacts in the music world – Max worked for an events company that staged concerts: rock, pop and classical. This particular Italian restaurateur employed impoverished music students to sing whilst the punters ate pasta. Sounds fun, but in reality, having someone draw up a chair and croon – or blast – Puccini in your face on your first date wasn't really ideal, and so we bolted down our spaghetti *al vongole* and beat a hasty retreat to Draycott Terrace.

Those first few weeks swept by in a predictable fashion: drink, eat and retire to horizontal activities, to be repeated again when energy levels recovered. After a bit, though, we emerged and became more inclusive. We spent time with friends, his or mine, at the Surprise, the Phene, the Admiral Cod, the usual haunts. I did tease him initially about his friends, who were the green-sock, tasselled loafers, Barbour-over-a-suit brigade, but apart from Coco, who drank, they turned out to be as normal and insecure about their looks and concerned about their love lives and their jobs as the rest of us. I grew to like them as much as my own crowd. My own friends knew Max anyway, but my college ones didn't, and circled him warily at first. Once they realized he brayed but didn't bite, they embraced him and, after a bit, even Mimi relaxed, and went out with a friend of his called Bertie.

His parents were heaven, and we drove to see them regularly in Hampshire, in their lovely Georgian farmhouse, complete with rambling acres, paddocks and sheep grazing beyond a ha-ha. Although clearly well off, they were steady, sensible people: his father was a local solicitor and his mother a housewife who organized charity events and gardened. She told me quietly one day as I was helping her deadhead roses that she was so pleased Max had met me, because, frankly, some of the girls he'd gone around with before had been a bit racy. Her delicate skin on her beautiful face had puckered thoughtfully, like tissue paper, as she'd paused, trug in hand. Not that any of them had been serious girlfriends, she'd added, resuming her pruning. He'd only had one proper girlfriend before me, an Australian girl called Tiggy who he'd met on his gap year and fallen for, but, geographically, it hadn't been ideal.

And, of course, he in turn met my mother, who adored him, principally because he played backgammon with her for hours on end and laughed at all of her jokes whilst pouring the vodka, all of which encouraged her no end. But he seemed to genuinely enjoy her company.

'Yes, I do,' he agreed, when I put this to him. 'She's good fun.' He nudged me. 'She's where your lighter side comes from.'

I'd grinned, but knew we were both wondering where the darker, more serious one came from. And, like other friends before him, Lucy in particular, he'd asked if I wasn't intrigued.

'Oh, I know the possibilities, I've narrowed it down,' I assured him, and reeled off the names of a captain of industry, a fashion photographer and a musician, and he'd tried to persuade me to discover more. The furthest I'd gone was to take him to a house in the Boltons, where we'd peered down into the well-lit basement kitchen together, where the musician, now a successful producer, was pouring a drink for his wife as she peeled potatoes. Two young children were curled up, watching television on a sofa in the corner.

'I'd be the worst sort of bad news,' I told Max as we stared. 'I don't want to be that. Don't want to be a nasty shock in a letter, or standing on the doorstep. Ruin four people's lives.'

'Change,' he'd said. 'Change their lives and, in time, they'd come to love you. You'd be the cool older sister.'

I made a face. 'Not for a long while, and not to the poor wife. I'd be a horrific jolt, and I don't want that. The other families are all much the same, incidentally. I've checked. Incredibly happy.'

'But what about you? What about your happiness?'

'But I wouldn't be happy, knowing I'd made everyone miserable. I'd be wretched.'

'OK,' he said slowly, 'but what about the truth?'

'It's just a word. Rhetoric. It's not an emotion. A feeling.'

'So not important?'

'Oh, very,' I said vehemently. 'But it doesn't take precedence just because it resonates on moral high ground. It doesn't beat wrecking a family. Anyway, I'm fine, I've got Mum.' I smiled, knowing he couldn't dispute this and that, despite her frivolity, he saw a different side to her: a brave one.

'Brave?' I'd said, astonished, as we'd left her house in Fulham one night after midnight. 'Reckless, you mean.'

'It takes courage to be that happy. Not to let regret overwhelm you. And she's solvent. She's done all that on her own.'

'Done what!' Mum hadn't worked since her early modelling days.

'Made her own money, invested it in property and managed to hold on to it. So far.'

'Well, all she did was stand in front of a camera . . .' I said dubiously.

'Does it matter if it's beauty or brains you're blessed with? Surely it's as much of a crime not to use one as the other? If a first-class brain who could be studying at Oxford was running a sweet shop, you'd say what a waste.'

'I suppose.'

'She's used her assets.' He shrugged. 'Same thing.'

'And had immensely rich boyfriends.' I thought of our fine Parisian years, with Philippe, who was then the French finance minister. I wasn't sure Mum had paid for anything when we'd lived in the beautiful apartment he'd bought for us in Montmartre: I was pretty sure he'd paid for me to go to school, too, in the darling little Madeline ensemble with cape and straw boater.

'Oh, sure, she's taken her chances, but a few years in Paris is just the same as accepting a sabbatical at Harvard. Getting a break for being clever.'

I laughed, loving Max's refreshing view on life, knowing he was good for me, that I could be too critical of Mum sometimes, too judgemental. But then I was allowed to be: she was my mother. And other people, with their cosy, deadheading, trug-wielding, Yorkshire-pudding-making mothers could afford to find her enchanting. They only dipped in.

Max was four years older than me, so I wasn't totally surprised when, after eighteen months, as he was approaching twenty-eight, he asked me to marry him. Girlfriends and I had already discussed this beneficial side effect of dating the slightly older man. Oh, we laughed as we said it, but there was a glaring reality, which obviously couldn't be repeated on the floor of the *Evening Standard*, where I was now working as a fledgling restaurant reviewer under the great Fay Maschler. And I was the happiest girl alive. I'd got my gorgeous Mad Max, who complemented me, just, as everyone said – Parrot, Lucy, Gus – I did him. I'd calmed him down a bit, apparently. I was the brakes, and my friends, who might have initially thought him a bit flamboyant, loved him too now. We happily planned an engagement pary, on my twenty-fourth birthday.

Unfortunately, I was felled by horrific stomach cramps for the two days leading up to it, and on the morning of the party, dizzy with painkillers, I collapsed at work and was taken to hospital. An already erupting appendix was removed from my abdomen and burst as it was placed in the kidney dish. Disappointing, obviously, but it was also a relief that it wasn't more serious. I rang Max drowsily from a phone a nurse wheeled to my bed when I came round from the anaesthetic, and he came rushing in. His face was pale and worried, and he held my hand tight, but gradually, as I talked, he was reassured and relieved, too. I told him to go ahead with the party.

'Don't be silly, it's our engagement party. And your birthday!'

'Yes, but everyone's been invited, and everyone's coming, and it's tonight. In four hours' time. Please, Max. I'll feel wretched if you don't. And it's only our friends in your flat, it's not like it's anything grand.'

Reluctantly, he did go ahead – the alternative, pre-texting and pre-Facebook, being to sit on the phone for the rest of the afternoon. The next day, when I was feeling much better and sitting up, a whole gang of our friends – Max,

Fiz, Lucy, Mimi – came in to see me and said it hadn't been the same. That they'd missed me terribly, but they'd toasted me at midnight and Max had made a short speech about his darling girl. I'd glowed.

The arrangements for the wedding, six months hence, began. I had a gorgeous few days trying wedding dresses on with Mum, who wanted me to go for something elegant and fitted and steered me, quite rightly, away from the shepherdess costumes. We had a heavenly girly time of it, tasting champagne and flicking through folders full of pictures of cakes: Mum, always defiantly feminine, can be quite traditional when she feels like it.

And then, one day, I was in the Coopers Arms in Flood Street, fingering veil material and waiting for Max, when I looked up and saw Coco, on her own, at a table in the corner, dwarfed in a huge camel coat. She looked dreadful and was clearly already plastered. I went across with my drink and sat next to her.

'The blushing bride,' she slurred, the corners of her beautiful mouth lurching with the effort of trying to speak.

'I hope you'll come, Coco? To the wedding?'

She looked at me through dull, dead eyes. 'It's made you bold, hasn't it? This engagement? You used to be scared of me. Now you're trying to be kind. Patronizing. Of course I'll come, he's my cousin.' She seized her drink and knocked back the remains of it. I smelled whisky. 'Who d'you think you are – Diana Spencer? Snaring the prince, so now we all have to cosy up to you? Be your best friend?'

I glanced around, wishing Max would arrive. She got up to go, thank goodness. Wobbled a bit.

'I'll be your best friend, Flora,' she said suddenly, placing both hands on the table for balance. 'I'll tell you something you should know, and that no one else will tell you. On the night of your engagement party, Max fucked Mimi. That's what you should know, and no one else will tell you.'

She staggered from the pub.

I sat, shocked, rocked and immobile at that table in the corner. A few minutes later, the door flew open, and Max arrived on a blast of cold air. He was full of apologies about the bloody Tube and his boss keeping him hanging on and wanted to know how long I had been here. Then he saw my face.

'What is it? What's wrong?'

I told him. And then watched as his face turned grey. And I knew. He sat down and put his head in his hands. Ran his fingers through his hair. Slowly, he looked up, ashen. The party had gone on quite late, he told me. And, eventually, he'd gone to bed, leaving a hard core staying up drinking, playing cards; telling them to let themselves out quietly. Sometime later he awoke to find a naked girl beside him. At first, in his confusion, he thought it was me, then realized it was Mimi. She was already on top of him, working her magic. He told me he had absolutely no excuse. Except that he was quite drunk and very disoriented.

'It was my birthday.'

'I know.'

'My engagement party.'

'Yes.'

'I'd been under the knife, having an operation.'

He didn't answer.

'You came to see me the next day. She came, too. She brought me flowers.'

The horror of the deception threatened to overwhelm me. I felt terribly sick.

I managed to leave the pub. Managed to walk, not home, but to Mum's. She took one look and poured me a very large drink and we sat whilst I cried and told her, and she held my hand. She didn't offer any advice, she didn't tell me what to do, she just looked very sad and very wistful, and once or twice she seemed to be a million miles away, back in her own past. I didn't want to be her in twenty years' time. Didn't want history to repeat itself. I'd never asked Mum why none of the men she'd been with had ever married her, I knew it was too painful.

The only thing she said, aside from consoling me, was, 'He's a very good-looking man.' Not implying anything, just a statement of fact. But I knew. Knew that I was OK-looking – pretty, with an open, friendly face – but that I'd been punching above my weight. I'd be looking over my shoulder for the rest of my life, wondering who was perching on his desk at work, who he was going on business trips with, or, if I was away myself, who was moving in on him at home.

I broke up with him. And, obviously, I broke up with Mimi, and moved back in with Mum, in Fulham. Max was heartbroken. He tried his hardest to win me back. He called me constantly, he loitered around outside my office, my house, but I wasn't having any of it. And the reason I wasn't having any of it, I realized one day on my way into work, was those flowers. Although there'd been other friends around, about five of them, Max and Mimi had approached

130

the end of my hospital bed together, almost as a couple, bearing gifts. The flowers were from Pulbrook & Gould, a very smart shop around the corner from Max in Chelsea, which I used to walk past – nowhere near the wrong end of Fulham, where Mimi and I lived. Somehow, I knew they'd bought them together. Had had breakfast together in his flat, coffee, croissants. And then they'd gone to select them, before coming in to see me. That she hadn't beat a hasty retreat first thing in the morning.

I stayed with Mum for a year – in many ways, she was more like a flatmate than a mother, anyway – and threw myself into having a raucous, non-stop, hectic social life. My friends were brilliant: they partied hard with me, encouraged me to do as much as possible, to accept every invitation. I didn't disappoint them. But towards the end of the year, in November, I overdid it, and broke a tiny bone in my foot, a metatarsal, trying to dance on a table in a nightclub, then jumping off it when the barman, who'd originally thought it a huge joke, turned ugly.

Lucy took me to St Thomas's. James was working in A&E at the time as a young registrar, and something about the way he handled my foot at two in the morning and observed that at least I'd been on the table and not under it, made me warm to him.

'Were you plastered?' He looked up at me with a smile, crouched as he was, tending my ankle.

'Not entirely.'

'Well you're about to be. I'll get a cast on that.' He straightened up.

'Apparently, a surgical boot gives you more mobility? Can't I have one of those?'

'It's a short cut. If you were my girlfriend, I'd want you to be in a cast. It'll mend much better in the long run.'

It made me want to be his girlfriend. To be looked after. To be there in the long run. And he had kind grey eyes, thoughtful ones – not twinkly, naughty ones like Max's.

My visits back to St Thomas's became the highlight of my social calendar. I dressed carefully for them, and when James asked me out for a drink when the original cast was changed for a lighter one, I hobbled off delightedly. His was the first name on my new ankle. With a kiss.

A year later, we were married, and then, not long after that, Max married Mimi. I nearly fell over when I heard. I hadn't even known they'd been seeing each other. Once I'd got over the shock, though, I was triumphant. You see, I thought smugly, pushing through a swing door at St Thomas's, where I had another appointment with James, but this time for a scan, as I was pregnant with Amelia, I'd been right. Of course I'd been right. I'd known all along. Max had never been the man for me.

Chapter Ten

Sally, unused to being the sideshow, was not appreciating the way my eyes and Max's had met in the outside lights of the chateau – me on the balcony, him gazing up – and held on tight. She was alive to the situation in an instant.

'Of course, you two need no introduction, do you? I'd forgotten you know each other.'

Speechless, I dragged my eyes away from Max and back to her, my breath short at the magnitude of her gall. *Forgotten?* Of course she hadn't forgotten. I'd told her the whole story myself, curled up on an ancient sofa in the morning room at Brechallis, when I'd first gone there with James, during one of our girly chats. Starved of company, she loved to drag me off for hours, wanting to know everything. She knew all about Mimi – obviously, she didn't know quite how heartbroken I'd been, because I was going out with her brother – but she knew it had been incredibly traumatic. Thriving on drama, when her life yielded so little, she'd wanted the story again and again.

'I couldn't stop her, Flora,' Rachel, beside me, said in a low voice.

I swung around to her. Her face was drawn in the glare of the outside lights. Sally and Max were getting suitcases out of the boot now, shutting car doors. We stepped back into the relative safety and gloom of the bedroom.

'But this is monstrous, Rachel. You must know that?'

She hesitated, looked wretched. 'I'm not sure Sally's up to that sort of treachery, she's not that deep. I honestly think he flirted with her, she was flattered, and when she realized who he was, she thought, Oh well, so what? It was years ago and he doesn't mean anything to Flora any more. And, I admit, she might have thought – it could be quite amusing.'

'Not to tell me –'

'Yes, that smacks of wanting to give you a surprise, but not a nasty one. Just a bit of a jolt. You know how insecure she is, how everything has to revolve around her.'

'But does she even realize that this has nothing to do with her at all?' I hissed furiously. My hands were shaking as I clutched the necklace around my throat. 'And everything to do with me? That he is here because of me? Is she that stupid?'

Rachel swallowed. 'I think that's taking it a bit far –'

'Oh no, Rachel, it is not!' I knew what he was like, knew his chutzpah.

She licked her lips. 'I know what you mean. It is a bit odd, from his point of view –'

'It's extraordinary!'

'Flora, we must go down,' she said anxiously as we heard noises below. 'It looks even more odd if we hang around up here. We must go and meet them, be normal.' She looked at me imploringly in the dim glow of the bedside light. She was right. Of course she was right. And she was helping me. I needed that. I nodded quickly and, together, we went down the corridor and descended the stone staircase. My heart was pounding. I hoped I wouldn't fall.

When we got to the bottom, they'd already pushed through the front door into the brightly lit hall and were gazing around in wonder.

'Ah, there you are! We wondered where everyone was. Thought you weren't coming to greet us!' Sally's newly bleached teeth glistened as she smiled broadly. She crossed the hall and enveloped me in a mass of lipstick, hair and scent. I managed to hug her back.

'I *do* hope you don't mind, Flora,' she whispered fiercely in my ear, and I actually believe she meant it.

'Sally! How lovely to see you,' I gasped. 'Everyone's still on the terrace, having drinks. You look amazing.'

I turned to Max, as Rachel embraced her sister. His eyes were alight, but it wasn't just amusement: he'd like me to think it was, but there was something else there, too.

'Flora. Lovely to see you.' He stepped forward, and we pecked each other awkwardly.

'You, too, Max. What a surprise.' I kept a bright smile going. I'm good at those. Suddenly, I agreed with Rachel. Sally wasn't deep. Giving me a jolt might be a thrilling by-product, but it wouldn't be her raison d'être for being with Max. She plainly just imagined that this very attractive man, who'd once gone out with her sister-in-law, was now in love with her, because she was so thin and beautiful. But I knew Max. Knew he'd never fall in love with Sally. He wouldn't fall in love with her head.

'Come and see everyone.'

'I thought they'd hear the car, come and meet us! I'm dying to introduce everyone to Max.'

I turned and led the way through the house towards the terrace. I could hear myself breathing.

'What a house!' Max was saying as we crossed the inner hall. 'Is it as amazing throughout?'

'It's pretty special,' I replied. I hadn't heard his voice for so long, it was bizarre.

'It's beautiful,' agreed Sally, stopping to gaze around. We stopped with her. 'Although it's not quite on the scale of the one I was in last year, of course, when I was with the Wards in Angus, which is the neighbouring estate to Balmoral.'

'Yes, I remember you showed me the pictures,' Max said lightly. 'Is that the coast we can see, twinkling away in the distance?' He'd moved to an open window.

'Yes, it is,' I said shortly, removing my tongue from the roof of my mouth, where it had seemingly taken root. I led the way through the kitchen and out to the terrace, where, under the twinkling lights and a velvet sky, my entire family were seated. I was glad it was dark so no one would see my horrified face until I'd had time to compose it. Neither could they hear my heart beating. I introduced Michel and Thérèse, who were clearing away the liqueurs and were the closest, and then as everyone got to their feet, exclaiming, Sally took over.

'Max, this is my gorgeous niece Amelia – and you must be Toby, I've seen your picture on Facebook. And this is my *other* gorgeous niece, Tara – so, by a process of elimination, you must be Rory!'

I stood by in a daze.

'What the hell . . . ?' James was beside me suddenly, staring as Sally went round the table, dragging her beau with her. 'Isn't that Max?'

'The very same.' I swung round to him. 'Did you know?'

'No, of course not!' He looked horrified.

'Well, she's your sister!' I hissed.

'Yes, but –' His face acknowledged this responsibility. 'God, Flora. I'm so sorry.'

'Oh my God, look at you!' My daughters were on their feet and shrieking, gawping at their aunt, circling her in wonder. 'How much have you lost?'

'Five stone!' said Sally proudly.

'But how did you *do* it? Was it the five-two thing?' Amelia demanded, clearly wanting to run off and do it instantly. 'Did you starve for two days?'

'No, I met this man.' She smiled and reached for Max's hand. 'It just dropped off.' She half-shielded her mouth with her hand. 'Plenty of sex,' she whispered, in a hideous aside to her nieces.

'When did you two meet?' asked Tara, giggling, but blushing, too, as Amelia, after rolling her eyes at me, made room for them to sit at the young end of the table, where they were handed bread, cheese, Calvados and olives by Thérèse and Michel, who, having been assured the late arrivals didn't want any proper supper, prepared to disappear. Max had paused to greet my mother, who had looked surprised but not incredulous. She introduced him to Jean-Claude. When his back was turned, though, she looked across at me and raised her eyebrows. Everyone settled down to chat, but after a few minutes Lizzie was up from her seat and down to my end of the table.

'Your mother says that's *the* Max.'

'The very same.' I reached for the dregs of someone's wine. Gulped it down.

'Do the girls know?'

'Not yet. They will soon, though. They're already au fait with his sex life. Apparently Sally's going like a train, no doubt with all the zeal of the recently converted.'

'But what's he doing here?'

'Search me, Lizzie.'

Mum was now sitting next to Amelia, and I saw her lean across and whisper in her ear. Amelia froze. She turned to gaze at me. Then, when she could decently pretend to withdraw from the conversation, she scuttled down. Pulled up a chair.

'Is that really your ex-boyfriend, Mum? Granny says it's the one you were engaged to!'

'Yup.' I reached to pour myself some more wine.

'But how do you feel? Isn't that so weird for you? That he's going out with Sally?'

Her face was agog. Max continued to talk to the others, but I knew he was going through the motions, was more intent on us. He couldn't hear us from that distance, though.

'It's more than weird, Amelia.'

'God, I can *imagine*. But he's divorced, apparently, and Sally does look amazing, doesn't she?'

'She does.'

'He's seriously hot, Mum.' She broke off to look at him again. Then back. 'Does Dad mind?'

'I very much doubt it.'

He wouldn't. Once he'd got over the initial shock, he'd assume that these things just happened. That life was full of curious merry-go-rounds and some ended up in your back garden. James didn't have a jealous bone in his body, which had sometimes annoyed me. He was far too relaxed

138

to get worked up about an ex-boyfriend, even if he had been my fiancé. Would I mind if James's ex-girlfriend pitched up? Of course I bloody would. Except, I knew he hadn't had his heart broken by Henrietta. He'd split up with her, so perhaps I wouldn't mind. Perhaps that was different. Yes, it was. But broken hearts mend, and mine had, I thought defiantly, looking at Max chatting and laughing with Toby, Tara and Jean-Claude. Did I honestly feel anything? No. Not in that way. But I was horribly jolted, which wasn't what I'd wanted on my one proper break of the year, particularly such a special one. It dawned on me that, actually, I was furious.

Max deliberately wasn't looking at me, no doubt feeling my eyes on him, but when he excused himself and went inside to go to the loo, I slid away and entered the house via a side entrance, knowing I could intercept him in the corridor. I slipped into the sitting room, which was in darkness, its open double doors giving on to the dimly lit corridor. He tried a few doors before he found the right one and, from my vantage point, I saw he'd put on a bit of weight around the middle. Good. I waited until he'd come out of the bathroom.

'Max, what are you doing here?'

He pretended to look surprised to see me, but I wasn't fooled. Max and I thought alike. He'd left the table deliberately. Had known I'd follow him, I realized with a start. One–nil to him already. His eyes sparkled mischievously in the gloom.

'I'm here with Sally, of course,' he said facetiously. 'I thought you knew.'

'Did you? Did you ask her to let me know?'

'Oh, I didn't do that, but you knew she was bringing someone. You could have asked.'

'I didn't imagine I'd know a man she'd met in Scotland.'

'Does it make a difference, Flora? It's been a very long time.'

'Of course not!' I blustered. 'I just think it's extraordinary of her not to say, that's all.'

He smiled. 'I think she wanted to surprise you.'

'Yes, she would.' So he knew that much about her. 'What are you doing with her, Max?'

'That's a bit churlish, Flora. She's a lovely girl.'

We stared at one another. He knew I couldn't gainsay that. I knew he didn't mean it. Or thought I knew. I couldn't actually read his mind, of course. And he clearly hadn't known her long – was I being paranoid? And horribly unkind?

'She's frightfully glamorous and great fun. Just what I need at the moment.'

I raised my chin. 'I'm sorry it didn't work out with Mimi.' I'd heard through Lucy that they'd parted.

'I'm sorry, too. But I shouldn't have married her. We married in a bit of a rush, for the wrong reasons.'

'What were those?'

'I think you know, Flora.'

'If you're implying for one second that it was my fault, and that you married her on the rebound, it doesn't say much for your character, Max.'

How odd. We'd slipped into talking very earnestly and personally to each other, in furious whispers, as if we'd last seen each other yesterday: this man I hadn't set eyes on for twenty years. As if I'd just picked up the phone when he refused to stop ringing me at Mum's, or bumped into him as he doorstepped me yet again outside her house on my way to work, launching into another row about Mimi. Him telling me she'd wanted her revenge, served cold, that he'd just been a pawn in her game. We both had. That we shouldn't let her win. Trying to persuade me to have a coffee with him round the corner, to listen to him for just two minutes.

'And you didn't?' He gazed at me intently.

'What?'

'Marry on the rebound?'

'Of course not! How dare you!'

'It was bloody quick.'

'A year.'

'Bloody quick. And I gather you were drunk for most of that time, partying hard.'

'Oh what, trying to forget you in a blur of alcohol and then marrying the first man who asked me out?'

He shrugged, his eyes mocking. He definitely had control of this conversation. But then he'd had a while to think about how it might go.

'You've got a nerve, Max. Turning up on my family holiday with a failed marriage behind you, trying to suggest there's anything wrong with mine.' I was shaking.

'You're livid, aren't you, Flora?'

'Yes, I am.'

'Which is interesting. Such a strong emotion. Surely you shouldn't give a damn if I'm here or not? Shouldn't give it a second thought?'

'It's the deceit, the duplicity. You're with a girl we both know is not your –'

'Max?'

Sally appeared at the other end of the corridor. Her feet echoed along it now. 'What are you doing in the dark?'

'Flora was just showing me where the loo was. Come on, darling, let's find our room. I'm bushed, aren't you?'

'Amelia's showing us, she's waiting at the bottom of the stairs. Night, Flora, and thanks so much for having us.'

'Yes, thank you, Flora, we couldn't be more thrilled to be here.' And so saying, he gave me another wicked smile before moving smoothly around to take Sally's arm.

Only when they'd gone did I realize my hands were trembling. I clenched them together hard. I took another moment, then started back unsteadily to the garden.

Most people had drifted on up to bed; it was late. I saw Rachel helping her father make his way slowly inside, his back bowed in his cream linen jacket. Only Mum and Jean-Claude remained seated, deep in conversation at the far end of the table. James was circling it, clearing the last few glasses and napkins in a haphazard fashion.

'Thérèse told us to leave everything, but I think that's a bit off, don't you? I thought I'd at least clear the ashtrays and take the cheese plates in.'

'Yes, I agree.' I gave him a hand, knowing it helped to be married to a man who knew what was OK and what was a bit off. A man of integrity, who would never dream of being manipulative.

'Is the Brig all right?' I formed the words: found a cloth and gathered some crumbs. 'Has someone shown him where he's sleeping?'

'The girls. They're loving being the hostesses with an enormous pile at their disposal.'

'Doesn't happen often.'

'Quite. Make the most of it. Are you OK, Flora?'

He'd paused and was looking at me intently as I frantically swept the table, glad of something to do.

I stopped. 'It is odd, isn't it, James?' I clenched the cloth and looked imploringly at him. 'You must admit?'

'It is a bit peculiar,' he said slowly. 'But I don't think it's some deliberate campaign.'

'I do,' I said vehemently.

'I know, that's why I said it. I knew you would. I just think they coincidentally met and he's divorced and happens to be going out with Sally, that's all.'

'But *Sally.*'

'Steady. She looks terrific.'

'She does, but – Christ, James, she drives *you* up the pole. Let's not pretend she's easy.'

He shrugged. 'I'm her brother. She's bound to be different with him.' He put his head on one side. Gave me a kind smile. 'Come here.' He held out his arms and I walked into them. Held on tight.

'I'm scared,' I whispered.

'Why?' He laughed into my hair. 'He can't hurt us, Flora, don't be silly.'

'I don't know. I just feel incredibly threatened. I want him to go. Now.'

He squeezed me. 'Well, that's not going to happen, darling. Come on, you just have to make the best of it.' He patted my back. 'And you really can't look too thrown, for the girls' sakes.'

'I know.'

I bit my lip as he carried on clearing up. I couldn't be hiding behind my dark glasses all day, skittery and on edge

143

because my ex-boyfriend was amongst us; what would they think? That I was vulnerable, that's what. But he was on my patch. It was outrageous. Imagine if the roles were reversed and James and I were divorced and I'd turned up on his and Mimi's family holiday? It *was* outrageous. Why was I the only one with eyes to see? As James gathered the place mats, I wiped them down. Tried to be sensible. Not so childish.

As we walked inside carrying the debris, we passed behind my mother and Jean-Claude at the far end of the table. Mum didn't turn, but she reached a hand out behind her back. I squeezed it gratefully. She'd looked after me that year before I met James, nursed me at her house. She'd sat on my bed as I'd sobbed. She'd asked me, more than once, if I wasn't cutting off my nose to spite my face. The rest of my life, even. Asked me, if I was so upset, so heart-broken, why I couldn't forgive him? Take him back? Get over my pride?

If anyone had eyes to see what came after pride, she did.

Yes indeed.

Chapter Eleven

'Oh God.' I swung around in alarm. 'I've put her next door!' I breathed to James as he closed the bedroom door behind us.

'Well, that's all right, darling. They're hardly going to be at it like teenagers, are they? Especially after a ten-hour drive. And, anyway, so what if they are?'

He was beginning to look a bit cross. I knew I had to keep my paranoia under wraps. Nonetheless, I found myself looking at our double bed, its headboard against the shared wall, as I knew theirs was too. While James was in the bathroom getting ready for bed, I tried to drag it across the floor. It was bloody heavy and I only got it a few inches. It also made a terrible racket.

James shot back into the room, toothbrush in mouth. He stared.

'I thought it might be nice to sleep under the window.'

He removed the brush. 'Flora, you're being absurd! I'm beginning to wonder why it would affect you so much to hear your ex-boyfriend in flagrante with another woman.'

'Shh!' I glanced at the dividing wall in horror. 'And, anyway, do you really want to hear your sister in the same state?' I whispered.

He looked appalled. Hesitated a moment, then put his toothbrush back in the bathroom and hastened to help me.

'Lift, don't drag,' he muttered.

With much puffing and cursing, we shifted the heavy bed to the other side of the room. It left behind an empty, dusty stretch of floor, which, framed by the great sweeping damask canopy, looked most peculiar. I solved that by dragging a chest of drawers across to fill the space. Or started to. James had to help, of course, in the blue T-shirt he wore to bed, his willy poking out beneath it.

'Happy?' he panted.

'Yes, much better.'

He stood up and gazed around. 'Camille will think it's bizarre.'

'Why will Camille know?'

'Thérèse is bound to tell her.'

'I'll just say I'm a fresh-air fiend. Have to sleep under a window.'

'You'll have plenty of it – we can't close the bloody curtains now.' He got on the bed and tried to yank them across.

'Yes, we can, just pull the bed out a bit. It's too close to the wall.'

We went to the other end and were pulling, bottoms up, when Amelia came in.

'Oh, gross, Dad.' She covered her eyes.

'Well, knock, damn you!' James stood up and pulled his T-shirt down.

'Sor-ry. Why have you moved the bed?'

'Your mother wants the air.'

'Oh.' She looked at the dividing wall. Her eyes widened. 'Oh, right. Important not to overreact, Mum. Um, Jean-Claude needs a room, obviously, which means there isn't one for Toby.'

I gazed at her, still panting with exertion, hands on my hips. Infuriating. For her grandfather and Aunt Rachel's sake, I'd insisted Toby nominally had a room. My mother's new boyfriend obviously had to have at least the semblance of separate sleeping quarters, too, since she'd only known him five minutes, which meant my daughter's boyfriend no longer had a smokescreen. I looked at James hopelessly. He shrugged and threw up his hands.

'You sort it out.' He stalked back to the bathroom, muttering darkly about the bloody women in his family.

'Yes, well, obviously, he'll have to go in with you, Amelia, even though it's not what I wanted.'

'It's not my fault.'

'No one's saying it is.'

'I don't see why you have to keep up this bonkers sense of appearances, anyway.'

'Because your grandfather is of a different generation, as is Rachel, in a way, and also, it's the thin end of the wedge. In a twinkling, Tara will be next, and I promised Rory's mother –'

'Oh, grow up,' she interrupted. 'Do you really think Rory and Tara are going to sleep at opposite ends of the corridor?'

And with that she flounced out, having got what she wanted. So why flounce? Why?

I brushed my teeth very hard and drew blood. I stared at it against the white porcelain. No. Over my dead body would my seventeen-year-old daughter disport herself thus. Eighteen was the rule in this family, with at least six months of dating behind them. I spat more blood, pleased with that. I'd just made a rule. A good one. Also, with Tara

147

directly opposite us, Rory would have to be pretty bold to sneak down here. And he was a good boy, I knew that. I got into bed, knowing I wouldn't sleep for ages, that there was too much in my head. After a bit, eyes shut but mind whirring, I heard footsteps padding softly down the corridor. Tara's door opened quietly. I froze. Then I heard her giggle. I leaped out of bed and flew to my door, flinging it wide.

Max was outside, talking to Tara, who was fully dressed at her open door. They stared at me.

'What are you doing?' I asked, wrong-footed.

Max regarded me a moment. 'Borrowing an adapter. I didn't bring one and your daughter said she had two.'

'Right. Where's Rory?'

I threw a wild glance up the corridor, then peered past Tara into her room. She recoiled in mock-horror, squinting in that 'You're so weird' way beloved of her tribe. 'In his *room*?' she suggested incredulously.

'Right. Good. Go to sleep,' I said, as if I'd sorted out something crucial.

I shut my door, but not before Max had managed to look me up and down, taking in my heavily night-creamed face, my very cheap, very short Primark nightie, eyes ironic and amused. His, not mine. I crept back to bed, feeling like a humped beast. Splendid. Oh, splendid.

'Might I suggest, if you're intending to leap up and down all night and patrol the corridors like something out of a French farce, you keep the noise to a minimum?' enquired James sleepily as I curled up beside him. 'God help us if Jean-Claude is down this way, too. Your mother will be here in a minute.'

'He is,' I said miserably. 'Toby's designated room was next to ours, and Mum will definitely do the creeping. So, far from having the quiet end of the house, we've ended up where all the action is.'

'Well, let them get on with it,' he grumbled, turning over on to his side, his back to me, and bunching up his pillow. 'Good luck to them. Everyone will be bonking away like rabbits, but you can rest assured there's one couple who won't be.' He gave a hollow laugh.

I didn't reply. Thought about giving a hollow laugh back, since it wasn't always me that was tired, but decided against it.

Instead, I listened for sounds next door: strained my ears. Nothing. I'd heard murmurings earlier, but only the motion of two people going to bed. And, anyway, why would I care? Max had been married to Mimi for eighteen years, been going to bed with her night after night – why would I care about Sally? I wouldn't. Care was the wrong word. The right word was ... I thought hard. For ages. When I did locate it, the word which summed up the way I was feeling, it took more than one. Out-manoeuvred. Out of control. Spiralling into the stratosphere. Almost to the point where I couldn't breathe. I knew I'd felt like this once before, when Coco, huddled in a huge coat in the corner of the pub like a fragile bird, had delivered her *coup de grâce*. It was the same flailing experience that I'd do any-thing to escape from. Next door, I heard Sally giggle. I shut my eyes tight and rammed in my earplugs.

The following morning, Sally came down to breakfast looking flushed and happy. I was already at the table under the trees with some other early risers, it being warm enough to eat outside. I smiled at her brightly over my coffee.

149

'Morning, Sally.'

'Morning, Flora. I say, James has finally told me who this place belongs to. I couldn't believe it! Camille de Bouvoir, the opera singer!'

'Yes, I know. He was asked not to broadcast it, and you know what he's like. His word is his bond, and all that.'

'Max was flabbergasted when I told him last night, we had no idea. Is she very glam?'

'I've only met her briefly, but yes, she is. Oh, *merci*, Thérèse.' I smiled up at Thérèse, who'd arrived with some fresh coffee. Sally wanted to know if it was Brazilian, Max's favourite, and when Thérèse said she wasn't sure, she asked her in an imperious voice to please check and, if not, to add it to her shopping list? I cringed and pretended to check my phone.

Most people were already up, it being after nine, aside from the teenagers, who wouldn't appear until much later. The Brig was seated facing the view, almost in a trance. The hazy morning light shimmered over the valley floor below us, heralding another hot day, and he looked sweetly delighted in his panama hat, mouth slightly open, as it often was these days, as he rested both liver-spotted, gnarled hands on his stick. Rachel, beside him, poured coffee for both of them. She was wearing an ancient blue shirtwaister which was already dark under the arms. It occurred to me that she really had tumbled into the carer role if Sally had broken free. Rachel had always done the lion's share but, to give her her due, Sally had never stinted. James and I were the slackers, I knew, but then we had a family and lived in the south. I wondered if Rachel minded. She gave so little away. Always a very private person, it was as if, as Tara had once commented, she concealed a lot of things: as if she carried her past around with her at all times. Lizzie, beside her, glamorous in a yellow-and-white striped sundress and gold sandals, provided quite a contrast, reading her emails on her iPad, slim legs crossed. She glanced up as Michel delivered a basket of fresh croissants. I saw him smoulder at her. Ah. Not just me then.

Max appeared, looking impossibly handsome in a pink shirt and khaki shorts, tanned legs beneath them. He smiled down at Sally as he took a seat beside her and she squeezed his leg, leaning in to whisper something. She was wearing a plunging halterneck sundress that revealed acres of bosom. Those hadn't reduced much, I observed as I sipped my coffee. Or dropped. Extraordinary. She really had turned into a very good-looking woman. Perhaps I had got it all wrong. Perhaps they really were in the first flush of love. I pretended to read a guidebook, taken from a pile which the Brig had brought out from the kitchen. Sally leaned diagonally across to me.

'Did I tell you Max and I are going on to St Tropez for a few days after this?' She helped herself to a croissant, then put it back in the basket.

I looked up, as if I had been miles away. Blinked. 'You didn't, no.'

'To stay with the Hamilton-Frasers. Remember I cooked for them when they took that shooting lodge in Perth? I'd love Max to meet them, they've become such good friends.'

'Oh, really?' I was surprised. I'd run into Felicity Hamilton-Fraser coming out of M&S on the King's Road not that long ago. We'd chatted and I'd asked how it had gone, and she'd said, 'Well, your sister-in-law is an excellent cook but we learned not to ask her for a drink. She's feet up in the drawing room making herself very at home, isn't she? And not just one drink, either!'

'Oh, sorry, Felicity.' I'd recommended Sally, who'd been at a very low ebb at the time.

'Oh, it didn't matter, we got quite giggly about it, actually. Put bets on how long she'd stay!'

I'd felt a bit cross then: I didn't want her to be the butt of their jokes.

'Probably just relaxing after all that cooking? It's hard work.'

'This was *before* dinner, Flora. We didn't get fed until well after nine.'

'Heavens! Oh, I am sorry, Felicity.'

'Oh, don't worry, we didn't mind. She was hilarious at the after-dinner games. Any excuse to strip down to her underwear!'

I'd scurried away into M&S. Hadn't told James. He'd have been mortified.

'They've replied, have they, darling?' asked Max.

'No, but they know we're coming. I emailed weeks ago. But you know Felicity, she's so disorganized. It's probably slipped through her net.'

Stupidly, I caught Max's eye.

'We might just see if she makes contact this week, hon.'

'Oh, I'm not fussed either way. We could have a couple of nights at that place you found in the Michelin Guide instead, if you prefer.'

'Yes, we might do that.'

Was she the butt of Max's joke, too, I wondered? That

would be cruel. And would make him a very unpleasant person, surely? Something I'd never known him to be. I thought of the lovely, crazy, funny Max I knew. I voiced this to Lizzie in the kitchen, when we went inside to make some instant coffee, which we preferred.

'It must be for real, Lizzie,' I whispered as we waited for the kettle to boil. 'It makes him the most terrible cad if not, don't you think?'

'Yes,' she said slowly. 'But then again, a marriage break-up does funny things to people, Flora. Makes them desperate. If his life has gone terribly wrong – which it clearly has – there's a temptation to lurch back to the past, when it was peachy. Look at the success of Friends Re-united. He may be here to banish a few ghosts, see you in the flesh and think – what was all the fuss about? She's just a middle-aged housewife carrying a few extra pounds.'

'Yes,' I said slowly. 'That could be it.' I remembered his amused eyes on me in my minuscule nightie last night, taking in my streaky fake-tanned legs. I had thicker ankles since childbirth, too. 'In which case, it'll take a matter of moments.'

'I honestly don't think he's here with the cold, clear aim of breaking up your marriage.'

'No. But . . . maybe to make trouble?'

'It's only trouble if you feel it to be. It's you I'm worried about, Flora, if I'm honest. He's awfully attractive.'

'Oh, you don't need to worry about me.' I hastily grabbed the coffee she'd made me. A bit spilled on my hand and burned me. 'I got over Max years ago.'

I sailed back out to the garden, sucking my sore hand.

*

It occurred to me as I went up later to change that I'd put mascara on for breakfast. And lippy. Something I'd never usually do on holiday. In the privacy of my bathroom, I wiped it off defiantly. Then I put on the shiniest, whitest, total sunblock – I burn very easily – which gave my skin a fishy look. Even the swimming costume I chose was an elderly Boden affair, slightly saggy at the waist and legs. It was very much third reserve for when I ran out of good ones. I added a dreary cheesecloth poncho, chose a trashy novel rather than anything cerebral, and, popping it into my beach bag along with a hat and more sun cream, sallied forth defiantly.

At the top of the stairs I glanced down and saw Sally and Max crossing the flagstone hall below, one step ahead of me, in their swimwear. Sally was in a gorgeous black bikini with a pink sarong tied low around her hips. She was already beautifully brown. Max's hand was resting on the base of her bronzed spine as they crossed the hall. I almost fell over the balcony. Was that *Sally*?

I dashed back to my room. Changed into my expensive new one-piece made from reinforced steel which pulled in all the bits that mattered, including the droopy tummy and the side boobs, as the Australian lady who'd sold it to me had promised. Then I wiped off the thick grease, found a slinky turquoise sarong, applied a touch of lippy and went down.

The pool was a short distance away from the house. To reach it, one had to cross the manicured front lawn, which was constantly watered by spiralling hoses, via a cinder path, duck under a spreading cedar tree, skirt a small lake with a single rowing boat on it, and enter through a charming green wooden gate in a tall, crumbling wall. Inside, there was a beautiful enclosed haven, which had once been an enormous walled kitchen garden. It still boasted large regular flowerbeds to one side, now full of bright dahlias and gladioli, the cutting garden for house flowers, rose-clad walls and a small orchard. Aside from the pool, the rest was laid to lawn, but such was the garden's size, there was even an area with a badminton net. At the far end, an ancient stone barn with a gaping façade had been converted into a pool house, complete with table tennis, drinks fridge and comfortable rattan armchairs with vast, squashy cushions. Behind the barn and over the post and rail fence, a pair of elegant chestnut horses nodded at the flies around them, already hot and bothered, ready to head for the cool of the trees. In the distance, beyond the parched pasture, was the neighbouring vineyard, then the hills of Fayence rose up gloriously in the shimmering heat.

The teenagers were already present and horizontal, having clearly grabbed a croissant and orange juice en route, judging by the glasses and jam-smeared plates dotted about. I'd have to make sure they found their way back inside and put a stop to that tomorrow. Why couldn't they pause for breakfast at the table? They were dozing around the end of the pool nearest the barn, which faced the sun, having bagged the best beds. The boys wore garish long trunks, the girls tiny bikinis, and all were plugged into their iPods, sunglasses on, a paperback apiece. I regarded my girls with pride. Amelia, who'd still like to be thinner, was much more slender than a year or so ago, and Tara had a great figure. Lizzie, in an orange bikini, was face up amongst them, and Max and Sally had not yet appeared. Perhaps they'd got lost.

I found a sunbed in a distant corner, abandoned by the children for being half in the shade, but that suited me. Arranging myself upon it carefully, top half in the shade, legs in the sun, I meticulously removed my sarong, but not until I was sitting down, and even then I let it drape a bit over my thighs, which, despite the fake tan, looked pasty and heavy. I bent my knees to make my legs look thinner and wondered if I could hold this position all morning. I did it for ten minutes and became increasingly uncomfortable and cross.

I hadn't envisaged anything other than total relaxation on this holiday, and having an ex-boyfriend wondering how my figure had changed in the twenty years since I'd last seen him was not in the script. Defiantly, I let my legs flop down on to the sunbed, just as Sally and Max appeared through the garden gate. I snapped them back up again, sharpish. They didn't seem to notice me, though, and took beds, as I knew they would, in full sun, at the more popular, fun end of the pool.

I watched from behind my book, dark glasses and the brim of my hat as they began to shed layers. Sally's legs were long and slim; the only hint of the colossal amount of weight she'd lost was in the slightly mottled texture of her tummy and thighs, but you'd have to be very picky to find fault. I saw Amelia pretending to read but looking with interest, too. Max, in long trunks, was lean and toned, with only a hint of a paunch where, once, he'd had a very flat stomach. He was in pretty good shape, and had a natural tan, which suggested this wasn't his first holiday this year. I realized he looked expensive. His trunks were a good, dusky green. His deck shoes were not tatty and Cornish like James's but sleek and Italian-looking, as were his shorts and shirt, which he folded in a pile beside him, together with a Rolex watch. It occurred to me he'd probably made a lot of money. I knew he was still organizing concerts and events, because Sally had mentioned it last night, but I had no idea how his career had panned out, because, I realized with satisfaction, I hadn't been interested enough to find out. Doubtless, I could have done, we still had one or two mutual friends – Lucy would have known, Parrot, too – but I'd never bothered to ask; had never googled his name, never investigated. You see? I was safe as houses. If he still had problems as far as I was concerned, which – I watched as Sally lay down beside him and they briefly held hands – I was beginning to doubt, that was his lookout. Having seen Sally in her bikini, I was now finding it farcical to imagine Max was here on my account. I smiled. Took my sunglasses off and shut my eyes. How ridiculous of you, Flora. So egocentric. Ridiculously vain. Thank God I could relax.

I have no idea why I fell asleep so easily and so early on in the day, although I suppose I'd had a pretty unsettled night, but I was woken by Tara, her face above mine, concerned.

'You're a bit red, Mum. And also' – she leaned forward confidentially – 'you might want to tuck yourself in a bit.' She glanced down at my bikini line: half my bush was flourishing the wrong side of my swimsuit; my legs were akimbo.

I sat up with a horrified jerk. Rearranged my splayed

157

limbs – one foot seemed to be on the *floor*, as if I'd been writhing in my sleep – and quickly wiped the dribble from the side of my mouth. I realized the sun had moved. I was now in its full glare, chest and face on fire. Damn. Why had I wiped that sun cream off? And how long had I been like that? I glanced across the pool. No sign of anyone. All beds had been abandoned. Plates, books, glasses and sun cream were littered about.

'What's the time?' I gasped, mouth totally devoid of saliva.

'I dunno, but it must be nearly lunchtime. You were snoring fit to bust, Mum.'

'*Was* I?' I was aghast.

'Come on, they'll be wanting to serve up. Dad doesn't want us to be late. You know what he's like about keeping staff hanging around.'

Tara sloped off, and I quickly found my hat. I wrapped my sarong around my waist and, feeling sticky and drenched in sweat, prepared to follow her. My sarong stuck to my legs. It was no good. I'd have to go in the pool. I was horribly hot.

Thankful no one was around to witness it, I stripped off the sarong and plunged into the pool, obviously not putting my hair under, just wiping my face with my hand. I swum a length of breaststroke in the cool blue water. Bliss. When I reached the other end I saw that, far from being alone, as I'd imagined, one couple was still here. Max and Sally had moved their beds around to the side of the barn, and Sally was naked. She was on her tummy, and around a discreet corner to be sure, but still starkers. I boggled. Max had his back to me and was sitting on his bed beside her, suntan lotion in hand. I watched, mesmerized, as he took a handful and began to cream her back. As he massaged it down her spine, lower, lower, gently into her bare bottom, he turned his head, looked me straight in the eye and smiled.

Chapter Twelve

'But don't you think that's peculiar? That he should be smiling at me while massaging his girlfriend's bottom?'

I was trotting to catch up with Lizzie, who'd spotted a stall she wanted to revisit at the far end of the market.

'Not if he only that moment realized you were there. What did you want him to do, scowl? Look horrified that you were spying? Snatch his hand away? I think, under the circumstances, a smile was quite resourceful of him.'

'It wasn't that sort of smile, Lizzie. Not a friendly one. It was more . . . implicit.'

'Implicit of what? "This is what you're missing"?'

'Yes!'

'Oh, don't be ridiculous. I'm surprised at you, Flora, letting it spoil your holiday like this. You're in a complete tizz about nothing. Rise above. Also, if you could drag your eyes away from your own life for a minute, Jackson emailed me this morning. He can't come, after all. He's too busy rehearsing, which probably means I've been too needy recently and he's relishing some time alone without me.'

'Oh, Lizzie, I'm sorry. I'm sure it's not that, by the way. Jackson's nuts about you.' I bit my thumbnail as she rummaged amongst the shoes on the stall. 'Sorry. I am a bit self-obsessed, aren't I?'

'If truth be told, we all are. Now, what about these? Too bright?'

She was holding up a pair of shocking-pink espadrilles with ribbons. When Madame's eyes were averted, she slipped them on her feet.

'No. I mean, yes. When you get them home, probably.'

Lizzie hadn't known us in the old days, of course. Me and Max. Hadn't known how close we were. She was the wrong person. Lucy would have been better. But, on the other hand, Lizzie was the right person, because Rise Above was just what I should do, and what I'd decided to do only this morning.

I narrowed my eyes and looked into the distance. The market was crowded and packed with stalls under brightly striped awnings which stretched right to the end of the long, gravel square, where, on quieter days, old men played boules and chewed the fat in the sun. Ahead of us, Mum and Jean-Claude were sampling olives from an array of vast wooden barrels on a trestle table. They'd got here much earlier and rung us to say we might like it, this rare afternoon market, very much for the tourists, but quite fun. Lizzie, James and I had driven across to the exquisite hilltop town, perched like a bird of prey hovering over a valley, and made our way in the heat up the little cobbled streets to the top. I'd been pleased to get away, to have a change of scene; James and I were not good at lying by the pool these days, preferring to poke around monasteries and art galleries, as befitted our age, and this was a beautiful place to come. A magnificent church dominated one end of the square, a phalanx of ancient steps running up to its open door, and to either side an avenue of trees with mottled grey trunks provided some welcome shade under a canopy of thick green leaves. Just beyond the right-hand row of trees a low stone wall ran the length of the square – and pretty much the town – in a typically casual French attempt to prevent one toppling down the dizzyingly steep hillside below. No barriers and hideous signs here. The stands were predominantly full of clothes and trinkets, the real commerce having been done yesterday morning, when steely-eyed madames had prodded glistening hams, plump artichokes and florid tomatoes with all the thoroughness of gem merchants. This was a far more flippant affair, and it occurred to me the girls would have liked it, but they'd been intent on their tans when I'd asked, forensically examining first-day white marks and studying factor numbers as if they were revising for exams, determined to go home bronzed.

The world jostled by in strappy tops, shorts and flip-flops under a blazing sun, but my tummy was tight. Up ahead I saw James, who wasn't a great shopper at the best of times, high on the church steps, probably contemplating taking a peek inside. It occurred to me that a moment's quiet reflection within a great dark chasm of peace was just what I needed right now. It might still my soul, bring a sense of proportion to my thoughts, which I knew was sadly lacking. Yes, a wander past the tombs of brave soldiers and Resistance fighters who'd had much tougher lives than me, the opportunity to light a candle for my family, with my husband by my side, could be just the ticket. I left Lizzie to her shoes and made my way through the crowd towards him. As I approached, I realized he was on his mobile. He was laughing and tossing back his head, running a hand through his fine fair hair. His face was alight, eyes bright.

I watched as he laughed out loud, then said, '*Au revoir*.' Au revoir? He pocketed his phone.

'Who was that?'

'What?' He turned. Looked startled. 'Oh, hello, darling. It was Camille.'

'Camille?'

'Yes. Just wanted to know how it was going.'

'Right. She rang yesterday, didn't she?'

'Yes, well, it's the first time she's let the house out. She's obviously keen to know it's all going smoothly.'

'She hasn't let it out, she's lent it to us. Surely Thérèse reports back?'

'I've no idea. Anyway, she'll be here this evening.'

'Here? With us?'

'Yes, she's coming for dinner.'

'But – but, James, I thought she was touring!'

'She is, but her rehearsals are in Cannes. After all, that's where the first concert is. Didn't I say? She said she'd be with us about drinks time.'

'But – do we want her?' I blurted. 'How long is she staying?'

'Well, obviously, the night, and then I've no idea.' He looked affronted. 'It's her house, Flora, be reasonable.'

'Yes, it is, but it's hardly our holiday at all, is it? Everyone assumes they've got carte blanche to invite whoever they please. It's a flipping free for all!'

I made to storm off, but he caught my arm. 'Flora, you're behaving like a spoilt child. Just because Sally has found some happiness and the girls have brought their boyfriends –'

'Oh, I don't mind about that –'

'And your mother has found a friend –'

'Who you objected to, originally!'

'Yes, but I had a good chat with him this morning, he's a nice chap. And now Camille is dropping by – what could be nicer? It's a huge house, and the more the merrier, surely? She's such a lovely, generous, warm-hearted person. I'm surprised at you.'

'Are you? Well, that's because you didn't realize you were married to such an unlovely, ungenerous, cold-hearted person, isn't it?' I stormed off, shaking my arm free.

I shoved through the crowds, boiling with heat and rage, knowing I was behaving very badly. Knowing if this was Amelia – oh, I knew full well where her temperament came from – I'd be livid. Stall after stall of pretty bedlinen, summer dresses, scarves, baskets, Provençal tablecloths in beautiful, colourful prints which, ordinarily, would afford me huge pleasure, passed me by. On I marched. I badly wanted to be alone, but there were so many people and it was so hot, it was impossible. In the tatty jewellery section of the market, where smiling, over-bronzed Mediterraneans sold tin under the guise of silver, Jean-Claude was fingering a faded pink cameo brooch. I made to duck past without him seeing me, but he turned, caught my eyes with a disarming smile.

'You think she like this?'

I stopped. Gazed. It was about the only pretty thing on the stand, and certainly the only thing with any age. I swallowed. 'Yes. Yes, I think she would, Jean-Claude. If you mean my mother.'

'I do. I wanted to thank her. It is so very kind of her to have me. And you, too, of course.'

'Oh, don't thank me, I'm just the tour guide,' I warbled. 'Anyway, I thought you were bound for the market at Aix, not this one? Some urgent mission?'

'I was, but no longer. I got here early when this market opened and all I need is here. Would you like to see? It's being kept for me.'

Oh, why not, I thought, not even bothering to show surprise about Aix: I'd known all along he was staying. He led me across to where another suntanned smiler had a clothing stall, brightly coloured slinky dresses dripping from a railed enclosure. The proprietor greeted Jean-Claude like a brother, her face creasing into a toothless grin, and Jean-Claude, having kissed her three times on both cheeks and indulged in some rapid formalities, moved across to whip away a blanket covering a huge mound in the corner. Beneath it were a cluster of applewood chairs, a pretty wrought-iron bedstead, a fruitwood table, an Aubusson rug, some tapestry cushions, a long length of faded velvet brocade curtain and a box of glasses.

'Oh!' Despite my demeanour, I found myself drawn to the fabric. I crouched down and ran it between my fingers, feeling its luxurious weight. Then I picked up a thick wine goblet, turning it in my hand. 'What lovely things. I haven't seen anything like this. Where did you find them?'

'It was all over very quickly, in the first half-hour. The antiques dealers, they have gone now.'

I picked up an ancient pestle and mortar, enormous and heavy. Gorgeous.

He smiled. Crouched beside me. 'You like your mother. You like these things.'

'It's a family weakness.'

I thought of my Clapham house, stuffed to the gunnels with just this sort of shabby-chic clutter, so that James complained that everything broke within seconds and the girls said they longed for the minimalist cool of their friends' houses, with clean lines and neutral colours and just the occasional flash of orange or lime green. But there was no soul in clean lines. No history. And I didn't like orange or lime green. I liked chipped ivory. Soft rose.

I straightened up. 'Mum had a boyfriend once, in Paris. Philippe. We used to spend whole mornings buying mirrors and pictures in the *puce* at Saint-Ouen. Then we'd have lunch in Montmartre. Philippe wasn't really interested, but he loved Mum. So much.' I remembered him watching with pleasure as she browsed the stands, long blonde hair framing her remarkably beautiful face, always smiling, always happy, other men turning to stare. Women, too. 'We'd spend hours trailing around with her. She'd buy whatever she wanted, and it was never expensive. An old book, a piece of lace. A china doll for me. It gets under your skin after a while.'

'Those sound like happy times.' He was watching me keenly.

I remembered being wrapped in an old fur coat of Mum's, a steaming *chocolat chaud* in front of me, at an outdoor table at Chez Pommette, a mottled mirror propped beside us, the three of us laughing as we played spotting the dog most like its owner, Philippe declaring the winner a poodle and his camp master who minced past as if the most horrendous smell were under their noses. Then we'd go back to our apartment up the steep hill, to our creeper-clad building, where Philippe would cook bouillabaisse, letting me help, showing me how to debeard mussels, clean clams. Make an aioli. I was reasonably convinced that my love of good food and cooking stemmed from these times.

'Yes. They were.' I remembered always feeling safe and secure. Always with Mum, never parked with a nanny, which was surely all one could ask of childhood?

'But yet you still wish it could have been otherwise?'

'How did you know?'

He shrugged. 'Just a hunch. A thatched cottage in the countryside, rows of running beans, the vicar coming to tea.'

I smiled. 'Runner beans. And yes, I probably read too much. And yes, you're right, Jean-Claude, she did her best and I was ungrateful. Have always been ungrateful.'

'That's not what I'm saying. I'm just saying it's not good to be always looking over your shoulder with regret, thinking what might have been. Or what might be, one day. It is better to enjoy the moment.'

'I never do that,' I said quickly. 'Look back, I mean.' Was this really what I wanted? An in-depth chat with Mum's latest squeeze on the nature of my shortcomings? But his eyes were kind. I found myself liking this man and marvelling, as always, that, despite the turnover, Mum unerringly went for decent men. She was never one to play a victim to some bastard.

'Let's get a coffee,' he said, sensing a shift in my mood. 'And a cognac, maybe.'

I allowed myself to be led out of the teeming melee to an equally crowded café on the fringes of the market, under the plane trees, beside the old stone wall which dropped away dramatically to the valley below. There was absolutely no chance of a table, except that, in the blink of an eye, and after some quick-fire conversation, Jean-Claude had procured one, out of the blazing sun, under an umbrella, right at the front so we could watch the world go by. He pulled up a third chair for my mother, who'd gone to look at some buttons, he told me.

'I never knew this market yielded such treasures. It's years since I've been to Fayence. And Aix is so overdone, of course.'

I was pleased he'd deliberately reverted to light chit-chat. I looked at him as he ordered for us. He was very attractive and aristocratic-looking. My French was good enough to know his accent was good: Parisian, not provincial.

'How come you've ended up as a *brocanteur* in a little village, Jean-Claude?' I asked when our coffee arrived.

He smiled and lit a Marlboro, offering me one. I took it, knowing I needed it, and the coffee, too. My nerves were shredded. And when I was upset, I lashed out. Which wasn't nice.

'I, too, grew up surrounded by nice things. My father was a diplomat and we lived in many beautiful places. We didn't own them, of course, the grand houses or the antiques, they were ambassadorial, attached to the house, but when my parents' marriage broke up and I lived with my mother, in very reduced circumstances in Brittany, surrounded only by ugly things, I vowed that one day I would surround myself again with attractive *objets*.'

'Attractive women, too.'

'Of course.' He blew smoke above my head and smiled, the smile reaching right up to his sea-green eyes. 'Why not?'

'So that's always been your career? Antiques?'

'No. Not always.' He paused. Seemed about to continue, then changed his mind. 'And you, *cherie*? You like what you do? Eating for a living?'

I laughed. 'Well, put like that . . .' I frowned. 'Actually, no. I don't like it much now. I used to. But I haven't for a long while.' It was odd to hear myself say it. Out loud. Not just to myself. 'I hate putting food in my mouth if it's not for pleasure, which, these days, it isn't, and I hate either hurting a restaurant's reputation and possibly its livelihood, or lying to my readers. It's a lose-lose situation.'

'So give it up.'

'Can't. We're broke,' I replied cheerfully. 'Well, not stony broke, but we certainly need the money. There's never enough. I could never afford to be a lady of leisure, like some of my friends. Not that I'd necessarily want to. I have to help James.'

'And James. He too is bored and disillusioned, I think?'

'Yes, you think right.' I smiled. 'But hey. So are most people, probably, if you ask them.'

He shrugged in a Gallic fashion, his neck disappearing right into his shoulders. 'And yet you have free will! You are not beasts of the field. You could change all that in *un instant*.'

'Oh, really?' I gave a mirthless laugh. 'How? And still pay the mortgage? And the bills? Educate the girls?'

'Oh, well, now you put up obstacles. You run scared. And subject yourself to the tyranny of middle-class values. And your girls are young women now, adults. You've done your job there.'

'Right. So what do you suggest we do, Jean-Claude?

Chuck it all in and run a vineyard or something?' I swung my arm over the ancient wall to the serried ranks in the valley below. 'Out here, perhaps?'

He shrugged. 'Yes, of course. Why not? If that's what would make you happy. Life is so simple. If you let it be. Ah, *cherie*! There you are, I was worried!'

My mother appeared, looking radiant, a straw basket over her shoulder full of hats, lace and oddments, bags in the other hand. She kissed us both as Jean-Claude sprang to his feet to help her with them.

'Such finds! Such beautiful stalls! And so lovely to come back and see you both sitting here.' She glowed with pleasure.

Jean-Claude was pulling out her chair eagerly, glancing up at the sun to make sure it was shaded. 'Good. I'm pleased you had success. I feel responsible as a Frenchman – as host *national*.' He placed a hand on his heart with a playful smile. 'It is important you English ladies are happy.'

I smiled and sank into my coffee as they chatted on. English ladies: one very beautiful, one not so, with only relative youth on her side. And how many times had I been in the very same situation? When a boyfriend of Mum's had tried to befriend me. Not in any scheming, Machiavellian way, not to worm his way in, just to help me. But I'd always resisted. Always felt tolerated. It would have helped if I'd been prettier, I'd always thought. To be beautiful was such a prize: to be escorted into a restaurant by a triumphant man – yes, as a trophy, but was there anything wrong with that? Surely only other women said it shouldn't be so? I remembered, after those years in Paris, after Philippe had died – I must have been thirteen – coming back to England and going to boarding school. My choice, not Mum's. I'd read about it: Malory Towers. Philippe had left my mother some money and she bought the pretty house in Fulham and, very reluctantly, let me go. I was deeply unhappy there, a fish out of water in this all-girl, upper-class, alien establishment. One night I overheard a girl in the dorm saying, 'Mummy says her mother's a tart.'

The following day was Sunday, and we were allowed out. Mum arrived with Gerald, her new boyfriend, whom I'd never met before, in his convertible Aston Martin, and they took me to lunch at a local country pub. I didn't speak to either of them. Mum looked flustered and deeply embarrassed as she tried to coax words out of me. I sat there, lumpen in my navy-blue uniform and thick woollen tights, hating her and Gerald, who, a rather nice twinkly banker, said quietly, when he thought I was out of earshot, 'It's too much for her, Susie. Too soon. Don't worry.'

'But she's so sweet, Gerald, darling. I want you to see her sweet.'

'I know. And I will.'

He did, eventually, after about four years, when I finally came round, but only when I'd almost left school. A London day school, which Mum had moved me to soon after that awful lunch, knowing I was miserable. I'd sulked for almost that entire time, which was such a waste, because Gerald was very nice. Unfortunately, his wife, being English, wasn't as accommodating as Yolande, Philippe's wife, had been, and when she found out about Mum, Gerald had had to choose. He badly wanted to leave his wife and marry Mum, whom he loved very much, but then his own daughter, Celia, who was a couple of years younger than me and at a similar London day school, attempted suicide. She slit her wrists in the bath. Obviously, he went home. And the whole family moved to a Jacobean manor house in Devon, as far away from Mum as they could get, and Gerald resigned from his bank and retired to become a high sheriff and shoot pheasant. They didn't need him to work any longer – he'd made plenty of money – and his wife kept a close eye. Which of course is how it should be, keeping families together. Not yielding to a 'home-breaker', which was another expression I'd heard applied to Mum at school.

Mum and Jean-Claude had broken off their conversation to watch me as I stared into space, my coffee cold before me.

'Darling? I said, did you buy anything?'

'Oh. No. I didn't.' Don't sulk. Not again. I could almost feel the scratchy woollen tights. Mum's eyes were anxious. I rallied. 'But I've seen all Jean-Claude's finds – amazing.'

My mother's face broke into a relieved smile, as if I'd actually said, I'm happy with your lifestyle, Mum, and I love your latest man.

'Yes, aren't they?'

Jean-Claude smiled at me over the rim of his cup, patting my back, I knew. Good dog.

And of course it was easier to behave these days; as an adult, not being alone. How I'd wished for a sister or brother when I was young. Yearned. But these days, with James and the girls, who couldn't give a damn, who showed me the light, it was simpler. Although, actually, I'd been shown the light before. Been shown that it was no reflection on me who my mother was and how she behaved. Max had done that. He'd taught me to embrace my exotic mother, to admire her, not to be ashamed. He'd done my small family an invaluable service.

I sipped my cold coffee and swam up from the past to the present. As I broke through the surface, I put my sunglasses on in defence. Glanced around at the bright, bustling market. My eyes snagged on a white dress I'd seen earlier this morning, with a plunging neckline. Sally was engaged in a heated discussion with a stout, wind-battered monsieur. So she was here, too. She held a brightly painted jug in one hand and gesticulated wildly with the other, leaning across his stall of similarly decorated crockery, pursing her lips, showing off, and arguing loudly in terrible French that it was far too expensive. Max was beside her but distracted, staring over the walls of the town across the valley to the luxuriant green hills beyond, hands in his pockets, as far away in his head, it seemed, as those hills. It was inevitable, of course, that I didn't look away quickly enough and that he felt my gaze upon him. There was no mistaking the look he gave me this time as he turned and our eyes met, not over Sally's naked bottom, but over the distance of years: of different lives, marriages, children, the death of his beloved mother, I'd heard, lives spent without each other. It was wistful. Indeed, I'd go so far as to say it was full of regret.

Chapter Thirteen

Camille arrived that evening, fresh from a sexy convertible Alfa Romeo driven by a minder, on a gust of warm Provençal air and Nina Ricci's L'Air du Temps. If she'd also trailed a four-foot Isadora Duncan-style silk scarf, I wouldn't have been a bit surprised. I'd forgotten how beautiful she was and what charisma she exuded. Petite but powerful, she swept across the drive towards the terrace, where we'd all gathered – assembled, perhaps, a little over-excitedly – awaiting her presence. She wore a silk fuchsia shift dress, and two little dogs on leads dangled from a tanned hand. Before she reached us she handed them to the driver, a thick-set individual with no neck and lots of jewellery, who carried her bag. He disappeared around the side of the house.

James had been at fever pitch for the past hour, consulting Thérèse as to which aperitif to serve, which canapés were her favourites, wanting to get everything just perfect. Quite right, I thought, keeping the bitch within firmly in its kennel. She's been so generous – although I couldn't help noticing he'd changed his shirt, twice.

Camille came up the terrace steps, took off her sunglasses and smiled around, taking us all in. 'Look at you, all gathered and looking so heavenly on this perfect evening! Have you found everything you need? All you require?' She went around, kissing everyone twice, whether she knew them or not, which of course she didn't, whilst James, as master of ceremonies, introduced everyone. Our girls and their boys coloured up in excitement, and when she'd turned away, I noticed Toby snap her profile on his phone.

'It's all completely wonderful,' I assured her when it was my turn. 'What a gorgeous place!'

'And you found the town all right? You'll want to go there, it's sensational.' Her voice was a low purr, and she looked deep into my eyes.

'We've been already,' James assured her, handing her a glass of chilled champagne. 'We went this afternoon, it's stunning!'

She made a face. 'But not, I imagine, at that time of day. No, no, *cherie*, you want to go in the morning, before the sun and the crowds. And Seillans is even better. Such hidden treasures, such colours – truly *charmant*. I'll take you tomorrow myself.' She bestowed a huge pussy-cat smile on him, employing her eyes, too. James swooned visibly.

'I say, my dear, you've been inordinately kind to suffer such an invasion.' The Brig beamed broadly at her. 'The last thing you want to do is take us round the ruddy sights. Particularly when you must know them like the back of your hand.'

'*Au contraire*, it's no trouble, and if I show James, then he will know where to take you all, you see?'

James was now hopping around like a Labrador on heat, flushed and delighted in his pink gingham shirt.

'You must be so proud to have such a talented son, Dr–rummond,' she said, pronouncing his name like a drum roll and settling herself down in the centre of the cushioned basket sofa as James topped up her already full glass. 'Thank you, *cherie*,' she murmured up at him.

'Oh, well, yes.' The Brig blinked, surprised. 'I mean, it's always nice to have a medic in the family, isn't it? And he's frightfully good on bunions and wot not. I suffer terribly, you know. But, talking of parental pride – look at you!' His eyes and mouth widened in delight. 'I gather you have a daughter – she must be *so* proud, and all your relatives must be beside themselves.'

Camille made a face. She patted the seat beside her. 'Sit.' The Brig obediently sat. 'My mother was a great opera singer herself, far greater than me, so I think perhaps it is not so extraordinary for them.' She patted the sofa cushion to her left and James also sat obediently; indeed, he almost sat on her hand, so snappy were his reactions. I badly needed a camera. Amelia caught my eye and grinned.

'Your own mother is dead, James? I notice she is not here?'

'Yes. Yes, she is.'

A silence fell. Camille, sensing she'd hit a nerve, turned and clasped the Brig's hand. 'I am sorry, it is still too new? Too recent, yes? I'm afraid I am very sensitive. I pick up on these things so quickly, my emotional antenna is very acute.'

'No, no, not recent. Many years ago, as it happens.' The Brig said matter of factly. 'It's just the circumstances were rather harrowing, so one does rather draw a veil.'

'Of course,' said Camille, pressing on to open the veil. 'Long illnesses can indeed be difficult. I know only too well. My own father died of cancer.'

'Oh, no, it wasn't anything like that. She was killed, you see.'

'*Alors!*' Camille looked stunned. Reared back and clutched her heart.

'Um, Camille, your daughter, she's not with you? Cheese puff?' I interjected, knowing, if pressed, that the Brig was only too keen to confess, and then to give a detailed account of life behind bars at Her Majesty's Prison Dartmoor, regaling anyone who was interested – and most people jolly well were – with an account of all the characters he'd met in there. Donaldson, his cellmate, featured particularly strongly; he was a shaven-headed Glaswegian who'd done time for murder, having knifed someone in a pub brawl. They'd been released at about the same time, and Donaldson had worked for Drummond as an odd-job man on his estate, living, until his recent death, in one of the cottages. They'd been very close. Oh, it was all very uplifting and heart-warming and right on, but I could tell by the look on my husband's face that his father the ex-con was not necessarily the first impression he wanted to give his new crush. I loved him enough to spare him that. Camille was still digesting this information, but I was right in her face with the cheese puffs and my question, so she couldn't ignore me.

'Agathe? Yes, she is here, but she got out of the car at the lodge to see Thérèse and Michel.'

'Of course, you popped in there first.'

She waved her hand dismissively. 'Agathe did, but I was keen to see how you were all getting on. And to see that my room is ready in the tower.'

'Ah, we wondered. Only there's a locked door at the far end of the corridor –'

'My private apartment,' she told me firmly, touching my arm and giving me a level look.

'Of course,' I was flustered. 'I didn't mean . . .'

'Your sister is very attractive, James?' she said, peering around me and waving my plate of canapés away with a bored hand.

'Oh. I suppose. Yes, she is,' said James, surprised, as we all were, not used to Sally being complimented thus.

'She never used to be. Used to be frightfully fat,' the Brig told her in a stage whisper, leaning in. 'But then she ate like a pig. Cooks for a living, you see. Temptation always there.'

'Ah. So your family are all interested in food?' She looked up at me. 'James told me about your job. It sounds so fascinating. And your other sister-in-law? She is in the food industry, too?' She looked at Rachel's ample behind.

Why did I feel she was laughing at us? And the trouble was, Camille had a carrying voice, and poor Rachel blushed. Not one to dissemble, though, she came across.

'No, in fact I don't do much at all, I'm afraid,' Rachel said. 'Daddy's fairly moribund these days, so I'm pretty much around to look after him.'

'Couldn't do without her,' the Brig said warmly. 'Particularly now Donaldson's gone.'

'Melon ball, anyone?' I asked quickly, finding another plate.

'Donaldson?'

'My roommate. Met him at Dartmoor. Splendid chap. Worked for me for years.'

'Oh, but Dartmoor is such a beautiful place! Agathe learned to ride there when she was in England.'

The Brig's face lit up. 'Did she, by Jove! Whereabouts?'

'Actually, her father took her.'

'Ah, splendid. Well, yes, it's a wonderful moor. And, of course, being low-risk and therefore at the top of the pecking order, I had one of the rooms on the top floor, with a panoramic view. Bars, of course, but still. People used to visit and say that, position-wise, it would be the envy of many a country-house hotel. Remember, darling?' He turned to Rachel. 'You never saw my cell, of course.'

'Are you rehearsing or performing, Mme de Bouvoir?' Rachel asked swiftly, seeing Camille look mystified.

'Oh, Camille, please. Rehearsing. The actual tour doesn't start until next week. But you must come. I'm doing one special preview night near here, in Cannes.'

'Oh, well, we'd love to, but I'm sure we wouldn't get tickets . . .' Rachel blushed, realizing she'd looked artful, which she wasn't.

Camille held up the palm of her hand like a traffic policeman. 'I have two. One of which, of course, James shall have; the other, if it is all right with Florence, I will give to you.' She raised questioning eyebrows at me.

'Flora. And, yes, of course it's all right with me. Rachel's very keen on opera.'

'You are?'

'Oh, well, recordings, and box sets,' I heard Rachel muttering as I moved away. 'I don't get to go, of course. Although once, many years ago, with the school, in Edinburgh . . .'

'What did you see?'

'*Madame Butterfly*. But I was only about twelve.'

'But it left an impression?'

It did, and she and Rachel embarked on an animated discussion, Rachel growing pinker with the attention. I wished I didn't dislike Camille. Everyone else seemed to love her. I passed around the nibbles. After a bit, Camille got up and went to talk to the teenagers and Lizzie, who were standing slightly apart, by the balustrade. They chatted for a while and I heard them roar with laughter. Camille stood back and admired Lizzie's dress and I saw Lizzie flush with pleasure at having her Stella McCartney recognized, at being acknowledged as a discerning fashionista. Even Mum and Jean-Claude fell under her spell, as she broke into enthusiastic French to talk to them, although I noticed she addressed Jean-Claude much more frequently than Mum, who, despite her age, was far too beautiful. Mum wouldn't have noticed. She never noticed – or acknowledged – anything unpleasant. Surfed nicely over life's inconvenient hummocks.

Out of frame, Thérèse and Michel were quietly loading the dining table at the far end of the terrace with our supper. Unparalleled delights were appearing from the kitchen. A huge platter of oysters sat on a bed of ice; curling pink langoustines lay between artfully arranged crabs; and there were bowls of tiny pink prawns. From inside, the most wonderful aroma of *lapin à la moutarde* drifted through. My appetite had certainly come back on this holiday, prompted by the joy of eating for pleasure.

'The stops,' Jean-Claude commented to me *sotto voce* as he topped up my glass, his eyes darting towards the laden table, 'are surely being pulled out tonight.'

I smiled. 'Quite.'

Dinner was indeed delicious. A lively, convivial affair, too, with everyone showing off a bit, wanting to be able to say when they got home, Oh yes, I know Camille de Bouvoir. Or even 'my friend Camille', which was how it must always be for the famous, I realized. I was seated well away from her, at the other end of the table, but watched her in action with James beside her. He'd organized the seating plan. She flirted shamelessly with him, but not, I noticed, with Max. Maybe when one was surrounded by attractive people all the time, they rolled off one's back, and someone as interesting and clever as James undoubtedly was – he was regaling her now with some amusing medical story – was perhaps a novelty? And no doubt, having established that Max worked in the music industry, she'd lost interest. She knew all about that. No, it was the operating theatre she wanted to hear about, and James had a good many stories, apocryphal or otherwise, to tell. I saw him reach back into his reserve for more as she threw back her head and roared with laughter, or gasped with horror, depending on which was appropriate.

Her hand went to her heart: '*Non! Mon dieu!* The wrong kidney?'

'It happens,' James assured her. 'And never have an operation at the weekend if you can help it. You get all the part-timers.'

'But surely all surgeons have passed the same tests? Performed the same operations? Surely they are equally good?'

'You'd think so, wouldn't you? But think of the tenors you work with. Some better than others?'

'*Mais oui.*' She pulled a disgusted face. 'Some can barely sing!'

'*Exactement!*' trilled my husband. '*Je n'ai rien à ajouter.*' He turned to Rory, opposite, who was listening. 'I rest my case,' he explained.

'Your French is excellent, James,' Camille said quietly, and, emboldened, he picked up her hand and gallantly kissed the back of it. They smiled at one another.

Oh, please.

Thérèse and Michel served us as usual, providing fresh plates for the rabbit dish after we'd eaten the fish, but I did wonder why they didn't join us. I knew James had asked them. And surely Camille would want to spend time with her own family?

'Apparently, they find it too stressful, cooking and eating. And, actually, I can understand that,' Lizzie, beside me, told me. 'When you've slaved over the bloody thing, the last thing you want to do is flaming well eat it.'

'That's true,' I said, remembering my own dinner parties. 'It's just . . . Camille and Thérèse are sisters. It seems a bit master–servant.'

'That's clearly the way it is,' she murmured. 'They work for her, come what may. Interesting dynamic, isn't it?'

'Very.'

'And where's her man? It can't be that heavy I saw lurking earlier?'

'No, he's in the kitchen having supper. She's divorced.'

'Yes, I know, and, apparently her ex is gorgeous. Thérèse told me. Rich as Croesus, too, comes from some huge landowning family in Grasse. No, I just thought someone like her would inevitably have a guy in tow. The gossip columns link her with Paul Merendes.' A famous film director. 'She certainly seems to have the hots for James.'

Camille appeared to be reading my husband's palm now.

'James saved her daughter's life, Lizzie. She's obviously grateful.'

Lizzie gave me a look. 'I think we all know he stabbed her with an EpiPen, Flora. Even I could have done that.'

In bed that night I snuggled under James's arm, an unusual move for me, since James took any form of bodily contact, even a pat on the hand, as the green light for sex. He gave me a cuddle but didn't seem that interested in pursuing matters.

'Camille's very entertaining, isn't she?' I remarked softly.

'Great fun. And so kind and inclusive, don't you think? She could easily have eaten on her own tonight. I mean, who wants to get involved in someone's else's family? But she seemed to genuinely enjoy us.'

'Well, she enjoys you, darling,' I said lightly into his armpit.

He laughed. 'Oh, hardly.'

I prodded his chest playfully. 'Laughs at all your jokes, hangs on your every word. Picks your medical brains, too.'

'That's because her voice is so important. She wanted to know the internal workings of the larynx and the effect of vibration on the thorax.'

'I'll give you vibration on the thorax,' I murmured suggestively, nudging him.

'It's all to do with the cumulative effect of the muscles, of course. Which I explained.'

'Well, of course. You're the man to do that.' Piqued, I rolled away. 'What with your particular area of expertise being at the opposite end of the human body.' There was a silence.

'As you well know, I trained in every single area of physiology before I specialized. The larynx is something I was particularly drawn to.'

'Depending on who it belongs to.'

He paused. 'Are you peeved, Flora?'

'What, that Camille de Bouvoir finds you fascinating? Not in the least.'

'Only there's an edge to your voice. You're the one usually telling me to stop telling everyone I specialize in athlete's foot and big up my medical credentials. And now that I am, you're squashing me.'

'I am not squashing you, I'm teasing you. Do calm down, James, you're reacting like a schoolboy.'

'I'm reacting because it occurs to me that you don't like not being the centre of attention.'

'Centre of att—?' I sat up. Snapped on the light. 'Centre of attention – me? When? When am I ever the centre of attention? When am I ever anything other than the girls' mother, your wife, Susie's daughter –'

'Oh, you're being ridiculous. And full of rather unattractive self-pity, too. I was right. Jealous.'

'*Jealous?*' I shrieked. 'What, because some heavy-breasted opera singer turns her headlights on you, and reads your palm and –'

'Mum.' The door flew open. Tara appeared, looking horrified. 'Can I just say, these walls are, like, paper thin. We can hear every word.'

184

'We?' I roared. 'Who's we, Tara?'

She coloured dramatically. Was about to stutter something, but not before I'd flung back the covers, reared out of bed and swept past her. I threw open her door. Inside, Amelia, Rory and Toby, all fully clothed, were huddled on her bed, watching a film on her laptop. I blanched. Pulled down the old Primark number which, as we have already established, was very short.

'Mum, you seriously need to have a word with yourself,' Amelia told me, her eyes cold. 'You're out of control at the moment. And you need to *stop* bullying Dad.'

Speechless, I slammed the door shut, which meant Tara had to open it again to get back in. She shot me a filthy look. At that moment, the door behind me opened and Sally appeared in a pretty pink camisole and boxer shorts. She smiled nervously, clearly wondering what all the rumpus was about, then retreated back inside to report.

I flung myself back into bed, snapping off the light, feeling murderous. I turned away from James, who already had his back to me.

'Caught them all at it?' he asked. 'Got it on video?'

I ignored him, my heart pounding. Then I clamped my eyes and my teeth shut and counted to a hundred. I tried to sleep, but my heart was racing. Also, what had started as light mutterings and muffled laughter next door had fallen mysteriously silent. I tried not to listen and wished I had my earplugs, which had fallen under the bed. After a bit, I heard more muffled laughter, then someone pulled the lavatory chain. A few moments later, the chain went again. I put my pillow over my head and tried to go to sleep.

When I awoke the next morning, James's side of the

bed was empty. A beam of bright light was streaming through a gap in the curtains. It was like being woken by the Gestapo. Indeed, it was so bright it must be quite late, I realized, turning to peer at the clock. Twenty past ten. Why hadn't James woken me? Oh. Yes. There'd been a bit of a row. Deflated, I gazed out of the open window. The sky was clear and blue and the scent of all things warm and Mediterranean wafted through. Voices, too, from the terrace below. Laughter. I was missing out, something I've never been good at. I dragged myself out of bed, reckoning I was averaging about six hours sleep a night, which wasn't ideal on what was supposed to be a holiday, and lumbered off to the shower.

By the time I got downstairs, nearly everyone had gone. As I emerged through the French windows on to the terrace, Drummond and Rachel were just getting up and leaving the table. The Brig greeted me delightedly, with a wave of his stick.

'Flora! How lovely that you slept in. We saved you some brekka.'

'Thanks, Drummond. Did you sleep well?'

'Like a log, my dear. Best sleep I've had for months. Must be the air. James and the others have gone to Seillans, asked me to tell you. Two cars – the whole shooting match went in the end. So kind of Camille. Even the *Kinder* got up early!'

'Oh. Right. Of course. I'd forgotten.'

'They didn't want to wake you. James said you'd had a bad night.'

'Yes. I see.'

'Plenty of time,' Rachel said kindly. 'We're here for ages. I'll come with you tomorrow, if you like? Daddy will be fine without me, won't you?'

'Right as rain! You girls go tomorrow. I'm happy as a sand boy under the trees with the *Telegraph*. Rory gets it for me on his laptop, you know – how about that?'

'Yes. It's . . . amazing.'

'Do you want to go today?' asked Rachel, ever sensitive.

'No, no. I think I'll – just go for a wander, actually. Round here. Around the vineyards, you know. Maybe go to that chapel we passed.'

'Well, don't leave it too late, the sun's getting up,' called Drummond as they carried on their way through the house and on upstairs to attend to their ablutions. I sat down at the breakfast table alone in the sun. It was a still life of broken bread, jam pots and hastily discarded coffee, all abandoned as people pressed on with their day. In my present mood, I realized, the tableau could easily lead to introspection, which was the last thing I wanted. I rose quickly and went to the kitchen to make myself a coffee, drinking it standing up, burning the roof of my mouth, but keen to get on.

Michel appeared from behind a door. 'Good morning.' I'd swear he winked as he said it.

Rude not to wink back, but I resisted and smiled brightly. 'Morning, Michel! A beautiful one.'

'Would you like me to warm a croissant for you?' he murmured, moving closer.

'Er – no, I think I'll skip breakfast. Do me good.' I patted my well-upholstered tummy out of nerves, and his eyes travelled over my body. Instinctively, I sucked everything in. Slowly, his gaze came up. He looked me in the eye.

'As you wish.' He shot me a look from under dark brows, and my eyelashes fairly sizzled with the heat. It occurred to me that if I'd said, 'But if you wouldn't mind popping upstairs . . .' it would be considered perfectly acceptable; all in a day's work for a Frenchman.

Instead, I hastily put my cup in the dishwasher, aware of his eyes still trailing over me, amused, no doubt at this pale Englishwoman's discomfort. I grabbed my phone from the island then escaped upstairs to find my purse, a sunhat and a couple of aspirins for the headache that was already threatening.

A few minutes later I was padding down another set of stairs at the far end of the corridor, stairs which I now realized led up to Camille's tower. I emerged through a side door into a vegetable garden I hadn't even known existed. Neat rows of beans and courgettes stretched out before me, and a gravel path ran through the middle. Presumably, it ran parallel with the drive. I took it and, after a moment, the front gate was in my sights. Who knows where I'll wander, I thought, with a vague sense of mounting excitement. It would be an adventure. A lovely morning alone in a vast, dreamy, Provençal landscape, the sights and smells of which would be enough to suffocate any niggling feelings of jealousy. Oh yes, James had been right, as he so often was. But jealous of whom – Camille? Not for one moment. My daughters, perhaps, with their newly burgeoning love lives? Happily, no, although some friends of mine ticked that box. My mother, then, with yet another beau falling at her feet, yet another exciting start? No.

Who, then? Sally? Was it she who was making my heart beat so fast, my head ache so ominously? I hastened on to the gate.

When I'd made it to the lane, on an impulse I turned left. I walked fast, swinging my arms briskly. Glorious vineyards lined my route, some with single rose bushes at the end denoting, what – the vintage? I didn't know. James would, I thought with a smile. I'd ask him. As I pressed on, the vines gave way to huge swathes of lavender, ready to be harvested, swaying gently in the breeze and humming with bees. The smell was unbelievable. I breathed deeply, taking it right down into my lungs. A tiny part of me was aware that I should take heed of where I was going, remember which turns down these country lanes I was taking, and on no account should I get lost. But I was walking quite fast, for the ridiculous reason that I was a tiny bit apprehensive. As I'd emerged from the vegetable garden I'd seen Michel, behind his green-bean canes. He'd watched me go. For some reason, I wanted to get a move on. Put some distance between us.

As I progressed down the lane, a silly thought occurred, which was that every so often, as I rounded a sharp bend, out of the corner of my eye I'd catch sight of the bright-blue cotton shirt Michel was wearing. I came to a junction and realized with relief that one lane was sign-posted to the village. It surely wasn't far. From there, I could get a taxi back, if I was exhausted. I took the turn gratefully. Now and again, almost testing myself, I'd turn my head quickly. No. It had been my imagination. I ploughed on down the hill. This had been a wonderful idea, I decided, still swinging my arms. Getting away from everyone. Away from the irritants of family life, giving myself time to regroup and come back loving them. I was so glad I hadn't gone to Seillans.

Down into the valley I plunged, the chapel just visible on the horizon, a silhouette in the distance. Too far to walk: the village on the main road was a much better idea. And I'd have a coffee in the shade. I passed a spectacular field of sunflowers, their huge yellow heads bobbing as if in greeting, and then the vines again, mile upon mile of them, as far as the eye could see.

Eventually, I came to another junction, happily still signposted to the main road, but this time, hot and exhausted, I sat for a moment on the small, parched triangle of grass at its base. I leaned my head back on the post. As I did, I turned. There, in the distance, an unmistakable flash of blue caught my eye, before it quickly disappeared behind a tree.

Chapter Fourteen

I got to my feet abruptly. I wasn't seeing things. That had been a blue shirt topped by a tanned face, and it had darted out of sight. I must have walked well over a mile by now, and I was in the middle of vast open countryside, vineyards stretching unceasingly, acres and acres of them, and Michel was following me amongst them. I'd press on. The sign said 'D234', the village couldn't be far, and maybe he was just walking there, too? Maybe that was what he did on a Monday. But something about his eyes in the kitchen and the way he'd looked at me when I'd patted my tummy – did that mean something in French? Take me? Give me a baby? – bothered me.

I hastened on, dry-mouthed, relieved I'd brought a hat. The sun was beating down. Every so often, I glanced around and, for a while, I wouldn't be able to see him. I told myself he'd gone another way. Then – oh God, there he was again, gaining on me: not running, but making up ground steadily, with a long stride. I hurried along the hot tarmac. The countryside was completely deserted, not even the rumble of a 2CV in the distance, not even a Jean-Pierre wobbling on a bicycle, although I had passed a man on one earlier. Suddenly, I remembered I'd walked blatantly through the middle of Michel's vegetable garden. Perhaps he thought *I'd* come looking for *him*? I went hot. Stumbled on.

Actually, it was fine, I decided: because just around the next bend, this road would yield houses, the beginnings of a village; the sign had suggested as much. I was on the right track. It wouldn't be far, and I was being stupid. Patting my tummy meant I was fat in any language, and I'd wager people took that short cut through his garden all the time. It was an obvious route from that side door. And he was undoubtedly going to the village himself, perhaps on an errand for Thérèse. He probably had a shopping basket. I turned. He didn't. His hands were empty. And he was gaining on me. Still not running, but walking very fast, determinedly. I'd never seen Michel move anything but stealthily and quietly; he crept up on one like a cat. Only last night I'd found him behind me in the dark corridor upstairs when I'd slipped up for my lipstick, not bothering to turn on the light. Camille had appeared from her room at the far end, and he'd disappeared, but the more I knew Michel, the more I realized his opening gambit that first day – 'The nights are lonely' – had not been a linguistic solecism. He knew the English for 'evening' and 'night'. I gulped.

Well, if he was going to the village, he certainly wouldn't follow me down this track, would he? My eyes darted left across the vineyard. On an impulse, I plunged through a gap between the vines, still heading in the right direction, but as if taking a short cut. I couldn't see if he'd followed – I was running now, under the relentless rays – because dripping grapes and dense foliage obscured my vision, but the fifth or sixth time I turned around, stumbling over ruts in the sun-baked clay, he was coming through the vines, too, jogging menacingly down the track behind me.

I was incredibly scared. I was running quite fast, and dripping wet. My hat flew off and I didn't stop – neither did he, I noticed, as I glanced over my shoulder, to see that he was gaining on me, his eyes intent and glittering with purpose. I wanted to shout, scream – *Help!* – but no one would hear me and I'd secluded myself totally with this screen of vines. I put my head down and sprinted, hearing him now – oh dear God – behind me. Abruptly, the tunnel of green yielded light, and I was on to a road, which would be empty of traffic, I knew, but was something other than this terrifying tunnel. I could almost hear his breath in my ear, and I raced as I've never done before. As I made it to the road, Michel almost upon me, almost able to grab me by the collar, a car, by the gift of God, rounded the corner towards us. I spread myself like a starfish in the middle of the road, found what little breath I had left and screamed, '*HELP!*'

It all but careered into me. It stopped, just short – only just – and I collapsed on to the bonnet, sobbing, clinging to the silver paintwork. In an instant the driver's door flew open.

'What the –?' Max got out. Max, in khaki chinos, a white linen shirt and sunglasses, which he whipped from his face. He looked horrified, pale under his tan. 'Flora! Dear God.'

He hurried around and I threw myself at him: clung to his chest, sopping wet, sobbing with fear and relief, unable to say anything except 'Michel' in a strangled gasp.

And Michel was indeed amongst us; bent double, clutching his knees, panting. Sally, too, as she emerged from the passenger seat of the car, elegant in a pale-blue dress. Her hand went to her mouth.

'Flora – what's happened?'

'Michel,' I managed. 'Followed me, from the house. Chased me. Through fields. Oh, thank God you've come.' I was still clamped like a limpet to Max. I had no idea I could feel so frightened.

'She took the wrong phone,' panted Michel, holding his side, his face wracked with exhaustion. 'Took Thérèse's, by mistake, from the island in the kitchen. I came after her. Thérèse worried she get lost; the Brigadier, he say she gone to the chapel. So far. Madness. Then she begun to run. I was worried, thought she'd gone mad. The sun maybe. Crazy lady ran through middle of vineyard' – he turned to point back to where we'd come from – 'she never find a way out. Like a labyrinth! I run after her, but she fled. I so worried, think she ill.'

He did indeed look incredibly concerned. All three of them did: Sally, in her pretty blue dress, sunglasses off now, peering; Max, whose chest I managed to prise myself from, gazing down at me with anxious, lovely eyes; Michel, still heaving, holding out my phone, bewildered.

I stared at it, trembling, stupefied. Put my hand into my skirt pocket. Brought out an identical iPhone, but not mine. Thérèse's. We swapped silently.

'You scared me,' I whispered.

Michel looked more than concerned now. He looked taken aback.

'I so sorry. You think . . . ?'

It took another moment for the penny to drop. I watched it clatter down. Watched him comprehend completely and look aghast. I felt so ashamed. Mortified.

'Camille, she will –' he stuttered.

'This doesn't have to get to Camille,' Max said firmly. 'Nothing's happened here. Flora had a fright, that's all.' He had an arm around my shoulders in a comforting, brotherly way. I could feel my trembling desist. 'But no harm has been done. She simply got the wrong end of the stick, as so often happens.'

Did it? Max and Sally shepherded me gently into the back of the car, as if I were a day-release patient. Then Michel got in. He'd resisted initially, saying he'd rather walk, but they weren't having it. He practically sat on the door, so anxious was he not to be near me. Do these things often happen, I wondered? Or was I losing my mind? Kind, thoughtful gardener, brother-in-law of generous hostess, hurries to give guest correct phone lest she finds herself hopelessly lost in unfamiliar landscape, whereupon she breaks into a gallop and fears she's going to be attacked. How common was that?

We drove back in silence. I felt numb, if I'm honest. So relieved it was all over, but knowing, somehow, it wasn't. That it was only the beginning.

On the gravel sweep in front of the house, the car stopped. Sally, annoyingly, nipped round and helped me out of the back. I tried to shake her off, but she insisted, and I'd swear she put her hand over my head, like they do in police dramas. Fear and shame were rapidly turning to a feeling that I'd been extremely foolish. And Sally was evidently enjoying herself. A shaken Michel got out, too, and Max had some quiet man talk to him, about how he wasn't to worry – no doubt, hysterical females featured; no doubt, he was apologizing on my behalf – I couldn't really hear. I was too busy trying to get rid of Sally, who was escorting me through the hall and up the main staircase, one arm round my shoulders, the other hand holding my elbow.

'I'm fine, Sally, thank you.'

'Have a shower and a lie down.'

'I will.'

'And drink a lot. You'll have lost fluid with all that sweating.'

'I know.'

'And a couple of aspirins.'

'Yes.'

'I'll get them for you.'

'I have some.'

'Mine are very strong. You'll need them.'

'I have strong ones.'

'Mine are prescription.'

'I'm married to a doctor. I've got fucking knock-out drops.'

'There's no need to swear. I know you're distressed, but you must stay calm. Try.'

Eventually, at my bedroom door, I shook her off. I showered long and hard, warm then cool. Then I wrapped myself in a huge towel and lay on the bed, staring up at the ceiling.

At length, James and the others returned. I heard the cars beneath my window and the doors slamming. Voices were high and exuberant, but then I heard Max's voice, quite low, and their voices lowered, too, to hushed tones. After a bit, there were footsteps on the stairs, and James came into the room, white-faced.

'Good God, darling, are you all right?'

I silently thanked him for that.

'Yes. I am now. Just got a fright.'

I propped myself up a bit as he sat on the bed beside me. 'Poor, poor you.' He took my hand. 'But why did you think . . . ?'

'I don't know. I just panicked, I suppose. He sort of . . . twinkled at me, in the kitchen. And before.'

'Twinkled?' He looked horrified.

'Oh, no, not that. With his eyes.'

'Oh.' His face cleared with relief. Then he frowned. 'And you thought . . .'

'Well, I didn't know what to think, James. This man, racing after me through the countryside.'

'But why were you rushing off alone anyway?'

'I wasn't rushing, I went for a walk. You'd all gone, and I didn't want a solitary morning by the pool.'

'Dad and Rachel were here.'

'Yes, under a tree, reading. Which didn't really appeal.'

'So you thought you'd stomp off in a show of defiance?'

'No! Not at all. I just fancied a walk.'

'It's three miles to the village from here, Flora. In the midday sun –'

'I had a hat, and sunscreen, and money and a phone. Or so I thought.'

He got up off the bed and crossed to the window. Gazed out. After a moment, he came back, lips pursed. He looked down at me. 'It's incredibly serious for a man to be accused of sexual harassment . . . you know that, don't you?'

'I didn't accuse him!'

'I know, but –'

'Whose side are you on?'

'I'm just saying that Michel is very distressed.'

'*I'm* distressed!'

The door flew open. Amelia came in. Nodded above the bed. 'Window's open, Mum. Calm down. We're all on the terrace.' She leaned across and shut it. Sat down on the bed beside me. 'Are you OK?'

'No, I am not. Your father thinks I've deliberately tried to incriminate an innocent man.'

'Oh, don't be ridiculous,' retorted James.

'Max said you were very scared,' said Amelia.

'I was. But I thought it was going to be kept quiet. Camille . . .'

'Michel broke down, upset. Camille heard. Max had to explain. And Sally helped, obviously.'

'Obviously.'

James turned to Amelia. 'Apparently, he twinkled at your mother.'

Amelia frowned. 'Twinkled?'

'Gave me the eye,' I muttered, feeling incredibly foolish.

'Oh God, he flirts with all of us. Frenchmen do that. Did he say anything?'

I cast my mind back to the conversation in the kitchen. 'Well, he – he asked me if I'd like a croissant warmed.'

James got off the bed. I saw him exchange a look with his daughter. 'I think we'll just draw a line under this, don't you? Forget about it. Come on, darling, come down. We're all going to have a late lunch. But I think you should apologize to Michel.'

'God, yes,' spluttered Amelia, in a voice that suggested her father had been far too restrained. 'This is beyond embarrassing, Mum. You need to get out more.' James shot her a warning look as, with a flounce, she left the room. He hesitated, then followed her.

The door, as he closed it, blew the window above my head open again; it had been shut, but not clasped. From the terrace, hushed voices drifted up: Amelia had clearly rejoined the young and was recounting the drama from my viewpoint. There was a pause when she'd finished.

'She's at that difficult age, of course.' My daughter Tara – the good one – observed.

'Does that send women bonkers?' Rory asked.

'Can do,' Toby replied soberly. 'My mum went totally mental.'

'Maybe she's fantasizing?' Tara said. I imagined a huge and general sucking in of cigarettes as they all gave this some thought. 'How did she look?'

'Awful. Crazy. And naked, but for a towel.'

I leaped up on the bed. Flung wide the window. '*I have had a shower!*'

Unfortunately, my towel dropped as I held the window. I snatched it up. Slammed the window shut and fastened the clasp. Silence from below.

I fumbled around the room, finding some clean clothes, my hands fluttery and trembly. As soon as I was dressed, I went downstairs and out on to the terrace. Everyone avoided my eye, even Tara, who could always be relied upon. The Brig and Rachel approached from the trees where they'd been doing the *Telegraph* crossword, and a general look flew around that they didn't need to know, and shouldn't be told. Camille and Lizzie were absent. At length, they emerged from the house together; they'd clearly been talking. Camille, with perfect manners, sat next to me and patted my hand.

'Poor you. What a fright.'

I glanced at her gratefully, but her eyes told me she didn't mean it. She was livid.

'I'm so sorry,' I stuttered. 'Feel such a fool.'

This helped a bit. But not much. She nodded. Didn't speak.

'I'll go and apologize.'

She held my wrist in a vice-like grip under the table. 'Not yet. He is very upset.'

Lizzie slid in on the other side of me. 'It's fine,' she muttered, flicking her napkin out on her lap. 'They're making a meal of it.'

I thanked her with my eyes. Mum and Jean-Claude drifted back late from Seillans, and as they sat down, chatting away about what a lovely time they'd had, we all tucked into huge platters of charcuterie and melon and tomato salad as if nothing had happened. Thérèse, though, when she came to remove the plates and replace them with fresh ones for a plum tart, banged mine down so hard it nearly broke. Everyone round the table jumped. Her eyes, when I glanced up at them, were glittering with fury, as I'm sure mine would be if someone had accused James of something similar.

Years ago, James had asked a nurse, in the operating theatre – in a pass-the-scalpel moment – if she'd had a good weekend. She'd replied that she'd had a lovely time punting with her boyfriend, and James had jokingly said he didn't need the details. She'd reported him to the disciplinary committee for inappropriate behaviour. James had come home ashen-faced. He'd gone straight to the sideboard and had a large whisky, which he never did. He'd actually had to restrain me from driving to the hospital and beating the door down. The disciplinary committee! My kind, gentle James! I knew how Thérèse felt and shrivelled under her angry gaze. I didn't touch my tart either, in case she'd spat in it.

After lunch I had a long discussion with Lizzie, not in my room, where the world clearly overheard, but at the bottom of the garden in the olive grove, where only a donkey grazed. In the shade of an ancient, crooked tree, perched on a heap of stones, amidst prickly dry grass and chattering cicadas, I cried, and she hugged me. I explained, and she got it, but no one else would. We were the only two middle-aged women here. Sally and Rachel didn't count somehow. But Lizzie understood.

'But you'll have to apologize, I'm afraid. Just so it doesn't look like you still believe it.'

'I don't.' I wiped my eyes.

'I know, which is why you have to.'

'I know.' I clutched my tissue. 'Will Thérèse be there, d'you think?'

'I don't know. But I'll come with you. Come on. Let's get it over with.'

We got up and went around the side of the chateau to the front drive. As we walked up to the lodge house, my heart pounded.

Thérèse came out. Perhaps she'd been waiting for us, watching from the window. Either way, she stood on the front step, tiny, inscrutable and, on closer inspection, quite lined, unlike her tanned, smooth-skinned husband.

She was wearing a printed dress with an apron tied firmly over the top, which I'd never seen her wear before. It seemed symbolic somehow: as if it were to remind me that they were subservient and defenceless. It occurred to me this could have been turned into a joke: 'You thought what? Oh, Flora, you are *priceless*! Listen, everyone, Flora thought he was chasing her for her body!' Why hadn't it been? It also occurred to me that at no point had Michel shouted, '*Votre portable!*' Waved it in the air. I spoke French. I'd have understood.

Thérèse listened as, falteringly, I explained, then she went to get Michel. I clearly wasn't to be allowed in. He came out and stood, head bowed, in servile attitude, as I apologized profusely, Lizzie beside me.

When I'd finished, he nodded, looked a bit sad, but said he accepted my apology and was sorry for having frightened me. Which was nice of him.

We turned to go but, as we did, Agathe appeared. She slid into the doorway to take her uncle's hand. As she looked up at me, I caught my breath. Side by side, I could see that her eyes were identical to Michel's. Her mouth, too: sullen, yet full and sensual. There was a striking resemblance.

'Lizzie, did you see that?' I breathed, once we were safely out of earshot, hurrying away down the drive.

'What?'

'The child, Agathe. So like Michel!'

She shrugged. 'A bit. But a lot of French children have that surly, Mediterranean look.'

'Lizzie – she's the *image* of him!' I was fired up.

Lizzie swallowed. She hesitated, then gave me a funny look as we approached the house. Paused a moment. 'Maybe don't lie by the pool this afternoon, Flora. I'd keep out of the sun for a while. You've had a nasty shock.'

She gave me a quick hug, but then went on her way to the pool, looking thoughtful.

Chapter Fifteen

Of course, it hadn't escaped my notice that I'd clung to Max like a barnacle. Drenched his shirt, no doubt, with my sweat, but he hadn't cared: he'd held on tight with strong, protective arms like men do in the movies. He hadn't peeled himself off. Not even when Sally got out of the car. Well, you wouldn't, would you? If someone was that distressed?

I thought about this, and about other things, as I sat under the walnut trees with Rachel, in her quiet spot. She was fair-skinned and only troubled the pool to swim once a day, when no one else was about; otherwise, she sat here with Drummond and read or sewed. He'd gone for a siesta now. Others had, too. Lizzie, Mum, JC, Max and Sally – the latter for a siesta *complet* perhaps, as James and I used laughingly to call it. And the young were catching rays by the pool. Rachel and I sat in companionable silence, her embroidering and me pretending to read, remembering occasionally to turn the page. Thank God for a quiet sister-in-law. What I wanted, more than anything, was to be alone, with my crackpot theories and ideas, to mull over my derangements in peace, but I knew I couldn't do that on a family holiday. Knew it would look odd. Look where it had got me this morning? I knew I couldn't self-indulgently draw attention to myself by going on another long walk, or by driving to a deserted monastery or finding a church to poke around; everyone would raise their eyebrows. I had to stay put, at least for a bit, and being with Rachel was the nearest thing to solitude, just as being with Sally was the nearest thing to being in a crowd. It was a wonder James was so normal with such siblings. Except, at the moment, I hated him, of course, so he wasn't. He was odd, too.

I watched surreptitiously over my paperback as Rachel stitched her tapestry. What passions boiled beneath that smooth, pale brow, I wondered, the one she presented coolly to the world? This wasn't the eighteenth century: surely it wasn't enough for her to be the unmarried sister, alone in a Scottish pile caring for her aging father, going to church, visiting the elderly in the village, dabbling with her watercolours? James and I had discussed it at length, and he'd always assured me it was, before changing the subject. His family was off limits. A closed book. We couldn't know everything about the person we were married to – I respected that – and I knew they'd suffered a terrible trauma, but I'd had an unusual upbringing too, and I was completely transparent. Too much so, probably. And although it all tumbled out of Sally, it was generally rubbish, as if she covered herself with garbage and hid beneath it, so one never knew what made her tick either. Both sisters were opaque in different ways.

I was rarely alone with Rachel, and if I'd been my normal self I'd have relished the opportunity to ask questions, enquire gently if she was happy with her lot, but I wasn't, so I didn't. I was the one with the problems, not her.

'I don't suppose you'd like to drive into Callian, would you, Rachel? There's a chateau that's supposed to be quite interesting. We could have a drink and be back in time for supper.'

'Flora, I'd love to, but I promised Daddy I'd go tomorrow, it's on the way to Seillans. He's really looking forward to it. Apparently, it's got a moat. We're going to set off early, before the sun gets too much. It might take the gloss off it if I'd already been with you. Come with us in the morning?'

'Yes. Yes, I might.'

We left it at that.

A little while later, probably twenty minutes or so, a shadow fell over my book. I looked up. Max was there in a dark-blue shirt. He smiled.

'Would either of you ladies like to come into Callian? There's a church worth seeing, twelfth century. We could have a drink.'

'And a chateau,' smiled Rachel, putting down her work. 'Flora and I were just saying; it's all in the guidebooks in the kitchen. Do go, Flora,' she urged. 'You'd love it. Don't wait for us.'

'Is Sally coming?' I shaded my eyes up at him. I absolutely knew I didn't want to go with him and Sally and frantically searched my head for an excuse.

'Sally's asleep. I think I'm going to leave her. Do her good to rest.'

Why, was she pregnant, I wondered wildly?

I nodded. 'Sure. I'll come.'

Why not. My heart was pounding, though, as I closed my book. I'd clung on to that shirt quite tightly. Not the clean one he was wearing now, the one in the bottom of his wardrobe, in a heap, or in a linen bag, if Sally was that organized.

'I'll get my bag.'

'OK. See you at the car. Let's take mine.'

'Fine.' As if it were a perfectly normal thing to do.

We walked back towards the house together, peeling apart as I went upstairs.

In our room, James was flat on his back on the bed, snoring for England, catching flies. I crept around, finding my straw bag, a hat, changing my shoes, looking in the mirror in the bathroom. My face was a little flushed, so I dabbed some translucent powder on. I brushed my hair, still long – too long probably, for my age, but heavily highlighted now to hide the grey. I studied my reflection, wondering why. Knowing why. I added some lipstick. Rubbed it off hastily. And no scent. But it was hot, so I did blast more deodorant under my arms.

I crept out, shutting the door softly. On the landing, I met Drummond.

'Going out?' he asked, looking at the straw bag over my shoulder.

'Yes, to Callian. Have a poke around.'

'Ah – with Max. Yes, he asked me earlier, but Rachel and I are going tomorrow. Nice chap. Have fun, my dear.'

And on he went. Right. So when Max had asked both me and Rachel, it was in the certain knowledge that Rachel would decline. I paused for a moment, uncertain, my hand on the polished banister rail. I wasn't far from my room, and the girls were right about the acoustics. I could hear James's snores as if I were right next to him. It wasn't the most seductive of noises. In a twinkling I was tripping downstairs – like Cinderella off to the ball, except in wedged espadrilles, not satin slippers, oh, and my new sundress,

which I'd quickly changed into in the bathroom but neg-
lected to mention just now – down the majestic stone
staircase, across the flagstone hall. Ancestors glared down in
a censorial manner from gloomy oils as I went, and I wondered how many far more glamorous mesdemoiselles had
escaped thus, under their disapproving gaze amid the crossed
swords and suits of armour, on secret assignations?

Max had put the roof down on his car, and I slid in
beside him. We exchanged a quick, hopefully not too complicit, smile. As we sailed down the long gravel drive,
through the iron gates at the end, and purred along the
lane between the vineyards, I felt exhilarated. Safe, too,
which was strange, given who I was with, but Max and I
knew each other extremely well: knew we could sit in
silence for a bit and not make small talk, just let the warm
wind whip through our hair, the heady scent of sunflowers and lavender wash over us. It helped that we'd been in
each other's company for a few days already, softening the
shock of being together again after all these years. As we
slowed down to go through a tiny hamlet, an old woman
dressed in black hobbled out to cross the road, her equally
elderly chihuahua on a lead beside her. Midway, the dog
decided to relieve itself. We waited. And waited. Madame
glared at us.

'D'you get the impression she's indignant we're even
watching?' murmured Max.

'Possibly the crossest Frenchwoman I've seen to date.'

'Steady. The competition for that title is stiff.'

'Oh, really? Are they notoriously bad-tempered?'

'Suspicious is more the word I'd use. But they have good
cause to be. Their husbands are rascals.'

'That's what Mum says.'

'Sensible woman, your mum.'

I smiled. Looked at his profile a moment. I took a strand of hair from my mouth. 'Max, I was really sorry to hear about your mother.'

He nodded. Didn't look at me, though. 'Lucy?'

'Yes.'

Finally, he turned his head. Gave me a sad little smile. 'Thanks, Flossie.'

His old nickname for me. It took my breath away for a moment, but he'd said it without thinking.

'Cancer?'

'Yes.' He looked straight ahead again. 'I gather you wrote to my dad.'

'Yes. I was so fond of her.'

'I know. Thanks for that. He appreciated it.' Madame finally achieved the other side of the road, and we drove on. After a while, Max's mouth twitched. 'Notice you didn't write to me, though.'

'Well, I –'

'Didn't want to give me ideas?' He turned and gave me his wolfish grin.

'Oh, don't be ridiculous!'

He roared with laughter. 'Still so easy to tweak!'

I shook my head wearily, but found it hard not to smile, and the mood in the car was light as we drove into the beautiful town of Callian. We climbed up and up, snaking around the steep hill to the medieval town perched on top. Both sides of the road were already chock-a-block with parked cars, some at crazy angles.

'*Centre ville*, d'you think?' suggested Max.

'You mean in the total absence of spaces?'

He shrugged. 'Fortune favours the brave.'

Miraculously, it did. As we approached the city wall, which was draped with pretty bunting to announce that the town was *en fête*, a car drew out of a space just next to the old gates. Max reversed in expertly, but it was tight. I swivelled round to help him.

'About two foot.'

'Thanks.'

'Stop – *cripes*!' He'd nearly hit the car behind. When he'd finished the manoeuvre he turned.

'Did you just say cripes?' he asked incredulously.

'I was going for Christ and changed my mind,' I admitted, busted.

'Thank you for not blaspheming, Flossie. I'm a sensitive chap and I'd have been truly shocked.'

I narrowed my eyes at him as we got out of the car. 'Don't push it, Max.'

'What d'you mean?' He looked at me with mock-bafflement.

'The Flossie business.'

'I called you that earlier!'

'That was different. Don't take advantage.'

'Why ever not?' He roared delightedly as he locked the car. 'Haven't you seen the flags?' He nodded up at the bunting. 'It's open season!'

More head-shaking and lip-biting from me as, together, we sailed on through the ancient archway into town.

Strange how the years rolled back. We could have been walking down Marville Road to Mum's for a drink in our old trainers, or coming back from walking the dogs at his parents' house, strolling down the lane, our hands brushing cow parsley heads, in time for lunch. No nerves, no need to explain anything, just a lot to find out. I think we both knew we weren't going to the chateau, which was on the other side of the hill, or the medieval church in the Latin quarter. Instead, Max headed for one of the narrow side streets off the main square, as yet not particularly crowded, its restaurants still laid with paper cloths for drinks, not white linen for supper.

We found a pretty place with a raised terrace and a pagoda dripping with grapevines. There were a few empty tables outside. The waiter arrived almost immediately, pleased to have some custom, and Max ordered a beer for him and a glass of rosé for me. When he'd gone, he took off his sunglasses, folded his arms on the zinc table and leaned across. He smiled. Right into my eyes.

'So.'

'So.'

'How have you been?'

'For the last twenty-odd years? Fine. Apart from today.'

'Oh, today.' He made a dismissive gesture. 'Crossed wires. A mountain out of a molehill. Too much fuss made about nothing. I'm not interested in that, I want to know about the rest of your life. Quite a lot to catch up on, one way and another.' Our drinks arrived and he took a sip of beer.

'Not really. Only if it's complicated,' I told him. 'Mine's pretty straightforward. I could probably do it in about five sentences.'

He smiled. 'OK. Go.'

'No, you.'

'What, from the beginning? In my case, we'll be here all night.'

'Edited highlights, then.'

He paused. And, as he did, I studied his face. A few lines, obviously, and he was going grey at the temples. His hair was swept back instead of flopping forward in a fringe which he used to push back impatiently. His cheeks were slightly more sunken, but that only highlighted the good bones. It suited him. He gazed beyond me in thought. Came back and flashed me that grin.

'Well, you dumped me, obviously.'

'Obviously. You cheated on me.'

'I made a tiny mistake.' He held his thumb and forefinger a centimetre apart. 'A small slip.'

I winced. 'Unfortunate analogy.'

He inclined his head, accepting this. 'Anyway, there was no forgiveness from you. No Christian mercy.'

'This is old news, Max. Shall we fast-forward? Reader, you married her?'

'Oh, you mean Mimi?'

'I imagine I do.'

He shrugged. 'What was a boy to do? You'd snared your medic by then.'

'Ah, yes, of course. The stereotypical bourgeois girl on the hunt for a nice professional man. Thank God I found one.'

'You always did like clever coves.'

'Didn't I just?'

'Did you love him?'

'Yes, of course I did. Do!'

'As much as me?'

Merest pause. 'Of course. More than you,' I retorted, to make up for that pause.

'*More* than me,' he repeated incredulously, eyes widening in mock-surprise. 'And yet we were engaged to be married.'

'This is childish, Max. I wouldn't be so rude as to ask if you loved Mimi.'

'But you'd still like to know. I did, actually. Mimi was a slow burn. She crept up on me. And was very sweet. She helped me get over you.'

'Which is weird, really, when you think that she instigated our split.'

Max waved a disdainful hand. 'That wasn't her fault. She was pissed. You overreacted.' His eyes twinkled. 'Because of your mo-th-er . . .' he sang, grinning.

'Ah. Mr Amateur Psychologist speaks.'

'Nothing amateur about it, I studied at the master's knee. Lesson one: do not repeat parental mistakes.' He wagged a stern finger. 'Do not replicate a behavioural pattern.'

'Shall we move on? Tell me more about Mimi.'

He shrugged. 'What's to tell? Mimi and I got married and we were very happy. For a bit.'

'Children?'

'A boy, Mungo. He's with his mum at the moment.'

I wondered at an only child, but didn't ask. 'And you're in the music business?' As soon as I'd said it, I wished I hadn't.

He blinked in delight. 'You know I am. You overheard me telling JC about it the other night. Your mind was not remotely on Lizzie's new shoes.'

I flushed, and when he saw, he became kinder, which he was.

'Yes, you're right. I put on shows, organize concerts. That type of thing.'

'Celebs?'

'Some.'

'Like who?'

'Robbie Williams?'

'Close personal?'

''Fraid not. Purely a business relationship.'

'So what went wrong?'

'With Robbie?'

'Obviously not with Robbie.'

He shrugged. 'Nothing cataclysmic. We argued a lot. Mimi's quite . . . controlling. And I went quiet on her when she nagged, which only made it worse.'

'About what?'

'What did she nag about? Promotion, mostly. How I should move on and up in the world. She's pretty ambitious. I don't know, what d'you want me to say? I should never have married her? Or – I married her because she worked on me night and day and she's a good-looking bird and she can be very entertaining and you'd married someone else?'

'Please don't tell me you married her to spite me.'

'Don't flatter yourself. Why would I wreck my life for you?'

I stared at him. After a moment he gave me that grin again. More indolent than wolfish this time. He sank into his beer. It struck me he was quite lazy. Capable of taking the line of least resistance. Part of his charm, in a way.

'What are you doing here, Max?'

He wiped some froth from his mouth. 'Courting Sally. What does it look like?'

'Old-fashioned word.'

'Old-fashioned girl. OK, shagging Sally.'

'Why?'

'Oh, hello, back to you. You mean, am I here on your account?'

I held his eyes. Raised my eyebrows, undeterred. Suddenly, a blowtorch smile lit up his whole face.

'Of course I am!'

I took a moment. Wrong-footed. 'You are?'

'Well, I didn't engineer it, if that's what you mean. But when Sally mentioned her brother was being lent a house in France courtesy of a grateful patient, and did I want to come, I didn't think, I couldn't possibly bump into Flora after all these years; I thought, great, why not? After all, my marriage had collapsed, I'd never really got over you, and I figured you might a) have the happiest marriage under the sun, in which case I'd go quietly, or b) be trapped in a monotonous, boring relationship and be going through the motions on account of the children, who are actually young women now, so pretty soon it'd just be you and the medic.'

He was laughing at me with his eyes. My mouth was dry, despite the rosé. 'And what have you decided?'

He lifted his beer to his lips, still holding my gaze. 'Jury's out, Flossie. Somewhere between the two, I'd have said when I arrived, but this last twenty-four hours . . .' He shook his head. 'I'm not so sure.'

Chapter Sixteen

'Well, you're wrong,' I said shortly. 'There's absolutely nothing wrong with my marriage. We're extremely happy.'

'Congratulations. No nineteen-year itch?'

'Not even a tickle.'

'I'm glad.'

I think we both knew we were stretching the truth: he certainly wasn't glad, but it was nice of him to say it without sarcasm, and I was exaggerating, but in only one respect. I had no itch with James, just with my life. With the relentless monotony of it – his word. The work which I increasingly disliked, the endless worry and bickering with the girls, the mortgage, the daily grind, the general keep-buggering-on-ness. That was the irritation. And sitting here, opposite an extremely attractive man, with whom I used to be in love and who was clearly still interested enough in me to want to join my family holiday, gazing deeply into my eyes on a balmy, Provençal evening under a vine groaning with swollen grapes, was really not going to help. Or else it really was, depending on how you looked at it. Temporarily, a little voice in my head said. Temporarily, surely, it's OK to relieve the irritation? Apply a little soothing balm? Forget everything for five minutes? Where's the harm?

'You're still easy on the eye, Flossie.' He looked at me narrowly.

Max didn't do conscious charm. I knew he meant it. But no middle-aged woman with cellulite and thread veins and the odd hair cropping up in unlikely places needs to be told that she's still attractive and hang on to her sanity. I felt mine slipping.

'Rubbish,' I muttered, meaning, *Tell me more.*

'You are. You've still got your own hair, your teeth.'

'Actually, these come out at night.' I tapped a front one.

'Ah. I thought I heard the rattle of porcelain in a glass next door.'

I thought of him lying awake in the adjoining bedroom, listening: not to that, but for anything else. I thought of me lying awake, listening, too.

'You're not being very kind.'

'To whom?'

'To Sally.'

'Sally knows the score. She knows I'm playing it for laughs. That I've come out of a long marriage. And I'm not serious. I was upfront about that.'

I believed him. 'Still. She doesn't know the whole story.'

'Oh, you're not the whole story, Floss, don't get ahead of yourself. I'm also here for the sybaritic free holiday. The wine, the *grande maison*, the Mediterranean sun – who'd turn that down?' He grinned.

'Not me,' I agreed.

'Think of yourself as an added bonus. The bonus ball. D'you want to do the chateau?'

'Not really. Do you?'

'No. D'you want another drink?'

'Yes, please.'

*

Back at the ranch, when we rocked up an hour or so later, drinks were in full swing on the terrace, and supper was being laid out. I slipped upstairs whilst Max strolled off to field any questions and wax lyrical about the chateau. Our first lie, I thought with horror, but also with a frisson of excitement as I looked at my flushed cheeks in the bathroom mirror, my bright eyes. I crept across to the window and listened to the chat and laughter below. Max was handling it beautifully; nobody was in the least curious or suspicious, it seemed. I had a quick shower, recovered my maxi dress from the floor of Tara's bedroom opposite, where, having tried it on, she'd discarded it, and went down. If I'd felt in control, though, I'd reckoned without my elder daughter's antennae. She saw me approach through the French windows and beetled across the terrace like a heat-seeking missile to intercept me.

'What was *that* like?' she whispered, as I helped myself to a drink from the tray held by Thérèse, who, incidentally, still wasn't smiling.

'What was what like, darling?'

'Don't be coy. A date with your ex.'

'Don't be silly. We went to look around a chateau. No one else wanted to.'

'Did you ask Dad?'

'Couldn't find him,' I lied. Second one.

'Well, come on. Give.'

'Fine.' Exhilarating. Unbelievably exciting. 'Nice to touch base again.'

'Is he still hot for you?'

'Don't be ridiculous, Amelia.'

'Did you talk about old times?'

'A bit.'

'What, like, how he broke your heart?'

'He didn't. I broke his. Where's Daddy?'

'Gone to the chateau with Camille and Sally.'

'Oh, right.' I felt myself flush. It broke out all over me. I gripped the stem of my glass. Met Max's eye across the terrace, which told me he, too, knew. Also that he'd deal with it.

'Didn't you see them there?'

'No, but it's a big place. Must have missed them.'

At that moment, tyres crunched on the gravel at the front of the house: car doors slammed and voices carried. Not long to think about how to handle this. In an instant, they were upon us, Sally most of all.

'Max, darling! We looked for you and couldn't see you. Rachel said you'd gone to Callian.'

'Yes, we did, but we couldn't park so we abandoned it. Just drove round it.'

'I thought you said it was a big place?' Amelia asked me.

'Callian? It is. Well, intricate, anyway. Lots of winding streets.'

'Oh. Right.'

She looked confused and I wondered why I couldn't just say, Look, we hadn't seen each other for almost twenty years, we needed a drink to catch up. What was wrong with that? Nothing. Unless there was something wrong with me. Which there wasn't. And I'd say it to James, later, in bed, I determined. No secrets.

James, though, didn't seem to have his mind on where his wife had been, or the spirit of full marital disclosure at all: he was too busy making sure Camille had a drink, that she wasn't short of olives or tapenade and didn't need her wrap. His own colour was pretty high, too, I thought: his eyes shining. Perhaps this was what our marriage needed – what any lengthy marriage needed – a little light flirtation? To oil the wheels, make us feel young and invigorated and sprightly again, so that when we came together, sparks flew? It was surely how the French operated, I thought, seeing Michel back to his old ways as he sidled up to Tara and asked if she was sure she wouldn't like *un petit feuilleté aux anchois*? Rory bridled when she giggled. Perhaps it was the climate? I knew, though, that there was no danger in James's flirtation: knew instinctively Camille wasn't serious, even if he was. In fact, I wondered what her game was. And when would the main event, her current beau – oh yes, Lizzie had done some digging and discovered she definitely had a love interest – appear? Would she then depart with him, I wondered, watching her circulate around the terrace, looking stunning in a long pink skirt and silky white camisole: finally exit stage left and leave us in peace?

She floated across the terrace towards me with a wide, welcoming smile. Why was I such a cow?

'Did you have a lovely time? Did you like my Callian?'

'Loved it,' I enthused, trying to make up for my treacherous personality. 'It's beautiful, Camille, you're so lucky to have a gem like that on your doorstep.'

'But you didn't make the chateau, I hear. Too busy?' She waggled her eyebrows knowingly at me.

I laughed. Fell right into the Girls Together conspiratorial trap. 'Oh, you know. It was nice to have a chat. Max and I haven't seen each other for years.' Why was everyone so interested?

'Ah, *oui*? I didn't know you were old friends? Ah, *cherie* — have you met Flora?' This to the quiet child who'd crept up on us stealthily, like a shadow.

'Only very briefly.' I smiled and held out my hand. '*Bonsoir*, Agathe.'

She took it and smiled shyly. Then turned to her mother. '*Maman* — couldn't you just for once come back and eat with us tonight? Not these complete randomers?' She wasn't to know, of course, that I spoke fluent French. Camille did, though.

'Agathe! *Ne soyez pas impoli!*' she chided. 'But yes, tonight, I will.'

And so she did, turning away, which was a relief. And what with her absence, and the time I'd had earlier with Max, I found myself feeling quite buoyant and being altogether delightful at supper: really rather funny and light-hearted for me. A person I remembered. I saw James smiling at me as I recounted some tale the girls loved to hear and prompted me to tell, about how I'd once lost a shoe outside Harrods, found it again in the crowd with my foot, only to discover, when I got on the bus, that I'd got odd shoes on, one of which didn't belong to me. 'It *has* to be one of Mum's fibs,' insisted Amelia, as she always did. 'No, no, quite true,' I declared, as everyone roared.

Oh yes, I thought, lifting my glass to my lips: she's still there, that person, the one you all remember. Just very hard to find.

I found myself saying yes to everything that night. Could Tara have a few euros to buy a dress she'd seen in the market? Yes. Could Lizzie borrow my new sarong tomorrow; she'd spilled wine on hers? Yes. Could my mother take our car to the lake for a boat trip with Jean-Claude? Yes. I even said yes to James that night. Quietly, though. Indeed, we made almost no sound at all.

The following morning, as usual, dawned bright and clear. Aside from Drummond and Rachel, who'd gone sightseeing, most people decided on a lazy day by the pool, and that suited me fine. I wanted to lie still, get a tan, pretend to be asleep and reflect on yesterday's conversation. Hug it to myself. Tell myself it was lovely to be admired again after all these years and that was that. It was a bit of a strain keeping my knees bent at all times in case Max should appear, but he didn't, taking the Reading Under the Walnut Tree option, along with James, who was not a sun worshipper. It occurred to me that not many men would be happy to sit with their wife's ex-boyfriend and discuss the new biography of Napoleon they both happened to be reading, but James was not many men. He was rather exceptional. Rather lovely, I told myself sternly, lest I should compare him in terms of physical attributes, in which department he might be found wanting, but which were not important.

Sally, however, had other ideas regarding my solitude and, unable to amuse herself for five minutes on her own, or concentrate on a book, lay down on the empty sunbed beside me. I groaned inwardly but smiled, tipping up my hat, which covered my face, for a brief second, before replacing it, hoping she'd get the hint.

'Flora, can I talk to you for a moment?'

'Of course.'

'I mean, girl to girl?'

Oh God. What had he said? I removed my hat and

looked at her. Her face was a bit drawn: worried. I felt my mouth dry.

'What's wrong?'

'Did you know that Max and Camille had had a thing?'

I stared at her. Sat up and turned to face her properly.

'*What?* They don't even know each other.'

'Yes, they do. Max told me last night. I think that's why we're all here.'

I stared at her for a long moment. 'Sally, I have no idea what you're talking about. Max and *I* had a thing –'

'Oh, yes, years ago, old history.' She waved a dismissive hand. 'I know about that, but this was six months or so ago, after his marriage had finished. She was the girl before me.'

'I don't believe it.'

'Why would he lie?'

'But – but they don't even look like they know each other, let alone had an affair.' My mind span.

'Because it was kept so quiet. She didn't want yet another relationship to get in the papers. Her ex-husband is threatening to fight for custody of the child. She didn't want to jeopardize anything.'

I put my fingers to my temples, trying to make sense of this. From the other side of the pool, Tara and Rory looked up, eyes trained on the intense whispers. I lowered my voice.

'How did they meet?'

'Through the opera. Max produced one of the shows she was in. It was in Rome, in St Mark's Square. Lots of famous classical names, plus some modern ones – Katherine Jenkins, Paul McCartney, the Opera Babes – it was huge. Televised on enormous screens in the parks. You know the sort of thing.'

'Yes.' I might even have watched it.

'She fell for him, and they had a fling.'

'Who broke it off?'

'He did.'

'Why?'

He said she was too intense and too spoilt. Wanted everything to revolve around her. And, of course, by that time, towards the end, he'd met me.'

'Right.'

'We weren't actually going out, but we were seeing each other. Also . . .' she hesitated. 'He's never quite got over an old girlfriend. He told me that at the time.'

I stared at her. Sat very still.

'Well, not you, obviously, Flora.' She laughed.

'Obviously!' I laughed back, but my head said, *fucking hell*. I was *engaged* to him, Sally.

'Max has had loads of girlfriends,' she said kindly. She patted my hand. 'He's a very attractive man.'

'Yes.'

I wasn't so sure. I knew Max much better than Sally did. He wasn't a roué. Had never been a player. I sniffed a man covering his tracks, littering it with phantom girlfriends.

'So . . .' I felt my way. 'After he and Camille split up . . .'

'There was nothing to split, Max said. It was just a casual thing on location as far as he was concerned. And when I got James's email saying he'd administered an EpiPen to a child on a plane and the mother had lent him a villa in France and would we like to come, I didn't think to ask who it belonged to, just squealed and emailed back, "Yes, please!" So that was all I knew to tell Max.'

Camille had also asked James to keep her name quiet. Claimed she didn't like people knowing where she lived.

'So Max didn't know who it belonged to?'

'Any more than I did.'

'But *she* knew.' I was thinking aloud. 'About you. She knew he'd probably come with you.'

'Exactly.'

I stared, horrified, as the full implication dawned. 'You think she engineered this whole thing? To see Max?'

'I do. Think about it, Flora. She asks for your email at the airport to send you a bread-and-butter thank you, and when she sees the name she thinks – hello: Murray-Brown. That's an unusual surname. She knows Max is seeing a Sally Murray-Brown. So she investigates. Asks James to lunch. Discovers he does indeed have a sister called Sally. So she suggests his entire family come out. But asks that he keeps her name quiet.'

'Odd.'

I recalled her at the airport: very much in a hurry at the baggage carousel, to which she'd arrived late, making for the exit and leaving her minions to collect the luggage. At the last moment spotting James and having no choice but to come across, but hardly on a mission. Then, suddenly, lunch at the Hyde Park Hotel, and then, lo and behold, the surprise holiday, hurtling down the tracks. I felt a nasty taste in my mouth. For us, as a family. For having been duped. And for my James. Who, even now, was probably mixing her favourite lunchtime Bellini in her favourite tall glass, with sugar on the rim, running around after her like a puppy dog, making, if I'm honest, a bit of a fool of himself. Which Camille encouraged in order to . . . what, make Max jealous?

'Does she strike you as the type to make a huge, magnanimous gesture?' persisted Sally. 'Or the type to casually write an email of thanks, not even a letter?'

'The latter,' I agreed.

'I reckon we're all here because she wants to try to get Max back.'

I shook my head, staggered. My heavens, she was cool. A very smooth operator. Although, of course, what Camille didn't know, I thought, my head spinning, was the subtext. That Max and I had once been together, had been very much an item and were quietly getting to know each other again. And that once he'd got over the shock of whose house he was in – I remembered Sally saying he was flabbergasted – he wasn't averse to spending his holiday here, because he, too, had an agenda. Had known all along I was coming.

'So . . . what is it that worries you, Sally?' I said carefully. 'I thought you and Max had a very casual relationship?'

'We do,' she said quickly. 'He was straight with me from the beginning, as I was with him. Absolutely no strings attached. We're playing this one for laughs. Otherwise, I wouldn't have got into it,' she said firmly.

'Right.' I was surprised at her vehemence. Rather admired it.

'I was just a bit shaken, I suppose. To discover the lengths she's gone to, to engineer this. And I feel a bit bad for James.'

'Me, too,' I agreed, as, at that moment, Max came through the gateway to the walled pool in swimming trunks and a pink shirt, a book and towel under his arm. As he peeled off for a swim, Sally got up and sashayed around to greet him. She rose up on her tiptoes to give him a kiss, then took up position on the bed beside the one on which he'd placed his book and towel. Max reached down and gave her hand an affectionate squeeze before walking around to the deep end to dive in. Just then, Camille appeared through the gate at the other end of the walled garden. I'd never seen her by the pool before. She wore a green silk sarong around her hips and a white bikini top, which just about encased her considerable bosoms. Her figure was to die for; slim and brown but curvaceous, she was a veritable pocket Venus, and in keeping with the mythological analogy, her blonde hair flowed in ripples down her back. If Max saw this vision of female pulchritude, he didn't acknowledge it. His eyes didn't flicker towards her. Instead, feet poised on the edge, he raised his arms and executed a neat swallow dive into the shimmering blue water, hardly rippling the surface.

Three pairs of female eyes watched intently as he travelled the length of the pool underwater. Before he made it to the other end, I quickly pulled mine away. Drew the brim of my hat defiantly over them. Oh, no. Count *me* out, I thought in horror. Count me *right* out of the equation.

Chapter Seventeen

That evening, as we dressed for dinner, I told James what Sally had told me. He listened, but I could tell he didn't want to believe me.

'Oh, no, I think that's just a coincidence, darling.'

'Do you?'

'Yes. You girls with your conspiracy theories. I'm sure Camille was as surprised as anyone when Max turned up.'

'But did you even know they knew each other? Let alone had an affair? I mean, they kept that very quiet, didn't they?'

'Well, for obvious reasons. He's with Sally now, and if Camille's going through a custody battle – I knew about that, by the way, she's having a terrible time with her ex. He's called Étienne de la Peyrière, and his family rule the roost round here. Own half of Grasse. I'm going to see if I can get her some help. Chap I was at Cambridge with is a brilliant family lawyer.'

'I'm sure she's got the best that money can buy already, darling.'

'Well, she seemed pretty interested.'

'Right.' I tied the strings of my espadrilles in a bow. 'Thérèse told the girls he's nice.'

'Who?'

'Étienne de thingy.'

He laughed hollowly. 'Not according to Camille, and she

should know. I gather he's a complete shit. Have you seen my blue linen shirt?'

'You didn't put it in, it was dirty.'

'Damn. And I've run out of contact lenses, which is annoying.'

'Why?'

'Well, I'll have to wear my glasses.'

'James, don't . . .'

'What?'

'Nothing. Come here.' I was sitting on the bed. I stretched out my hand and he came across. Sat down beside me.

'We're all right, aren't we?' I asked him.

He laughed. 'Isn't that the sort of thing they say in *Friends*?'

'But aren't we?' I persisted.

'Of course we are. And last night was lovely.' He kissed me perfunctorily. 'And you're enjoying catching up with Max?'

'Oh, yes. We went for a drink last night, which is why we didn't make the chateau.'

'Yes, that's what I assumed. And the thing is, Flora' – he hesitated – 'it's making us much better together. Getting out more, I believe it's called. Mixing with different people. Sparks us up a bit.'

'Yes, that's what I thought, too. A couple of days ago. Yesterday, even. It's just . . .' I still had his hand.

'What?' He brushed my fringe from my eyes. An affectionate gesture.

'I just think we should be careful.'

He laughed. 'Oh, don't be silly, darling, we're not seventeen.'

'No.'

'I'm really not worried I'm going to find you snogging in the undergrowth with Max, if that's what you mean.'

'I don't mean that.'

'Nice man. I like him.'

I nodded. Odd man, my husband. Plain *odd*.

'Camille has got tickets to an Andrea Bocelli concert in Cannes on Friday,' he said. I now had no illusions about Camille leaving us. She was here for the duration.

'Has she?' I got up and found my earrings on the dressing table. Popped them in and turned. 'You go. You know I hate opera. How many tickets?'

He hesitated. 'Two.'

I smiled down at him. 'Honestly, go. You know I don't mind.'

I didn't. Did that make me odd, too? No, because I knew why she was here, even if James didn't believe it. Would I have minded if I'd thought she really was after my husband? Yes, of course. I quickly added some blusher. Caught my own eye in the mirror. But she wasn't.

Supper that night – a barbecue, which made a pleasant change – found me placed next to Max. I won't pretend I didn't engineer it. Once a noisy conversation was under way at the other end of the table, Amelia and Toby on either side of a debate about legalizing cannabis, both waving spare-rib bones at each other, everyone else lining up to take sides, I came straight to the point.

'I gather you and Camille are not exactly strangers.'

He grinned. 'Sally didn't waste much time.'

'But why did you pretend you didn't know her? I can

understand not wanting to appear over-friendly, but we didn't even know you'd met.'

'To tell you the truth, I was so bloody shocked when Sally told me whose house it was, and then, when she appeared on the terrace that first night, I didn't quite know how to handle it. She pretended she didn't know me, so I took my cue from her. Let myself be introduced. After all, it's her custody battle.'

'So you know about that.'

'She told me in Rome.' He shrugged. 'I assumed that was the reason for blanking me here in front of her family, her sister.'

I speared a tiny caramelized onion thoughtfully with my fork. 'You realize we're all here on your account? Every single one of us?'

'Bollocks.'

'It's true. For once, I agree with Sally. Camille has master-minded this whole shebang. You have no idea how manipulative women are, Max.'

'Oh, I think I do.'

I'd forgotten he'd been married to Mimi. I wondered, for a moment, what it must be like to be Max. To be so attractive that women fought to get close to him. Arranged their lives around him. Not this one, I thought, ignoring the fact that his blue eyes looked even brighter now his face was tanned, his hair slightly flecked with gold. And, anyway, part of me thought that he was really only inter-ested in someone as ordinary as me because I'd resisted him.

I was conscious of Amelia's eyes on me towards the end of supper and, after pudding, she followed me into the kitchen, as I helped take some dishes in. She stood over me as I stacked the dishwasher under the island by the sink. Could have helped, of course, but she had other things on her mind.

'Tara and I really aren't happy about it, Mum,' she said pompously.

'About what?'

'You flirting outrageously with Max, and Dad being knocked sideways by Camille.'

Tara appeared, hastening to her sister's side from the table. This was clearly a pre-arranged pincer movement. She nodded solemnly and they both looked po-faced. Any minute now some arm folding would go on. They folded their arms.

'I'm not flirting, Amelia, and anyway, you were really rather interested yesterday.'

'Yes, but it's too much now,' said Tara. 'It's all a bit – you know – weird. And Dad's even worse.'

We turned to look through the open French windows. James was rocking with laughter at some comment of Camille's – one supper with her own family in the lodge had clearly been enough, and she was back with a vengeance. He was looking, I have to say, quite attractive as he embarked on yet another orthopaedic anecdote.

'Dad's just having a nice time. Enjoying the attention.'

'He looks like he's going to stick his tongue down her throat. It's gross. Anyway,' went on Amelia, 'I think she's secretly after Max.'

'What on earth makes you say that?'

'She keeps sneaking him furtive glances, and he is really good-looking. How come you snared him, Mum?'

'Thank you, Amelia. I had my moments.'

'What, in the Wimpy Bar? With your flared jeans?'

Lizzie had joined us now, sensing girl chat. She took out her Marlboro Lights and leaned against the draining board, but misjudged it and staggered slightly.

'Frankly, I'm just jealous no one fancies me,' she pouted. 'I'm the bloody single woman here. You might have invited some sex-crazed Lothario on my account, everyone's shagging except me.' Her mouth lurched at the corner as it did when she was pissed, and she fumbled to light her cigarette.

'No one is shagging, Lizzie. And anyway, yesterday you said there was a glimmer of hope on the Jackson front.'

'False alarm. He's still up to his eyes with work. Speaking of which, did you get Maria's email?' She blew out a thin line of smoke and attempted to fix me with swimmy eyes.

'Yes. I did,' I said shortly.

'And you're not going back?'

'No, I'm bloody not.' Ever, I thought to myself, wondering if I meant it, or if it was just holiday bravado. I took a slurp of the Cointreau she'd brought in with her.

'Going back where?' demanded Tara, ears pricked.

'Maria's calling a meeting. The magazine's been taken over, so . . .'

'You knew that. That happened months ago,' objected Amelia. 'You said it didn't matter.'

'Yes, but the knock-on effects are now rippling out. The implication is that anyone who wants to keep their job had better show up for this meeting.'

'But you're on holiday.'

'I know.'

They looked thoughtful. 'You could just go for the day?' suggested Amelia. 'Get a plane from Nice?'

'Yes, that's what I thought I might do,' agreed Lizzie.

'Oi, are you lot coming or what?' Toby's voice floated across from where he and Rory were shuffling cards at one end of the table, ciggies and candles lit. The girls drifted off to play Vingt-et-un, bored now that we were talking shop and not men.

'Watch yourself, Mum, OK?' was Amelia's parting shot to me. I rolled my eyes theatrically.

'But not you?' asked Lizzie, her mind still on flights home. 'You're really not going?'

'I'm really not going. If they want to sack me, they can jolly well get on with it. Give me a nice fat redundancy package. I'm not going back to grovel.'

My eyes were on Max, at the table, helping Drummond, who could be jolly stiff, to his feet. He steadied him, found his stick and then stayed with him a moment as Rachel came round from the other side of the table to take him inside and up to bed.

'Night, all.'

'Night, Drummond.'

'Night, Grandpa!'

He gave a cheery wave to the young with his stick, still brimming with delight at being here, amongst his family, in the warmth, which he can't have felt on his skin for years: since his days in Africa probably, in the army. Thanking his lucky stars for being alive when so many of his contemporaries weren't, before shuffling in.

'Right. Well, I don't have the luxury of choice, so I might. Go back.'

'It's not a luxury, Lizzie, I don't have that either. We need the money as much as you do. It's just . . . I've come to the end of something with that magazine.'

I had. Had known it for some time now but had been in denial. Because I used to love it so. And I'd made myself believe I still did, but I didn't. I still loved the food: was still excited when something new hit my taste buds, some innovative combination of flavours. That moment when I realized there was someone highly creative in the kitchen was still a thrill. I remembered discovering Antoine Edelle in a tiny restaurant in Tooting, being struck by his prodigious talent, praising the young chef to the skies and being delighted when, a few months later, he opened in Greek Street to rave reviews. The delight in all that was still there. And it more than made up for the mistakes I couldn't help noticing, like Thérèse putting too much wine in the marinade tonight or balsamic in the vinaigrette. And the food was good here. Or last night, how the creamy morel sauce was just slightly too rich, badly needing a dash of lemon to cut through it – I'd seen Jean-Claude's face after his first mouthful, knew he knew, too: he approached food with a great solemnity, I'd noticed. Yes, most evenings I noticed something, but it didn't taint my pleasure. Noticing flaws was an occupational hazard, and I was proud of my training, my finely tuned palate. It defined me. But I wanted to turn it in another direction now. Do things differently. I knew how, too. Just couldn't quite admit it. Even to myself.

I swam up from the depths of my reverie. Helped

myself to another slurp of Lizzie's Cointreau. 'To be honest, Lizzie, I think it's all just a storm in a teacup. Maria's holiday in Tuscany got cancelled at the last minute because her husband had to go to New York. She's probably a bit jealous of us all lying here in the sun.'

'I know, I wondered that. She's really pissed off, apparently. I spoke to Colin. Serve her right for marrying an über-rich banker.' She sighed. Stubbed her cigarette out in a cheese plate. 'Perhaps I'll play it by ear. See if we get any more missives tomorrow.'

'Exactly. I would.'

Lizzie had been standing with her back to the draining board, facing the garden. She focused her gaze on the candlelit table. 'I say, James is having fun, isn't he?'

I turned. Dried my hands. My husband was on his feet now, mimicking someone with an exaggerated limp. A hunched back, too, apparently. Was he Richard III? Camille was laughing prettily, clapping her hands with delight.

'Is he making a fool of himself, Lizzie? The girls think he is.'

'Of course not, he's on holiday. I haven't seen him like that for years, it's really lovely. He's such good company.'

I glowed. Lizzie had sat next to him at supper.

'It's good for us, isn't it, Lizzie? All of this?' I looked out at the lively table, a game of cards at one end, explosive laughter at the other, the lights strung so prettily through the trees on the lawn.

''Course it bloody is. Christ, we're not dead yet. Let the young shake their heads and suck their teeth, I'm not reining in. Not for one moment. In fact, I'm going skinny-dipping with Sally.'

'Is that where she is?'

'Yes, starkers in the pool. Come on. While the kids are playing cards.'

She grabbed my arm and, full of Cointreau, we hastened off. Giggling like schoolgirls, we ran out through the side door and then around the other side of the house. We picked our way across the sloping lawn, through the spinney in the dark, and under the cedar tree to the gate in the old walled garden. A few minutes later I was beetling back alone, eyes wide, fully clothed. Mum was in the pool, too.

In the pitch black, my mind not on the route I seemed to have veered from, I cannoned straight into someone in the dark. I shrieked.

'Oof – steady!' Arms came out. It was Max.

'Oh – God, it's you!' I clasped my heart with relief.

He laughed, steadying me. 'Who did you think it was, the bogeyman? Word is the girls have got their kit off down at the pool. Couldn't get down there quickly enough.'

'Yes, but, actually, maybe not, Max. Mum's in there.'

'Oh. Right.' He turned about abruptly.

'Exactly.'

We went back up the cinder path together. I grinned up at him in the dark, lurching only very slightly. 'Odd, isn't it? Amelia and Tara would be horrified if I went in, but I think I'm still young. So why am I aghast at my own mother?'

'I think it depends,' he said carefully.

'On what?'

'On whether the pool has underwater lights or not.'

I giggled.

'Do you still smoke?' he asked.

'Occasionally. But, like skinny-dipping, not in front of the children. I operate a strict regime of hypocrisy.'

'Let's have one over here, then.'

He drew out a pack and we wandered off the beaten track a bit, towards the horses' field beyond the spinney. It was a moonless night, with just a sprinkling of stars above, like diamonds tossed carelessly on to black velvet. The horses came ambling across the field to greet us, and we stroked their velvety noses. Let them blow into our hands. Max lit two cigarettes the way he always used to and passed me one. We leaned back against the fence.

'You haven't lost that habit, then,' I observed.

'I have, actually. Haven't done that for years.'

Instantly, I was transported back to the many times he'd done it for me: on the top of the number 19 bus as we rumbled back from the West End after the cinema. Inside the cinema, in the days of little ashtrays between the seats. In the Italian bistro afterwards, him lighting both from a candle dripping with wax as we argued about the film, never agreeing on anything we'd seen. And then, of course, in bed, at his flat. Flicking ash off the navy-blue sheets into a small pewter ashtray on the floor beside us that had belonged to his grandfather. Burning a hole once. I could tell Max had gone to these places in his head, too. We didn't speak, just smoked in silence. At length, Max cleared his throat.

'I miss you,' he said simply. 'Miss those days.'

I swallowed. Kept my face free of expression. 'You're idealizing them, Max. Because it was our youth. That's what people do. Because we were young and carefree, we look back fondly. But we can't recapture it.'

'You do, too?'

'Look back? As a rule, no. But I did just then.'

'We were good together, Flora. We never stopped laughing.'

He'd deliberately conjured up a very seductive image: one that was hard to resist and one which, when I was young, when he'd betrayed me, had been the hardest. Max and I would laugh until the tears rolled down our faces. Until our sides hurt and we had to sit down. About anything. Nothing. Someone in the street going so fast they were bent at right angles. Max would suddenly mimic them, going right up beside them as he did it. A shop assistant or waitress with a funny turn of phrase, which we'd employ for the rest of the day, in a Sybil Fawlty voice – 'Ta ever so.' 'Will you be wanting sauce with that?' 'If Madam would kindly desist from smoking.' So many things collectively tickled us, and life was so serious now. It seemed to consist of a series of problems to be solved in rapid succession, popping up like moles the moment the last one had been bashed on the head.

'Nothing's that funny now,' I observed.

'It can be.'

He reached up and brushed the hair from my eyes, something James had done earlier, but this time an electric current shot through me. I steadied myself on the fence, knowing I was full of Cointreau and giddy on warm Provençal air under a starry sky. That this wasn't real life. We stubbed our cigarettes out simultaneously and glanced at each other. Or I did. I was aware Max had been watching me for some time. I was shocked by the intensity of his gaze: by the depth of feeling. Suddenly, all the years rolled back in a snap, as if I'd let go of a roller blind I'd been hanging on to, to keep the darkness in place. The light flooded in and, with it, a myriad of other memories I'd shut out. Bright, sunlit ones, like playing football with his small cousins in Hyde Park, Max in goal, deliberately letting them shoot past him, their shrieks of delight. Driving to the coast in his convertible MG, me hanging on to the surfboard we'd tied above our heads which threatened to disappear at any minute. Running down dunes in our swimming costumes into a freezing North Sea. Lying on our backs in the sand, windmilling our arms to warm up. Sleeping on his roof terrace in South Kensington during a heatwave, being woken by thin clear light and the rattle of milk bottles below. It might have been twenty years ago but, right at this moment, it felt like yesterday. So when he took me in his arms and kissed me, it felt entirely natural. In fact, it felt like the most natural thing in the world.

Chapter Eighteen

At length, we pulled apart, our hearts racing. I say at length, because the kiss was a long one: I'd like to tell you it was brief and hurried, but it wasn't. It was also highly charged and emotional; full of longing on his part and high excitement on mine. Afterwards, we held each other tightly and I could hear his breath roaring in my ear. Then, as one, we stepped back in shock. Gazed at each another. 'Blimey' sprang to mind, but happily not to my lips.

'I've got to go,' I muttered, and he nodded quickly in agreement.

It occurred to me, as I saw the shock in his eyes, that he was as taken aback as I was. This hadn't been premeditated. He hadn't planned this in any way. He'd just meandered down to the pool full of food and booze, as I had, with a cheeky desire to surprise some naked women. He hadn't followed me or engineered it, any more than he'd engineered us dipping out of sight of the teenagers to have a cigarette. It had just happened. But . . . had it been lying in wait all these years? Ready to ambush us? Had it been tucked away in our minds as something to do one day? To finish what was started – and ended so brutally – all those years ago? It seemed to me I'd just melted into his arms and turned my lips up to his without a second thought.

No time to speculate further, though, because as we emerged from the spinney, the house was in sight, lit up in all its glory. My adrenalin was pumping fast as we walked up the sloping lawn and I felt the words 'Adulterous Witch' writ large on my face as we rounded the corner and approached the post-dinner table to sit – rather conspicuously, in retrospect – as far apart as possible. Neither of us got a second glance from the others. They carried on drinking and laughing and playing cards, as if we hadn't been missed at all. Max went to the far end to watch the game and I pulled up a chair beside Jean-Claude, who was talking to Thérèse. It was all too easy, wasn't it? I thought, picking up a stray drink, my hand trembling ever so slightly. An extramarital affair? So simple. No wonder it happened so often. Not that it was ever, *ever* going to happen to me.

James was opposite me, beside Camille, who was talking to Jean-Claude and Thérèse now.

I smiled. 'I'm off to bed,' I told him. There. Quite normal, that two-timing voice of mine.

He smiled back, and something in his eyes told me he remembered our conversation in the bedroom earlier. About us being all right.

'Me, too,' he agreed.

We got up as one, as a happily married couple, and said goodnight rather generally. I didn't look at Max or my daughters. Together we walked through the house to the hall. Up the curling staircase we went, James pausing to collect a paperback he'd left on the landing windowsill. I waited for him as he riffled through the pile. My heart was still pounding and I was terrified he'd hear it. Once in our room, I brushed my teeth, slipped quickly into bed, then turned away and shut my eyes. James was only just behind me. He turned out the bedside light.

'Night, darling,' he said sleepily.

'Night.'

He, too, turned over and was asleep and snoring in moments. I lay there for what seemed like hours, waiting for my heart rate to come down, waiting for my breathing to return to normal. Wondering if I'd ever be the same again. Well, I wouldn't, would I? I'd kissed another man. I'd irrevocably changed, in the space of ten seconds, the nature of our marriage. It would never be the same, I'd seen to that. It's very fabric, intricately woven over many years, had been yanked, and when a loose thread revealed itself, pulled apart. What would happen now? How would this change manifest itself? I was so transparent – everyone said so – would he guess? Would I have to tell him? We told each other everything. Always had done.

The following morning I awoke with a start. Abruptly, as often happens, when something extraordinary has happened. But, strangely, in the soft warm light that streamed through a gap in the shutters, what had felt so momentous and painful and totally wonderful all at the same time a few hours ago suddenly seemed faintly ridiculous. What a fool I'd been. To get pissed like that. And how stupidly I'd behaved. It had been late and dark and all my senses had been skewed with drink, but really. In the excitement of the moment, and in the middle of the night, it had felt far more portentous than of course it was. Just a stolen kiss with an ex-boyfriend in a dark wood. Stupid, Flora. But not the end of the world. Move on. Don't, whatever you do, breathe a word to James – I can't believe you considered that last night – and never, ever, let it happen again. There. Job done.

James stirred beside me. He turned over and hugged me from behind so that we slotted together like spoons. Sleepily, he kissed my shoulder. My eyes bulged slightly at the opposite wall as he kissed me again. I wasn't entirely sure this was what I wanted, but on the other hand . . . maybe it was. To prove that last night had indeed been an aberration. A silly deviation from real life. James pulled me in closer and I acquiesced. Yes, last night had just been a ridiculous episode not to be repeated: to be put down to drink, holiday madness and happenchance.

Ten minutes later James was bounding around the bedroom like a teenager, humming loudly and running me a bath. He was fresh from the shower, stark naked, towelling his shoulders vigorously, his love life a positive riot at the moment.

'This holiday has done us the world of good, darling,' he declared heartily, bending over the bed and planting a kiss squarely on my lips. 'It was clearly just what we needed!'

Clearly, I thought guiltily as I watched his bare bottom retreat back into the bathroom. I wasn't convinced it would necessarily feature in any agony aunt's advice on how to reignite a tired, marital sex life, though. I wasn't sure kissing an ex-boyfriend and letting your husband have his ego massaged by a sexy soprano would necessarily be amongst Graham Norton's Top Tips in the *Sunday Times*.

Speaking of that very same sexy soprano, the sound of her dulcet tones began to filter up through the floorboards. Except they weren't dulcet and the floor wasn't providing much of a filter. They certainly weren't pleasant. She was belting out scales, at full volume and at an increasingly high pitch, whilst accompanying herself on the piano. As they got higher and higher, they became shriller and shriller. Then came the arpeggios. *Screeching* arpeggios. She was certainly very good, but very, *very* loud. I had no idea one person could sing to that volume; it sounded more like a fully blown choir. Would the windows shatter, I wondered? Instead, our door flew open. Tara, tousled and astonished, put her head around.

'What is that *terrible* noise?' she whispered.

'It's Camille practising.'

'Make it stop,' she begged.

'You're lucky to be hearing it at all,' retorted James, appearing from the bathroom with a towel around his waist. 'People pay good money to hear that.' He cocked his head appreciatively as the floorboards rattled.

'*La – la – la – la – LAAAAAA!!!!*'

The whole house shook. And must be awake, too.

'Sounds like she's being stabbed,' Tara said. She shuffled back to bed and I pretended not to hear Rory muttering to her as she closed the door.

On and on it went.

'Bloody *hell*!' I heard Sally shriek from next door, then she dissolved into giggles. I wondered if her sex life had been pepped up, too? As a result of last night? I shut my eyes tight. No, I did *not* want to think about that. Instead, I leaped into the bath James had run me and agreed that no, I didn't think Camille would mind if he went down and slid quietly into the room to listen, keeping to myself the view that he would be in a minority of one. I visualized him, creeping into the drawing room with the grand piano in the window, polishing his glasses and perching on a sofa to listen adoringly. Indeed, when I went down later – the noise too deafening to do anything else – this was the scene I encountered. Except it wasn't Camille playing the piano, as I'd imagined, but Michel.

He scowled slightly at being interrupted, even though Camille hadn't seemed to notice. James frowned and motioned me away, as if he was acceptable at an operatic masterclass, but I wasn't.

So Michel was rather talented, I thought, closing the door quietly, as Camille broke into the aria from *Madame Butterfly*. It was one thing to thump out scales but another to play this. Not just a gardener. At the end, James applauded loudly.

'Bravo! Oh, bravo!'

I cringed for him and, unfortunately, he burst into the kitchen glowing when I still had two fingers down my throat in mock-disgust.

'What are you doing?'

'Got something stuck.'

'Oh. Isn't she marvellous?'

'Marvellous.'

'And guess what, she's been asked to perform that aria on stage tonight, with Bocelli, practising as a preview for her tour. So I'll actually see her in action!'

'Oh that's great, James.' I really was pleased for him. He was having the time of his life. 'So' – I suppressed a smile – 'she'll step up on to that stage, vacating the seat beside you – and everyone will think . . . she's with you!'

'Yes!' He squealed. Then realized. 'I mean – no.' He looked worried.

I laughed. 'Don't worry, darling. It's only one night. Why shouldn't you look as if you're escorting a celebrity? I'd be chuffed to bits if I was, and it was – I don't know, Michael Bublé, or someone.'

He shot me a grateful look, and I knew in his head he was already wondering if she'd kiss his cheek before she got up from the seat beside him, like they did at the Oscars, enjoying his fantasy to the hilt.

The next visitor to the kitchen was not so euphoric. Lizzie swept in, smartly dressed in a navy-blue jacket and skirt, clutching an overnight bag.

'Just as well that dreadful caterwauling woke me up. I'm going to catch the 11.50 from Nice, if I can.'

She dumped her bag and clip-clopped in her heels to the cappuccino machine in the corner.

'Oh really, why?' James looked surprised.

'Hasn't Flora told you?' She glanced around. 'It's the day of reckoning. Maria is summoning the troops.'

James raised his eyebrows at me.

'Lizzie's exaggerating,' I said smoothly. 'Maria's pissed off because she's stuck in the office, so she's trying to wreck everyone else's holiday. You frighten too easily, Lizzie.'

Lizzie arched her eyebrows at this: it was patently untrue. She really didn't, as a rule, and I really did, but right now, our roles seemed to have been reversed. Generally, it would be me getting the first plane back and Lizzie who'd be dragging her feet and telling me not to panic. But not today. Today, as she bustled about behind me, finding her iPad, checking timetables, I sat at the kitchen table sipping my coffee, watching the morning sun cast a shimmering haze over the lawn, heralding a beautiful day and the

247

promise of more heat to come. Today, I was happy to let the real and stressful world wash over me in a liberating manner, as I gave myself up to the delights – which, let's face it, were coming in many unexpected guises – of my much-needed Provencal holiday.

Sally and Max were next down, and we all greeted each other cheerfully, as if a starlit snog had never happened.

'Morning!'

'Morning, all! A lovely one, as ever.'

Max's eyes snagged on mine and then darted away, but you'd have to be very acute to notice, and no one did. Jean-Claude and my mother were next, looking stricken.

'Terrible, *terrible* noise!' Mum whispered, coming in, clutching feebly at the furniture in mock-horror and looking appalled.

I frowned as Camille came in through another door on a cloud of Diorissimo, in tiny white shorts and a strappy top. For an opera singer, she was minutely built and I wondered where the strength and power of that voice came from? All in the spectacular lungs, I imagined.

'My darlings, I hope you don't mind fending for yourselves tonight, I've secured a few more tickets for tonight's performance. Michel and Thérèse are coming with me.'

'Oh, no, not at all!' we all chorused instantly.

'Of course not, you've been so kind,' I said, as she ignored us anyway and swept on out to the terrace, taking the coffee Lizzie had just made for herself, leaving her looking startled.

A cosy camaraderie prevailed in the kitchen: a palpable relief at the thought of being on our own tonight, without any member of the de Bouvoir family.

'We could go out?' suggested Sally quietly over her coffee as she sat down opposite me.

'Or I could cook?' said Jean-Claude, joining us at the table. 'I'd like to.'

'Really? Would you?' I turned to him in delight, always keen to reject the Eating Out option these days. And we were so happy here, weren't we? In our womb-like existence. Our own little world. I wanted no intrusion from the outside world, no reminder of reality, no piercing of my bubble. Indeed, I'd almost forgotten the chateau belonged to Camille at all.

'Of course, I would enjoy to do it.'

'Splendid!' declared the Brig, who'd just appeared. He settled himself down at the table, too. 'I do find restaurants so damned uncomfortable these days. And they nearly always have a battery of steps for me to fall down.'

'I'll shop for you, if you like?' I offered. 'I'd like to do that.'

Jean-Claude smiled. 'Ah, but you are forgetting I won't know what I am cooking until I have gone to the market. Until I have seen the meat and smelled the fish. *Alors*. You make the lunch, *cherie*. Let us do all of the cooking today, so that Michel and Thérèse have the whole day off.'

'Perfect!' I said happily. I liked cooking, too. So did James. Adored it. Maybe we'd do it together? His eyes told me we would.

'That would be really nice, darling,' he said.

So, with Michel kindly taking Lizzie to the airport – she left with regret and promises to be back soon, muttering darkly about there being no way she was spending more than a day placating Maria – James and I, having looked at the map, and James having been assured by Thérèse it was the best place to go today, prepared to set off for yet another exquisite hilltop village, this time that of Mons.

Amelia appeared through the front door just as we were loading up the car. Her eyes were bleary from sleep and she picked her way gingerly in bare feet down the steps and across the gravel drive, but she looked pleased.

'Where are you two off to?'

'Sightseeing and food shopping in Mons.'

'You crazy kids.'

'Want to come?'

'Nah. Have fun, though.'

I smiled, knowing she was pleased to see her parents together and looking happy. As I threw in a couple of straw baskets I'd found in the pantry, I caught a glimpse of Max, who'd moved further down the garden to sit under the walnut tree with a book. He was watching us go from under the brim of his hat. That must never happen again, I thought, as I slammed the boot shut. Never. Nevertheless, a glance in the rear-view mirror as I drove to the end of the drive told me he'd watched the car all the way down, and I felt an unmistakable tingle of excitement. It was a long time since I'd been watched by a man. Aside from traffic wardens, of course.

'We'll probably leave at about four, Camille says,' James was telling me as I turned down the lane, excited at his own plans, oblivious to my world. 'Otherwise, the traffic builds up. We'll have drinks by the sea first, and then supper, which she's booked.'

'Lovely, darling.' I turned from behind the wheel and smiled at his evident pleasure. I always drove on holiday, and James map-read. The other way round, and I felt sick in minutes and we ended up lost and having a flaming row.

'Turn right here,' he told me. 'And I imagine we'll be back quite late, so don't wait up,' he said, casting me a furtive look.

'No. I won't,' I assured him with a smile. 'You know Max is going, too, don't you?' I said, hoping he did. Hoping it wouldn't burst his bubble.

'Yes, in an official capacity,' said James pompously. 'His company is organizing the concert and, since he's here, he thinks he ought to put in an appearance.'

'I can see that.'

'Oh, yes. Me too.'

I was glad he could see it. I, on the other hand, could also see Camille, surrounded by adoring men. I was convinced Michel was not immune to her charms – my own thoughts on that, I heroically kept to myself – and, of course, James was beyond hope and she wanted Max to witness this. As we'd cleared the breakfast table, Sally had told me that Max had felt the pressure to go, but that she hadn't been invited.

'Perhaps there are only a certain number of tickets?' I'd suggested. Rachel, I'd noticed, originally the first to be invited, seemed to have been forgotten. Naturally, she hadn't said a word. 'James says it's sold out.'

'Except you'd think the star of the show would be able to wangle one more, wouldn't you?' she'd said crossly.

Or even the organizer, I'd thought privately, but I didn't say. I couldn't meet Sally's eye as it was.

James and I parked easily halfway up the hill to the village, remarking as we got out how in England we'd have to search high and low for a space. We walked arm in arm up the steep little cobbled street, dodging pots of geraniums and bougainvillea littering front steps, cats sunning themselves and neighbours strapped into pinnies discussing the business of the day. The sun was high in the sky now and, as we climbed, it cast a rich, warm glow on the scattering of red roofs which began to reveal themselves in the depths of the dizzying valley below, in the vast dramatic expanse of the dusty plane peppered with olive groves. As we strolled ever upwards in the sunshine, passing a clutch of old men playing pétanque in the mottled shade of trees, sipping their pastis, it occurred to me that I hadn't been happier in a long while. Before we embarked on the market, we stood for a moment, still arm in arm, on the terrace at the top of the promontory, by a cooling fountain, gazing down at the panoramic view, the abyss freckled with tiny farms nestled amongst groves and vineyards, banking right up at the sides to oak- and pine-forested slopes, then through the valley floor to the sparkling sea beyond.

'I could stay here for ever,' I told James, as we stared, surprising even myself. 'Never go home. I love it.'

He laughed. 'People always say that when they're on holiday.'

'We don't.' I reminded him.

'That's because we always go to Scotland.'

'True. We should do this more often.'

'I know.'

But we both knew we wouldn't. That this was a one-off. A treat to be savoured. Knew, that with crippling bills – shoring up the house before it slid down the hill had hit us badly – and a mortgage, we'd be in Clapham, and periodically Scotland, for the rest of our lives: watching anxiously as James's private practice dwindled and younger men leaped ahead, hoping we could limp on until he retired and drew his ever-decreasing National Health pension, which was, oh, only another fifteen years or so. As if the sobering thought had struck us simultaneously, we turned, as one, away from the seductive view, the other world it presented, and with a certain forced jollity now, strode away to the market to squeeze the melons.

Salad Niçoise, James had decided, with fresh tuna, which he was sure we'd find easily. Also, some delicious plump black olives from a barrel, freshly laid eggs, green beans, tiny new potatoes and tomatoes you could smell at twenty paces – oh, and some asparagus tips, too. This was to be a salad unlike any you could make at home.

The market was well under way and bustling with critical intent, for, unlike the one for tourists the other day that was full of handbags and dresses, this was for serious gastronomes only. Every local French housewife worth her salt was here; the place positively bristled with them. They sniffed and prodded the abundant displays of brightly coloured peppers, vibrant green courgettes and creamy chicory heads which looked, to our eyes, spectacular, often dismissing them and certainly bartering energetically, before they deigned to make a purchase. James and I got into the swing immediately, food shopping and cooking being one of our great shared pleasures. Cheeses being his speciality, he beetled off, nose twitching, to some creamy, blue-veined Roquefort he'd spotted. *Saucisson* and other charcuterie were also on his agenda, whilst the fruit, veg and fish were mine. As I went slowly past a string of stalls, squeezing and smelling, not ignoring misshapen, lumpy tomatoes, knowing looks were not a guarantee of ripeness or flavour, buying a fat bundle of white-and-mauve asparagus here, an irresistible orb of purple aubergine there, I wondered if I'd ever tire of a market like this. Ever stop marvelling, as I entered the fish stalls, at the baskets of scallops heaped on the floor beside the tables, the tiny pale shrimps in buckets, the vast, pale-pink langoustines, bright-red mullet, clams, plump soles, oysters like silver medals in their creamy, corrugated shell beds, soft crabs, boxes of winkles, everything ripe for bouillabaisse, which, personally, I'd have made but I had wanted James to choose the menu. Would I tire? I thought not. This was what I loved about food, what I missed: the instinctive sensory pleasure, not having to rate it out of ten. Eventually, I found what I looking for and seized upon the perfect tuna. Having examined the pink gills and bright eyes, I deemed it unmistakably this morning's catch and ordered a large slice.

Before we left, with our bulging baskets, happy with our purchases, we stopped for a drink, in the square, under the trees. I had a coffee, dark and bitter, and James had a beer. Together, we sipped and watched the world go by: two people content not to speak, just to be. The previous night flashed briefly through my mind but, already, it seemed like a dream. Something that might never have happened. Perhaps it hadn't? Perhaps I'd imagined it all. I manoeuvred my legs into the sun, making sure my face was shaded by the umbrella.

'Have you noticed how much slimmer the people here are?' I said after a while as the crowd flowed by.

'It's the diet. Less McDonald's.'

'And the way of life. The fact that they shop for fresh food every day. That's exercise in itself. No Ocado deliveries here.' I smiled. 'Are we turning into Francophiles, d'you think?'

'You always have been. All those formative years. It's in your blood.'

I sighed contentedly. 'It speaks to me, James, this country. I don't know why. I feel at home here.'

There was the smallest of pauses. 'Then we must come back more,' he said lightly.

I didn't answer. As I drained my *café noir* I narrowed my eyes at the church at the far end of the square, huge and looming, dominating proceedings and refusing to be ignored, as French churches do. I nodded towards it.

'Shall we pop in? Take a look?'

'Why not? Or – tell you what, darling, you go. I'll watch the bags. Don't be long, though, we need to get back and get this fish out of the sun.'

'Oh. OK.' He was right, I supposed. It was a lot to cart around, but it would have been nice to go together.

'I'll get the bill,' he told me as he waved to the *garçon*.

I put my sunglasses on and wandered off, pushing back through the market and pausing only to make an irresistible purchase of tapenade, the gleaming Provençal olive spread, to ladle on to crusty fresh bread and pass around before the salad. After I'd climbed the steep phalanx of steps, worn smooth by generations of pilgrims, and crossed the ancient threshold into the vast, brown chasm, candles flickering at the far end by the altar, the cool, the gloom, the peace and the emptiness enveloped me. I felt, not sadness, as Lizzie always said she did with a shiver, if I was with her, already making for the exit, but tranquillity and calm wash over me. I sat in the nearest pew and said a little prayer. Then I went to the tray of tiny candles. Popping my two euros in the box, I took a taper. As I lit a candle, I shut my eyes. Prayed hard. But not a small duty prayer this time, not a thank you for getting us here safely, a proper Please God one. I prayed for longer than I expected, because I had quite a lot to say. There was a bit about forgiveness, obviously, but then other things. Things I didn't even know were on my mind. Things no one had asked me about in a long time but which I felt a sudden compulsion to share. To divulge.

After a while, I sensed a presence beside me. I opened my eyes and raised my head. It was James, with the bags.

'Thought you weren't coming in?' I said.

'Changed my mind. What did I interrupt?' His eyes were kind. Soft, grey eyes I loved. 'What were you praying so hard for?'

I smiled. Linked my arm through his. We made for the door. 'For us. For the rest of our lives. For some sort of guidance through this crazy, uncertain world in whatever way,' I glanced up and gesticulated, open-palmed, to the heavens, 'that He sees fit.'

Chapter Nineteen

Jean-Claude cooked for France that night. James and I thought we'd acquitted ourselves pretty reasonably at lunchtime, the tuna having been seared to pink perfection and served on a bed of pale-green endive so springy it fairly exploded in the mouth, with soft-boiled eggs, plump anchovies and olives accompanying, but it was nothing to the meal Jean-Claude produced and I wished my husband had been there to witness it.

Escargots were first flamed in cognac then added to sautéed ceps and shallots and served with a cream, mustard and tarragon sauce. Then came a perfectly pink rack of lamb with a fragrant herb crust. It was accompanied by a truffle and Madeira sauce, dauphinoise potatoes, tiny shelled peas and blanched artichokes. All this was followed by a sublime chocolate fondant, surely the ultimate test for any chef. Mum acted as sous-chef, chopping and washing ingredients as he quietly got on with the main event. He issued a few low instructions to her, but he also thanked her every time she put a row of prepared vegetables in front of him, I noticed. I'd been perched at a stool in the kitchen, having my nails painted by Tara. She liked this man, and he liked her, I could tell. Watching them took me back to the days of Philippe: not just the cooking, which they loved to do together, but the way Philippe would look at her when she stopped to stroke a dog in the street or gave money to the beggars who gathered at the foot of the steps to Montmartre. It was the same tenderness Jean-Claude had on his face now as she dithered, on the point of putting the snails in front of him, then dashing back to the sink to give them a second wash. She was happier than I'd seen her in a long while. Not that Mum ever presented anything other than a cheerful façade to the world, that wasn't her style. But as she shimmied around the kitchen in the pretty dress she'd found in Fayence, popping out proudly to announce each course to the assembled family on the terrace, who cheered and clapped each announcement – Mum dropping a low curtsey as if she'd cooked it all herself, then executing a pirouette, arms above her head, to make her granddaughters laugh – I saw a light in her eyes I hadn't seen for years.

There was certainly a less formal atmosphere that night, without Camille, and without being waited on by Michel and Thérèse. Spirits were lighter and more frivolous. I liked it. In fact, I wished we didn't have the de Bouvoir family watching over us all the time. Wished we could have more nights like these – but then, I reasoned guiltily, we wouldn't be here at all if it wasn't for them. It was also something of a relief, I realized, not to have Max here. It gave me a respite from my feelings, anyway. I wondered if he'd disappeared on purpose. Sally had said it was a spur-of-the-moment decision to go to the concert: had he deliberately given us both some space? It would be a kind gesture, and very like him. I sank hastily into my wine.

At the end of the meal we all clapped like mad and raised our glasses to Jean-Claude who, flushed and smiling, appeared from the kitchen, framed in the French windows. He'd barely eaten a thing, so intent had he been on getting each course to the table, hot and perfect. After a self-conscious little bow he finally sat down beside me and gratefully accepted a cognac.

'That was unbelievable, Jean-Claude,' I told him. 'And I mean that from a professional point of view, not just as a grateful and greedy holidaymaker.'

'I told you.' He smiled. 'All Frenchmen can cook.'

'Don't give me that. You're professionally trained.'

He smiled and swirled his cognac around in its glass, avoiding my eye. 'Perhaps,' he admitted at length.

'Where?' I demanded, turning in my chair to face him properly. 'And what's with the bric-a-brac — lovely though it is,' I added quickly.

He laughed. 'Only so very recently you applaud my artistic tastes. Admire my finds in *brocantes*. Now you prefer my culinary skills?'

'You've clearly got taste in spades,' I told him, 'be it antiques or haute cuisine, but even I could source a few bedsteads and lamps. I certainly couldn't cook like that. Come on. Give.'

He sighed. Shrugged. 'I trained with Thierry Dupuis in Paris. I work for ten years under Hugo Monfleur in L'Escale before finally opening my own restaurant just off the Rue Saint-Honoré seven years ago. I gain two Michelin stars in three years.'

My mouth dropped open. 'You're kidding.'

'I'm not.'

'What happened?'

He spread his hands, palms up, in a hopeless gesture. 'I got divorced. The recession bit. I owed people money. I had to sell the restaurant to pay my wife. I opened another, in a less elegant part of the city, in Jardin des Plantes, and it didn't work.' He shrugged expressively. 'These things happen. It's happening all the time, all over Paris. London, too. You open, you close. Oh, and did I mention that the maître d' had his fingers in the till? And, because I was so busy in the kitchen, I didn't notice until it was too late? Until we closed, in a blaze of bad publicity, orchestrated by my ex-wife, who works for *Paris Match*, and who saw to it that the magazine covered my fall from grace?'

I stared as he gazed, narrow-eyed, into the distance. Hurt eyes. Right. A glimpse of this man had been apparent these past few days, but I'd had no idea. I'd noticed him tasting dishes with critical relish, thoughtful as he savoured a mouthful of soup; it was something I recognized. And I'd seen him assiduously picking over *moules* in the kitchen, considering himself unobserved, but now I got the complete picture. And to have had a restaurant in such a prestigious part of Paris. I wondered if I'd heard of it.

'La Terrasse,' he told me when I asked.

I had. One of the premier establishments on the Right Bank, very much in the vanguard of a new wave of French cooking: I had no idea it had closed.

'But it is a mistake to cook and also to own and manage. I couldn't do it. Couldn't trust anyone, but couldn't do it all on my own.'

'You do need a good manager,' I agreed.

'*Exactement*. But everyone is in it for themselves these days, siphoning off what they can. You have no idea.'

I looked at his tired, much-travelled, handsome face as he massaged his brow with his fingertips. I visualized him years ago, as a young man, in the heart of Paris. A chic, cultured, good-looking man. Walking in the Tuileries Gardens perhaps, with a glamorous wife in a Chanel coat, two small children in private-school uniforms. I knew he had two boys, grown up now. A little dog maybe: the ultimate Parisian family. Living the dream. Then the fall from grace.

'Oh, I know shit happens, Jean-Claude. I'm in the same business, remember? I see restaurants open and close all the time, sometimes by dint of my pen. So then what? After the divorce. Your wife kept the house?'

'She did. In the Marais. Her father was a divorce lawyer, which helped, and anyway, I just wanted to get away. I left her nearly everything. I'd had an affair, after all, so of course I felt guilty. And when the second restaurant closed, I felt such a failure. Very . . . how you say – humi—?'

'Humiliated.'

'Exactly. So I came down to the south. Decided to move right away from Paris. I wanted to get away from food. Find a different life.'

'But you miss it?'

'I didn't, for two whole years. It was a relief. But, you know, when you create for a living, and then you stop, at first you relish the peace, but then, you itch. Your fingers, you know?' He waggled them ruefully. 'Because it's not a job. It's not an occupation. It's in the blood. Like breathing. For me, cooking is like breathing. So you see, the oxygen, it is gone. And cooking for you tonight . . . ah, *mon dieu*!'

I saw something in his eyes which only came from talking about something – or someone – you adored.

'Would you ever go back to being a chef? Now?'

'In Paris, *non*. I'm done with that city. For ever. But down here, in the south . . .' He shrugged expressively, his head disappearing into his shoulders. 'Who knows? I think it is unlikely, because I don't want to work for anyone else, and to open again on my own – with what?' He spread his hands in an eloquent, empty gesture. 'Buttons, as you say in England? Everything boils down to money, *ma cherie*.'

'I know.' I did. I sighed. 'And what happens when Mum goes back? To England.'

My mother came to sit beside us, glowing with pride for her man. He took her hand.

'I hope she won't go too quickly. I've asked her to stay on for a bit with me, in Valence. Have a bit of a holiday. Maybe help with the shop.'

'Oh. Right.' Controlling as I could be about my children, I could hardly tell my sixty-something mother it was out of the question. And how happy she looked.

'You didn't come through Digne, did you, darling?' Mum lit a cigarette, beaming. 'James said you took the autoroute, but it is complete heaven. A charming, bustling little town with a terrific café society – a bit like Aix, but much smaller. Not nearly so crowded. I thought I could go off to the markets while JC is manning the shop and look at things he doesn't do yet, maybe branch out into linens, antique tablecloths. A bit of lace, that sort of thing.'

Jean-Claude squeezed her hand fondly, but he made a face. 'Except the rest of the south of France has already branched out that way. But we will see.'

'Or maybe dried herbs? In bags? No reason why it has to be exclusively antiques?' she suggested.

Jean-Claude and I roared. 'Herbes de Provence, Mum?

Yes, that's novel. What, in little sacks? I'm sure no one else has thought of that.'

She pouted good-naturedly. 'You tease me, but you wait. I'll think of something. Something to give him an edge.'

I envied them for a moment: their adventure, their happiness. Knew it could end in tears, this holiday romance of Mum's, as all her affairs did, but there was something different about this man. For a start, he was no longer married. A first, for my mother.

The evening slipped on. The children, entirely of their own accord, washed up, and then sauntered off for a swim. Mum and Jean-Claude had an early night and I sat with my in-laws, playing bridge, something I hadn't done for years. It took me back to the days when I first went to Scotland, when James took me home. We'd been going out for some time – might even have been engaged – and I'd been dying to meet his family. He'd cautiously described his sisters on the long drive up, explaining why they hadn't made the move to London, or Edinburgh, or indeed any town at all, as most young people did, why they were so resolutely at home with their father, trying not to make them sound odd. I'd been intrigued. We'd played bridge after supper that first night, and I'd weighed them up. Rachel, I could just about understand: quiet, but with an inner strength, which James told me stemmed from her religious beliefs. But she also seemed to have a strange and misplaced sense of duty, which certainly Drummond didn't expect or encourage. It was as if she, as the elder, less attractive sister, was happy to have an excuse in her widowed father to stay where she was, for ever. Sally, I could never fathom. Already a size sixteen, in dresses that looked like tents, she seemed to grow daily, with every huge meal she cooked and ate furiously. I'd never seen anyone shovel food in so fast; it was as if it were a daily challenge. There was a terrible moment on the last day of our visit when she couldn't get out of a dining-room chair, a carver with arms. We'd had to help her. But I'd always known there was a very attractive woman in there. It was as if Sally were determined she would never emerge. And yes, she was silly and unpredictable – hysterical, sometimes – but she could be bubbly and charismatic, too. Why would she stray no further than the surrounding glens? Never work further than Perth? I'd asked James on the way home. Surely she could come and stay with us? Perfect her culinary skills at one of the London colleges? She was still young; it was never too late.

He'd laughed hollowly. No, no, Sally was better off where she was. And anyway, that would leave Rachel on her own. Sally was fine. And she'd certainly seemed it as she'd clucked excitedly around me on that first visit, thrilled to have a visitor, a potential sister-in-law, showing me every inch of the huge, dreary house, the sterile, windswept garden, where nothing grew except a few hardy shrubs; she was proud of everything. But I'd sensed an underlying nervousness, too. And she'd seemed almost to have to steel herself to go into Kincardine, the tiny town twenty minutes away – twenty minutes to the nearest pint of milk. Now, though, as she laid down the dummy hand opposite me on the bridge table, pretty stacking rings glittering on her tanned fingers, the metamorphosis wasn't just amazing, it was extraordinary. Yes, she was still excitable and watched over carefully, I realized, by Rachel, who had always kept an eye on her, interrupting her sometimes when she was getting out of control, when her voice rose too shrilly, smoothing over conversational faux pas – but there hadn't been many of those this holiday. She'd been much calmer. Better company. What had happened to spark the transition? To make her slim down, leave Scotland, have her first proper boyfriend? Something must have, I was convinced. I watched the sisters as I played cards with them, both so impenetrable and guarded in their own ways.

After another hand, Drummond yawned, and I used it as my cue.

'Yes, I'm tired, too. In fact, I'm ready for bed,' I said, stretching. 'Sorry, everyone, to break up the game.'

'Don't be silly, my dear, I'm ready, too. I'm thrilled you played a couple of hands. Just like old times, eh?' He patted my shoulder. 'I'm off. *Bonne nuit*, everyone.'

Drummond got unsteadily to his feet and both his daughters went to help him, holding his elbows. Rachel reached for his stick, which was propped against the table. She was making to move off with him and take him upstairs, when I said, 'Um, Rachel, you wouldn't give me a hand laying the breakfast table, would you? Only Thérèse and Michel usually do it, and I thought maybe we should . . .'

'Of course!' Rachel, ever solicitous, was shocked she hadn't thought of it herself. She flushed a bit as Sally took over Drummond. I wished I'd had the presence of mind to think of something else, something that wouldn't have made her uncomfortable.

'I'll take Daddy,' Sally assured her, already making steady headway towards the house with her father. 'I've been looking forward to an early night, since Max is out. Toodle-oo!'

'Night!' we both called, as Rachel began busying herself, clearing the debris of ashtrays and glasses from the table. I stayed her hand.

'Rachel, that's not why I asked you to stay. It was all I could think of.'

'Oh?' She paused. Looked down at me enquiringly.

'Sit down a second.'

She sat. Blinked. Looked nervous. 'What is it?'

'I'm just so intrigued. By Sally. Last time I saw her, at Christmas, she was enormous. Played clock patience constantly by the fire, ate tin after tin of Quality Street, barely left the house except to collect the groceries, got terribly upset when she thought someone had taken her favourite cushion from her bed – cried, even, remember?'

'Yes,' Rachel admitted, as we both recalled her running into the drawing room, shaking with sobs, accusing everyone until it was finally found, not on the bed, but under it. She was like a child.

'And now here she is,' I went on, 'slim as a blade, looking gorgeous, a handsome man in tow, off to visit friends in St Tropez – what's happened?'

She laughed. 'Yes, it's amazing, isn't it? Such a turnaround.'

'But what precipitated it, Rachel? Something must have done.'

She shrugged. 'The weight loss, I suppose. If you lose five stone, it's bound to make a big difference.'

'But what galvanized her to do it? To lose it in the first place?'

'No idea. She just did.'

I felt she was being evasive but couldn't be sure.

'What, she just woke up one morning and thought, I know, I won't have four Weetabix for breakfast, I'll go for a run?'

'I suppose . . .'

'It was January, wasn't it?'

Rachel blinked rapidly. Looked beyond me. 'Yes. January. The fifteenth. Just after Donaldson's funeral.'

'Donaldson?'

Her eyes came back. She gave me a peculiar look. 'You remember, Flora.'

'Yes, of course I remember Donaldson.'

He'd been Drummond's right-hand man. His batman, almost. Orderly, I believe it's called in the army. The man he'd brought out of prison with him. The man he'd been close to and had given a cottage on the estate in return for manual labour. Drummond had adored him. They'd shared a cell, and Donaldson, a seasoned convict, a reoffending prisoner, had helped him through some very dark times. They'd been released within six months of one another, and Donaldson had arrived at Brechallis almost immediately. He was a reformed character who spent all his time mending fences, tending the sheep, which he'd learned to do, turning them upside down and clipping toenails, dagging and shearing them, clearing streams. But I'd always been a little scared of this tough, heavily tattooed, inscrutable man. He'd keeled over in a ditch, just after Christmas, trying to release a ewe from some brambles. Heart attack, apparently. Drummond had been terribly upset. He wasn't that old, either; must only have been in his late fifties. James went to the funeral, I remember, but I didn't. But why should his death be the catalyst for Sally to lose weight? I opened my mouth to voice this.

'Coincidence, I'm sure,' Rachel said quickly. She got to her feet. 'I've no idea why I even mentioned it.' She brushed some imaginary crumbs from her lap, not looking at me. 'Sally just got to a stage when she couldn't look at herself in the mirror any longer, that was all.'

'She hadn't been able to do that for a long time,' I said slowly.

It was one of the things I knew about Sally. She avoided mirrors. There were none at Brechallis, except in Drummond's and Rachel's bedrooms. I'd had to put one in the guest bathroom. We all knew Sally didn't like seeing what she'd become; it was common knowledge, even if no one ever mentioned it.

Rachel swallowed. 'Yes. Well. I think it just all came to a head. Anyway, I'll go and get the place mats for breakfast and then I think I'll turn in, Flora. Goodnight.'

She turned and went quickly inside, the conversation over, a curtain firmly drawn. And there was absolutely no chance of reopening it, of that I was sure.

Chapter Twenty

The following morning I awoke late, as seemed to be my wont these days. I'd heard James returning in the early hours, full of the joys, slightly pissed and making just a bit too much jolly noise as he said goodnight in loud stage whispers to his opera comrades on the landing. Faux tiptoeing around the bedroom, he'd banged into furniture and shed his clothes before falling into a noisy, snoring slumber beside me, no doubt dreaming of being on stage in tights and a codpiece, singing his heart out to his leading lady. I, meanwhile, despite the earplugs, couldn't go back to sleep. I tossed and turned, finally waking – I peered at the clock – at a quarter to ten. Annoying. A waste of another day. On the other hand, what was the rush? What, apart from the sun, which even now was streaming in through the shutters James had left ajar, did I have to get up for?

I sat up, stretched languidly and reached for my iPad. I tried not to read emails on holiday, but a glance at the recent additions told me there was one I really should open. I grudgingly complied.

Dear Flora,

Since you didn't feel inclined to attend the crisis meeting I called, and since, as you know, I have to lose at least three members of the

*team in order to ensure the magazine remains viable, I am afraid
I have no alternative but to make you redundant. It goes without
saying that your hard work and loyalty to* Haute Cuisine *over the
years has been exemplary, as has your commitment. I had hoped
not to end our working relationship by email, but I'm afraid you
left me no choice.*

*I do hope we can remain friends and wish you all luck for the
future.*

*Best wishes,
Maria*

I stared, shocked. In fact, I had a bit of an out-of-body
experience. Almost felt as if I were floating up on the ceiling, looking down at myself. I wasn't sure I'd had such a
jolt before. Oh yes, of course. In the pub. In Chelsea. With
Coco. Now, though, despite the world wobbling briefly
and me observing it from on high, it righted itself soon
enough. I floated back down. Because part of me had
known. A small part of me had thought, Don't go back
with Lizzie. Then Maria will have to make you redundant.
Just a small part. One I hadn't even properly admitted to
myself, let alone to James. And a mighty big part of me
realized now that I was relieved. It was sad to hate a job I'd
loved so much, but I did, and I'd wanted someone else to
make the decision for me. To push me. My lip curled,
though, when I reread the email. Crisis meeting? What crisis meeting? She hadn't originally couched it in those terms.
And when had she previously mentioned making anyone
redundant? Never. And if she'd hoped to have the conversation in person, well, then, she'd already decided my fate,

hadn't she? I'd have returned to be informed by Maria, in that little-girl voice of hers, as she peered over the spectacles she wore for effect – we'd all sneakily tried them on – from the other side of her vast, glass-topped desk, and looking down her nose, so tiny after so much surgery it was a wonder she could still breathe through it, that there was no way she was responsible for this decision. That the powers that be – Didier in particular, from the parent magazine in Paris – was forcing her hand and she wished it could be otherwise. Then she'd flick back a sheet of expensively highlighted blonde hair, cross her minuscule knees in her tan leather Christian Lacroix skirt and wait for my reaction.

I thought for a moment, heart pounding, bolt upright in my Primark nightie. Then I reached over the empty expanse of bed for James's phone, which was on his bedside table. Reading the number from mine, I rang Maria's mobile. She answered immediately in her breathy whisper.

'Hello?'

'Maria, it's Flora.'

Shocked silence. Had she known it was me, she wouldn't have picked up, but I knew she wouldn't recognize James's number.

'Oh, um, Flora,' she faltered. 'I'm so sorry.'

'Don't worry, it's not your fault. As you say, it's out of your hands. Can you tell me what the redundancy settlement is?'

'Of *course* I can, darling. Hang on.' I heard her mobile clatter down on the glass desk as she riffled nervously through some papers. She returned a few moments later and mentioned a sum of money so large it made me blink.

271

'Right. A year's salary, then.'

'I'd have liked it to have been more – you've worked for us for nearly eighteen years – but it was the best I could do, Flora.'

'It's fine, Maria. More than I expected. Thank you.'

I doubt if anyone had ever thanked her for firing them. She became expansive in her relief.

'Well, I told them there was no fucking way I was letting you go without a fight, and without a decent package. In fact, I was in the boardroom for two hours on your behalf, giving them what for.'

'And you'll give me good references? Explain the economic imperative for letting me go?' I asked briskly, cutting through the crap.

'Of *course*, darling, glowing references. I suspect you'll get a job on a rival magazine in moments, *and* pocket a year's salary.'

'We'll see,' I said shortly. 'Anyway, I must go.'

'And we'll meet up?' she said urgently. 'We've been friends for years, Flora. No hard feelings?'

'None at all,' I told her, before saying goodbye.

We'd been colleagues for years, not friends. Maria was far too brittle and self-absorbed for me: I doubted I'd ever see her again. But my own phone was ringing now and I lunged to answer it, recognizing the number.

'Lizzie.'

'Oh, Flora, I'm so sorry!' she wailed. 'I feel such a heel!'

'You kept yours?'

'Yes, but only just. I had to creep and crawl around her office for hours, until I thought I was going to be sick all over her carpet, all over her Manolo Blahniks. I just feel so bad for you.'

'Don't,' I told her. 'I half expected it. Half . . .' I paused. 'Wanted it?'

'If I'm honest,' I admitted. I swallowed. 'I'm tired, Lizzie. Tired of doing the same old thing, hammering out copy about another bloody artichoke or another steak tartare and pleasing everyone except myself. I want to go. It's time.'

She was silent on the other end. 'Have you told James?'

'Not yet. Only just heard. Might go and do that now. Are you coming back?'

'You're joking! I'm doing all your bloody restaurants now. Forget the editorial column, I've got breakfast at The Connaught, followed by lunch at Le Caprice and dinner at La Rochelle – they've sacked Henry, too. I'm eating for three!'

I smiled. 'You'll be the size of a house.'

'Don't. I've already googled bulimia. We're all going to miss you so much, Flora. Everyone's devastated.'

This did threaten to choke me. The band of brothers in the little office on Charlotte Street, up those rickety stairs, crammed into our cave, whispering about Maria as she sat in splendid isolation in the room above, united in our common dislike of her. Years ago, we'd all bashed away at word processors, the air full of cigarette smoke and expletives as we mistyped, ashtrays overflowing. No cigarettes now, of course, and only laptops and iPads, so much quieter, but always laughter: me, Henry, Lizzie, Colin, Fatima, Sue, Blodders, Pat, Toenail – I'd miss them all. Miss the banter. The camaraderie. But let's not get too carried away. Let's not oversentimentalize. These days, a lot of copy was written at home; journalism had become a lonely business. Still, I put the phone down feeling sad and nostalgic, and promising I'd ring Lizzie for a proper chat later and, yes, come in and have lunch with them all. At Bellingdon's, our favourite haunt on Charlotte Street, which she'd organize. For Henry, too. Poor Henry. His partner, Graham, had recently been made redundant as well. Then I got out of bed to have a pummelling, invigorating shower and threw on some clothes.

I found James in the drawing room with Camille. I'd followed the music. The hills were alive. There he was, like a dutiful gnome, but taller, on the edge of his chair. This time, she was at the piano, swaying slightly and singing softly as she played.

'Oh – darling.' He got up as I came in, just a bit too quickly. Gave me a hug. Unusual.

'Did you have a good evening?' I asked.

'The best,' he told me warmly as Camille continued to play, not deigning to stop and greet me, I noticed, or even turn and smile.

James put a finger theatrically to his lips, and we crept out. He led me through the open French windows to the garden, where a few people were still having breakfast. He shut the glazed doors quietly behind us.

'It was an amazing evening,' he told me, glowing. 'Gosh, she's got an incredible voice, Flora. It's not until you actually hear her sing, in the flesh, that you realize how extraordinarily gifted she is. Ask Max.'

He and Sally were at the breakfast table in the garden in the sun. I turned.

'Oh, she's quite something,' Max agreed, glancing up from his iPad. 'It's a phenomenal feat to project a voice across three or four thousand people, plus an orchestra of about seventy-odd instruments, with absolutely no amplification at all. One forgets.' There was genuine respect in his voice, and I wondered if Camille had wanted this: for Max to see her at her very best. We didn't meet each other's eyes.

'The whole place erupted when it was announced she was going to make a guest appearance,' went on my husband, eyes gleaming, extraordinarily star-struck. 'No one knew, you see, and you should have heard the roar when she got up to take to the stage – they went berserk! I've never heard such applause! First, she did the duet from *The Magic Flute* with José Carreras – he was also making a guest appearance – and then she sang an aria from *Carmen*. And my God, when she'd finished, you could have cut the air with a knife. Could literally have heard a feather drop. We sat in complete silence. I'm not ashamed to say I cried I was so moved, and even Max here looked a bit moist as we clapped away. We all got to our feet – the whole place was on its feet, wasn't it, Max? – cheering and stamping for ages. Extraordinary!'

'It must have been.'

'And they *implored* her to do another one, wouldn't let her go back to her seat. So she sang "*Un bel dì*" from *Madame Butterfly* – you know?'

'No.'

James and I never went to the opera. I didn't think he liked it. Plus, we couldn't afford it.

'Yes, you *do*.'

'I don't, James. Why would I?'

'It's always on the radio.' He put his hand to his heart. Stood up straight. '*Un bel dì, vedremo, levarsi un fil di fumo, sull'estremo confin del mare,*' he warbled loudly, and only half ironically. James can't sing. At all. He's tone deaf. I felt my eyes widen. Max looked away. '*E poi la nave appare –*'

'Da-ad!' Amelia, at the far end of the table, let her mouth drop theatrically. 'God, stop him, Mum. It's embarrassing!'

Tara was pink, too, but their father was in the grip of an infatuation. He simply laughed at his daughters' distress.

'You girls should get out more,' he joked, gaily plucking a croissant from the basket. He tossed it in the air, bouncing it on his arm like a cricket ball before catching it and munching away heartily. His eyes shone. 'Get some culture.'

The girls made weary eyes at him, and I sneaked a look at Max. James was not normally so foolish and susceptible, and Camille was a very beautiful and talented woman. Max surely couldn't be totally immune to her charms if my husband was so bowled over. As if on cue, Camille appeared through the French windows in a crumpled little white dress. If anything, she looked slightly tired and vulnerable, always a winning combination with men. James gazed at her as if he could eat her up and even Max gave her a longer look than he would normally. He glanced quickly away, but I wondered if her magic was finally working.

'Pool, d'you think, darling?' asked Sally, perhaps wondering, too. 'Another hideous day in paradise?'

'Why not?' Max agreed, getting to his feet and gathering his iPad and book. It was Camille's turn to watch him go. Plan her next move.

Agathe, the ghost child, appeared out of nowhere beside her. She tugged her mother's arm. As Camille bent down, she whispered in her ear, cupping her hands around her mouth, something I'd always told my children was incredibly rude.

Camille nodded grudgingly and allowed herself to be led away. Agathe cast us a glittering, menacing look from her dark eyes as she tugged her mother towards her sister's cottage.

'Pool for you, too, darling?' asked James, gathering up his own book. *A History of the Royal Opera House.* Dear God.

'In a mo. Or I might drive into town. Actually, James, have you got a sec?'

'Sure.' He looked surprised, catching something in my voice.

He made to go back into the house with me, but, knowing the acoustics of our bedroom, I turned and walked the other way, off down the sloping lawn towards the olive grove, chewing my thumb. James caught up with me, and I was aware of Amelia's eyes following us. When we'd gone through the little gate at the bottom, into the longer grass of the orchard, I turned.

'I've lost my job, darling. Maria's made me redundant.'

'Shit.' He stopped. Looked aghast. We stared at one another under the dappled shade of an olive tree.

'But I've got a year's money.'

His face cleared a bit. 'Well, that's something, I suppose. You'll find another job within a year. But what a shaker, Flora. Right out of the blue. Are you OK?'

'I'm fine, actually. And it wasn't so out of the blue. I half expected it.'

'Oh? You didn't say?' He frowned; looked searchingly at me.

'Well, only half,' I said quickly. 'And I didn't want to worry you.' If pressed, I could feel rather guilty about wilfully reducing the family fortunes, not going back to fight my corner. 'And the thing is, James' – I felt my way carefully – 'I may not get a job in the same field.'

'We can't afford for you not to work, Flora.'

'I know. It's just, I don't know if I want to do the same thing.'

He raked a hand nervously through what remained of his hair. 'Well, I'm not sure *I* want to do the same thing, removing bloody bunions day after day, hoiking out ingrowing toenails. But there is something of an economic necessity. A bit of a bloody mortgage to pay, and –'

'Not much.'

'What?'

'Not much of a mortgage left.'

'No, but still. We can't afford for you to do frigging Pilates classes or wine-tasting courses. Flog cashmere gloves at Christmas fairs like some of your friends.'

The wives of rich bankers, he meant. I knew that. And I didn't want to either. Knew I'd tire of that sort of life in seconds.

'No, but the thing is, James, there are other ways. Other . . . hang on.'

Tara and Amelia had made their way down the lawn and were even now picking their way through the field of sharp grass in their bare feet, towards us. We waited.

'What's happened?' asked Tara, before they'd even reached

us. They looked alarmed. Clearly, they'd been watching us from the breakfast table.

I swallowed. 'I've lost my job, darlings.'

'Shit.'

Why did all my family say that?

'Told you,' muttered Amelia.

Tara put her arms around me, hugging me tight. 'Oh, Mum, you must be devastated!'

'Not too devastated, if I'm honest. And don't worry, they've given me lots of money.'

'Oh, well, that's a relief.' She let go. It obviously was.

'How much?' asked Amelia.

'Never you mind,' said James. 'Your mother's being very brave about it, but it's clearly been a terrible shock.'

'Did Lizzie keep hers?'

'She did.'

'But you'd been there longer?'

'Not much. And, anyway, I'm pleased for Lizzie. She needs it more than me. She's on her own.'

'And your mother will get another job in no time.'

'Of course you will,' agreed Amelia. 'Didn't that chap at *Gourmet* headhunt you only last year?'

'Of course!' James struck his forehead with the palm of his hand. 'Well remembered, Amelia. Give him a ring, darling.'

'Well –'

'Or Malcolm Harding? At the *Sunday Times*? He was always bothering you, always wanting you.'

'I just might give it a bit, James.'

'Oh yes, a couple of days.'

'She's in shock,' Amelia told him sternly. 'You're rushing her, Dad. This is huge.'

I felt bad that it wasn't that huge. But then I'd always told my girls a career was so important. The cornerstone of their life. Marriage and babies slotted in. Why? When I'd never really believed it? Marriage and babies were far more important.

'Come on.' My elder-statesman daughter took my arm. 'I'm going to make you some tea. With lots of sugar in it.'

I allowed myself to be led away to be fussed over, feeling a bit of a fraud, if I'm honest. But it was a rare experience in my household, and one I was unwilling to pass up.

Word spread fast. One by one, people came up to commiserate and squeeze my shoulder as if I'd suffered a bereavement. I wondered if this was how people felt when someone they loathed had died and, inside, they were quietly rejoicing. Guilty. But, on the other hand, why should I dissemble?

'I hated it,' I told Max defiantly, when he came to find me. 'I was longing to go. This is a blessed relief.'

Mum was with him. She understood immediately. 'You'd done it too bloody long,' she told me, lighting a cigarette and handing it to me. I dragged hard. 'Everything has a shelf life.'

'Exactly,' I said gratefully. My mother had skipped from one passion to the next all her life and was the happiest person I knew.

'And work is so overrated,' she told me firmly, rather undoing the wisdom.

Camille, after all of half an hour with her own family,

was back amongst us on the terrace. She approached my chair as if I were in A&E, took my hand and pressed it between her two, bird-like ones. 'Your heart is breaking quietly, I know,' she said softly, crouching down. 'It is your life. Your career. You've given your best years. And for women, because we battle so hard, because we smash through the glass ceiling, it is so much harder to bear. Rejection. It cuts us, here.' She pressed my hand to her heart, which was beyond embarrassing. Her breasts were enormous.

I cleared my throat. Extricated my hand with an awkward wiggle. 'No, actually, Camille, you're wrong. It was time for a change.'

'Quite right. The show must go on.' She gave a brave smile and leaned forward to kiss my cheek. 'Such courage,' she whispered, before fluttering away, all male eyes upon her.

That evening, however, I'll admit, I hit the bottle. Despite my relief that the decision had been taken out of my hands and that I'd been generously compensated, there was a need to drink and reflect on how I'd spent most of my adult life: in restaurants, getting to know lovely patrons like Fellino, forging relationships that spanned years. With friends like Lizzie and Colin, meeting deadlines – just – scribbling copy, in editorial meetings. It was goodbye to all that and hello to a different way of life.

Unbeknownst to the rest of my family, I knew this for sure. Felt something click firmly into position within me. I knew I had to be strong, though, to follow through. To really mean it, and deliver. I'd talk to Jean-Claude later. Not tonight. Tonight I just wanted to reminisce and tell my stories. About the time I'd found a wedding ring in my soup, or the waiter who'd flambéed not only the crêpe Suzette but his wig, too. We'd had to stamp it out. The time Lizzie and I had got so disastrously pissed she'd thrown a bread roll at the disapproving couple on the next table and we'd been evicted. Less amusing stories, too, like the time the IRA had planted a bomb in Hyde Park when I'd been at the Berkeley. The horrific scene that had met my eyes as I ran out at the blast. Those enormous brave horses on their sides, the terrible carnage, the young soldiers. Or the time a man had sighed deeply at the table beside me, clutched his heart, fallen from his chair and promptly died. Or when a young man had run into Boulestin, interrupted a couple at the next table and presented a ring to the girl. She'd got to her feet and run off with him. My job, played out as it was in public places, had a certain theatrical element to it; a certain – curtain up – which made it unpredictable. It was live. It was a performance. As was the food. And sometimes it was unbelievably amazing, and sometimes – rarely, thankfully – memorably bad, to the point where I'd have to spit it out. Always, though, I was the revered guest, the star attraction. The red carpet would be rolled out as I was ushered to my table by the maître d', his poker face giving nothing away. Time for someone else to have that thrill, I thought, raising my glass of Sancerre to my lips. Time for some younger – cheaper – reviewer, to be giggly and incredulous, as James and I had been in the beginning at this free lunch for life. Time to move on.

In the moonlight, sitting as I was at the head of the table, I watched as an owl soared up into the dark velvet sky, hooting softly, circling the trees. As it landed on the branch of an oak, it seemed to be in pursuit of something. A mouse? A mate? I was more than a little pissed, but as the owl took off again it suddenly seemed imperative to see if he'd achieved his quarry. Toby and Rory were talking across me now, not rudely, just animatedly, about cycling in London, which Rory did and Toby didn't; a conversation in which I'd previously been participating, adding my two pennyworth. They could manage without me. I stood up – slightly unsteadily, it has to be said. Without disturbing them, I moved quietly down the garden towards the olive grove for a ciggie with the wise old owl: a lean against an ancient, gnarled tree, which had seen a few of life's sea changes. For some time alone, to think.

As I tiptoed down the slope, not wanting to disturb the table, I stopped, abruptly. Snagged on a sound. Muffled voices were coming from my right. I turned, and in the faint half-light of the moon saw two figures, locked in an embrace, in the little gazebo where the barbecue was. At first I thought it was Thérèse and Michel. Then I realized, with a sickening thud of my heart, that it wasn't them at all. It was James and Camille. My husband was kissing Camille with all his might. His eyes were shut, his arms wrapped tightly around her as he towered over her, clasping her to him, giving the embrace every ounce, every fibre of his being.

Chapter Twenty-One

Perhaps if I hadn't been so inebriated I might not have charged in quite so precipitously. Might have given it some calm and measured thought; taken a moment to consider and reflect. Instead, I resorted to immediate intervention and robust rhetoric.

'*What the fuck are you doing!*' I roared. Very loudly.

The whole world stopped. My world, my daughters' world – if I'd thought about it – my mother's, James's. I couldn't have been more destructive if I'd tried.

James and Camille sprang apart like repelling magnets. Camille disappeared out and around the side of the gazebo, melting into the darkness – with a degree of practice, I felt – like a spirit of the night. James stood there, rooted, dumb and horrified, caught in the headlamps that were my eyes and in the elaborate wooden structure – more Gothic temple than garden shed – like a fly in a web. I marched towards him, incensed. He backed away, into the barbecue: tripped over a gigantic set of tongs lying on the floor and fell over backwards with a terrific clatter. As I stood over him, fists clenched, speechless, both daughters rushed up.

'What's happened!' cried Amelia breathlessly. 'Why were you yelling? Oh God – Daddy! Are you OK?' She and Tara lunged to help him. With great presence of mind, I swam to the surface.

'Your father's drunk,' I managed. 'I found him flailing around in here.'

'Well, help him!' retorted Amelia, gently helping her shaken father to his feet. Tara found his glasses. 'Bloody hell, we've all been in that state, including you! You're not such a model of sobriety yourself tonight, Mum. I thought something terrible had happened!'

It had.

'You frightened us,' Tara told me angrily, rounding on me. 'Dad blundering around plastered hardly warrants you yelling like that.'

'Poor Daddy, did you hit your head?' asked Amelia gently.

'Yes,' he bleated.

'Bastard!' I couldn't resist roaring.

Amelia swung around. 'Mum, you have seriously got to stop thinking that the world revolves around you. If Dad decides to get drunk on his holiday, so bloody what. Get a grip, live your own life and *leave him alone*! Come on, Daddy, let's go and find you a chair. Black coffee for you.'

James, blinking in terror in the moonlight and sheltering cravenly behind his daughters' misapprehension, willingly allowed himself to be led away up the garden path to the top of the sloping lawn. As they reached the table under the trees, Amelia turned and cast me a last black look. A space was made for her father to sit down, the boyfriends muttering incredulously at my over-the-top reaction. Sensible James. Safety in numbers, of course. Even at this remove, though, I could feel Max's eyes upon me from the opposite side of the table. I wondered if he knew what had happened. But how could he? From that angle, it would be impossible to see around the corner into the dark gazebo. I just felt that Max had extrasensory perception, somehow: that he was extraordinarily tuned into me and knew I wouldn't scream if my husband were merely drunk. Mum, too, gave me a searching look as I approached. Bidding everyone a shaky goodnight, I went up to my room, trembling, I noticed, to wait for James.

The length of time he took to reach our room was important, I knew. If he was ages, hoping to sneak in when I was asleep, or had calmed down, it was bad news. If he practically followed me up, it was better. Almost as I'd shut the bedroom door and went to sit on the bed, clenching my hands tight, the door flew open. James appeared, white-faced.

'Oh God, Flora, I'm so sorry,' he breathed, shutting the door and crossing the room quickly. 'I don't know what came over me.'

'You fucking bastard!' I spat between clenched teeth. Real spittle, I noticed, shot out.

'Yes.' He looked shattered. Really devastated. 'Yes, I am. I know that. And you have every right to say it. I am so, so sorry, Flora. I regret it with all my heart. I wish to God it hadn't happened.' Bravely, he crept to sit beside me on the bed.

'And what else has happened, eh? What else, James? How many stolen kisses in the moonlight? Or worse!'

'None!' he yelped, leaping off the bed beside me. 'None, ever! That was the first – and last – and absolutely nothing more than that. Nothing worse, I promise!'

I could read James like a book. Knew he was telling the truth. He was incapable of lying. If we didn't want to go to a dinner party, I'd tie myself in knots, thinking of an elaborate excuse, as he'd say, 'Can't we just tell them we don't want to come? That it's too far and we're out the night before, which we are?'

'No, of *course* not,' I'd tell him. 'We'll say you're on call.'

So I could lie and he couldn't. And looking at his frightened, wide eyes behind his glasses as he perched tentatively beside me, I knew the whole story. That his infatuation had led to one stolen kiss in the moonlight, on a balmy Provençal evening, with a very beautiful, very famous woman. But no more than that. Why, then, did I continue to vent my spleen?

'Oh, so you say!' I roared. 'But how can I tell? How do I know what you were really up to last night in Cannes?' I couldn't resist it. I held all the cards, you see. It was so rare. Such a novelty. Such a pity to waste them.

'Nothing!' he whimpered, terrified. 'Honestly, nothing happened – and, and Max was with us the whole time! Ask him!'

Max. That did give me pause for thought. Or slowed me down, at any rate. But not to a grinding halt. Still I swept on, with a valid point, this time.

'And what if I hadn't spotted you, James? What if I hadn't pottered down to have a quiet ciggie in the olive grove? Would you have allowed yourself to be led off to her private quarters? You certainly seemed to be enjoying yourself!'

A mental image of her wrapped in his arms, his eyes shut, face suffused with rapture, came careering back to both of us. He took a moment.

'I don't know,' he said honestly. See? Can't lie. I held my

breath as he thought earnestly. 'I hope not. Believe not.' He looked beyond me as he considered it truthfully. His eyes came back to me. 'No. I agree I was loving that terrible, stolen moment, but the instant it changed to something much more duplicitous, to being led by the hand, creeping round the house to the back stairs, for instance – something would have kicked in. I know it would. In fact, I'm sure of it. I honestly believe that, Flora.'

I did, too. No way would James sneak off to Camille's bedroom up in the tower on a family holiday; locking the door behind him, shedding clothes, hopping round the room trying to get out of his trousers, glasses off, blind without them as Camille waited patiently in bed – no. Banish that image. We both knew it wouldn't have happened. Any more than I would have succumbed to – well. You know. I swallowed, alive to the parallels. To the fearful symmetry. But that was different. Was it? Yes. Definitely. Max was an old boyfriend. I'd kissed him before. It hardly counted. Or did it count more? Surely there was more latent emotion, more feeling between the two of us than there could be between Camille and James? James was ridiculously flattered to be courted by her, and Camille . . . what *was* she up to, I wondered?

'You've been an idiot,' I told him coldly. 'You've been taken in and used. She's in love with Max, James. She's trying to make him jealous. You've been a pawn in her game.'

This hurt, I could tell, and I wished I hadn't said it. I'd never deliberately hurt James, but I was a bit out of control. And a bit out of my depth, situation-wise, too. What did one say or do when one's husband was caught with his trousers down? Surely one got out the big guns? Surely the little ones wouldn't do? I had to make a *bit* of a scene, surely? Couldn't just climb into bed and read as usual? James gazed at the carpet, ashamed. But I wasn't finished.

'I'm disgusted with you, James. Absolutely appalled. That you could betray me like this, and our children, on a family holiday.' Yes. This was the stuff. This was more like it.

'I know, Flora. I'm so sorry.' He gulped. His hand crept along the bedcover and found mine, gripped it hard. He turned huge, pleading, pale-grey eyes upon me, blinking rapidly behind his spectacles. 'Please don't say anything terrible, please. Something that can't be unsaid. It will never happen again. I'll do anything. I'll go home, if you like. We can say the hospital rang, that Peter Hurst's been taken ill and I need to go back. I'll do anything to save us, to recover this. I love you more than anything in the world – you know I do. It was just a silly infatuation, an idiotic mistake, but it will never, ever, happen again. I've been a vain, gullible fool, but please God don't say anything terrible. Words we've never said before.' He was near to tears, and I realized I was, too. I thought of his look of rapture as he kissed her. Something I hadn't seen for a long time – because marriage wasn't like that, was it? Particularly a nineteen-year-old one. You didn't go around in a state of unadulterated bliss, gazing into each other's eyes, holding hands.

I sighed.

If we'd been in London, I realized, if this had happened at home, we'd have slept in separate bedrooms. But we couldn't do that here. I could, I supposed, go to Lizzie's room, which was empty, but that would involve making a scene, and I didn't want that. Instead, we both went separately to the bathroom – not together, as usual, one having a pee whilst the other brushed their teeth – then, night-clothes on, we stole into bed and turned away from each other. I tried not to think about what might have happened if I hadn't intervened. The next kiss. I was sure there would have been one of those. The panting and the mutterings before he resisted the bedroom in the tower. Tried not to imagine James's lovely heart beating rapidly, so smitten, his passions so aroused, but it was hard. His heart and mind and soul and sex drive – sex was very important to James, he took it seriously – had been mine for so long. I couldn't help but feel hurt, even though my head told me this episode was a nonsense. Couldn't help but feel wounded in the moment, not yet an hour after the event.

Eventually – and I knew James wasn't asleep, heard none of the rhythmic snoring I usually did the moment his head hit the pillow – I got up, took a sleeping pill in the bathroom, came back and fell into a dreamless coma.

When I awoke, a cup of tea was beside the bed. A few sprigs of lavender, too, in a tiny vase. The tea was a bit cold, but I drank it. He obviously hadn't wanted to wake me. When I went down, quite late, he and his father were at the breakfast table.

'Hello, darling.' James's eyes were anxious.

'Hello.'

'Thérèse has made some pancakes. I kept a couple warm for you. Would you like them?'

'No, thank you.'

I helped myself to coffee and a croissant.

'Would you like a little trip today, darling? Shall we go into Grasse, perhaps? It's the centre of the perfume industry, apparently. You could try a few out?'

'It'll be terribly crowded, James.' I was trying to be nice, but it was hard.

'Camille's ex owns one of the scent factories there, apparently,' Rachel said, joining us, sitting down.

Silence at the mention of her name.

'Or Tourrettes, perhaps? There's a glorious view from the top of the hill?'

'Yes, perhaps.'

Or perhaps some time alone, to think, I wanted to say. Not about anything drastic, just some time apart. Surely that would do us good. But James was a bit frantic. A bit scared. I could be a bit chilly, you see. A bit scary. But sometimes, when I was in a corner, I didn't know how to be anything else. And him being scared made me worse.

'Or there's an art exhibition in Seillans, I keep seeing the posters advertising it. You'd like that, wouldn't you, darling?'

Rachel wasn't stupid. She looked from one to the other of us. Didn't say anything.

'Lovely,' I said faintly. 'Let's do that, then.'

'Leave in about twenty minutes?'

'Perfect.'

It was as if we had a date. Drummond glanced up from the iPad he'd been engrossed in. Getting the *Daily Telegraph* every day courtesy of Rory had made his holiday. 'To a gallery, you say?' Drummond was fond of art.

'Yes, but let's let James and Flora see if it's any good first,' said Rachel quickly. 'You know what these Provençal shows can be like. All vibrant colours and cubist disasters. Cézanne gone wrong.'

'Oh. Yes. Ghastly.' Drummond shuddered. 'Quite right. Can't be doing with all that.'

He went back to his newspaper, and Rachel and her brother communed silently, James thanking her with his eyes. They were very close, these two. Sometimes, over the years, it had surprised me how close, because neither was demonstrative about it. There was no big hug, or 'Lovely to *see* you!' when we went to Scotland. But James would go out on the hill with her a lot. Long walks. She wasn't a night bird like Sally, who would stay up until three drinking and talking, but she liked walking and James liked her company. She hardly ever came to London – in fact, I could count on one hand the times in our married life she had – but if I lost my phone and borrowed his, or vice versa (oh yes, that happened regularly) Rachel's was possibly the most recent number I'd see. They talked. It occurred to me he might conceivably tell her about last night. Which would be fine. She'd be good. Was quietly good at most things in life, even though she didn't lead a busy one, or a married, complicated one. But perhaps that gave her special insight? No, I wouldn't mind if he talked to Rachel.

The children appeared. James endured a certain amount of teasing about his condition last night and the state of his head this morning. Drummond roared with laughter. Happily, he'd been in bed and was none the wiser. And he loved their jokes.

'Was your father a bit squiffy last night, then?'

'He was off his head, Grandpa. Fancy a nice glass of

beer, Dad? Or perhaps a few press-ups and a jog around the block?'

'Bugger off, you lot,' James said good-naturedly, pleased to have their presence, which diluted their mother's. 'When *haven't* you woken up with a hangover?'

'Not often,' agreed Toby seriously. He straddled a chair backwards and got out his tin of tobacco, reading the situation wrongly, as usual. 'And, actually, I sometimes wonder if I ever draw a sober breath. One day just merges into the next, you know? It's like a total blur, man.' There was a silence. 'I mean – out here,' he added quickly, glancing up from his tobacco and seeing James and I join forces in the stony-look department.

'How's that management-consultancy application coming on, Toby?' asked James, uncharacteristically. It was the sort of thing I might have said, or badgered him to ask, but he wouldn't. Would regard it as interfering, or controlling. I realized he was doing it to please me.

'Yeah, I've almost filled it in,' replied Toby, surprised. He put the lid back on his Golden Virginia. Swung his legs round and sat properly on his chair. 'Sending it off when I get back.'

'Good.'

'Great,' said Amelia, under her breath. 'Two of them now. Happy days.'

'Life is not all beer and skittles, Amelia,' I told her, wondering why. This was surely entering a battleground I neither needed nor wanted on holiday. Perhaps I was supporting James. Showing I appreciated his solidarity. To my surprise, she didn't flare up or stalk off.

'I know, but do you know why we all think it is? Why we all regard it as one huge bowl of cherries?'

'No, do tell?' asked Drummond delightedly. He adored Amelia. Admired her spunk, he said, which always made her giggle.

'It's because you've kept us as children for too long. Poring over us, controlling us, always so interested in our lives, wanting to look at our Facebook pages – we're incapable of functioning on our own. If fifty is the new forty, eighteen is the new fourteen. I'm just a baby.' She widened her dark-brown eyes. 'It's not my fault I'm so reliant on you, Mummy, so helpless. You've made me that way.'

'Your generation grew up much quicker,' Tara agreed. 'You were left to sink or swim, so you swam.'

'That's true,' agreed Drummond quietly.

'You've coddled us,' said Amelia, warming to her theme. 'So now we can't grow up. You'll have to look after us for ever.' She gave a bolshie grin.

'I might have known it was my fault,' I said.

'Actually, it's the fault of technology,' said Rory. 'The only reason my mother can get hold of me every day is because of my iPhone.'

'Does she?' I asked, surprised.

'No, because I've turned if off. Told her there's no signal. But she would. Not every day, but a lot. She can't stop herself. And it's not healthy.'

'No,' I agreed, thinking of my own upbringing. James's. Were either of those any healthier?

'I think there's some middle ground,' said Rachel sensibly, 'which perhaps the next generation will find.'

'You mean when we have children?' Tara asked her.

'Exactly.'

This sobered them up a bit, as they contemplated how they'd do it.

'I'll let them do exactly what they want,' said Amelia predictably. 'Make their own mistakes. Learn by them.'

I smiled. No point even being drawn into this one. It struck me that James and I could never part. Never go our separate ways. This was such a two-pronged effort. Such a struggle.

'Yes, well good luck with that,' James said shortly. 'I hope you enjoy clearing up the mess.'

'So many children are still living at home at thirty,' Rory said. 'Did you know, in Spain, the average child leaves home at twenty-eight?'

'Exactly, because our development has been stunted,' Amelia told him. Nothing was ever her fault.

'No, because of economics. Your generation could buy your own houses. We'll never be able to do that,' Toby told us.

James's eyes sought mine in mock-horror. I didn't respond, though. The thought of thirty-year-old Toby and Amelia living with us was indeed appalling, but I wasn't ready to join James on any jovial level yet. I drained my coffee and made my way back upstairs, leaving them to their discussion, which would go on for ages, round and round in pointless, rather boring circles, with Amelia feeling more abused and aggrieved at every turn.

No sign of Camille, of course, I noticed, pausing a moment at the tall window halfway up the stairs, where all the discarded books seemed to gather on the sill. I gazed out down the front drive to the lodge. She'd made herself very scarce. Had gone into Cannes with Max, Sally told me, when I'd run into her just now at the foot of the stairs. Sally had been on her way to the pool. I'd been startled, but she hadn't looked remotely concerned.

'They had to tie up a few loose ends, business-wise, after Wednesday night's performance. The sponsors wanted to have lunch with her, take some photos for PR, that kind of thing. It was part of the deal, apparently. And she didn't want to go alone. Obviously, Max had to go because he's the promoter.'

Obviously. Or was Camille's plan working? I knew Max had been alive to the fact that something had happened last night in the gazebo. Were these men, one by one, falling like flies, slotting perfectly into her grand plan?

'And, actually, it's lovely to have a quiet day without the boyfriend around,' Sally giggled. 'I've put a treatment on my hair – it feels like straw with all this sun.' She patted her oiled locks. 'And I'm going to bake all day and read a crappy book. No need to impress Max with a Booker Prize winner today!' She flourished a fluorescent paperback gaily before sorting through the basket on the hall table where all the sun creams were tossed, ready for a peaceful day by the pool.

I watched as, suntan lotion retrieved, she appeared beneath me now, and went through the front door and down the steps. She padded across the gravel drive in her espadrilles, a basket swinging from her shoulder, hat in hand, long legs already brown and unbelievably slim. As she went, she passed Michel coming in the opposite direction, down the box-lined drive from the lodge, towards the house. He carried some vegetables in a trug. They smiled and exchanged a few pleasantries before moving on. Sally tracked right across the sloping lawn towards the walled garden and the pool. As he came closer to the house, Michel stopped. He looked up at the tall window where I was standing, and gave me a very direct look. A very cold look. Flustered, I moved away. But it had chilled me. Why, I didn't know. Clearly, he had just glanced up, sensing someone's eyes upon him, that was all. I hurried on up to my room. Quickly, I changed my shoes, found my basket, slicked on some lipstick and made to go back downstairs. Before I did, I closed the shutters against the sun to keep the room cool. In the front drive I saw James already waiting, leaning against the bonnet of the car.

I put my dark glasses on as I went down the front steps into the gravel and the glare of the sun. I might not be looking forward to this little trip, but I was glad we were doing it. Could see the sense, actually. It would clear the air. Draw something of a line. James had parked on the far side of the fountain under the trees in the shade, and I didn't hurry as I crossed the drive. Trailed my fingers a moment in the cool water. It was hot and, anyway, he'd kissed another woman last night. Let's not forget that. He could wait. As I reached the car and put my hand on the door handle I caught sight of his face across the roof. It wasn't the Flora-pleasing one of last night: the abjectly apologetic, craven one. It wasn't even the nervous one of this morning at breakfast, let alone the scared one. It was a furious one. Indeed, it was pale with anger. I blanched with shock as his eyes hit mine, glittering behind his spectacles.

'Get in,' he said tersely. 'We have a lot to talk about.'

Chapter Twenty-Two

We shot off up the drive at speed. Shocked, I put my hand out on the door to steady myself. Gravel sprayed beneath the tyres. My husband did not drive like this; like something out of an American cop drama. And why was he driving at all?

'So,' he said curtly. 'You and Max.'

I inhaled sharply. Felt the blood drain from my head. Had he really said that?

'What d'you mean, me and Max.' See? I can lie. Instinctively. Reflexively.

'Don't try to fib your way out of it, Flora. You were seen. Grappling and panting in his arms the other night. Michel saw you.'

'Michel?' I repeated faintly, my head spinning.

'Yes, he was going back to his cottage. You weren't quite careful enough, you see. Away from the house, sure, but not from the staff.' James's face was dangerously pale as he whipped a glance across at me. 'You disgust me. In so many ways.'

'How did you? I mean –' I was horrified, and hot with shame at being caught. I was scared, too. More so than James would have been.

'How did I find out? He told Camille, who's just rung me. Don't try and deny it, Flora, you know full well what happened. And who knows what else, too.'

I recalled Michel's face just now. Vengeful. That was the look I'd been unable to place. And, of course, I'd accused him of something terrible earlier on in the week. Revenge was surely a dish best served cold.

'Nothing else,' I whispered as we sped along the lanes much too fast, vineyards flashing by. The sun was beating down, hotter than ever, a furious heat, it seemed. Sunflowers glared and nodded accusingly at me, their enormous, round faces scarily nightmarish: not so pretty today. I somehow found my voice. 'Honestly, James, just one kiss. I swear to God. Swear on the girls.'

He glanced at me at this.

'I – don't know why it happened. A warm night, too much to drink – who knows. It was a nonsense. Just like . . . well.'

'No, nothing like me and Camille. And no, we are not all square, not remotely, if that's what you were going to dare to suggest. In the first place, you haven't even had the grace to apologize and you made me crawl.'

'I'm sorry, James.' I looked down at my hands.

'Really crawl.' His lip curled.

'I'm truly sorry. It meant nothing. I promise.'

'And, in the second place, which is far more pertinent, I don't believe it meant nothing. There is a world of difference between a stolen kiss with a famous opera star with whom I am childishly infatuated, and falling into the arms of a man with whom you were once head over heels in love and engaged to.'

'I disagree.'

'Oh really? Don't be fatuous, Flora. Even I, who don't fit into the jealous-husband mould, can see that he still

299

adores you, which, up until now, has given me something of a perverse pleasure this holiday, I'll admit. Something of a gratuitous kick. Knowing you're mine and not his. But now I know the pleasure is all his.'

'Of course it's not! I told you, it was a drunken one-off.'

'And you felt absolutely nothing?'

'I –' I tried to answer honestly, as he had last night: knowing James would demand nothing less. Would see through anything else.

'I – yes. I felt something.'

A muscle went in his cheek. I lunged for the lie instead.

'I felt transported back in time, that was all. A trip down memory lane.'

'You wanted him.'

Why was it all about sex, for men?

I sighed. 'No. That I can answer truthfully. If you mean – did I want to charge upstairs and take all my clothes off – no. It was more . . .'

James thumped his chest with his fist. 'More in here?'

I felt panicky. He wanted me to be honest, and what was the result?

'I was moved, OK? Touched. God, James, who wouldn't be?'

He nodded. 'You got a glimpse of the life you could have had if you hadn't settled for second best.'

'Oh, don't be absurd!' I turned to him in horror. This was very unlike him. James was famously self-assured. Not arrogant, but happy in his skin. 'You're saying that out of anger – you've never felt that, I'd know it. You're saying it because you can, because it conveniently fits the argument.'

'I don't think you're in any position, Flora, to determine what I can or can't say.'

'No. I realize that.'

'You didn't even have the decency to let me off the hook last night, knowing you were in the same boat. That's disgraceful.'

'I know.'

'It makes me dislike you as a person.'

'Don't say that, James,' I said quietly.

'It's true.'

We drove on in silence. I sensed a clenched calmness sweep over him. Knew he was livid, which rarely happened.

'I think we need some time apart.'

I swallowed hard. 'You said last night we shouldn't say anything terrible. Words we'd regret. That's something terrible.'

'I know, but it's what I feel. I don't know you at the moment, Flora. Can't bear to look at you.'

'You mean a day or two? A week? I could go to Mum's when we go back.'

'No, I mean one of us goes home now. I can't bear this situation. Won't be able to cope. I'll take you to Nice this afternoon. When we get back. There's a flight at six. We can tell the girls you've decided to fight for your job. Gone to see Maria.' He pulled sharply into a layby beside a field of lavender, jerking to a halt. 'Something you should have done anyway, like Lizzie.' He turned in his seat behind the wheel to face me properly, his eyes furious. We were clearly not going to an art exhibition in Seillans. 'You need to think about what you want, Flora. Do you want to continue to support this family, to make it a joint effort, or d'you want to play the frivolous frustrated housewife instead? Chuck in your career and have an affair with an old boyfriend? Or even make a life with an old boyfriend? After all, he's single, and it's clearly why he's here, which is pretty elaborate when you think about it. He obviously has no feelings at all for my poor sister.'

It was my turn to flare up. 'Well, that's not my fault! And I'm insulted you'd suggest for one moment that I'd disappear with him. You're being totally disingenuous. You know that's not true. I told you, it was a stupid indiscretion, and yes, I should have gone easy on you last night, under the circumstances, but human nature isn't always like that. I *was* incensed, still *am* incensed at the thought of you kissing another woman, because I love you, James.'

We were silent a moment, both inwardly fuming; both very hurt. Both having hurt each other and knowing it had changed our marriage in some way which felt irreparable at the moment, and terribly sad, but reason also telling us it was only the here and now, sitting in this car fighting, not the reality long term. So why did I have to go home? The thought appalled me. A kiss each. Stupid, but not a tragedy, surely? But I couldn't see into James's mind completely. He'd always kept a tiny bit back. Not his love, just a part of him, which made him special, I thought. Interesting. He was less heart on sleeve, warts and all, than I was. But what if that something was a slight meanness of spirit? He turned away from me now, to look out of the window across the fragrant mauve valley, his face a mask. There'd been a handful of times when I couldn't see into his soul and this was one of them.

'Come on, James.' I reached for his hand. 'Let's sleep on it. You've just found me out, and you're incensed, as I was incensed last night, but I'm calmer now, after a night's sleep. Can see it for what it is. A silly mistake. Ruining everyone's holiday is not going to help.'

'We wouldn't be ruining everyone's holiday, just yours.' He said this coldly. He really did despise me right now. 'I can't help it, Flora. I can't stop seeing you in his arms. I want to kill him.'

And James was such a mild man.

'And we can't ask Sally to leave, to take him away. Can't tell her what you've done. Which is pretty atrocious behaviour towards your sister-in-law, incidentally.' He started the engine again. 'No. You'll have to go home.'

We drove on in silence.

In point of fact, we did go to Seillans, or at least we parked outside the gallery, up on a pavement in a tiny side street. James went inside to get a brochure to prove we'd been. I sat still, staring ahead. He was right, I wasn't a nice person. I'd betrayed him, and also betrayed Sally, and then been a total hypocrite last night. Home in disgrace was the best I could hope for. But I was still shocked by his decision.

I thought of the house in Clapham – musty and dark, north-facing, but I'd never really minded; had resolutely painted it creamy, light colours to compensate, but it seemed gloomier than ever somehow, these days, and always much darker, of course, after a sybaritic holiday in the sun. But Clapham was the truth, the reality. This was just a dream. I gazed around at the ebb and flow of beautiful, tanned people in holiday mode on the cobbled street which led down to the main square, where pretty bunting stretched between the mottled plane trees beneath an azure sky, and where waiters were setting tables for lunch around the fountain. This wasn't real. Except, for some people, it was, I thought, singling out those who clearly weren't tourists: those with their basketfuls of groceries, with more purposeful looks on their faces as they dodged the ambling crowd, tiny dogs trotting beside them on leads. Of course, they had their dramas, their disappointments, their tragedies even, but didn't this glorious setting, this heavenly climate, make everything more bearable? Being tired and cross here wasn't the same as being tired and cross in the Southside Shopping Centre, or trudging up Lavender Hill in the rain with shopping, or sitting on the South Circular in a traffic jam. And I had to leave. James knew it was a punishment. Knew I'd feel it keenly. He was being deliberately harsh.

I watched as he came out of the gallery a few minutes later, shutting the door on the predictable blaze of sunny landscapes in the gallery window, his face set and angry. Of course, he was still in shock. He'd only just found out. He was bound to be upset. I felt nervous, though. James didn't make empty gestures. He didn't order his wife home from holiday without meaning it. And, however it might look to outsiders, he wore the trousers in this marriage. I might make all the noise as I flapped about with the smaller sails, rushing from side to side shrieking, as one boom after another swept over, threatening to decapitate us, narrowly missing us, but James's was the hand on the tiller.

We drove home in silence, my mouth inexplicably dry. James took a detour through a couple of unfamiliar villages to give us time: to enable us to tell the folks back home we'd had a lovely time at the gallery. I knew it was giving us time, too, as we purred slowly past the old men playing boules in the main square, or sitting outside a bar with a café cognac, their wives gossiping on doorsteps or outside shops: I also knew from his taut, clenched face that, instead of calming down, if anything, James's quiet fury was gaining momentum.

'You tell them I'm going,' I told him when we reached the chateau, pulling up at the open front door. 'I might burst into tears and give the game away. You tell them I'm going back to see Maria.'

'Sure,' he said, as if I'd asked him to tell them they were having pizza for lunch.

I knew he'd be fine, too. Knew he'd make it so casual and low key they wouldn't bat an eyelid: *Oh poor Mummy, what a bore, but she'll be back in a couple of days*, I could hear Amelia saying, before going back to her iPad, or her book, in the sun. And then, when I didn't come back, he'd say I was working things out with Maria, and they'd nod, knowing Mummy was being responsible, as adults had to be sometimes – not them, of course, not yet. They were the new fourteen. And James would wander off to read his book under the trees, mission accomplished: which made him quite a consummate liar, too, really, didn't it? Quite the deceiver. And why was my crime so much more atrocious than his, I thought defiantly as I climbed the stairs to my room. So much more heinous? Because we both knew it meant more, I reflected, packing a bag, wondering if I should take the lot: if I'd be back. Would James summon me, after a decent length of time? Probably not, I thought, with rising terror, but still, I only took hand luggage. Let him sort the rest out. Odd that I wasn't fighting this, I pondered as I packed my sponge bag in the bathroom. Not putting my foot down, saying, Don't be ridiculous, I'm not a child, of *course* I'm not going home. Just going quietly.

As I was rooting around for my passport in the bedside drawer, zipping it into my bag on the bed, the door opened. Tara came in, pale-blue eyes wide.

'Daddy says you're going home.'

'I think I should, darling,' I said, forcing a smile. I might have known this one wouldn't go straight back to her iPod. 'I've had that job for eighteen years. Can't just throw in the towel. If I was in London, I'd march round and have it out with her, so I think I'd better march home and do the same now.'

'I suppose.' She bit her thumbnail and sat on the bed in her bikini, slim and brown. I threw a few more bits in my bag. 'Except yesterday, you said you didn't mind.'

'Shock, I suppose.' I kept the bright smile going, making myself look at her and trying to appear as cheery as possible. Her blue eyes in her tanned face looked worried. 'Is everything OK? Daddy seemed a bit ... you know. Clenched.'

'I think he's a bit cross I didn't think of it sooner. I mean, going home,' I said, trying to stick as close to the truth as possible: the best way to lie. 'I should have been the one to see our finances wouldn't survive this, but I was a bit swept away with the glamour of being here. All of this!' I swept my hand to indicate the high-ceilinged room, its elaborate cornice, the canopied bed, the chandelier, the view out of the open window to the hills and the sea beyond.

She nodded. 'And you'll be back?'

'Of course I'll be back, darling!' I gave her a hug. Squeezed her tight. 'Now, I'm going to put you in charge of making sure people don't treat the place too much like home: empty the odd ashtray, chivvy the others to stack the dishwasher occasionally to help Thérèse ... d'you think you can do that?'

'Of course.' Tara did that sort of thing anyway. She walked to the door with me as I picked up my bag. 'Rachel says she'll take you to the airport.'

'Oh, really?' I stopped short of the door. 'Not Daddy?'

'No, he's gone to the vineyard to get some more wine with Sally and Grandpa. He said he'd told you? Said good-bye already?' Her brow puckered and her worried eyes searched mine.

'Oh, yes. Yes, of course he did. I forgot. I thought he meant he was going later, after supper.'

'But he said goodbye?'

'Of course he did, darling, stop worrying!' I laughed, squeezing her shoulders as I went on, but only my mouth was smiling; my head was spinning. Crikey. Where was James? In his head? Shot of me already?

I prattled on about it being good to be able to give the plants back home a watering, that I was pretty sure Maddy, our neighbour, didn't get round to it as often as she might. About how I'd have lunch with Lizzie, maybe launch a sustained attack on Maria, a show of force – 'girl power!' I joked, raising a clenched fist. Tara raised a thin smile.

At the foot of the curved staircase, in the cool of the limestone hall, Rachel was waiting with her handbag and her car keys. I got a shock when I saw her eyes. Scared.

Knowing. Had he told her? My heart jumped. What had he told her?

'Bye, darling!' I said brightly to Tara, giving her another quick hug. 'Say goodbye to the others for me!'

'Aren't you going to? They're only out there.' She pointed to the terrace, which could just be seen through the French windows of the inner hall, where some of the party were gathering for lunch. It would be odd not to say goodbye to my other daughter, who was ambling across in a sarong, book in hand. She saw me through the open door and came across.

'Ma. Gather you're deserting us.' She took off her sunglasses. Looked surprised. So I'd got that a bit wrong, too.

'Yes, off to grovel,' I chortled, giving her a hug.

'Unlike you?'

'Oh, I have my obsequious moments.'

'Well, if she says no, spit in her coffee.'

'Will do. Bye, everyone!' I tripped across the hall and stuck my head around the door, but didn't set foot outside. The boys went to get up, but I was too quick for them, gave them a cheery wave and darted back.

'Say goodbye to Mum and JC for me, will you?' I asked Amelia as I returned to the front hall.

'They're only by the pool.'

'I know, but we've got to hustle if I'm going to catch this plane. Toodle-oo!'

And, with that, we were off, Rachel and I, leaving my daughters standing together on the front steps watching us go, their boyfriends, unperturbed, already back to their game of cards. But blood was quite thick, I thought, as they shaded their eyes with their hands, waving uncertainly as Rachel and I drove off. And their faces said it all as I studied them in the wing mirror: how unlike Mum. Totally unlike Mum. But I could put it down to age, or hormones, or, of course, their father.

As we swept up the drive it occurred to me that Rachel's fingers on the steering wheel were tight. She'd barely said anything. Her mouth was pursed, too, as she stared straight ahead at the road. I felt cross suddenly, at this melodrama. OK, nothing much happened in Rachel's life, but could she please get a sense of proportion? Could everyone get a sense of proportion? Including James?

'Rachel, what's he said to you? James? You look like I've fallen so far from grace there's no hope of redemption for me in this world, let alone the next. As if I'm a scarlet woman!'

'You're not, are you?' She glanced at me.

'No, of course I'm bloody not! I kissed him, for God's sake, after a drunken evening. Just as James . . . anyway. And now I'm being sent home in disgrace like a fourteen-year-old.'

'He can't help it, Flora. I know it seems like a huge over-reaction, but it's not his fault.'

This annoyed me. The sister knowing more than I, the wife, did.

'Well, he *can* help it, if only he'd give it a bit of rational thought. He's jolly lucky I'm complying and not staying for a stand-up, knock-down fight.'

'He was so sure of you, you see. Knew you'd never stray. This is shattering for him.'

'A kiss,' I said weakly, knowing she was right. That James was shattered. That I couldn't have stayed.

'It's what it symbolizes. And who it was with. I think

he was almost enjoying having Max here, knowing he was desperately in love with you and that you wouldn't give him a second look.'

I was silent. It was indeed so terribly different to him and Camille. I licked my lips. Swallowed. We drove on in silence. I knew they went deep, these siblings, but I wondered how deep. Deeper than with me? I felt jealous. Knew it would take so long to undo this. I also felt utterly exhausted.

The magical scenery swept by. At length, though, the vines, the sunflowers and the lavender gave way to villages, then ribbon development, then solid urbanization. As we reached the outskirts of Nice, where washing hung from tenement windows and stray dogs trotted purposefully along pavements, a couple of women, tottering in mini-skirts and heels, shoulder bags on chains, stepped out in front of us at a pelican crossing. Rachel stopped sharply. We watched as they made their way across, cackling with laughter, leg muscles bulging from the strain of the heels, faces over made up, on their way to town. As she shifted into first gear, Rachel said softly, 'It's to do with Mum.'

I gazed straight ahead. Nodded. 'I know,' I said, equally quietly. We drove on.

I did know. About James, Rachel and Sally's mother. Drummond's wife. Of course I did. I watched as the two women disappeared from view in my wing mirror. About how she'd tottered – or driven – into town with a faceful of slap. Until Drummond had had enough. They'd all had enough. I blinked rapidly as Rachel took the slip road up to the airport. And of course I'd been conscious of the nature of our bond in the early days: how we'd clicked so quickly. Why, perhaps. Why I wasn't shocked by his

childhood. Because I'd endured something equally uncon-
ventional, with my own mother. Why he totally understood
about me being unable to forgive Max's infidelity. As he
was unable to forgive me now. He'd always said he'd be
incapable. Made that clear. I used to joke and ask what he'd
do if I ran off with the milkman?

'Oh, tuck a child under each arm and head for the
wide-open spaces,' he'd say. Meaning it.

'My children, too!' I'd retort, knowing it would never
happen: that I never would.

'You'd have to fight me for them.'

A grim courtroom drama had flashed through the banter like a sharp knife. He'd already contemplated it.
Thought it through. And now, here he was, making me
head away from my children; my girls, standing uncertainly
together in their bikinis and sarongs in the drive, shading
their eyes to watch me go. What was he putting in motion?
When all the time . . . the ecstasy on his face as he kissed
Camille swept back to me in a rush, like the tide surging up
the beach: the complete and utter abandonment.

'I'm sorry!' I said to myself as we approached the terminal building, but actually aloud, too. 'No, I'm sorry, it's
just not on!'

Rachel came to a halt behind a row of cars outside
Departures. She didn't speak.

'It's not fair, Rachel. And I won't tell you why, but it's not.'

She looked neither surprised nor startled by my out-
burst. In fact, she didn't look at me at all. We both got out
of the car and she waited while I went around to the boot
and got my bag. I came back and kissed her. Thanked her
for the lift.

'I'm sorry. None of this is your fault.'

'And none of it is yours, either, really,' she said ruefully, so ruefully that I caught on her tone. But she was already getting back in the car, putting on her seat belt, glancing in her rear-view mirror to pull away. And then she was off.

I stood for a moment, mid-pavement, the warm breeze snaking around my bare legs, watching her go. I turned and walked towards Departures. As the glazed doors slid open automatically I felt the chill of the air conditioning. A blast of reality. I was still musing on Rachel's words as I glanced up at the screen to check my flight. Delayed. Oh, splendid. By how long? It didn't say. And it wasn't the only one, either: many were, I noticed. Resignedly, I joined the queue behind the familiar orange easyJet desk.

The commuters were the usual suspects: middle-class, middle-income families disgruntled at being herded like cattle, with only a distant memory of the glamour of a bygone era of air travel, too poor to upgrade to a better, classier airline. As I queued, I became increasingly incensed by Rachel's words. *Not your fault.* Too right, it wasn't my fault. We'd both had a difficult time, a difficult upbringing. Both been true and loyal throughout our married life and both had a minor indiscretion, astonishingly, within days of one another. Wherein, then, lay the difference? All of a sudden, I caught my breath. Not in the same queue but leaning languidly against a desk at the next counter was a more urbane, sophisticated sort of traveller. One in a crisp chambray shirt, stone-coloured chinos, with a deep tan and very deep-blue eyes. It was Max. Watching me. Waiting for me, even. I swallowed. Left the line of passengers and walked towards him. Herein, of course, lay the difference.

Chapter Twenty-Three

'You are absolutely the last person I need to see,' I told him, dropping my bag, practically on his foot. 'You are the reason I've been sent home in disgrace.'

'I know.' He tried not to grin. Failed. His eyes sparkled naughtily.

'What are you doing here?'

'Waiting for you.'

'You knew I'd be here?'

'Sally told me.'

'Well, I'm on my way home, Max.'

He affected a long face. 'Shame.'

I narrowed my eyes. 'And my marriage may well be over.'

'I doubt it. Come on. Let's go and have lunch.'

'Use your eyes, please. I'm getting a plane.'

'I know, but it's delayed, they all are. Baggage handlers' strike, didn't you know?'

'No. I didn't. Shit. *Bugger.* I'll ask,' I cast about wildly.

'I already have. At least five hours, they say. Most are leaving tonight, though. You'll be OK.'

'Will I?' I said grimly.

'Come on, I'm starving. Let's go into Nice.'

'No, thanks. I'll get a sandwich here and wait.' I sat down on my case. A bit like Paddington Bear. But it was small and squashy – hand luggage, remember – so I wobbled precariously.

'Oh, don't be absurd, you've got hours! The only reason this lot aren't going anywhere is because they haven't got some knight in shining armour waiting to whisk them away for a slap-up meal. Where's the harm, Flossie? I'm not going to jump on you. Don't get ahead of yourself.'

The harm, as we well knew, was in the chat, the drink, the banter, and how it would look to James. But, actually, I was becoming increasingly furious with that man. It occurred to me that I had broken away from Max of my own volition: would he have broken away from Camille if he hadn't been interrupted? Forget running up to her bedroom in the tower – we all knew he wouldn't do that – but what about a lengthy grapple in the gazebo? Not one kiss but several? A spot of first base? He'd have been up for that, I bet. How dare he send me home?

'Wait here,' I muttered. I strode off to find an orange-clad easyJet official, no mean feat at the best of times, but particularly impossible in an airport packed with furious commuters. Eventually, I tracked one down. He indeed confirmed that nothing was leaving the tarmac for at least five hours, but most would go before midnight. Hopefully. Maybe. Fingers crossed. I came back.

'OK, you're on. But I warn you, I'm in a filthy mood, Max. And if I had to choose anyone to have lunch with right now, you wouldn't be top of my list. In fact, you'd be right at the bottom.'

'You've completely charmed me, Flossie. I'm putty in your hands.'

'Oh, sod off.'

'Where did you learn to flirt like that?'

'Funny.'

Outside, in the short-term car park, we found his silver Mercedes, which, through the miracles of modern technology, converted to the roofless variety in seconds flat. I slid nervously into the passenger seat, aware he was still laughing at me.

'I might have known you'd end up with a car like this.'

'I haven't the faintest notion what you mean.'

'An incredibly obvious crumpet-catcher. A topless model.' I dragged a scarf out of my bag and wrapped it around my head, then put on some dark glasses.

'You're travelling incognito?'

'You're public enemy number one, Max.'

'And you know so many people in Nice.'

'I'm not taking any chances.'

'You look a bit like my cleaning lady.'

'It's a look I rock regularly.'

We set off.

In the event, we didn't go into Nice. The centre would be impossible, he told me, far too crowded, and there wasn't anywhere remotely acceptable on the outskirts, so we'd drive along the coast for a bit, to a little place he knew. Of course he did, I thought, watching him out of the corner of my eye as we swept along the coast road. His older, now familiar face was tanned and handsome, blue eyes narrowed behind sunglasses, a cornflower-blue shirt conveniently matching those eyes and the sea beyond – his underpants, too, no doubt – brown arms and hands muscular on the wheel. The wind was in our hair – I'd ditched the scarf by now, as it threatened to throttle me – and the sun on our faces as we flew along at speed. A vast stretch of Mediterranean swept away to the horizon on our left: tiny sailboats bobbed, speedboats trailed snakes of white foam and girls waterskied in bikinis. It was a long way from Clapham. Riviera Radio played the while, and some French crooner sang, not quite 'The Girl from Ipanema', but something impossibly similar. Then came the adverts, asking if we were all right for drinks cupboards aboard our yachts? If our Ferraris could do with a service in Cannes? Everyone here, it seemed, was rich: basking in the sunshine and their wealth. Including Max, of course, I thought, glancing at the rest of his sartorial ensemble – chic chinos, Italian shoes – comparing it again to James's ancient Crew Clothing which he dragged from the bottom drawer year after year. I sighed. But then, in a highly uncharacteristic move, I decided to surrender to the moment, reasoning it was highly unlikely I'd ever be in such a car again, with a man as handsome as Max, in such an utterly sublime setting. Defiantly, I leaned my head back on the expensive blond leather headrest. Occasionally, I caught Max glancing at me, amused. The next time he did, we both smiled. But not in a clandestine way, more in a 'This is OK' sort of way.

The restaurant was well off the beaten track, which pleased me. We drove up a narrow lane into the hills, navigated a series of hairpin bends, then climbed, almost up a dirt track, through pine woods. A few goats turned to stare amongst the sweet-smelling needles. Cicadas sang their deafening music. Right at the top, we parked on a promontory. I stepped out of the car and turned. Gasped. The most beautiful sea view met my eyes. The restaurant and its terrace were perched perfectly to make the most of the sun-drenched bay below. I felt sure someone out at sea aboard their gin palace must even now be sipping a Martini, shading their eyes up at us and murmuring, 'Darling, that must be a terrific place to eat. What a position. Let's go.'

And here I was. Of course, I shouldn't be, I thought, as I followed Max inside, but no one would ever know.

'This is gorgeous, Max,' I conceded.

'It is rather special, isn't it? The patron is a huge fan of Camille, which is the only reason I've secured a table.'

'He thinks you're coming with her?'

'Yes, you're going to be a colossal disappointment.'

'Story of my life.'

I whipped out my lippy and hid behind Max as he explained, to a swarthy maître d', in perfect French, that I was Camille's personal assistant, and we were hoping she might show up for coffee, but that she had a terribly tight schedule. It was something James would never have done and, as we were shown to our table, although I was cross with my husband, I was pleased about that: I mentally notched up points in his favour.

'You haven't lost your devious ways,' I told Max as chairs were pulled out with a flourish at what my practised eye told me was the best table on the terrace. The only free one, too; all the others occupied by beautiful people sipping champagne and eating oysters under a burgeoning pagoda of trailing vines and pale-blue lobelia.

'Needs must,' he told me airily.

We sat and admired the view, although, once he'd glanced at it, he removed his glasses and smouldered naughtily in my general direction. I remained resolutely glued to the seascape but caught his expression out of the corner of my eye. Too obvious, I told myself. Who wants a man who smoulders?

The trouble was, after a couple of glasses of rosé, which was chilled and delicious and slipped down an absolute treat as we waited for our escargots, smouldering didn't seem so terrible. In fact, it seemed really rather welcome. And, apart from anything else, I reasoned, as I listened to his entertaining music-world chatter, about which I'd asked in order to steer him away from more personal matters, when would I next be sitting at a table like this, obsequious waiter filling up my glass and hovering solicitously, in light of my recent dismissal? Max must be quite a big deal in his own right, I realized, for them to be sanguine about him appearing without the star herself. What exactly was his relationship with Camille, I wondered? I asked him.

'Oh, you mean you're no longer interested in the logistics of a two-month tour of the States complete with sound crew and diva? You're cutting to the chase?'

'I needed to ease myself in. Ten minutes on how you decide which venues to play and which to resist has helped enormously. That and two glasses of wine.'

'Excellent news. Well, as you already know, Camille and I had an affair.'

'Had?'

'Definitely past tense. But I was certainly bewitched by her, I admit that. Entranced. As James is now.' He grinned at me. 'She has a tremendous ability to ensnare men.'

'In an incredibly obvious way.'

'And when you hear her sing, you're lost. I was, for quite a while. And then, of course, there's the vulnerability; the little girl lost in a world that's only after her talent. You want to protect her, look after her.'

'And you left Mimi for her.'

He frowned. 'How did you know?'

'I worked it out. Never quite believed the fling-on-tour bit. Men always leave their wives for another woman. They rarely step into a vacuum.'

'Aren't you the wise old sage. Yes, all right, I left Mimi for her. I was besotted, at the time. Flattered, too, I suspect. But then, little by little, you see the other side of Camille. The ego, the arrogance, the self-absorption.'

'Little by little?'

'I know. Women see it sooner.'

'But then we're not trying to get into her capri pants.'

'True.'

I paused. 'So . . . were you in love with her?'

'I think I was, for a bit. But it's funny how, once that goes, it disappears remarkably quickly.'

'And it has gone.'

'Yes.'

It wasn't at all what he'd said before. Before, he'd said he'd felt very little for Camille. I was pleased, in a way. Max wasn't a shallow man. I'd been perplexed by that.

'So now?'

He shifted in his seat: a regrouping gesture. 'Now I'm thinking of working with Jonas Kaufmann, in Italy. He's asked me.'

'That would be good, surely? He's equally famous?'

'He is, and it would get me away. I could delegate Camille.'

'And Mimi?'

'Yes, well. That's another story.' He looked beyond me, into the distance. Leaned his elbows on the table and massaged the bridge of his nose wearily.

'Would she have you back?'

'She would. Just. We'd have to work hard, obviously.' He leaned forward and played with his fork. His face had dropped. 'It wouldn't be easy. I'm realistic about that.'

'But at least she'd forgive you. At least – your family, your son . . .'

'I know,' he said quickly.

'A second chance, surely?'

'Yes, but you can never snap right back to where you were, Floss. This isn't a fairy story. There'd be days when she'd still hate me, find it hard to forgive. Gloomy Monday nights in January when she'd rehash what I'd done. There'd be sulks, rows, bitter recriminations.'

'You could have counselling?'

'*More* counselling.' He groaned. Rubbed his eyes again. Then he sighed. 'Yes, we could. And it might work. But it's never going to be exactly the same.'

I remembered thinking that the other night: that James and I would never be the same, that we'd sullied our marriage. But one kiss each. Come on. It was nothing to what Max had done.

'But I got it wrong in the first place, you see,' he said into his plate of snails as they arrived. '*Merci*. If I'd got it right with you, none of this would have happened.' Blue eyes flashed across the table to meet mine.

'That suggests other people are at fault. It shifts the blame. I'm not so sure it wouldn't have happened anyway.' I refused to be seduced.

'You mean I'd be a shit whoever I married?'

'No, because you're not. But I'm not convinced you can abdicate responsibility like that. Say, Oh, if I'd been with her, I'd never have strayed.'

We ate in silence for a moment, attending to the tricky business of eating escargots but also alone with our thoughts.

'You know this is my last throw of the dice, don't you, Flossie?'

'I know.'

'That, despite all the banter, if you said yes, I'd forget Italy, forget Kaufmann, forget going home. Follow you wherever. Do whatever you wanted.'

I concentrated on extracting a snail from its shell but, actually, I didn't need to. Knew I could look up into those deep-blue eyes, heavy with meaning, and love, actually, and have no problem saying what was in my heart. I put down my fork.

'The thing is, Max, you felt I got away from you. And I'm not saying I felt I'd had a lucky escape – I loved you very much at the time – but I married the right man. And I knew that the moment I walked down the aisle with him. I haven't spent the last nineteen years with you burning a hole in my heart, full of what ifs.'

He met my gaze. I held it steady. Max nodded slowly. 'Whereas I have. James is a lucky man.'

I swallowed. 'Not really. I'm a shrew. And a nag. And I'm preachy and full of ridiculous neuroses. I drive my family mad. And I haven't aged particularly well. I've put on too much weight and my chin is a bit droopy. That surely helps, Max?'

He laughed. 'No question.'

'But it's true, isn't it?' I insisted.

'You mean, have I enshrined something – someone – in my heart who doesn't exist? Is it a relief to see her for what she really is, all these years later?'

'Yes. I mean, come on.' I rolled my eyes expressively. Almost held up my bingo wings. Not quite.

'You never were an oil painting, Flossie.'

I threw my head back and laughed. 'Thanks!'

'But not every man goes for arm candy.'

'No, but many men are distracted by it. And I think I'd have spent my life looking over my shoulder if I'd married you, Max, something I've never done with James. Women . . .' I didn't say – like Mimi – didn't want to dredge that up 'will always home in on you.'

He played with his spoon. 'I'm not asking for violins to be played, but it can be a curse, sometimes. For a man. Not to be taken seriously.'

Good looks, he meant. I thought about it. About people like Robert Redford and George Clooney, wanting to be famous for directing rather than acting.

'Nah.' I shook my head. 'Sorry. Given the choice, you'd never give it back. Never look any other way.'

He smiled. Very attractively. Eyes creasing with laughter lines – he, of course, had aged terrifically. 'Maybe not.'

The waiter came to take our empty plates and shells. Provided finger bowls, which we used. Asked if we'd like more wine. I declined. He left us alone. Max's eyes met mine. Held them.

'So that's a no, then, Flora?'

I smiled sadly. 'It's a no, Max.'

'Not even a moment's hesitation.'

'Not even a heartbeat. But I'm very flattered. On the other hand, you didn't leave Mimi for me. You didn't break out of a long, comfortable marriage out of passion for Flora Murray-Brown. You broke out for Camille. Then, when you realized she was shallow, you thought – shit, now I'm single. Hm, I wonder how old Flora's doing? Always liked her. Got a bit of depth. Ooh, look, here's her sister-in-law. Might ease in there, tag along on their family holiday, see if there's still a spark. Oh hello, yes, still fancy her. Even if she hasn't aged brilliantly. And although Mimi says she'd have me back, she's going to be bloody furious. I could have a fresh start with Flora. She's a laugh. We've always got on. Let's face it, we were engaged, should have been married. And she knows me very well. There'd be so much I wouldn't have to explain. We could have fun for the next few years together; maybe not get married, just see how it goes. And I feel like a change.'

I looked at him steadily. He held my eyes and, this time, didn't try a grin.

'We're all fallible, Flossie,' he said softly at last. 'All human. And maybe you're right. Maybe that encapsulates it. But is it so terrible?'

'No,' I said slowly, 'it's not terrible. It's reasonable, at our age. And realistic. But don't dress it up as something else. As a grand passion. You know very well that if we ran away together – which there isn't the slightest chance of our doing – we'd still end up getting on each other's nerves. Cracks would appear, as they have with you and Mimi – me and James, for Christ's sake. Nobody's perfect. There are no fairy-tale endings. You just have to keep buggering on.'

He nodded. 'You're right. You are preachy.'

'Which you'd forgotten. See? And, after a bit, it would irritate you. Drive you mad. Ask James. My daughters. They'll tell you. Go back to Mimi, Max. And give her my love.'

His eyes widened at this. 'She feels that she shat on you from a very great height.'

'Did it bother her?'

'Of course. She's not a bitch. She was just . . .' He shrugged.

'Overtaken by something more important than our friendship. I know.'

I did know. Mimi and I had been friends. Shared a flat. And I'd forgiven her years ago because, in a way, she'd delivered me to James.

'I'm going to preach again.'

'Jesus wept.' Max put his head in his hands.

'Sometimes the hardest route is the most worthwhile.'

'Wait. Hang on.' He folded his napkin lengthwise. Leaned across and put it round my neck, like a dog collar. 'Go on.'

I pulled it off. 'I mean it, Max. You're scared of going back to Mimi because she's a strong woman and you know she's not going to be pathetically grateful to have her man back and give you a hero's welcome.'

'I'm not saying she'd make me pay . . .'

'No, because, as you say, she's not a bitch. But you're going to have to put your back into it, not just swan in being suave and charming, and that makes you nervous. But it'll be worth it.'

The waiter brought the bill. Max paid in silence and I

watched him: loving him, in a way. Not like James, but just in an incredibly fond, 'What a shame I don't see you any more, I was extremely close to you' sort of way. And if he really searched his heart, I think that was actually the way he felt about me. He'd deny it, but I'd say it was so.

We walked to the car in silence. He had his arm draped around my shoulders, and that felt entirely right. We got in and he started the engine. The car bumped slowly back down the goat track, then navigated the zigzag lane through the pines, before we sped back along the coast road. The forested hills were to our left this time, the glittering expanse of water to our right, the sun beating down. When we stopped at some lights I could see he was deep in thought: it was almost as if I weren't in the car any more. I took a strand of hair from my mouth.

'What are you going to do about Sally?'

He turned. 'Hm? Oh, you don't need to worry about Sally. You'll be surprised to hear she wanted even less from this relationship than I did. No strings. I should think she'll be glad to see the back of me.'

I recalled her skipping gaily off to the pool with her book and her oily hair. For a day, I'd thought; but perhaps Max was right. Perhaps she didn't want anything. We'd all just assumed she did. But Sally didn't subscribe to that Darwinian instinct to settle eventually on one person. Like Rachel, she preferred her own company, but she was less straightforward about it: dressed it up differently. Assumed a more elaborate disguise, a camouflage of constant chirruping, in order to appear – well, like everyone else.

'I'll ring her this evening. Tell her I've got held up with work in Cannes and won't be returning. Then I'll have dinner with her when she gets back. She won't mind a bit.'

No. She probably wouldn't. Might even be relieved. She was a strange one, Sally. The only person she'd possibly ever been close to, outside of the family, had been Donaldson, but although my girls had wondered about that, Rachel and I had always thought no. No, this wouldn't shatter Sally.

We drew up at the airport right outside the Departure doors, Max ignoring the drop-off zone. He got out and went round to take my bag out of the boot. When he came back we stood facing each other: no embarrassment, just smiling. He opened his arms and I walked into them. He hugged me and I laid my cheek on his shirt, still smiling. When we drew back, he looked quizzical.

'By the way, did you ever contact your father again?'

My mouth dried. I retreated quickly into myself, behind my eyes. Closed the shutters. An angry horn blared loudly, a taxi driver behind us, outraged at Max's audacious parking. He was shaking a Gallic fist and shouting, leaning almost out of his window in rage. Max threw up his hands in response and a furious exchange broke out between the two men, with absolutely no serious intent on either side. Max came back to me. Grinned.

'Better go.'

'Yes.'

He held me again. 'Take care of yourself,' he whispered.

'And you.' I whispered back. 'Great care.'

Then he turned and went.

Chapter Twenty-Four

I joined the easyJet check-in queue for the second time that day. It snaked for miles and, on another day, at another time, I'd have found an official, asked questions, demanded answers – been embarrassing, my daughters would say: 'doing a Mum'. Right now, though, I just took it on the chin. I was feeling numb, so standing in a daze in a queue of complete strangers, thoughts chasing around my head, suited me. I welcomed the complete inertia in my body to counteract my very fast brain.

The man in front of me turned and gave a wry smile. 'Not much we can do about it, is there?'

I gazed at him. Middle-aged, nice, open face, balding. Actually, there was.

'Excuse me,' I muttered, sort of to him but also to the young chap behind me, who was weighed down with an assortment of backpacks and was blocking the way. I muscled past and through the throng, in the direction of the main concourse. Then I span around, looking for signs. Ah. That way. Down the escalator I went, following directions to the station. In the end, I had to get a taxi across town, as the station was not situated within the airport, it transpired, and then, when I reached it, I spent ages trying to work out a French timetable. In the end, I gave up. I explained my destination to the girl at the window, through the grille, and was told that '*Bien sûr*', it was indeed possible to get a train, or at least in that direction. There was one to Grasse in half an hour, but from there I would have to get a taxi, or a bus. No trains. '*C'est difficile.*' Lots of shrugging. It was not an accessible place. I'd manage, though, I decided, bag clutched on my knees half an hour later, as the train, with surprising punctuality, departed.

The journey was beautiful. If I'd had a mind to appreciate it, I'd have experienced the route swooping up over mountains dense with pine and then dropping down dramatically through tunnels to emerge into fabulous countryside. Even in my dry-mouthed, shallow-breathed state, I sensed the drama of my surroundings. After the Massif Central came hilltop villages, old men staring at the train as if they'd never seen one before as they herded sheep or goats. After an hour or so, we trundled into Grasse and I realized I hadn't released my grip on the handle of my bag the entire journey. My hands were white. I flexed them gingerly. As I got off the train I tested my knees, too, stiff from holding the exact same position, a heavy bag resting on them.

The taxi was sick-making. The car was old and very proximate to the ground. None too clean either, and the driver smoked continuously. I opened the back window and gulped down air, hoping I wasn't going to throw up, but relieved, in a way, to have something else to concentrate on. We lurched on for miles, swinging around bends without slowing down, me being thrown around in the back. As we drew closer, finding the chateau seemed to be entirely my responsibility, despite my giving the driver the address. Lots of raised hands – both of them off the wheel at the same time – as I directed him into another wrong turn, and another. Plenty of '*Merde!*' and murderous glances at the meter, which I'm sure he was not disappointed to see rocketing but wanted me to be aware of, aware that this was all my fault, in case I quibbled, no doubt. Finally, he flung me around yet another hairpin bend, but this time on to a dusty lane I recognized.

'*Alors – ici!*' I told him, leaning forwards. '*Au bout de cette voie – là-bas!*'

'*Ah, oui,*' he muttered, as if he'd known all along. I got the distinct impression we'd been carefully circumnavigating the house for some time.

'*Ici – ce côté de la porte,*' I told him firmly and, obediently, he stopped short of the gates.

I paid him, practically all the money I had, then waited a moment for him to go. I inhaled great mouthfuls of fresh air. Before turning around, I composed myself a moment, in the dust the taxi had left in its speeding wake, which hung, suspended, then I turned and walked through the tall iron gates to the chateau with my old blue bag. I felt a bit like Maria returning to the abbey. Or had she been fleeing from it? I could never remember. Was always in too much of a drunken haze on Christmas Day, just about coming round for 'Edelweiss'.

As I passed the lodge cottage perched at the end of the drive, I saw Michel and Thérèse bent double in their vegetable garden. They straightened up when they saw me, yellow corncobs in their hands, staring as I went by in that blatant, French way. I didn't greet them, and they didn't acknowledge me either. Agathe was with them, a basket full of tomatoes over her arm as she shaded her eyes to watch. On I strode, feeling, not like Maria now, more like

Clint. Yes, in some spaghetti western: a gun on each hip, ready to shoot from both. I hesitated, though, when I got to the front door, flung wide, as usual, to reveal the ubiquitous tangle of flip-flops, paperbacks, sun cream and hats strewn on the hall table and the floor. Should I go inside and upstairs to my room to ponder what to do next? Let people find me? Spread the word themselves? Or should I go round the back, brazen as you like, to encounter them all on the terrace or under the trees, announcing, quite simply, that I'd had a change of heart and wasn't going home at all, and did anyone know what was for supper?

Upstairs to my room.

I crept up the stone staircase, feeling a bit foolish now. It had seemed so right at the airport. Also on the train. Less so in the car. And now . . . I wasn't sure I could pull it off. I left the bedroom door ajar so that I might be seen or heard. Sat down on the bed. But nothing happened for a long time. I could hear voices below on the terrace. I coughed. Coughed again. Still nothing. Finally, I opened the shutters, which had been shut against the heat of the day, with a bit of a bang. Silence below. Then murmurings. At last, footsteps on the stairs, and Tara came in, eyes as wide as when I'd left her, still in her pink bikini.

'Mum! What are you doing back?'

'I had a change of heart, darling.' I bustled around the room being busy, unpacking my bag, which I'd deliberately left full to give me something to do, popping creams back in the bathroom, nightie under my pillow. 'Decided I could say everything I wanted to say to Maria on the phone and that it was pointless going all the way back just to have a conversation.'

'Right.' She looked stunned. 'But what about doing it in person, all that "much better face to face" stuff?'

I felt weary already. Had I said that? I could never remember my own web of lies.

'Well, yes, of course. Ordinarily, that would be the way forward but, you see, there was a baggage handlers' strike and I wouldn't have got a flight until the early hours. I didn't fancy a night on the airport floor.'

'Oh God, no.' Tara and Amelia had passed swiftly through the age of finding it fun to sleep on the floor of a soggy marquee after a party; indeed, my elder daughter had been known to book herself into a B&B after an eighteenth in deepest Wiltshire. Why hadn't I thought of that earlier? The truth?

'So will you go back tomorrow?'

'No, I think not. I shall ring Maria now. Tell her my position.'

'Which is?'

'Well, I'll . . . give it some thought.'

'Presumably you've been thinking of nothing else!'

'Yes, but –'

'Blimey – what are you doing back?' Rarely have I been so pleased to see Amelia.

'Baggage handlers' strike,' I told her.

'And she's changed her mind about the face-to-face bit,' put in Tara.

'Well, as I say, I can do it on the phone.'

'Oh, right. What about the sustained attack with Lizzie? "Girl power"?' Amelia raised her eyebrows.

'She'd have to have spent the night at the airport,' Tara said helpfully.

'Oh, gross.'

They watched me bustling around for a bit then turned to go, satisfied – or bored, perhaps – just as the boys appeared in the corridor. Their eyes were large as they peered over their girlfriends' heads at this strange woman, totally unlike their own mothers – I'd met neither, but the spectre of Rory's plagued me constantly – who boomeranged back and forth on a family holiday. The girls tactfully turned them around, and I sat down wearily on the bed, rubbing my aching brow with my fingertips. I listened to them amble downstairs. Knew they'd eventually spread the word, but knew it could also be a while, so dull and inconsequential was I, only really useful as a provider of food or fresh laundry, and since that wasn't necessary with Thérèse to do it, of no real consequence at all. They wouldn't rush to find their father.

I lay down on the bed to wait. Sat up, almost immediately. Swung my legs round and braced myself as his familiar footsteps sounded up the stairs. For the first time in my life, I felt scared. I remembered his fury on the way to Seillans. His taut, white face. But as he came into the room and shut the door behind him, I knew. Five hours alone had cooled his temper, just as it had mine the day before. He was no longer ablaze. On fire. That sort of combustion and momentum cannot be maintained unless you're a certain type of person, and James wasn't.

'What happened?'

'There was a baggage handlers' strike. I could have gone much later tonight, but I changed my mind.'

'Oh?'

'Yes, I've had a long time to think about it. Also, Max

was at the airport, James. Waiting for me, I think. Well, yes, he was. I was so furious with you for sending me home, I had lunch with him. After all, I had five hours to kill.'

James didn't say anything. A muscle went in his cheek, though, as he stared down at me.

'And I knew I no longer had any feelings for him, which was why it was all right to go, and I don't know if you'll understand that, but I'm telling you anyway. It's the truth. We had lunch in a very beautiful place overlooking the bay, with delicious wine and seafood, and he's terribly attractive, and I felt absolutely nothing, except an old bond of friendship and familiarity and a wish that we'd remained friends.'

'Bully for you. How nice of you to come all the way back to share that with me.'

'The point is, James, I never did feel anything. It was just a silly, drunken, summer-holiday indiscretion. I haven't been hankering away all these years for Max.'

'Again, my thanks to you for clarifying that.'

'But that's not what I came back to tell you.'

He stared at me. Didn't speak.

'I came back to tell you that – that –' Unaccountably, my knees began to shake. Physically tremble as I sat there. I put my hands on them. Began to feel tears sting behind my eyes, streaming down my face. A lack of air.

'I came back to tell you about my father.' I felt the air rush out of my lungs as if from a vortex. 'I've known all these years, but I've blocked it. I've blanked it.'

And then I broke down. Dissolved. I felt James sit beside me. He didn't say anything. Didn't put his arm around me, not that I was expecting it. I wasn't going for the sympathy vote here, that hadn't even occurred to me. I knew it wouldn't occur to James either. I just knew I couldn't keep it in any longer and that there was only one person I could share it with. I sobbed quite loudly and violently, and he got up and shut the windows. The shutters, too, plunging the room into deep gloom. Then he sat down again.

'Years ago,' I blurted out, quite loudly, 'Max and I went looking for him.'

'I know. You told me.'

'But I didn't tell you we found him.'

'No.'

'Because – well, you see –'

'You don't have to tell me.'

'I do,' I said fiercely.

'Right.'

I gulped. 'We tracked him down through his sister, in Brighton. Max and I went through Mum's things one day, in her bedroom, when she was out with Neville at the races, like a couple of budding detectives. We thought we were so clever. We found letters. Not from him, but from this sister, referring to someone called Tom, who was so sorry. And this sister – Sonia, she was called – was wondering if there was anything she could do. Max and I knew it was my father; we were convinced. Mum had clearly been left in the lurch with a baby and, for some reason, had never breathed a word. We got the train down to Brighton, to Sonia. She was still living with her parents, a mean-looking, closed-up couple. Sonia was better. The house was horrible, though, James, almost a slum. Max and I were horrified.' I took a deep breath. 'It turned out

Tom was in prison. For drugs. Not just possession, for supplying. Young people. But also for conning old ladies out of their savings to buy the drugs. He'd become notorious in Brighton. When her parents finally left the room, Sonia showed us the newspaper clippings. The trial. My mother beside him, looking shocked. So young. A baby – me – in her arms. He was very good-looking. Chiselled features, wavy, dark hair. He'd hit one of these old ladies, one of the ones he preyed on, and she hadn't died but was very shaken up. This was all reported as the trial went on. After that, Mum wasn't by his side any more with me in her arms. There was a picture of the old lady in her hospital bed, with black eyes, bruises.'

I was shaking, my voice rising hysterically. James's arms were around me now, holding me close as he sat beside me. It was only now I'd even noticed.

'He was charming, apparently. He'd worked his way into the old ladies' lives, their homes, by valuing their antiques. He was a dealer. In so many ways. It was mostly widows with death duties to pay. He'd sell their paintings and then keep most of the profits, giving them only a fraction. Then he'd sell more and more of their possessions, until this old lady – Cynthia Chambers, she was called – refused to part with her silver. So he beat her up. That's my father. That's my father, James.' I shook and sobbed as he held me.

'Max asked me about it as I left, said, "Did you ever contact your father again?" I couldn't speak. Hadn't let myself think about it for twenty years. Just ignored him. But I did follow it up.'

'And?'

I struggled.

'Don't say. Not if you don't want to.'

'I *do*!' Vehemently. I licked my lips. 'Max and I left the house in Brighton shocked and horrified. He asked if I wanted him to come to the prison with me. Meet him? I said no. But later, I went on my own and didn't tell him. I was so ashamed. So embarrassed. Max's parents were lovely. And, obviously, I didn't tell Mum.'

'Not even that you knew?'

'No. I decided she was so appalled and horrified she'd tried to protect me. Her one bad apple. All the others were so lovely, James. Philippe, Neville . . .'

'I know.'

'I didn't want to hurt her.'

'No. But you went to see him?'

'Yes.' I shuddered. 'Horrible. Unbelievably horrible. Again – I blanked it. A queue of women outside, a sort I was so unfamiliar with. Scary-looking. Bleached blondes chewing gum, chain-smoking, although most of them looked scared, too. We were shown to a big room with small tables and a chair either side. A complete stranger came in and sat down opposite me. Tried to take my hand.' I shook my head. 'I'm not sure I can even tell you about it, James.'

'Then don't.'

'But it hurt that Max knew and you didn't.'

'Yes. But that was timing. Circumstances.'

'Yes.'

'And he doesn't know this. Don't rehash it. Don't pick that scab. It's not healthy. You've told me, and I know. That's all that matters.'

'Don't you want to know where he is now?'

'Only if you want to tell me. You don't have to.'

'He lives in Singapore. With his third wife. She's Thai. I have half-brothers and sisters. I have no idea how many.'

'No.'

'I don't have to, do I, James?'

'No, you don't have to.'

'I was so scared that if I told someone – you even – I'd have to find out. That those were the rules. Wasn't allowed to just – let it lie.'

'Although your mother did. Sensibly.'

'Yes.'

'There are no rules, Flora.'

'Amelia would disagree. Tara even, they'd –'

'Be forensic, I know. Pore over it. And be aghast you hadn't looked into your new family, dug it all up. It's fine, Flora, leave it.'

'He may even be dead now, for all I know.'

I felt calmer, suddenly. Shattered, but calmer. It was out. And it had been in there for so long: buried very deep. With a heavy boulder on top. Max had been sworn to secrecy years ago and I knew he'd never share it with anyone. Max was genuine. And I didn't blame him for bringing it up just now. I might easily have done the same. But he had no idea what reaction those few words would provoke: 'Did you ever contact your father again?'

He'd unwittingly lit the blue touchpaper. And I'd quietly gone up in smoke. Imploded inside, in that easyJet queue, perhaps the combustion more tremendous for being buried for so long. And then I'd run to the one person in the world I knew I needed, come what may. James.

We sat on the bed together, side by side, and I knew exactly where we both were, in our heads. In Bistro Vino,

337

South Kensington, many years ago. Nineteen, to be precise, after I'd happily agreed to marry him. After he'd told me about his father and his mother, and after we'd agreed, holding hands in the candlelight, the wax dripping down the bottle, to so many things: mostly that we hated duplicity more than anything in the world; that we would never deceive one another. That his mother had hurt his father too badly for James ever to marry anyone who might eventually be capable of such a thing. That I had been a child of a one-parent family for too long not to want a forever marriage. And Max had deceived me and I never wanted to feel like that again. We didn't go into it deeply, we weren't heavy about it, but it could have been written in blood.

But there'd been another pact, too – an implicit, tacit one – that night. I'd been the one gingerly to broach it, wondering if two people, however much in love they were, needed to know absolutely everything about each other? Wondering if a person could still possibly have, not a secret, but something they felt they never wanted to share with anyone in the world? Meaning my father. Because, once shared, I'd gone on hesitantly, it was out there for real. Enormous. Uncontrollable. And before I'd even got to the end of the sentence, James had agreed. I remember the light in his eyes in the flickering candle flame: those eyes as they seized on something they recognized completely.

'I agree,' he'd said quickly. 'As long as it's not something that affects the other, why should anyone own the other completely?'

'Yes,' I'd said, surprised at his alacrity, and the way he'd put it. But so, so relieved. Knowing I wasn't ever going to be probed but had at least admitted to owning something he'd never know. And he'd never asked. As I had obviously never asked him.

But it was different now. I'd told him my secret. And, childishly, I wondered if he'd tell me his. I felt so much better having divulged, I realized. Exhausted. Shattered. Spent. As if I'd been sick, actually, which in a way I had, I'd spewed it out, but – it was all so long ago. It had felt huge then, in Bistro Vino – enormous. Had become more so because I'd hidden it, I realized. But now that it was out – why, it wasn't that momentous at all. My father. Just a sad old loser – a violent old loser – who'd procreated carelessly and produced quite a few children along the way, one of them being me. But I'd been lucky enough to have my mother. I breathed in deeply. Let it out slowly. I realized I felt almost evangelical about how much better I felt. I reached for James's hand. And maybe . . . just maybe.

But he was getting to his feet. Walking around to the window. Leaning over the bed to open the shutters. Then the window. Light poured in. He stood, staring out. Letting the air, the voices, the world, flood back in. No longer cocooned here in the dark, in our closed-off, womb-like world, everything changed. I licked my lips, knowing another opportunity might not come my way for years.

'James . . .'

'Come on, Flora. Have a shower, freshen up, or whatever, and then come down.'

He turned from the window to look at me, his eyes so guarded, so blank. I felt afraid.

'Yes,' I whispered. 'Yes, I will. And . . . thank you, James.'

He gave me the ghost of a smile, but didn't hesitate for a second. In another moment, he was gone.

Chapter Twenty-Five

I did as instructed and showered, changed and then went
down. It was almost drinks time, almost six o'clock, and I
needed one very badly. I felt exhausted and utterly drained,
but so, so glad not to be back home in Clapham. I avoided
the kitchen, where I could hear people talking, and instead
walked down the corridor to access the terrace via the
drawing room, deep in thought. Unfortunately, as I pushed
through the door, I realized I'd chosen the same room my
mother and Jean-Claude had elected for a quiet tête-à-tête.
They were sitting on one of the long, creamy sofas, holding
hands.

'Darling, how lovely!' Mum jumped up and clasped her
hands together prettily, eyes alight. Jean-Claude got to his
feet, too. He clapped me on the back as Mum hugged me.

'First of all, I couldn't believe you'd gone, and now, like
a miracle, you're back!'

Particularly without saying goodbye, she meant, but was
too nice to say it. Mum never emotionally blackmailed, or
applied pressure, she was too generous for that: just
focused on the good things, like me returning. Not for the
first time, I hoped I'd mostly inherited my mother's genes
and not Tom's. Obviously, this had preoccupied me at
times. Was it why I was impatient? So volatile? The girls
had often said, 'You're so different to Granny!' And I'd
cringe. Amelia would go on to say sagely, 'You're probably

like your father.' It hadn't frightened them, this mythical grandfather, because, naturally, they'd glamorized him. A French count whose aristocratic family Mum had protected. A diplomat with a high-profile career. A film star, already married with a family. After all, Granny had been so beautiful, her men so exotic. They'd never thought of a low-down crook. How disappointed they'd be. And, naturally, I worried for their genes, too. Why did Amelia have a temper? Tara, so indecisive? Or was it all nonsense anyway and far more to do with nurture than nature? I hoped so. And, of course, there'd been Sonia, who'd done the right thing, reached out to Mum. Tried to help. Maybe they weren't all bad apples in that family. And maybe Tom – I could never, even in my head, call him my father – had just taken a wrong turn? Some of the children's friends took drugs, I knew that – Toby, probably – it was not unusual. And if Tom had become addicted, well, then the natural extension of that was . . . no. No, it was inexcusable. This was where Tom and I always parted company. When he hit the old lady.

I gasped as Mum held me now, not from the pressure, but at the thought of how she must have suffered, on her own. She held me at arm's length, eyes dancing. 'I am *so* pleased,' she said.

'And I'm glad to be back, Mum,' I said, with unusual warmth. She blinked, surprised.

I wasn't always very nice to her, I knew that. Was impatient; scornful. But what a brave decision she'd made not to share Tom with me. Not to burden me with that baggage. If only I hadn't gone looking. I could have luxuriated in the same blissful ignorance as Amelia and Tara.

Something in my make-up, though, meant I'd always have searched. Without Mum's bedside box, I'd have found him anyway. Tracked him down through Interpol or DNA. I have that relentless, probing nature.

'And you're staying? Not dashing off again? Amelia said there was a baggage handlers' strike or something . . .'

'Oh yes, I'm staying. This place is too gorgeous to leave, Mum.'

'I know. Which is why . . .' she glanced at Jean-Claude, who nodded. 'Why I need to tell you my news, too.'

All at once, I realized her eyes were shining for other reasons.

'Oh?' I felt myself harden. Hated myself for it. But I knew what was coming.

She still had my arms. Made to sit down, but I remained standing. She hesitated.

'Darling, I'm going to stay in France, with JC. Move back over here.'

'We want to give it a try,' said JC, who'd seen my face.

'What, for ever?' I said, not liking my voice. 'I thought you said a few weeks?' What was wrong with me? Why was I like this? But I was upset. And this was always my knee-jerk reaction: to lash out.

'I miss France,' she said sadly. She perched on the cream sofa. Instead of standing stonily above her, I made myself perch beside her. Jean-Claude went to sit opposite. 'I realize that now. I had so many happy years in Paris, and down here I feel . . . well, I'm much more myself. I'm much more Mediterranean than English, Flora, this place speaks to me.'

'It speaks to me, too,' I said, before I could stop myself.

'Everything about it. The way of life, the people, the accent on prettiness and charm – I love prettiness and charm. I'm possibly even twee – is that so terrible? In England, I feel I'm constantly saying sorry for the way I am, for being feminine, rather than feminist. I don't like feminists, they scare me.' She hesitated. 'And I like men. I love the difference between men and women – *vive la différence!* – why not! I'm freer to think that sort of thing here. You'll scoff, Flora, but I know I'll be perfectly happy bagging up lavender bags and tying pretty ribbons on them on a sunny doorstep, cooking for Jean-Claude in the evening. It's my idea of paradise. And I wouldn't have to apologize all the time.'

To me, she meant. The apologizing bit. She'd phrased it as if she needed to apologize to the whole world, or at least the whole of England, but she meant me. Sorry for being scatty, for not having a tidy house, for feeding the birds in the park every day. For tie-dyeing all her T-shirts, chain-smoking, taking in stray cats, wearing ribbons in her hair, baseball caps, for always being in the pub with a man, playing canasta, roaring with laughter, at her age. I was a drudge. Always her brakes. And she wanted to get away. Or was I being paranoid? Was it absolutely nothing to do with me? I'd miss her so much, though. A huge lump filled my throat. So much, it hurt. She'd always been round the corner, always. Just there, for me. *Me.* So much, I'd taken for granted. I felt panicky. Thought I'd grown out of that feeling. The terror of Mum dying. When I was young, I'd awake bolt upright in bed, covered in sweat. I knew I had to be grown up now. Let her go. But if only it were Paris. Not so far. Deep in the south of France.

'It's a plane ride away,' she said gently, knowing.

'Yes.'

Up to now, though, I'd see her three times a week. Four, sometimes, if I popped in on a Sunday. Didn't I mention that? And yes, I usually went there. Oh, she came to Clapham, but mostly it was me making the journey. Well, you know, a lot of my restaurants were in her neck of the woods: Chelsea, Belgravia; I'd pop in after lunch. No reason to shop in M&S in the King's Road, though: there was one much closer to home. I looked at Jean-Claude, who was watching me.

'I'll look after her,' he said gently. And I knew he would. Knew she'd chosen another good egg, and that, even though they'd only known one another a short while, there'd been an instant rapport. They'd recognized each other. But Mum knew I wasn't worried about that.

'If it doesn't work out, I'll be back,' she said, to keep my panic at bay.

'It will work out,' said Jean-Claude, more realistically. The truth, which I needed. I looked across at him gratefully.

'And will you carry on with the shop?'

'Of course!' said Mum in surprise. 'But I'm going to make the outside so much prettier. Paint all the window frames a dusty pink and have a little reopening party. Invite the locals, get to know them all. It'll be so much fun!'

'Despite the crowded market?' I wasn't talking to her now. She sounded too much like a character in *Miranda*, or *Ab Fab*. 'The other night, you said it was so seasonal?'

'You're right, it is.' More truth from JC. 'And sometimes, I think . . .'

'What?' I said quickly.

'Nothing. Because that's a crowded market, too. And I don't want your mother to put money in. She can buy the pink paint,' his mouth twitched, 'but that's it.'

'Oh, but JC, that's how we're going to expand!' Mum exclaimed, lighting a cigarette, crossing her tiny knees and blowing smoke out excitedly. 'Buy another shop, in the next village perhaps, or –'

'If you touch your savings, it's off. *Fini*,' he said firmly. 'I'm not interested.'

She pouted. He turned back to me.

'And I don't think she should sell her house, either.'

'But I'll go to Flora's when I'm in London, I won't need it. Why would I –'

'Rent it out,' he told her, interrupting. 'Rent the London house, don't sell. That way you'll have an income.' He turned to me. 'You tell her, Flora. Never get rid of property, especially in a capital city. Lease it.'

I sighed, at a loss against his rational argument. How could I tell her she was being foolish, when she had someone more sensible than me at the helm? All I could do was nod, agree with JC, give them my blessing and hope my highly emotional state – I was now on the verge of tears – had more to do with the past twelve hours than with me, a happily married woman with two children, being unable to live within a ten-minute drive of her ditsy, impossible, highly irritating mother.

I should be delighted she's having another chance, I thought as I went out to the terrace. Too many people were gathered there, so I slipped through the French windows to the kitchen. A life in the sun with a gorgeous man who loves her. I shouldn't be helping Thérèse lay the table for supper – I delved into the cutlery drawer – with stupid, shaking hands. I doggedly put the knives, forks and spoons around the table on the terrace, ignoring Thérèse, who sighed and clucked, following me out and replacing them with the spoons she wanted – pudding, not soup – and sharper knives for steak.

But, actually, I'd known this was coming. Had known the other day, when, although they'd talked in terms of a holiday, a few weeks, they'd meant a lot longer. I'd had a while to get used to it. Mum had carefully seen to that. I knew I couldn't trust myself to talk about it yet, though, and since I couldn't sit quietly in a corner on my own without drawing attention, activity was best. I began to clear up the terrace, plumping cushions, collecting stray glasses, retrieving clothes from the floor, books from under chairs. The girls caught my mood and, assuming it was a bad one rather than an upset one, quietly got up from their comfy chairs to help. They were slightly in the dog house anyway, since I'd caught them coming out of Camille's room in the tower earlier, having a snoop. They went to the kitchen to fill water jugs, find glasses for the table, giving each other 'What's up with her?' looks.

James had bought a bottle of port from the vineyard he'd got the wine from and was showing the boys how to decant it properly, straining it through a piece of muslin he'd found in a drawer. Mum, pleased to have told me, to have got that over with, skipped off down the garden to pick some flowers for the table. JC sat on the terrace and watched her go with a fond smile. She was younger than me, in spirit, I thought as I paused in my clearing up to watch her bend down and gently pluck nasturtiums from their base, gathering them in a bunch. Always had been. Lighter. Kinder. Nicer. I got Tom. Aware I was in trouble now, I hummed away to the music Rory had put on the iPod in the kitchen: Jack Johnson, or Mumford & Sons, chosen, diplomatically, to appeal to all ages.

Sally appeared in a wafting blue kaftan-style dress, more the sort of thing she used to wear in Scotland. I realized I hadn't given her a thought. She looked happy and relaxed, though, helping her father down the step to the terrace. Drummond, bathed, florid and fragrant with Trumper's aftershave, looked even more delighted than usual.

'My dear!' He raised his stick exuberantly. 'So glad you're back. Excellent decision. Wretched magazine. Their loss, not yours.'

'I'm glad, too,' Sally said warmly. 'And I gather you had lunch with Max,' she went on, and boy, was I pleased I'd told James. Imagine how that little revelation could have ricocheted around the terrace.

'Yes,' I said breathlessly, as James continued instructing the boys, not turning a hair.

'He rang earlier,' she went on. 'He's got so much on at the moment, I don't honestly think he'll be back.'

'No, he – sort of said.' I was nervous of knowing more than she did. Of being better informed. But she was so nonchalant. Happy, almost. I believed Max now – not that I hadn't at the time – but I was glad of this clarification. Their liaison had meant possibly less to Sally than it had to him. Just because I, Flora Murray-Brown, took every relationship seriously, whether it be a blood tie, a best friend, an ex-lover, my neighbour, my cleaning lady even, it didn't

347

mean everyone did. Some were happy alone. Better alone. Stronger, perhaps.

Rachel appeared. It occurred to me that, for once, she didn't look so composed, so serene, but she wouldn't meet my eye, so I distracted myself by listening to the general chatter as we sat down to fillet steak, hollandaise sauce and salad. Camille had gone for good, it seemed, back to Paris, according to Thérèse, so when Mum shared her news, it was with family and friends. With people who knew and loved her. The girls were surprised and delighted.

'But Granny, that's fantastic! You and JC are just made for each other. Tara and I have said so all along, haven't we?'

'You're one of those soul-mate couples, you know?' Tara said earnestly. 'That you read about? Who sometimes take years to find each other, but when they do, you just know it's right.'

The older members of the party smiled at their plates.

'It's brilliant, Mum, isn't it,' she went on, turning to me. 'Don't you agree?'

'I do,' I said carefully. 'But Granny's going to live in France, don't forget.'

'Oh, Granny, we'll miss you!' Despair now, and real shock, as the implications dawned. But youthful idealism and enthusiasm returned as Mum quickly outlined her plans.

'No, because, look, on easyJet it costs practically nothing and they fly straight to Nice, two flights a day. And you can come out every holiday, not just in the summer. Imagine having a granny in the south of France! How glam is that? You'll be in St Tropez in a jiffy. And, anyway, I'll be back and forth.'

'Will you?'

'Of course I will! And think how brown you'll be – a year-round tan!'

'And we could come out and revise with you?'

'Exactly! Bring your books and laze in the sun.'

They were loving this already. In their mind's eye, they'd recreated a luxurious setting just like this one: a huge garden full of tropical palms, an infinity pool, a view of the sea, whereas the reality would be a tiny back yard, or even just the front step of the shop, in a provincial, dusty town, above which, Mum and JC would live. Not that it would bother Mum. She'd make it pretty. Fix windowboxes, fill them with trailing plants, add a balcony, perhaps. Arrange pots of herbs around the front door, bring the antiques outside and sit amongst them in the summer, sewing and chatting to new friends, playing backgammon, basil and thyme wafting. She'd persuade the girls when they came out that it was charm, not glitz and glamour, that was important: get them sewing, too. For now, though, as they adjusted to Granny not being round the corner, where they often went straight from school or college, or later on in the evening for a glass of wine and no doubt a cigarette, baring their souls in a way they never would to me, she let them think they'd be jetting out every other week to join the smart set. In reality, of course, flights to Nice not being cheap, once a year they'd drive to Portsmouth, put their old Clio on the ferry and drive mile upon mile to see her. They'd miss her so much. More than they knew. We'd all miss her so much. She was, quite simply, the lynchpin of this family. Just as she'd been in my small one, years ago. James caught my eye in sympathy, and I was grateful.

Supper rattled along and I held my own with Mum and the girls, exclaiming, delighting in their every plan and idea for her new life, but I was glad when it was over. There was a limit to the extent that I could say, 'Yes – terrific idea!' or 'Why not sell greeting cards, too?' and sound like I meant it. Now, with pudding over, I could leave them to their cheese and port and legitimately help Thérèse in the kitchen, even though I could tell she didn't want me. All the while, whilst I was pottering about and getting in her way, putting the dishwasher on when it wasn't quite full, causing her to tut and open it again, I kept an eye on the table. If someone had a plan, I had one, too. One that would help, I knew. I was waiting for the one who I was sure would go early to bed, with her book. Who'd rise quietly from the far end of the table and slip off. Ah. There. As she duly bid goodnight to everyone and came through the kitchen, I intercepted her.

'Rachel – could I have a word? Before you go up?' My voice was a bit breathless.

She looked surprised. But then – not so surprised. Instantly, the shutters came down. 'Well, I was just going to help Daddy . . .' She turned. Drummond was a few steps behind her.

'Oh, nonsense,' he roared. 'You fuss too much. I'll be absolutely fine! Anyone would think I was an old crone. Go on, Rachel, you girls go and have a natter and a glass of something. You never have a night with the younger crew.'

'Because I'm happy with my book.'

'It won't take a mo,' I pleaded, and anyway, Drummond was already on his way past us. Waving his stick in a backward salute, he successfully negotiated the step up from the kitchen to the hall, and was shuffling eagerly – showing off, almost – across the limestone floor to bed. Rachel looked scared.

'Let's go through here.' I knew I had to be firm. Seize the initiative and the moment. Not let her dither. I led her down the corridor and through the door to the drawing room, but it was a huge, formal room, the only light, when I flicked it on, being the bright, overhead chandelier. I hesitated in its glare. Rachel, to my surprise, wisely crossed through and opened the French doors to the terrace on the west side.

'I'd rather be outside,' she told me, as we slipped out into the night.

In the dark, I decided she meant, and my heart began to pound. I'd thought, given half a chance, she'd run, but there was something decidedly collaborative about her now.

We walked down the sloping lawn, away from the house, in silence. On we padded, distancing ourselves from the chattering family around the table, from the twinkling lights strung between the trees. The buzz of voices became more muffled in the still night air. I realized we were heading for a tiny terrace the children smoked on, a round, stone one, which came equipped with a small iron bench. It was in a natural hollow just short of the orchard; a sunken space that someone – Camille's landscape gardener, no doubt – had realized would make a delightful sanctuary to catch the setting sun. The evening air was heavy now with the powerful scent of the rosemary bushes he'd planted strategically in a circle around it. There was a tiny candle on the little mosaic table and a lighter the children had left. I went to light it, but Rachel stayed my hand. The faint glow from the house made our faces just visible, and that was enough for her tonight. Also, I realized, it would threaten our privacy.

We sat down on the bench side by side, and I wondered how to embark on this. How to phrase it. Rachel, I knew, was not going to assist me. It helped that we weren't facing each other. I could study my hands. I licked my lips and dived in.

'Rachel, I know – have known, for years – that James has been keeping something back from me. But, out of respect for his privacy, I've never asked him what it is. I asked him tonight for the first time, but he wouldn't tell me.'

There was a silence.

'And now you're asking me.'

'Because I feel I need to know.'

'Why, so suddenly?'

'Well . . .'

'Because you divulged something yourself?'

I turned. Blinked at her. 'How did you know?'

'I don't. I'm guessing. But, often, people don't question a secret if they have one themselves. But now that you've shared yours, you feel you have a perfect right to know his, is that it?' Her voice was uncharacteristically hard. I was startled.

'No. No, of course not. I just –'

'And now that your mother's deserting you, you want to clutch at another security blanket. You need to be sure of

James. You don't want this loose end. You want to claw something back, for you. Have all of him.'

I stared, shocked. Her expression was not one I recognized. It was tough. Unfriendly. All of a sudden, though, it collapsed back into the Rachel I knew.

'Sorry. I didn't mean that, Flora. Well . . . I did, and I didn't. I didn't mean it to sound so harsh.'

I gulped. Nodded. 'No. But . . . God. You're right, I suppose. I do feel a bit like that. A bit quid pro quo. A bit – now it's your turn. And I am upset about Mum. I hadn't analysed it to that extent. I suppose I am being a bit desperate.' My breath was becoming shallower. 'And I shouldn't be asking you, Rachel. It's James's secret and, if he doesn't want to tell me, I've no business going around his back. No business –'

'Except, it's my secret, too,' she interrupted.

I held my tongue. Held my breath, too. In the still night air, the cicadas paused in their chattering, and it seemed to me that, should a feather drop from a passing night owl, should a field mouse scuttle by, I'd hear it.

'And the thing is, Flora, I've always thought that one day you would know. That it was really just a question of time. A question of when. And I imagine that moment's arrived.'

Chapter Twenty-Six

We sat in silence for a moment before Rachel spoke again. At length, she cleared her throat. Her tone, as she went on, was contemplative, reflective.

'D'you find, as you get older, Flora, that you're more accepting of others? Their foibles and habits? Faults, even?'

I blinked, wrong-footed. 'Up to a point, yes. I try to be less judgemental, if that's what you mean.'

'I think it is. When you're young, everything is so black and white. So categorical. People are honest or dishonest. Trustworthy or unreliable. Good or bad. And, once that label is there, it sticks. We press it down hard with the heel of our hand. But I'd like to think I've become more accepting – more realistic, anyway – as I've got older.'

It occurred to me to think Rachel had never been anything other. At least, that was how she presented to the world. It was me who was quick to judge, to proclaim on someone.

'You've always been generous-spirited, Rachel.'

'No, I haven't. I was very hard on Mummy.'

I glanced at her. I'd never heard her say that. Only refer to her as 'our mother'.

'She was not so terribly different to your mother, Flora.'

I must have looked shocked: felt it, too.

'Who is completely delightful and enchanting,' she went

on quickly. 'Which Mummy wasn't, always. I'm just saying, there were some similarities. Both high-spirited
women, young at heart – young, full stop, in my mother's
case. Light-hearted. Fun. I was serious-minded and book-
ish. And I minded very much about her frivolity, as I saw
it then. I was hard on her.'

'You were very young,' I reminded her.

'Yes. But I was . . . priggish. I hope I'm less so, now.'

It occurred to me that a young, bespectacled Rachel in
dreary clothes and constantly with her nose in a book
could have been described so.

'Sally was more like Mummy. But I was so disapproving,
I even turned Sally against her. A bit. And Sally always
looked up to me. Sally would say – Oh, but it's so dull here,
Rachel, we know that. Mummy dresses up to go into town
occasionally, to have some fun, buy clothes and have her
hair done, just because she's bored: what's wrong with
that? But I told her it was more than that. That she was
staying out late, drinking with local men. Coming back
very drunk in the small hours. Driving whilst drunk.'

'Which she was,' I reminded her.

'Yes, but I could have protected Mummy more. I told
James, too. Went on about it. In a way, I think I poisoned
them against her.'

'But she was out of control, Rachel. You had good
reason. And why should you shoulder all that knowledge
yourself?'

'Some older sisters might have done. But we were alone
a lot in that cold, echoing place and, sometimes, stories
were our only company. And, don't forget, I read a lot.
Lived through stories, really. So I'd embellish. Say she was

355

a disgrace, even though, on that particular day, she might only have been seeing a girlfriend for supper. My imagination ran riot. And Mummy and I didn't get on. I adored my father and hated his sadness. But . . . there were only two people in that marriage. I shouldn't have got involved. Shouldn't have taken sides. It was for them to work out.'

I shrugged. 'OK, but I think it's inevitable. Eldest child, you love them both, but side more with one –'

'Yes, but I didn't really,' she interrupted. She twisted round on the bench to face me. 'Love them both. I came to hate Mummy, and I idolized my father.'

I waited. Wondered what was coming.

'The night that . . . Mummy went into town, I told them about Darren, the builder she was seeing.'

'Told who?'

'James and Sally. Upstairs in my bedroom. Aunt Sarah's old room. We were all under the bedclothes, hugging our knees in the dark in that huge, spooky room, which hadn't been decorated since Daddy's childhood, with the big brass bed. I told them she was sleeping with another man.'

'Which she was.'

'I . . . don't know.'

She looked scared for a minute.

'Well, Rachel, everyone in the village said she was, it all came out in court. Darren's wife said so. It was in the paper I found.'

'Yes. It's just, I didn't know for sure. I was guessing. And came down against her. In a child's mind, that is obviously the ultimate treachery. One parent cheating on the other. Your mother sleeping with someone other than your father. They were incredibly shocked. Sally sobbed. She was only eleven. James shook, I remember. Physically shook with rage. Sally and I had to hold him. He went so white. I hurt him very badly. Couldn't have hurt him more if I'd stabbed him.'

I gazed at her, imagining it. Three children in their nightclothes, huddled together in bed.

'Anyway, that was the night Daddy got so drunk. I went down to the kitchen and tried to take the bottle away from him, but he wouldn't have it. Just sat there at the table with his whisky, staring at the door, waiting for her to come in. I went back upstairs and told James and Sally how upset he was, and nobody went to bed that night. We sat on my bed, frightened, in the dark. Squished together, still holding James, who was trembling.

'But you went to sleep eventually? I thought –'
'No.'

Thought the shot had wakened them, I was about to say. That's what I'd been told. I stared at her.

'Eventually, we heard the car, coming up the drive. I got out of bed and ran to the window. I remember seeing her get out of the car, staggering about. James was beside me. We saw her swaying in her high heels, which she took off. She was barefoot as she approached, clothes all askew. Sally was still crying quietly in the bed. We watched as she came stumbling, giggling even, towards the house. James was completely rigid beside me. Then we heard her come in. Obviously, she tried to creep in the back door to the kitchen, but she was met by a terrible roar from my father. We clutched each other as we waited for what would happen next. Daddy called her all the names under the sun – a whore, a tart, an adulterer, a cheap and trashy

357

tramp. Mummy was shrill, defensive at first, but then derisive – abusive even. Very drunk. She was caustic and cutting. I remember hearing, 'Compared to you, *old man*.'

Then we heard a scuffle. We ran to the landing. James and I fled along the passageway and down the back stairs to the kitchen. They were fighting in there, really fighting. Wrestling. I remember racing to separate them and, as I did, I passed Daddy's gun, at the foot of the stairs, which was unusual. It was always in the gun safe, always – he was meticulous about that. But the fox had been prowling round the chickens the last few nights. He, or James, had put it there for easy access.'

'James doesn't shoot.'

'He did. Loved it. Rabbits, pheasants. Grouse, even. I saw James glance at it, too, but for longer than I did. Really stare.'

Oh dear God. I went cold.

'I don't remember much of what happened next, because I was so intent on separating them. Daddy had a hand round Mummy's throat and her knee was up in his groin. Daddy gasped in pain and I remember pushing him back hard, in the chest. He let go of Mummy, but she still had his hair. Chunks came out in her hands, but I managed to push them apart and give Daddy a superhuman shove, back against the wall. And then a shot rang out.'

Both hands flew to my mouth in horror.

'But how – it was Drummond!'

'No.'

I gazed at her. 'James shot his mother?' I breathed. 'Jesus Christ, Rachel – it was James?'

She stared back at me, her face like porcelain in the

darkness. 'Mummy was face up on the floor, arms and legs splayed out, blood gushing out of her mouth. Pumping. Her chest was covered in blood, too – soaked. At the foot of the stairs was Sally, in her pink nightie. The gun was in her hands.'

I went silent in horror. When I came to, both my hands were clamped over my mouth. At length, I extracted them. '*Sally* shot her?'

'Yes. James was frozen, still halfway down the stairs. I'd thought he was behind me. Had felt someone on my heels. But it was Sally. It was her glance I'd felt rest on the gun and, in the confusion, I thought it was James.' She swallowed. 'There was a moment when we were all suspended in time like that. The entire family, in the kitchen, in total shock and disbelief. And then the whole scene came to life. Jerked horribly back into action. Although, bits of it, I've blanked. I remember Daddy rushing to Mummy, bending over her, but there was so much blood. He was slipping in it. An unbelievable amount of blood. I remember lots and lots of screaming. Me, I think, mostly. Hysterical. James was still frozen. Then I remember Daddy taking the gun from Sally, who'd lowered it but still had it in her hands. He wiped it with a tea towel. Then he clutched it hard, before tossing it aside. I remember him dashing for the telephone. Ringing the police, the ambulance. Saying there'd been a terrible accident, to come quick. Then I remember him breathing very hoarsely, like a death rattle, herding us back up the stairs, to my bedroom.

'Up, *up!* Go! Quick!'

We ran to my room. Away from Mummy. Terrified. And, once he'd shut the door on us, he raced back down.

The police came very quickly, considering we were so remote. It all happened very fast. But they came by helicopter, you see, from Dundee. I remember it hovering outside the window, the trees all whipped up and important-looking, like something in an American movie, the long grass rustling as it landed. Daddy's footsteps were pounding up the stairs again. He flew in.

'Is she dead? Is she dead?' I shrieked, knowing she was. I was hysterical. The other two were silent.

'Yes, she's dead. The gun went off by mistake in my hands. I only meant to frighten her.'

I remember the three of us staring at him in the darkness, bewildered.

'But . . .'

'Yes, that's right, went off in my hands.'

'But – you didn't have the gun, Daddy.'

'I did, I had the gun. Remember that. If you do anything for me this night, you'll remember that. Rachel?'

'Yes, Daddy.'

'James?'

'Yes, Daddy.'

'Sally?'

'Yes, Daddy.'

She shuddered. 'None of us will ever forget that. As the police banged on the front door, down he went. And there we stayed, huddled and terrified, as I, Daddy's natural supporter, rammed it home. Sally, in prison? Unthinkable. Of course, I didn't know that might not have happened.'

'Daddy shot her by accident, yes, James?'

'Yes.'

'Sally?'

'Yes.'

We were so scared.

A kind policewoman came up, and we were wrapped in blankets and helped downstairs. Sally was carried. We were taken down the front stairs, not the back ones to the kitchen, but outside to the front drive. We passed Mummy, on a stretcher. She was covered in a blanket, about to be taken to the helicopter. I remember her face. There was no blood on it now, it was pure white above the red blanket. Daddy was talking to a policeman. We were driven away in a car. After that, it's all a bit of a blur. At the police station, we all told the same story. We were in shock, deep shock, and doing exactly as we'd been told, which was something we'd always done. We always obeyed my father. Never questioned him.'

She breathed deeply: gave herself a moment. 'And then we went to Aunt Sarah's, in Kent. She came and got us. And it all became sort of . . . surreal. Otherworldly. As if we'd simply come to stay, which, of course, we never did. In this nice, creamy, Edwardian house in a row of other houses outside Tunbridge Wells, with a big back garden and a cedar tree. It was as if . . . nothing had ever happened. I remember one day, at teatime, our cousin Paul said something about Scotland, and Aunt Sarah shot him such a look. It was never, ever mentioned again. It was as if our parents had been airbrushed from our lives. We even went to school with Paul and Anne for a couple of months. No mobiles, of course, in those days, and I don't even remember us talking to Daddy on the phone. Perhaps we did. I don't know. As I say, I've blanked a lot.'

I stayed very still.

'After that, of course, there was the court case. They decided not to put us in the dock, not to question us further, since my father had made a full confession. The gun had been there for the fox – of course, it shouldn't have been loaded, or out of the safe, he was genuinely culpable in that respect – and in the heat of the moment he'd grabbed it and it had gone off in his hands by accident. We thought he was going to be charged with manslaughter, and it was a terrible shock when they changed it to murder, which carries a mandatory life sentence. But life sentences vary – the shortest, at the time, being nine years, which Daddy got. I remember Aunt Sarah taking the phone call in the hall by the front door. We hadn't been allowed near the court in London, and no newspapers had been allowed in the house. I remember her coming back through and collapsing at the kitchen table.

'Nine years!' She covered her face with her hands. 'Nine years!' she sobbed. I rushed to comfort her, horrified. Then I looked up and saw Sally, white-faced, in the doorway.'

Rachel swallowed. Blinked rapidly into the dark night. 'After that, we went back to Brechallis, and Daddy's other sister, Belinda, came over from Ireland.'

'The spinster.'

'That's right. The teacher. She took over. Became our carer, I suppose. And we all went to boarding school. Just came home in the holidays, when Belinda would appear from Ireland. And, again, it was never mentioned.'

'Not even between the three of you? In the holidays?'

'Never. Because that would have given credence to the truth. It would have made it real, and Daddy didn't want that. The weird thing is . . . we almost came to believe it, I think. In our minds. Again, we didn't discuss it, but I think we all believed Daddy had killed Mummy by accident. That was definitely what had happened. Once, at school, someone in my dorm said, "Golly, poor you. And your poor father. What a dreadful thing to have to live with." I remember having to go to the san. Spending the night in there.' Rachel shut her eyes. I sat by quietly, shocked.

'Anyway' – she composed herself – 'we would go and visit Daddy at Dartmoor and, as you can imagine, he was always on good form. Always made light of it. Showed us his tapestry, or whatever he'd been doing, said the food was tremendous, that sort of thing. He was in charge of the vegetable garden eventually, had a team working for him. Said it was just like the army – well, you've heard him.' I had. Often. 'And time – years – just sort of drifted by. We got on with our lives. What else could we do? As we got older, I'm sure we all realized that Sally wouldn't have gone to prison, but . . . would she have been taken into care? Would we all have been taken into care? What would have happened? She would surely have been all over the papers, revealed as the girl who shot her mother, how would that have affected her? As it was, she was growing up OK. Or so it seemed. She never . . . formed any real attachment to anybody, though. No schoolfriends, nothing. But then I didn't really, either. James was better. Brought friends home, went to stay with them – but you were the only girl he brought back.'

'But not the only girlfriend.' I knew that.

'No, but the only one we met.'

My breathing became quite rapid. I tried not to think

about my poor darling James. To concentrate on what she was saying.

'Anyway. Daddy did form a close friendship. Inside.'

'With Donaldson.'

'Yes. Who'd also been in the army. As a private. And they formed this sort of officer–orderly bond, which suited them. And when they were released at much the same time – Donaldson was a lifer, too – as you know, he came to live on the farm.'

'Yes.' He was a surly, rather scarily brooding man, but quite good-looking in a dark, rough sort of way.

'What we didn't know, until much later, was that Daddy had broken the pact. The sacred, unshakable rule that the rest of us had kept.'

I stared at her, mute. Found my voice. 'He'd told him.'

She nodded. 'And what James and I also didn't know – in fact, I'm not sure James even knows now; I only found out by accident – was that Donaldson used it. With Sally. Let her know he knew. Turned the screw. Taunted her with it. Sally had always been the most panicky and nervous of the three of us, but I'd thought that was only natural. Had thought she'd be better when Daddy got out. So I'd stayed at the farm, thinking – all will be well when he's back. I can go. Have a life. But, if anything, it got worse, and I didn't know why. Couldn't work it out. She was even more teary, more fluttery – hysterical, at times. He bullied her, you see, and I think . . . blackmailed her. Certainly, she has no jewellery left. I think Sally realized she could never escape her past. And she got fatter and fatter, as if in defence. Ballooned to – well, you know.'

'Yes.' I inhaled sharply, remembering her cramming the

food in: standing right inside the pantry, taking it straight from the shelves to her mouth – pork pies, cold potatoes – so scared and unhappy. 'Oh God, Rachel, you couldn't leave her.'

'No. And she couldn't tell our father. He adored Donaldson. It would destroy him. Break his heart. Daddy had done so much for Sally, anyway.'

'And then, finally, Donaldson died.'

'Yes. Six months ago. And Sally escaped. Up to a point. In a manner of speaking. She lost all the weight, anyway – that was miraculous – and she worked further away from the glen. She made a few friends, too, proper ones, not just boasting about people she worked for. And then she met Max. But I knew she'd never form a proper relationship. She was too damaged for that, a psychologist would no doubt say. Which I think suited Max, too.'

'Yes,' I agreed. 'Although not in such a complicated way.' God, Max was a simple creature compared to this.

'No. No, of course not.'

'And James?' I asked, with a lump in my throat. 'D'you think . . . I mean . . . is he damaged, too?'

'You mean, enough to ever properly connect?'

'Yes!' I whispered, scared.

She covered my hand with hers. 'Oh, come on, Flora. Do you even have to ask? Of *course* not. Why are you even saying that? You know that's not true.'

I felt relief flood through me. 'Yes. I know that's not true. It was – well, it was that nightmarish tale you've just told me still speaking, I suppose. I was still in it.'

Still with that little twelve-year-old boy, frigid and terrified on the stairs. Keeping the real story of what had happened that night to himself, all his life. What *must* that be like? Terrible, but not as terrible as it had been for Sally. Of course not. But still. A ghastly secret. And secrets have to be kept. It's imperative. Because, look what happened when Drummond told only one person? Donaldson? It spiralled out of control. They *have* to be kept. So that if a bit of me was even remotely hurt that he hadn't told me – which it wasn't – I knew why.

Rachel and I sat together in the heavy, warm air, the fireflies playing in the tree lights which twinkled in the distance. I thought about what true love really meant. It meant sacrifice. As Drummond had done for Sally. And as Rachel had for Sally, too, never leaving her. It was something visceral, unspoken and profound that could never be put in Valentine cards or whispered in ears, because it was so completely silent and unutterable.

After a while I turned to her. 'Are you going to tell James you've told me?'

She barely missed a beat. 'Yes.'

I was so grateful. I told her so. 'I – don't think I'd be able to hide it, you see. The fact that I know. We're so in tune with each other. So tight. I'd find it impossible not to say. It's so huge, and I am so transparent. It would be all over my face.'

'I know. And the thing is, I always thought it would come out one day. That you'd know the truth. Even though James and I never discussed it. Because you two are so strong. I didn't think he'd be able to keep it inside for ever.'

'Except he did. You told me, Rachel.'

She turned to me properly in the darkness. 'But the

thing is, Flora' – she gave a small smile – 'he asked me to tell you.'

I felt my eyes widen. 'James did?'

'Yes. Said he wasn't sure he'd be capable of doing it. Without breaking down. And don't see that as a sign of weakness, Flora, that he asked me.'

'I don't.' I was so relieved. James had wanted me to know. Just hadn't been able to tell me himself. My eyes filled with tears.

'When did he ask you?' I whispered.

'Tonight. Before supper. He came and found me in my room. He said he owed it to you.' I inhaled sharply. She went on. 'I wanted to give myself some time to compose myself, think how to put it. He'd said at some point would I talk to you; he didn't mean tonight. In the next few months I think he meant, maybe when you came to Scotland. But you stopped me in the kitchen and there was no escape. I could see it in your eyes. I knew you wanted it now. And perhaps it's better this way. That it's over. Done.'

We sat very still. There was no sound, apart from the odd cicada chattering in the long grass, but I sensed something, or someone, close by. Slowly, I turned my head towards the sea. There, in the darkness, just below us in the olive grove, a small candle in a jar in his hand, was James. Waiting. He'd known I couldn't wait, too.

Rachel got to her feet. She reached out for both my hands in a swift movement and took them in hers. We held on to each other for a moment. Held each other's eyes, too. Then she turned and slipped away, into the night.

Chapter Twenty-Seven

I made my way towards him, through the rough, spiky grass in the orchard, which prickled my bare ankles, picking my way in the dark around the hassocks which would suddenly rear up in clumps. As I approached, he put the candle on the ground and held out his arms. I walked into them, and we held on tight. For a moment I was transported back twenty years: to when our love was new and he was a junior doctor at St Thomas's and I was a budding young journalist on the *Evening Standard*. It was that same intense, enveloping embrace of those early days. We held each other fiercely. After a while, our grip loosened and I lay my head on his chest. I could hear his heart beating. His voice, when it came, was a bit thick. Muffled.

'I'm not sure I'll be able to talk about it, Flora.'

'There's nothing to talk about. I know everything. There's nothing that needs to be discussed.'

I knew he wouldn't want me to say, God, James, how *awful*! Poor you. Poor Sally! How have you kept it hidden all these years? So I didn't. Waited for his cue, if there was to be one.

'There is one thing I do have to say, though,' he went on, more calmly, having cleared his throat. 'And that's that you must never tell a soul. Not the girls, not anyone.'

'James, that goes without saying.'

'Yes, but it needs saying. Because I believe by law – I

don't know, but I have a fair idea – the three of us, me Sally and Rachel, and you too, now, might be complicit.'

I raised my head.

'What d'you mean?'

'There's something called an accessory after the fact, which, as I understand it, makes it a positive duty to report a crime.'

'Oh, James, that's absurd! Your father's already served a life sentence. And Sally was eleven!'

'Yes, you may be right. I don't know. I've never asked and have never even trawled the internet for information. Because I don't want to know.'

'No.' I was scared suddenly.

'But, as you say, she was eleven, so perhaps not.'

'I agree, though,' I said quickly. 'About never telling a soul. Especially not the girls,' I added fiercely, protectively. I lay my head on his chest again.

A silence flooded between us.

'That's the thing about secrets,' I said, breaking it eventually. 'I was thinking it earlier. They're better kept.'

'Yes, but once you'd asked me, I knew you'd be hurt if I didn't tell you. I didn't want it smouldering away in the background of our marriage.'

'And it would have done.' I lifted my head: we'd given ourselves enough time now. Could look at each other properly in the faint moonlight. I took a step back and searched his eyes. They were hurt and pensive. Like a small boy's. As I gazed, I realized that, actually, there were some things I would like to ask him. Like whether he thought that not being involved that night was what had saved him? Emotionally? The rest of his family – Rachel, delivering the shocking news to her siblings about their mother's infidelity; Drummond, leaving the gun out and loaded at the foot of the stairs; Sally using it – had made huge mistakes, were all, in different respects, responsible, something they'd never recover from. They'd carry it to their graves. But James had been an innocent bystander. A spectator. Was that how he'd escaped? Been the only one able to lead a normal life? I didn't ask. And never would.

What I did know, though, was that the two of us had changed. That in the wake of these revelations we'd be subtly different for ever. Perhaps more gentle with one another. More understanding. Perhaps not, in time. Perhaps things would just return to normal and it would all disappear into the ether again.

'D'you want to walk down to the headland?' he asked.

'What headland?'

'The one further down the hill, with the best view of the sea. Haven't you been?'

I knew he was teasing me. Was pleased. I became jocular, too. 'No! Who have you been with? Something else you're not telling me?'

I might have chosen better banter. Nerves, I suppose, but James smiled, knowing I meant well, that I was rallying. Joining him in lightening the mood. Being stoic about it.

'Amelia, actually. She was taking pictures down there. With her proper camera, not that stupid one on her phone.'

'Oh, good.'

'She showed me some. They're not bad.'

I smiled. 'Try telling her that.'

'Well, at least she's finally decided to go to art college.'

'I know,' she told me. 'Northumbria, apparently.'

'Which will no doubt change.'

Normal humdrum conversation, which helped. We walked on together, using the candle to light our way to the other side of the orchard. Through the gate we went, shutting it on the donkey, who'd followed, and then down a little lane in the dark, a couple of pilgrims with their juddering candle. We needed some time, you see. Couldn't go straight back to the others, not just yet. The change of scene, the walk, clinging to motion, helped us to get our breath back. Helped distance us from any nightmarish scenes, to return from the past to the present. When we'd found the headland he meant, just a flat rock really, which we climbed up on to, it did indeed have a bird's-eye view of the sea, lights twinkling from boats. In fact, it was so beautiful, it was almost impossible to be anywhere else except the here and now. It would do the trick. We sat with our arms around each other, facing the view, soft breeze on our faces.

'It's funny,' I mused at length. 'In no time at all we'll be back home. Getting on with life. And these things, which neither of us knew anything about before we left, will be there with us, in the house. Around us in our daily lives.'

'Yes, except in a way, they'll be smaller for each of us. Certainly not bigger. Because they'll be shared.'

'Yes.' I turned to him, pleased. 'You're right. I hadn't thought about it like that. We've diminished them.'

'Waved our swords at them.' He smiled.

'Chopped their heads off!'

'Exactly.'

We squeezed each other. Turned back to the view.

'It's funny to think of being back in Clapham at all,' he said, after a while, with unusual despondency.

'Yes, isn't it?' I turned back to look at him. Couldn't gauge his expression. But then it was dark. 'James . . . you're not thinking . . .'

'What?'

'Well – I'd stay here in a heartbeat!'

'Oh, Flora.' He laughed. 'How could we? I've told you, that's just holiday talk.'

'No, but think about it, James. We could. I have no reason to go back now –'

'Yes, but I do!'

'But you hate it.'

'Well, of course I hate it. It's work. Lots of people hate work. But that's life, my darling. That's the deal. You work hard, you keep your head down, and if you're lucky – you make it through to the other side. To your retirement package.'

'Which is tiny. And also, a good fifteen years away.'

'Fourteen.'

'And it won't be much, James. We know that. They've whittled away at your job – taken away all the good stuff, the stuff you like, the interesting operations – and now they're hacking away at your pension. And they'll probably change the rules again before we get our hands on it. You'll probably have to work another five years, till you're sixty-five or something, before you even get a sniff of it. Do millions more toenails and corns, bugger on till then.'

'Yes. Thank you for reminding me. I know what my job description is. But what's the alternative?'

'Well, there *is* an alternative, don't you see?' I turned to him eagerly on the rock. Took a deep breath. 'There is always an alternative.'

He gave a hollow laugh. Dropped his arm from around my shoulders and drew up his knees. Hugged them. 'You're just intoxicated by this holiday, Flora, that's all. It's been too much for you. Too much for all of us. Too spoiling. We should have had a week in Bognor,' he said gloomily.

'But so many things have happened out here.'

'Yes, quite enough, if you ask me. Just drop it.'

He meant that. Had said it quite tersely. Changed the tone. And we'd been so close a moment ago. I knew I was ruining the moment. Nevertheless, I wouldn't drop it, because something told me that this *was* the moment. Something told me this was the night. When souls, already laid bare, emotions, already running high, were open and receptive. I had to seize my chance.

'So many life-changing, perspective-altering things have happened,' I went on in a low voice, trying to keep it steady. 'Don't you see? It's made *us* different. Made *me* feel differently about –'

'Life?' he offered sarcastically.

'Yes, OK, if you like,' I said defiantly. 'Life. About needing to grab it.'

'With two hands?' he offered, eyebrows raised.

'James, listen, please!'

He sighed. Removed his glasses and rubbed the bridge of his nose wearily. Replaced them again. 'OK. So what do you suggest? Buy a vineyard? Make our own wine and try to sell it? Flog it to derisive Jean-Pierres, like every other idiotic, idealistic English couple who've ever read *A Year in Provence*?'

'No, not a vineyard. A restaurant.'

'Ha!' He threw his head back and barked out a laugh to the stars. 'A restaurant!' His face, when it came back, was delighted. 'In France! *Les ros-bifs anglais?* Les Feesh and Cheeps? You must be mad!'

'Except we're not *les ros-bifs anglais*, are we, James? Cuisine-wise, we're as sophisticated as they are. Both of us. And, anyway, we'd have a French chef.'

'Who?'

I paused. 'Jean-Claude. He's brilliant. And I should know, it's my job to know. Trust me, he's out of this world. First class. He cooked for us the other night. It blew me away. It's what he did before the antiques.'

'Yes, I know, but –'

'In Paris, James. Rue Saint-Honoré. La Terrasse.'

'Off the Tuileries?'

'Right there. And then in the Jardin des Plantes.'

'He didn't say.'

'He wouldn't, to you. He's modest. And broken, too, by the experience. I had to prise it out of him. But you know me.'

'I do.'

'He was screwed over by the staff, who had their fingers in the till, and then by his ex-wife. He lost all his money. Took his eye off the ball. He's never got back in. He had two Michelin stars.'

James gazed at me. I licked my lips, knowing I had his attention.

'He has no business acumen whatsoever. None at all. You have loads.'

'Well, I –'

'Yes, you have. You know you have. You run your private practice yourself —'

'Such as it is.'

'Exactly, such as it is. Vanishing daily. But no other surgeon does that. They all have help. You could run that entire hospital if you felt like it — you've often said it's the side you should have gone into. A restaurant would be a piece of cake. And I know people in Paris, James. Influential people on the best magazines, newspapers, who'd write it up for us.'

'You want to do it in Paris!' he cried.

'No, down here, in Provence. But Paris is where the reviews will come from. I can get it on the map.'

'And where will the money come from, eh? To run this exclusive, Michelin-starred eatery? I presume that's what you're going for? Fine dining? Top end? How are you going to pay the staff, the waiters?'

'We'd have to sell Clapham, obviously.'

'Right!' he yelped, rocking back on his haunches.

'Probably for about two million pounds.'

He barked out another laugh. 'Oh, don't be absurd!'

'I promise you, James, you have no idea. That is what four-bedroomed houses south of the river like ours go for, even though we bought it for diddly squat twenty years ago. But we wouldn't spend it all on the restaurant, we'd buy a house, too, with some of the money. There'd be enough — it's cheaper out here. Mum would help with the restaurant.' My mother could do that. She'd been left a healthy inheritance by Philippe. Not as much as his wife, but a substantial amount. Some of which she'd used to buy Fulham, some of which she still had.

'How d'you know she'd want to?' he asked defiantly, but there was less conviction in his voice. Mum had to be constantly restrained from spending her money, from giving it all to us, which James found emasculating. She'd wanted to pay the school fees, but he hadn't let her. She'd clasp her hands with glee at this, sink in all of it, not that we'd let her. We'd have to rein her in. Somewhere small, I was thinking, in a bustling market town. Not remote. Passing trade was crucial. I'd even wondered about Jean-Claude's current premises, in the middle of a busy town, Mum had said. We'd walk to the market for the produce. I would. With Mum. Baskets over our arms. Meat and game, we'd source from local farmers. Just twenty covers, perhaps. And a few outside on a terrace. A small menu. Three choices for lunch, four for supper. But with the menu changing daily, according to what was bought. And I'd buy the best. Had spent twenty years training for it. Tasting for it. Moving, unknowingly, towards this day.

Word would spread, derisively at first – 'Les Anglais, they've opened a restaurant!' But when they came to mock, they'd eat their words. And how many French restaurateurs did I know in London who said they only employed English staff these days, not French, because they worked harder? And boy, we'd work hard. James would work his socks off, I knew, although, in time, I hoped he wouldn't have to. As I say, we'd keep it small. To begin with. After that – who knows? A larger premises? More covers. But no. For the minute – *petite*. Manageable.

James jumped off the rock. He was pacing about, hands in his pockets jingling his change, keeping his face averted in an effort to show he was not infected. Like so many foodies, we'd sat in countless restaurants over the years discussing the winning formula, how to do it properly, what would make a place really stand out. But we'd only ever dreamed. Had never really meant it.

'And the girls?' he said, forcing some sarcasm into his voice. 'They'd commute from London?'

'The girls are only with us for the holidays, James. Tara's in her final year, and now that Amelia's finally decided to go to college – yes, they'd commute, if you like, in the holidays.'

'Which they'll tire of. The novelty will wear off. All their friends are in London.'

'Except Mum's going to keep her house. Jean-Claude has persuaded her to do that. They'll always have a base there.'

'Oh, great, two teenagers living it up in Granny's Fulham pad. It'll be a drug den in no time!'

'No, because, if they are there, I'll go back. They'll come to France for the first couple of holidays, but when, as you say, they want to be in London, I'll be there, too. The restaurant will be up and running by then. You won't need me all the time. And I can do some good PR in London, go and see reviewers, travel writers. Spread the word.'

I'd thought this bit through very carefully. The girls were my top priority: always had been. But I could still make use of my time back home with them.

'And, anyway, they're not children, James. Amelia's nearly nineteen. They're young women. Plenty of their friends have parents who live abroad.'

'Plenty?'

'Emma's in Cyprus, Polly's in Dubai –'

'Well, yes, army. Or work.'

'*We'll* be work,' I said fiercely, clenching my fists. 'Working abroad. And crikey, they've had all their young life with us. It's not as if we shunted them off to boarding school at ten.'

He massaged his forehead hard with his fingers. Kneaded it. 'I don't know, Flora. It's such a risk. To give up everything, my work, my whole career. All my medical training.'

'You hate it. Hate what you do. What you once loved has turned around and bitten you hard on the bottom. You are so disillusioned. And this is not a risk.'

'Of course it's a bloody risk! It could so easily go wrong. Go tits up and leave us penniless! God, I don't even know why we're talking about it. This is silly talk. Forget it. Forget I even discussed it with you – indulged you. I was caught up in the emotion of another moment, one that happened thirty-odd years ago. Vulnerable to – to emotive chatter.'

'It is not emotive chatter.'

'Oh, trust me, it is. It's holiday-itus. Crap. Pipe dreams. Forget it, Flora. We go back as planned, to our boring but salaried jobs, next week. Or, at least, I do.' He shot me a flinty look. 'You'll look for another. I'm cross you even made me talk about it. Took advantage of the situation.'

He turned angrily on his heel and stomped off along the lane towards the olive grove, leaving me on the rock, looking out to sea, a flickering candle at my feet. I watched him go. Saw his tall, familiar figure wend its way up the hill, along the zigzag path, through the gate to the orchard. I lost sight of him then. But knew he'd march crossly. Go

378

back up the sloping lawn to the house, shoulders hunched, up the terrace steps and straight to bed. I turned and looked out at the vista before me. The soft lights of the few farms freckled in the valley beneath me glowed whilst the twinkling lights in the bay beckoned. The heavy night air was soft on my face. I stayed there, on my rock, hugging my knees, breathing in the scents of Provence, gazing a while. At length, I climbed down, picked up the candle in the jar and, having given him some time and some distance, followed my husband thoughtfully back to the house.

Chapter Twenty-Eight

We were awoken the following morning by a terrible rumpus. I'd been fast asleep, having finally dropped off in the small hours, my head too full of the night's events to fall precipitously into the arms of Morpheus, so it was an almighty jolt to hear shouting — swearing, even — all in French. It took me a moment to wonder where I was. It didn't help that the voices were unfamiliar or, at least, the protagonist's was. An angry, voluble man. Livid, even. I sat up in bed, realizing I was covered in sweat. Throwing off the sheet for some air, I tuned my ear into the incredible row beneath me. Who could it be?

'What the hell's going on?' growled James, still half asleep beside me.

Amelia burst into our room, wide-eyed in her pyjamas. I pulled the sheet up quickly.

'There's this really fit guy in the kitchen, right, looks like Johnny Depp, who's clearly Camille's husband. He's kicking up shit with Michel and Thérèse.'

'How d'you know he's Camille's husband? Pass me that T-shirt, please.'

She tossed me one from a chair. I wriggled into it. 'Because Tara and I crept into her room in the tower when she wasn't there, remember? Had a poke around, found a few photos — we showed you, so don't pretend you don't know.'

'Oh. Right,' I said guiltily. I'd been cross, but interested, too. 'Is Camille down there?'

'No, she left. You know that.'

'I just wondered if she'd come back with him.'

'Why would she do that? They're estranged, remember? Duh. No, they're down there fighting over the girl, Agathe.'

'How d'you know?'

'My French is not that limited, Mother. I did get an A at GCSE. You'd be better, though. Go on, Mum, go suss it out.'

'Don't get involved,' mumbled James sleepily as, with as much of a nose for gossip as my daughter, I tumbled out of bed. I slipped into my dressing gown – pausing only for a quick pee and a ruffle of my curls, should Johnny Depp be interested in the over-forties bedroom look – and crept down the passage towards the gallery. The landing ran right around the kitchen and drawing room on the first floor, affording a perfect view. Obviously, I kept well back from the action and slid against the wall, crouching down low, as the shouting, if anything, got more furious.

Tempers were indeed frayed: someone was incensed and, actually, I think I could have crept right to the edge and dangled my legs through the spindles and no one would have noticed. From a distance, I could just see, as Amelia had so rightly said, the top half of a very attractive dark-haired man with fine Latin features. He had slightly hooded light eyes in a narrow face, and a very straight nose. More of a young Alain Delon than a Johnny Depp, actually. He was sitting at the kitchen table by the open French windows in jeans and a blue linen shirt, sleeves rolled up to the elbows. His profile was towards me and he

381

was firing off a stream of invective, his face, under his tan, pale with anger.

'She's an animal!' he was saying, in a cultivated Right Bank accent, spitting out the words. 'She let's me discover, through a DNA test, when she already knows the result. Let's me take it, because she hasn't the guts to tell me herself. What sort of a woman – what sort of a *mother*, is she?'

Michel and Thérèse sat opposite him, dark heads bowed in silence. Thérèse had her apron on over her dress and Michel was in his *bleu de travail* overalls. They didn't look at him. Gazed down into their laps.

'And you two – you go along with it. Duping me, selfishly, just to get what you want, neither of you having the courage to tell me, when I've been so kind to you. Letting you see Agathe as much as you want, because I know you adore her – and now I know why! The reason! You're filth. You . . . *you*!' – he swung round to Michel – 'disgust me.' His lip curled, but it was quivering, too. He turned to Thérèse. 'And you – you let him. Let him sleep with my wife. Your own sister!' At this his voice cracked with pain. Horror, too. He threw back his head and gave a primeval cry.

'You have no idea, Étienne' – Thérèse's voice, when it came, was low, trembling with emotion – 'how much that cost me. How much. But you also have no idea – *tu ne comprends pas*' – she clenched both fists on the table and leaned forward, her face contorted – 'the lengths a woman will go to to have a child.'

'There are other ways,' he whispered angrily, leaning forward also, right into her face. His fists were balled, too. '*Were* other ways, available to you.'

'Expensive ways.'

'Which Camille paid for. Don't give me that crap!' He flung himself back in his chair.

'Yes, she did, four times. But the last time, when it didn't work, the doctors said they wouldn't do it again. That was my last chance. No more IVF.'

'There was another hospital. Where they said they'd do it again. You told me.'

'Sharks, at a private clinic, with their eyes only on Camille's money – the hospital told us that, too. Told us private clinics would let us go on for ever, compounding our grief, our disappointment. But it wouldn't work. Not for us. This was the best way. The only way.'

'Why didn't she do it properly, then?' Étienne lurched forward across the table again, right into her. 'Be a surrogate mother, have all the tests, go through the motions, all the procedures?'

All three faces at the table knew why. Said it all. 'Camille wouldn't do that,' Thérèse said eventually. 'I knew. And I wouldn't ask. She'd paid for all the IVF . . . done so much already.'

'She'd throw money at something, but she wouldn't consider putting herself out,' spat Étienne. 'Wouldn't put herself through it, all those hospital visits, hoops to jump through, tests to take – but a quick fuck with her brother-in-law, who she's always fancied – *pas de problème*. It would amuse her. Appeal to her warped sense of humour. And to be granted permission?' He gave a hollow laugh. 'What could be better? She's sick, I tell you.'

'I didn't care. Still don't care, now,' Thérèse said defiantly. 'I told you, I'd do anything.'

'I bet she didn't even think she'd get pregnant. Thought

383

it was just a quick shag. I bet that was a nasty surprise. After all, she never did with me.' His voice lurched at this. He couldn't look at Michel. Turned away.

'Maybe. And, yes, I think you're right. She told me she thought she couldn't,' said Thérèse. 'But she did. And she selflessly had the baby for us – she didn't have to do that.'

'Selflessly!' Étienne lunged right across the table, his face twisted and I saw spittle fly from his mouth. 'Camille never did anything selfless in her entire life. She never wanted children, I knew that when I married her, but I thought I'd talk her round, I was so in love with her. I couldn't believe it when I did, when my campaign prevailed, when, so suddenly, almost overnight, when she'd been adamant about not having any – only the week before – she agreed. But she was already pregnant by then, and she knew it. Of course, I didn't question that it was mine. And, in a way, once she'd got used to the shock, it must have suited her. She'd have the child, which would satisfy me – my irritating, persistent pleadings – and round off her public persona in one fell swoop. Make her profile warmer, more accessible, more *human*. A constant complaint of her PR people. Too much the ice maiden, they said. But she'd never really have to look after Agathe. She would always be with you when it was her turn for custody. An equal share, the judge said, but I didn't understand that. Why shouldn't Agathe be with me the *whole* time, when, in Camille's care, she was always with you? So when I fought it, eventually, in the courts, stupidly – oh, *so* stupid.' He screwed his eyes up and thrust the palms of his hands into them. 'You all watched. Stood by and watched.'

He removed his hands. 'And, at first, it goes well for me. The judge is sympathetic, I can tell, until Camille, knowing she's about to lose, knowing the judge will side with me and knowing, too, what that will do to her image: Camille de Bouvoir loses custody of her child – imagine! She insists I have a DNA test. *Merde!*' He hit his forehead with the heel of his hand, his face tortured.

Two figures crept to join me: Amelia and Tara, in their pyjamas.

'Is it good?' whispered Tara, crouching down beside me.

I made an anguished face. 'So sad.'

They hugged their knees.

'Thank God they had the humanity to let me know out of court, privately, when the results were in. But *you* knew. You could have told me the truth. Instead, it comes like a grenade, landing in the middle of my life. And, immediately – I know the rest. Know the father. It comes to me like another bomb, an unexploded one this time, one I've been sitting on for years. I wouldn't let myself believe it at first, would not let myself consider it. The horrible truth.' He gave a strangled sob and his head dropped into his hands. Tara gripped my arm. 'So now, I lose Agathe completely,' we heard him say in a muffled voice. 'I am worse off than when I started.'

There was a terrible, chilling silence.

'Never, Papa.' A small voice made the three of us jump. Our heads swung to the left. Through the French windows at the opposite end of the room, from the garden side, a small figure in short, floral pyjamas had crept in.

'Agathe?' whispered Tara, who couldn't see. She craned her neck. I nodded. Put my finger to my lips.

'You will always be my Papa – always. Now and for ever. I don't care what a court says. If you don't.'

Étienne clearly couldn't speak, so overcome with emotion was he. But in an eloquent gesture, as she approached, he drew her to him with an outstretched arm. With the other, he wiped his face, which was wet with tears. She stood beside him, her arm around his shoulders, his around her waist.

'And Thérèse and Michel will be my uncle and aunt, even though Thérèse has been like a mother to me, always, and Michel, a second father. That is how I'd like it to remain. As it's always been. The three of us. Just as it is now. During the week with Papa in Grasse, the weekends here, with Thérèse and Michel. Just as always. But I don't want to see *Maman*. Don't want to go to her in Paris, in the holidays.'

Tara squeezed my arm. 'Quite brave,' she whispered.

Étienne swallowed. He composed himself. 'At all, *chérie*?'

'She scares me,' Agathe said in a small voice. 'When I know I'm going there, when you drop me off, I sweat. And when I go up to her apartment, she never comes to greet me – her maid lets me in – and when I do see her, she says, "How long are you staying?" I know she doesn't want me. She's happy when I'm in my room, or watching TV. If we go out, we go shopping, for her. Chanel. Saint Laurent. I sit on a chair. And I never say the right thing. And always she tells me to speak up. And, sometimes, when I'm there, I wet the bed. That makes her very angry. And she's right, I'm too old, I shouldn't. But she doesn't like me,' she finished sadly.

'She never liked anyone very much, *chérie*,' said Thérèse

softly. Her own sister. 'It's just how she is. She can't . . . trust. And if I told you, as a child, she, too, wet the bed . . . Our mother, you see. Your grandmother. Camille was so pretty. Too pretty for her. With this brilliant voice. Like our mother. It was not the same for me. But that's another story.'

So many stories. Tragic ones. Stretching back and back in time. Affecting so many children. How many more, I wondered? Sally. Rachel. Camille, too, it seemed. James and Thérèse were survivors. Me, too. By the grace of God and the skin of our teeth. The ones who got away. I squeezed my own children's hands tight.

'But if that's what you want, *ma chérie*, I'm afraid I am not the person to implement it,' said Étienne sadly. His voice was broken. 'Not in a position. I am weaker now than I ever was. I have no claim on you.'

'No, but I am in a position,' said Michel, speaking for the first time.

The girls and I shuffled along the wall a bit on our bottoms, in a bid to see his face properly through the banisters. It was pale and tense. Determined. 'From now on, what you want, Agathe, is exactly how it will be, with no one telling you what to do, or where to go. In our hearts, we have always acknowledged and regretted the terrible wrong done to Étienne. And I know you will love her now, Étienne, as you always have done, because you are a good man. We are her aunt and uncle, you are her father. Her mother will not care one fig; she will be relieved. She is not maternal. The situation will remain unchanged, but Agathe, you will never have to go to Paris again. If she objects, wants you as an adornment, to be photographed with her, like she did in London, taking you out of school for two days, I will tell her that I will go to the press. Tell them the real story. I do not care. But she will. Very much she will care. You will be with your father and your aunt and uncle here, in Provence. Not go to Paris.'

'I'm ten, anyway, next month.'

'Exactly. Next month you are ten. In a few years, a teen-ager. A young woman.'

'And can I still come on holiday to Antibes, in September, before school, like I was going to, with you?' She turned to Étienne.

He shrugged, unable to hide his sadness. 'If Michel –'

'No, not if Michel,' Michel broke in. 'I told you. Every-thing will remain the same, with this' – he flicked a dismissive hand at the piece of paper in Étienne's hand – 'as if it had never happened.'

Thérèse got up. She whipped the sheet from Étienne's hand. Walked to the island and lit the gas on the stove. As the flame leaped into life, she held it within. Burned it, before the three of them.

'DNA,' she said scathingly. 'What is DNA to ten years of love and devotion. Ten years of unconditional love.'

A silence enveloped the four people below us; they were suspended there like characters in a play. Up in the gallery, we, too, turned to stone, hardly daring to breathe. The silence was finally broken by Agathe. Her voice, when it came, was shrill and unnatural. It had a crack in it.

'And you will love me just the same, Papa? Even though . . .' She didn't make it to the end of the sentence.

'Don't say it,' Étienne whispered fiercely, and equally brokenly, holding her close. 'No one knows it. Except the people in this room. And your mother. Who won't want anyone to know. So don't say it.'

She nodded, and they clung on to each other tightly. Agathe had both arms around his neck, hiding her head in his shoulder.

Upstairs, I glanced at the girls and saw them both blink away tears. My own eyes were full, too. We silently got to our feet in the shadows, feeling horribly like interlopers now. Quickly, we slid back along the wall, swallowing a bit, and, like spirits, disappeared out of sight, back down the corridor, fleet of foot, to our rooms.

The girls crept into mine and sat on the bed, which was empty. We could hear their father showering in the bathroom.

'Wow,' said Amelia.

'What a bombshell,' agreed Tara. 'So Agathe is Michel's, is that it? Did I get that right, Mum? They were speaking so fast.'

'You did. And she is. But we keep it to ourselves, OK?'

'Definitely. We shouldn't have heard it at all. Bloody hell, though. Who would have thought?'

Well, I had thought. In what I imagined was a mad moment. And I wondered how many more people might have done, or would continue to do so, over the years.

'So Camille shagged her brother-in-law,' said Amelia. 'How weird is that?'

'Or magnanimous,' I told her. 'Depending on how you look at it.'

Amelia gave me an arch look. 'Crap. I bet she loved it. She's like that, I can tell. And Michel is very good-looking.'

'They're both amoral,' Tara said. 'Similar types. Thérèse is the only decent one in that family.'

'Except Michel was generous to the husband, just now,' I reminded her. 'About seeing Agathe.'

'Oh, yeah. I meant sex-wise, that's all. I agree, he was good about Agathe.'

'I want one of those,' said Amelia wistfully, hugging her knees to her chest and gazing into space.

'What, a child?' I said, alarmed.

'No, a Johnny Depp lookalike with a six-pack and a heart of gold.' She shivered, her eyes on fire. 'Wasn't he amazing? All heart and soul and stunning good looks.'

At that moment, Toby blundered through the door, which was ajar. He was in his boxer shorts with a minuscule T-shirt which bore the legend 'Keep Calm and Marry Harry' stretched taut across his chest. Unshaven, as he had been for days, he reeked of stale bed. He scratched his balls.

'Oh, man, what time is it? Why are we all, like, awake?'

Amelia looked him up and down. Her lips pursed. She looked older, suddenly. 'Toby. Why the fuck have you got my T-shirt on?'

Toby glanced down in surprise. 'Needed a slash. Down the corridor. It was all I could find.'

'Well, take it off!' Amelia leaped off the bed.

Toby saw something in her eyes and, in panic, started to wrestle his huge, hairy torso out of the tiny T-shirt. Quite a lot of tummy protruded over his shorts.

'Not here, you fool!'

She turned him around and hustled him back to their room, but the T-shirt was stuck over his head so he couldn't see. He walked straight into our door.

'Ooof! *Ow!*' he roared plaintively, doubling up in pain.

Totally without sympathy, Amelia continued to steer him on. Before her own door shut, we heard her mutter darkly, 'Shut up, Toby. You'll live.'

I sat there a moment with Tara. We pulled the sheet up over our knees.

'Do you really think Michel's amoral?' I asked her.

'God, yes. He's the biggest flirt ever. A pest, actually. You certainly wouldn't want to be on your own with him. Apparently, he made a move on one of Camille's opera buddies when she came to stay, followed her down to the pool on her own.'

'How d'you know?'

She flushed. 'We found a letter on Camille's bed, complaining about him. It was recent. This summer.'

'Right.'

'Why?'

'Oh, nothing. Just wondered.'

She laughed and got off the bed. 'Still wondering if he was after you in the vineyard, Mum?' She regarded me kindly. 'It was from Atalanta Guggenheim, the American soprano? Legs up to her armpits? Face of an angel?'

'Oh. Right.'

She seized a dress from a chair in the corner. 'Is this mine?' she asked incredulously.

'Might be. I was trying it on.'

'It's way too small for you.'

'It's Lycra, Tara.'

'Yes, but that doesn't mean it's elastic! I hope you haven't stretched it.' She gave me an outraged look and flounced out.

James came in from the bathroom, toothbrush in his mouth. 'What was that all about?'

'I borrowed a dress of Tara's.'

'No, the rumpus downstairs.'

'Oh. That.'

I hesitated. He had been so smitten so very recently. I wasn't sure he was ready for the object of his desire to be quite so tarnished.

'Camille's husband's here. Raising merry hell about how little he sees of Agathe.'

'Ah.' He nodded. 'Well, she's a very devoted mother, of course. Likes her daughter with her as much as possible.'

I nodded. 'Right.'

James turned and wandered back to the bathroom, still brushing his teeth.

I smiled to myself in the empty room.

Chapter Twenty-Nine

The Murray-Brown family sailed for Portsmouth five days later. Our bodies were rested and tanned – and possibly a little plumper, having supped copiously at the land of milk and honey and done little more than flop by the pool – and our hair was a shade or two lighter but, most of all, our minds were made up. In particular, James's. There'd been a bit of a sea change. A bit of a Damascene moment, two days after Étienne had appeared. He'd stayed, Étienne – after all, it was his house, too: the divorce had yet to be finalized and Camille wasn't there – only for a few nights, and in the lodge with Agathe, not in the chateau, but he'd stayed. And God he was nice. He did little more than introduce himself that first evening, strolling slightly self-consciously on to the terrace, ruffling his hair and saying he couldn't really be next door and not say hello, and also did we mind if he used the pool? We'd all got to our feet in a flurry, lolling as we had been in chairs, saying, 'Of *course* we don't mind,' and golly, it was far more his pool than ours. Then we'd persuaded him to stay for a drink. We'd all liked him immensely, then, and the odd times we'd bumped into him in the grounds over the next few days. He was so courteous, so friendly, so *charming*. Or, at least, the female members of the party thought so, possibly because he was the best-looking man we'd ever seen. I'd had to kick Tara to stop her staring with her mouth open when he'd passed us on his way to his car, and Amelia seemed to have urgent business tidying up the pool house when he took his evening swim.

The men couldn't really see the attraction. Toby sulked, but James liked him very much, principally because he got the internet working again. It was temperamental, Michel had explained, with his lugubrious shrug one morning when Drummond had been unable to get his *Telegraph*; and he was not technical, he'd said apologetically. Neither were we. But Étienne knew precisely which provider to ring and harangue in his native tongue, and then which buttons to press. And James, who was the least web-oriented of us all, who didn't even own an iPhone, just a cheap supermarket model, seemed, strangely, the most grateful.

I crept down in the early hours one night, having woken and found the bed empty beside me, to discover him in the study, where the main computer was, staring at the screen. He cleared it quickly when he heard me come in. Stood up, shielding it.

'What are you doing?' I peered around him.

'Nothing.'

'Well, of course it's not nothing. What were you looking at?'

'I was bored. Couldn't sleep. Came down to read my emails.'

'I don't believe you. You hate doing that on holiday.'

'OK, I was looking at . . . porn.'

'Porn? You? Don't make me laugh.'

I pushed past him and sat down.

'What's so funny about that?' he yelped. 'I do have a sex drive, you know.'

'Yes, but you hate porn. What were you looking at, James?'

I tried to see if he'd minimized anything. He had. I pulled it up.

Restaurants à vendre en Provence.

I caught my breath. Stared.

'I was just – just looking out of curiosity,' he faltered. 'Just window shopping. No real intent, no –'

'And last night, too,' I breathed, ignoring him. 'I heard you get back into bed. What have you found? Oh, what have you found, James?' I swung around to him on the chair, my eyes shining.

'Well, no, Flora, nothing. You are not to get excited. It's just that – well, OK, this one . . .' He shoved me across on the chair and scrolled down with the mouse. 'Near Seillans, right, has a view . . . and also a terrace . . .'

And there we sat, bottom to bottom, a middle-aged couple in our jim-jams, poring over a heavenly-looking stone building in an olive grove beside a river, with covers for thirty. Too remote, though, we decided, scrolling back to another he'd found, this time in the centre of a very pretty village, opposite the *hôtel de ville*, which came with a separate house. And then another, so big it was a restaurant within a house, really: beautiful, shuttered and chateau-like, again, *centre ville*; the owners had simply converted their huge hall to accommodate tables, just twenty covers. This one, we loved. It had two kitchens, one for the private family side, one for business. We sat salivating over it until four in the morning, before dragging ourselves up to bed. We slept until noon.

'What have you two been doing?' asked Amelia, when we finally joined them by the pool, having grabbed a coffee en route. She peered at us over her book and sunglasses as we skirted past them.

'Just having a lie-in,' I told her.

'Oh, gross. Too much information.' She went back to her book.

'Better than sex, actually,' muttered James, as we lay down together on adjoining sunbeds on the opposite side of the pool. I giggled.

'They're *giggling*,' Tara told her sister in horror.

Amelia sat up. Regarded me from across the water. 'Don't get pregnant, will you, Mum? You told me the other day your Mirena was running out. I'm not going to have to talk to you about contraceptives, am I?'

She was showing off for the boys' benefit, to demonstrate that, unlike some families, we did pretty much talk about anything. The boys giggled, suitably bug-eyed with awe at Amelia's neck. I told her to wind it in, in no uncertain terms, but it did occur to me there were some things that would have to be talked about and, in a way, surely better done out here than at home?

The following evening, our penultimate one as it happened, we managed to corner them whilst the boys went to help Michel at the bottle bank.

'Won't take you a mo, boys,' I'd said cheerily, engineering the whole thing. 'And Michel will be glad of the help.'

Michel looked like he couldn't think of anything more irritating than having two grunting teenage boys along for the ride in his pick-up, but they settled in the front seat beside him and set off in a crunch of gravel, several weeks of louche living rattling in bin liners in the back.

I grabbed a bottle of rosé from the fridge as James shepherded the girls to a quiet spot at the bottom of the garden: the round stone terrace where Rachel and I had talked. As I approached with the wine and the glasses, the girls were sitting side by side on the bench, opposite their father.

'What's going on?' asked Amelia with wide eyes, not fooled for one minute.

I poured the wine and then we explained, between us, James doing most of the talking, for a change. About our careers. About how mine had obviously hit a sudden buffer and how Daddy's was – well, not entirely what he'd imagined it to be as an idealistic young medical student. And how, now that we'd educated them, got through the worst bit – school fees, etcetera – seen them through all of that, and now that they were young women, almost –

'Shit. You're not splitting up, are you?' said Tara.

'No, of *course* not. Of course not, darling.'

'Bloody hell. Yesterday's lie-in really would have been a last hurrah if they were,' observed Amelia.

James ignored her and carried on. Said how, of course, careers didn't always live up to expectations – one had to be realistic – but how it was also important to recognize it was possible to do something about it. Take a view. Maybe make some changes, before it was too late.

'Don't tell me. You're running away to the circus. You'll throw knives at Mum, who'll be spreadeagled in a bikini. Paul and Debbie.'

'Shut up,' muttered Tara, who was more intent.

'No, we're going to be restaurateurs,' James told her.

She gaped. 'Restaurateurs?' She had to think about it. 'What, run a restaurant?'

'Run and own a restaurant. Out here. In France.'

'How?' They both blanched.

So we told them. About how we – I – had all the experience under the sun to ensure it had the right ingredients to make it a successful enterprise. About Jean-Claude, who we'd talked to last night, and who had once been one of the most celebrated chefs in Paris, and about Mum. About how we all spoke French. How it could work. Would work. How brilliant it could be.

'What did Jean-Claude say?' asked Amelia.

'He leaped at it.'

He had. I recalled how James and I had broached it with him, gingerly at first, but he'd caught on like a forest fire, halfway through James's semi-prepared speech: had jumped to his feet, eyes shining: 'You mean you'd finance it? Run it? I'd just cook, be in charge of the kitchen?'

'In total control of the kitchen, yes. We'd do the rest.'

'Everything I hate, can't do. Loathe. The business side, the politics, the hiring –'

'I'm good at that,' said James firmly.

'And I know people in France. Magazine critics, contacts –' I'd told him.

'So do I,' he'd said vehemently, turning to me. '*Moi aussi.* Friends, who regret now what happened. Have some shame.'

'Exactly. Of course.'

'But not in Paris. I can't go back yet.'

'No, not in Paris.'

'But . . . maybe one day.' His eyes gleamed, remembering what he'd lost. What had been taken. Some unfinished business.

'That's a long way down the track, JC,' James had told him firmly, but his eyes had gleamed a little, too, perhaps at some unfinished business of his own. His own, unfulfilled career. 'Let's start small. Build a reputation. Here, in the south.'

'The best reputation. I would never let you down, never. You'll see. People will come from miles.'

'From Paris?' James had joked.

He'd turned a serious face on him. 'Of course. *Bien sûr, mon ami*. When they know I am cooking again.' His back straightened.

I'd breathed in sharply. Golly. I looked at my mother, who'd been silent the whole time.

'Mum? What do you think?'

I wondered if she'd seen herself more quietly: on the steps of the shabby-chic antique shop, painting chairs, mending old lace, her legs in the sun. But I was wrong: her face suddenly wreathed into smiles.

'Of *course*, yes, darling, of course! I'm in shock, that's all. My one, my only reservation about coming here with JC was leaving you behind. We've always been within minutes of each other, but to be here with you *both*.' Her eyes sparkled, and I realized they were full of tears. 'It's too much to hope for, at my age. All my life,' she admitted, 'I've never dared hope too much. Then you get through, you know? If you don't expect too much. Don't think too much. Don't go deep. Have only happy thoughts. See only nice things.'

It had always been her defence mechanism, I knew. And who was I to knock it? My mother had never been down, subject to depression or moods; she just didn't allow herself. She skated across the surface of life.

'But what about the girls?'

'They'll come, too,' I told her quickly. 'That's the only condition. In the holidays. Or, if they hate it, we'll go back to England then, and you and Jean-Claude will hold the fort. But, having said that, if they're not up for it at all' – I looked around at everyone – 'it's a deal breaker. The whole thing's off.'

Jean-Claude looked shocked, but Mum didn't. She looked very knowing.

I wished I felt half as knowing as James and I sat with our daughters now at the round mosaic table in the sunken terrace, the girls' faces not so jokey now, not so flippant. Digesting. Absorbing. Watching us closely.

'So, basically, we'd move to France,' said Amelia flatly.

'Yes. We'd sell Clapham, buy a place out here – you get more for your money, so it would be nice – and this would be our base. Provence.'

'But . . . what about all our friends? Tara and I don't really speak French.'

'We'd keep Granny's house. In Fulham.'

'Oh!' Having both looked tense and worried, they brightened considerably.

'You mean Tara and I can go there in the holidays? It'll be empty?' Already she was filling it with friends, loud music, everyone spilling out on to the pavement, smoking, drinking, neighbours banging on walls, the whole street vibrating, throwing the best parties in London, the coolest place to be: *Are you going to Amelia's? Her parents have, like, given her this house . . .*

'No, not empty, because, if you're there, Daddy and I will be, too.'

'Oh.'

Tara looked slightly relieved, though. 'So we can choose where we want to be?'

'Up to a point,' said James, more sensibly. 'The family won't be totally dictated to by you. We'd like to think a couple of weeks at Easter here in the sun, perhaps bringing friends; likewise, six weeks in the summer might be very pleasant, at the restaurant's busiest time. Grandpa might be persuaded to come, too. Whereas Christmas, we might spend in Fulham, whilst Granny and JC hold the fort.'

'Yes, and we could pop out for the odd weekend in term time. Pippa Foster does that, to her parents' in Guernsey. It's the same, really, isn't it?' said Tara.

'Exactly. As much as you want,' I agreed.

'And you'll pay?' said Amelia, naturally.

'Within reason,' said James firmly, knowing how inclined I was to promise the earth.

'Say a couple of times a term?' suggested Amelia, keen to firm things up.

'Yes, perhaps about that.' James couldn't help smiling at his elder daughter, whose negotiating skills were akin to his own.

'So, two weekends a term – perhaps with friends –'

'Or perhaps without,' said James crisply.

'Easter and the summer in the sun – and home for Christmas.'

'So we don't miss the parties,' agreed her sister.

They shrugged.

'Cool.'

Their eyes were alight, though. Not so cool. I could see we'd sold it to them. But they had to be realistic.

'Clapham will go, our home for twenty years, and that will be sad. But you'll have a bedroom each at Mum's.'

'We could sell Granny's and keep Clapham?' suggested Tara, but Amelia frowned. Fulham appealed to her. I'd always suspected my daughter of being a closet Sloane.

'We could,' I said, 'but I want Mum to have her independence. In case . . .'

'. . . it all goes wrong with JC?'

'Yes. But I don't think it will,' I said quickly. 'Even though they've just met.'

'It won't,' Amelia agreed. 'They've, like, found each other. After so long. I can sense it. It's amazing, isn't it? That it can actually take so long, a lifetime perhaps, to find the right person? Who you truly click with?'

'Yes, Amelia.' Her eyes were on the pick-up truck appearing in the distance, a cloud of dust behind it. A slight cloud appeared in her own eyes, too. 'It can take a very long time, my love.'

Important to get it right, though, I thought.

And so we were going home. Drummond, Sally and Rachel were leaving the same day, but Rachel was driving to Relais Saint Jacques, she thought, to break the journey, attempting it in one go being too much for her father. I'd sat looking at the map with her very early that morning in the kitchen, a pot of strong coffee between us. She'd looked around wistfully.

'It's so sad to leave. This has been such a – well, a cathartic place to be. Like a retreat, or something. It's as if we all needed it.'

She and I were alone, cases packed beside us.

'I think we did need it. And, sometimes, you have to step right away from your life before you can see it properly. I think we all did that here.'

'Toby! Will you stop arsing around and get out of bed!' floated down from the gallery upstairs. We smiled. A door slammed.

'I know. I definitely needed to get out of the glen.'

'For good?' I asked tentatively.

'No, of course not. Daddy would never sell. But . . . well, I've persuaded him to sell a few of the cottages and buy a flat. In Edinburgh. In New Town. He's so enjoyed getting away, and he can see how remote we are now.'

'Oh – so you and Sally can have a bit of city life?'

'With him, too, yes. Or without. I'm going to employ a housekeeper. A sort of – carer,' she said bravely.

I leaned forward and hugged her. 'Well done.'

'I interviewed one before we left, actually. Didn't have that particular epiphany here. I've been thinking about it for a while. She's called Heather, and she's a tall, handsome Geordie of about fifty. Divorced. Daddy thought she was a friend of mine who'd come for tea. He liked her enormously. Flirted, even. But she can handle that. He asked me, casually, the other day, if my friend Heather would be back?'

'Yes, for ever!' I gave a snort of laughter.

'Well, for three weeks at a time. And then a week to her mother in Durham. For a break. Which she'll need. Then either Sally or I will take over.'

'Or he could come to Edinburgh?'

'Yes, if we're working. Or studying.'

I paused. 'Studying?'

Her cheekbones coloured slightly. 'I've . . . applied to an art school there. Leith's.'

'Oh, Rachel, that's brilliant!' Rachel spent so much of her time painting on the hill, and not just watercolours. Oils, these days. She was good.

She shrugged. 'I haven't heard yet so, who knows, I may not get in.'

'You will.'

'But I thought – you know. Meeting people. And . . . I don't know. Something about your mother, Flora, has inspired me. Something about it never being too late.'

Through the window, we could see Mum and JC, packing their car.

'It isn't. Ever.'

'She is rather tremendous, isn't she? You're so lucky.'

'She is. And I am.'

'Always – in the words of Monty Python – looking on the bright side of life.'

I smiled. 'Quite. And Sally?'

'I'm persuading her to apply to the Jamie Oliver Italian in Edinburgh. Her agency work is a bit unpredictable – she'd be better with a stable job, where she gets to meet people for more than a week or so, don't you think?'

I agreed, but it was said with caution. I think Rachel and

I both knew it might end in tears, and that Sally would never be quite right: but she could be better. And stability would help. One thing was for sure, Rachel was too good and too special to devote her life to Sally and her aging father. I'd always thought the church would claim her one day, and maybe it would. But not yet. Not until her father had died. James would be pleased with her plans, I thought. I got up and busied myself, wiping down the draining board, knowing she didn't like too much attention. Now I knew the truth, I understood why James had felt such guilt about Rachel: why he always went so quiet at the mention of her name. So thoughtful. She'd been left holding the baby. Quite literally.

'She's the eldest, darling, and unmarried, so why not?' I'd once said, to which he'd replied, 'Yes, but I'm the man.'

I hadn't understood. I did now. We'd both help Rachel to get away. If not to Leith art school, then somewhere else. Out to France. Painting holidays. Sally, too, if she'd come, but maybe not together. Separately, to give Rachel a break.

'When are you going to break it to your father about Heather? That she's not an old mate from school?'

'Oh, I already have. Last night. When he'd had a couple of cognacs.'

'What did he say?'

'He said – you mean that rather fine-looking woman with the strapping thighs? Does it include a goodnight kiss?'

'Oh, God! Poor Heather.'

'Oh, don't worry.' Rachel grinned. 'She'll cope. Comes from a long line of demanding Geordie men, she tells me.

She won't take any nonsense.' She gave me a long, clear look as I leaned against the draining board. 'And you, Flora? You found some peace out here?'

Amelia came storming into the kitchen, dragging her case, fuming about the use of a sodding boyfriend who couldn't even pack his own *things*.

'Oh, yes.' I smiled. 'I've found some peace. I've found a great deal, actually.'

'Would you like some 'elp with that, Amélie?'

Étienne appeared in a pink T-shirt and putty-coloured shorts. Really rather tailored ones.

'Oh, gosh, thanks so much, Étienne. That would be super,' simpered my daughter, in textbook Fulham, pausing to flick back her hair. She had lipstick on, something I hadn't seen her wear for ages, not since she'd embraced a more earthy way of life. Also, a pretty top of Tara's.

'And Amelia? Has she found her more feminine side?' murmured Rachel as we watched her follow Étienne out to the car, swinging her handbag.

'Perhaps.' I smiled again. 'Perhaps.'

On the ferry, the long drive behind us, we sat up on deck in gloriously warm evening sunshine, gliding gently over the calmest sea I'd ever seen, skimming smoothly over a glittering English Channel. James and I were offered a *Daily Mail* by the couple beside us, who were getting up to go inside, and James took it with thanks. Behind us, in the second row of chairs, were Toby and Rory and, across the way, Amelia and Tara faced due south to get the last of the rays, both in shorts, both listening to the same iPod, an earpiece each.

Tara, I noticed, was reading the magazine she'd found abandoned on her chair, the one in French. She was so quick. And her French wasn't bad anyway. She'd pick it up in no time. Amelia's, if anything, was better. I tried not to let my imagination run away with me, tried not to let it gallop off to a long trestle table in daisy-strewn grass under the trees, a gingham cloth covering it. Both girls were jabbering away in perfect French to a table full of friends and relations: good-looking twentysomething boys, middle-aged couples – new friends of ours – and Lizzie, too. JC was coming out of the stone farmhouse with a huge platter of seafood to tremendous applause, Mum beaming proudly. I shook my head, banishing the vision, knowing I couldn't get too far ahead of myself. James had yet to resign. Had yet to tell the hospital what they could do with their Monday-morning list of bunions. I sighed and narrowed my eyes to the sun. Earlier, Rory had popped his head over to ask if we'd like a drink, and he returned now, with a tray of gin and tonics. As I poured my tonic into the wobbly plastic glass, James harrumphed beside me.

'What?' I asked.

'Look at this.'

He held the paper out in front of me. Page three of the *Daily Mail* had a colour photo of Camille, in a full-length emerald gown, on the arm of a handsome blond man in a dinner jacket. It was clearly some sort of a gala opening. I read the headline: 'CAMILLE DE BOUVOIR ATTENDS THE PREMIERE OF *DER ROSENKAVALIER* WITH SASHA RAIMONDI.'

'Who is he?' I peered at the photo.

'Some famous Italian conductor, apparently. Never heard of him.'

'Me neither.'

'No doubt poised to inject a little spice into her life.'

'Said with bitterness?'

'No, not at all. Relief. I was a fool.'

'No more than I was. And, actually, James, what we did discover was that our lives did indeed need an injection of spice. It was time. We were both just looking in the wrong places.'

He smiled. We toasted each other with our eyes and then our gins. And then we kissed briefly on the lips, before taking a sip each. As I swallowed happily, I caught the girls' eyes, their heads turned towards us. They rolled their eyes at one another before going back to their magazines. I smiled and lifted my face to the sun. A dazzling whelm of blue sky and sunshine made me squint, and I lowered the sunglasses perched on my head to my eyes, then regarded the glittering sea below. As the ship skimmed ever onwards on its stately bows, I had a feeling, as I gazed down at the water dividing two worlds, of having never been closer to the life I really wanted, with the people I most loved.

Read on for an extract from
Catherine Alliott's
new book

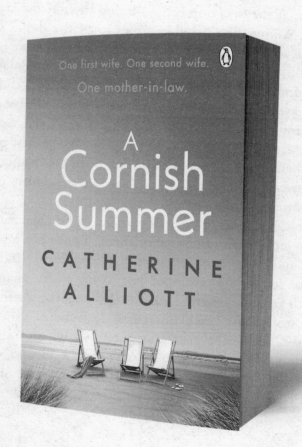

One first wife. One second wife.
One mother-in-law.

A
Cornish
Summer

CATHERINE
ALLIOTT

I

Celia peered nervously through the rain-spattered wind-screen at the towering hedges lining the narrow lane we were snaking along. Sodden trees formed a dark canopy overhead. She wrapped her vintage silk shawl more tightly around her bony shoulders and gave a mock shiver. 'Remind me again why I'm coming with you?'

I gave a small smile. 'You know very well. To paint the swirling seas and the billowing blue skies – your words, I believe, to persuade *me* to let you come in the first place.'

'I had an idea it would all be bathed in golden hues and honey-coloured light, that's all,' she said petulantly, gazing out into the gloom.

'It is, for about ten days a year,' I told her cheerfully. 'If we're lucky we'll catch one of them.' I gave her a bolshie grin and her eyes widened in genuine alarm. 'And – for moral support,' I reminded her. 'Your words again. For which I'm super grateful. And don't worry, the weather will perk up. It's always a bit mercurial down here.'

'Yes, well,' she rearranged her shawl and slid her bottom forwards in the passenger seat beside me, setting her faded orange espadrilles on the dashboard. She lit a cigarette. 'Can't have you entering the lion's den on your own, can we? Might never see you again. And anyway, I've heard too much about this famous family to pass up the chance.' She dragged on her cigarette, narrowing her eyes contemplatively. 'Actually, I might paint the old girl, Belinda, while you do Roger the Dodger. They won't know I only do landscapes, will they? I could do a Francis Bacon on her,' she said suddenly, sitting up delighted. 'All naked and bloody and flagellated – the final reveal coming to light in a dramatic spin of the easel! Can't you just see her face?'

'She'd faint clean away,' I told her as I hit the brakes. A speed camera heralded yet another grey, damp little village with opposing rows of blank-faced stone cottages, punctuated by the ubiquitous green Spar at the end. 'Roger, on the other hand, might like it.'

'Oh? Is he into bondage?' She glanced at me, encouraged. 'Bit of a Max Mosley? The gentry often are.'

'I've no idea what his sexual predilections are, but he's certainly not the crusty old buffer you're imagining. He's quite open-minded.'

'Oh good. I'll twinkle at him.' She grinned. 'See if I get a response.'

'Do not,' I said nervously, knowing Celia's charms of old. Twinkling was mild within her repertoire.

She chuckled darkly, flicking ash out of the window. 'Don't worry, I'll be demure and saintly. I'm on my best behaviour, remember? Your ex-father-in-law is safe with me.'

'Is he an ex?' I wondered aloud. 'I mean, Hugo's my ex, sure, but Roger is still Peter's grandfather, and I haven't remarried, so technically . . .'

'Yes, but Peter's his blood, you're not.'

'True. Ridiculously, I still think of them as my in-laws. Isn't that weird?'

'Beyond bonkers,' said Celia cheerfully. 'But then I think you prolong the whole relationship just to get up Christina's nose.'

'Absolutely not,' I replied vehemently. 'And anyway, nothing could get up Christina's nose,' I added, somewhat ruefully.

Christina, my ex-husband's second wife, a lovely, gracious creature, the soul of kindness, actually, had been nothing but tremendous to me and Peter: so inclusive and generous and uncomplicated, never questioning that I might want Hugo to go to every single rugby match at Peter's school, every parents' evening, every house play – with me beside him, of course – even *persuading* him to pitch up, and not to worry if it clashed with their own children's events, she'd go on her own; they were too young to mind. I told Celia so now.

'Making sure he's perceived as the model divorced father,' she said caustically. 'Just as Belinda and Roger are keen to be perceived by one and all as the model ex-in-laws and grandparents. They're a calculating lot, those Bellingdons.'

'And you, Celia Lonsdale, have got a nasty mind. They were all totally beside themselves at how it turned out, as well you know.'

'Guilt,' she said primly, flicking ash out of the window again which promptly blew straight back in. 'They all know they behaved badly and are praying you'll find a new man and be happy. Belinda is on her knees most nights.

3

The deliciousness is that you categorically *won't*, so they can't all relax, dust off their hands and say, "There. How splendid. Flora's found someone *at last*." '

'Only because they want me to be happy,' I replied uncertainly.

'Bollocks.' She snorted. 'As if they care.' But this last was said softly and I ignored it. I was well ahead of her, anyway.

'She will ask, you know. Belinda. About my love life.'

'Oh, I don't doubt it. And you'll say it's all going swimmingly, when in fact we both know it's Tim when you're really bored, and Rupert when you're feeling up to the banter.'

I took a hand off the wheel and bit the skin around my thumb. 'Thing is, Cele, I don't really fancy either of them. Wouldn't actually care if I never saw either of them again.'

'I know,' she said quietly.

It was all there, in those two little words: and I'd thought it such a state secret. Such a revelation. I was pretty sure I talked the talk about them both when I came back from dates, said what a marvellous time I'd had. Clearly I wasn't going to win a BAFTA. Celia stared diplomatically out of the window, knowing, occasionally, when to stop. Knowing not to say, get *on* with your life, Flora Bellingdon, fifteen years — yes, *fifteen* — after your husband has left you. Hanker no more for a man who's happily remarried with two children. I also knew the real reason Celia was coming with me. To stop me making a monumental fool of myself in the bosom of my ex-in-laws, which, trust me, I would only do if I was catastrophically drunk, and those days were over. Sort of. As we rose to the top of a hill and the countryside opened up tantalizingly around us before disappearing as we plunged once more into a valley, I recalled Celia's eyes, some weeks ago, huge and horrified in the studio we shared, when I'd told her where I was going this summer. She'd lowered her brush. Turned slowly from her easel to face me.

'Sorry . . . *sorry*, Flora. Run that by me again? You're going to paint Hugo's father, in Hugo's family pile, to add to the groaning collection of oils in the ancestral hall, when we all know—' She broke off, stunned. 'Why in God's name did they ask?'

'Because I'm the natural choice, surely?' I'd said defiantly. 'They want to commission a portrait and – well, I'm a penniless portrait artist. I'm also Peter's mother. Of course it should be me. Imagine if they *hadn't* asked me, you'd be up in arms about that,' I finished triumphantly, which was true. Celia would certainly have had something to say. Then again, she had something to say about most things.

'Yes, but they expected you to turn it down, don't you see?' she'd implored. 'They expected you to say – I'm incredibly touched, Belinda, but I've got masses of commissions this summer, why don't you try so-and-so, I hear he's terrific. I mean, sure, if you were neatly remarried, or at least attached . . . but this is supremely insensitive under the circumstances.'

'Oh, they won't know that, will they?' I'd muttered. 'They don't know how I feel about Hugo.'

'Belinda does, you've seen to that.'

Belinda, like Christina, had been on the receiving end

of one or two of my more shameful, demented phone calls. But not for a good few years, as I'd told Celia.

'I know,' she'd said quickly. 'I just think they could quietly get someone local and you'd never know. Or even someone super famous like Nicky Philipps – they've got the dosh, and you wouldn't question that. You'd just think, ah yes, well, of course.'

'Well they haven't, have they?' I'd said shortly. 'They've asked me. And anyway, it's only the two of them rattling around on their own down there. Hugo and Christina are sailing round the Greek islands or something.'

'Great. While the ex-wife works her butt off for his parents.'

I hadn't responded. And I was quiet now as I navigated the lanes, remembering the two spots of colour which had risen in anger in her cheeks, her sharp eyes fierce as she'd resumed work on her canvas. We drove on in silence. At length the rain abated. The sky began to clear and, as we reached the top of another hill, the sun finally came out. In a blaze of glory, the beauty of the Cornish countryside suddenly unfolded dramatically around us: a panoramic sweep of granite walls, sheep-dotted fields flowing over lush green hills and flooding into valleys: countryside I knew so well, having grown up here. Not in one of the pretty, low-lying farms, or in a grand house overlooking the sea like the one to which we were headed, but a stone cottage on the outskirts of a closed-looking village, similar to the ones we'd already passed through.

My mother no longer lived here, having darted instinctively to London to be near me when Hugo had left me and Peter was small: she knew viscerally I needed her, even though I had funds enough for all the help in the world. There she still was, round the corner from me, this born-and-bred countrywoman, in a one-bedroomed flat off the Wandsworth Bridge Road, a good twenty minutes' walk from a decent patch of green, traffic roaring past her window every day. Our old home, or indeed, just Home, was coming up in moments but I wouldn't tell Celia. She'd be far too fascinated and want to stop and peer, but I'd have to do it with several boulders in my throat. Instead we cruised on past the plain granite house, set back from the road, with its four sash windows and garden at the back, plus a small paddock for the pony which was all I'd ever wanted in life.

The field and the pony had been rented and bought for a song respectively by Mum when my father had died, in some vain attempt to plug an enormous gap, which, to our intense mutual surprise, it did. Mum was so like that, I thought, as the house disappeared in my rear-view mirror: making impulsive decisions which confounded all expectations and turned out to be dynamite. I certainly couldn't do without her in London, but I knew she missed her friends, her own life, her little decorating business, which had worked so well down here, but was harder to set up in town with all the competition.

'Oh nonsense, I've got heaps of friends and loads of clients,' she'd say, if I even vaguely suggested her returning to Cornwall.

I knew she had friends – Mum made friends wherever she went – but on the client front there was Mrs Farr downstairs who she did curtains for, Charlie and Anna who adored her and I suspect invented work for her, and

7

Odd Brian who liked to change his walls as regularly as his boyfriends and got Mum in to supervise. But choosing paint colours doesn't pay the bills, and what little money she did earn was mostly from tutoring History of Art, which, years ago, she'd taught. Sometimes she'd pass a few students on to me, particularly if they were rich Russians, claiming she had far too many, but really I knew she worried I didn't make enough from my portrait commissions, about which she was not wrong.

Fortunately, that only affected my own finances. Peter was superbly looked after by Hugo, whose career, after he'd taken over from his father as head of the family water company, had soared to stratospheric heights. I never had to worry about school fees or his holidays, which were coming up, now that school had ended. Hugo was supremely generous – too generous, I sometimes thought. Belinda and Roger, too, showered him with birthday money: a car, I knew, was coming for his eighteenth. None of them could have been kinder, I thought with strange mixed feelings as I gripped the wheel. We plunged down yet another steeply banked lane, one which I knew led eventually to the sea. And as Peter had got older – well, he'd appreciated the finer things in life. Of course he had. His expensive boarding school, and Hugo's alma mater, had seen to that. So if his friends took him scuba diving in the Caribbean, leaping from their fathers' boats, well, it was only natural he'd repay their hospitality at either his grandparents', or his father's, in Hampstead. I mean, naturally they came to me, too, had always come when he was younger: Jamie, Sam, Freddie – all the gang. But Freddie's parents lived down the road from Hugo, and Sam's

just across the Heath, which made it far more conveni-
ent to be at his father's when he only had a weekend from
school before heading back on a Sunday night. He'd felt
uncomfortable, though: and when it had been two weekends at Hugo's on the trot, and then potentially half-term,
I remembered him ringing from school.

'The thing is, Mum, Sam's asked me sailing in Nor-
folk for a few days, and I'd really like to go. And then
Phoebe and Minty have both got parties near Dad's, so I
thought—'

'Yes, of *course* stay with Dad, makes *complete* sense,' I'd
said quickly, never wanting him to feel awkward, ever,
about a situation that was not remotely of his making. I'd
vowed long ago never to play the guilt card.

'But I thought maybe I could pop over on the Sunday,
before I go back?' he'd said, nevertheless feeling that guilt.

'Oh, that's mad, Peter – it's no "pop", as we know. Tell
you what,' I'd said, making it up on the spot, 'I need to
go to Green and Stone for paint that week, why don't we
meet halfway and have lunch in the King's Road?'

He'd agreed happily, relieved. And I'd taken him to the
Bluebird. Even though Peter went carefully for pasta and
not a steak, and I even more carefully went for a salad,
what with a glass of wine each and then two tubes of
oils in the ruinously expensive paint shop opposite – he
insisted on coming with me so I'd had to buy something –
I'd had to ring Mum on the bus on the way home and grab
a Russian, pronto, to pay.

It had been lovely to see him, though; we hadn't drawn
breath. Luckily, Peter wasn't of the grunting, laconic
school of teenage boy. He was open and chatty about

9

school, work, mates, sailing, which he loved – girls, even – and I'd drunk in his floppy blond fringe, huge smile and creasing blue eyes over lunch. So like his father. And I'd almost fainted with pleasure when he'd asked me to look around Oxford with him.

'But don't you want Dad to do that? He'll know far more than me about colleges.'

'Exactly, and I know he'll push Brasenose – and why not, I might well apply – but I kind of wanted to look with my own eyes. And actually, I thought you might like to.'

'I'd adore to,' I'd beamed. Of course I'd adore to. The culmination of all my motherly pride and his hard work – the final hurdle. I couldn't stop smiling, actually, and had recklessly ordered us another glass of wine on the strength of it.

'What are you looking so happy about?' Celia cut into my reverie as I wound down a now extremely familiar lane, brimming with red campion and orange *crocosmia*, to the coast.

'What? Oh, I was just thinking about Peter and me looking round Oxford.'

'Oh, right. I thought you'd already done that?'

'We have. I was just remembering us creeping round Christ Church. We weren't supposed to go in but a door was open and we got lost and giggly up a staircase. Some crusty don threw open his door and barked so ferociously we nearly fell down the stairs.'

She smiled. 'You've done a good job there,' she said candidly, which was high praise from Celia, who mostly said I obsessed about Peter. 'Or the school has. But at that price they bloody well should. Is that the sea or the sky?'

'The sea,' I said happily, my heart rising inexorably at the sight of it, and also, at getting Celia off the thorny topic of the iniquities of a private education, despite the fact she'd had one and I hadn't. 'It'll flit in and out from now on, but keep your eyes on that gap in the hills.'

She did, and buzzed down her window too, sticking her sharp little elfin face out to feel the air, which, now that the rain had cleared, was fresh and soft, full of that just laundered smell of soaking wet grass upon which the sun has settled to steam dry. You could practically see it growing by the roadside from that heady combination.

'So we must be nearly there, then,' she said, bringing her head back in and taking her feet off the dashboard, edging to the front of her seat like a child. 'Didn't you say they lived near – oh, hello.' She lurched towards me in surprise.

I'd taken a sharp left turn through a gap in the hedge into seemingly open country and was driving my poor ancient car at some speed down a red clay track with grass growing down the middle, bumping her up and down along the ruts. Celia clutched her seat and looked alarmed. But I was determined not to ease her in gently. She was such an urbane fount of knowledge in London where she'd grown up; such a sage generally about life, the mind, the heart, despite – or perhaps because of – her own disastrous love affairs. Sometimes I wanted to shake her out of her cool, implacable composure. I knew I had the upper hand in the country, and I wanted her to get a sudden eyeful of Trewarren, with no warning. The back drive, coming as it did across the home farm, afforded that better than the front. I wasn't immune to the grand old estate's charms either and, as we drove under the tall avenue of chestnut trees, the lush green pastures stretching away in an erratic jigsaw of low stone walls, it cast its shimmering, ambiguous spell upon my heart.

I had to slow down, though, when a heifer blocked our way.

'How many bulls *are* there in this field?' Celia asked nervously, closing her window. 'Surely they fight?'

'Cows,' I told her. 'Highland ones, hence the horns. Roger's into rare breeds.'

'Like his wife, by all accounts.'

I shot her a reproving look. The shaggy blonde moved slowly away, looking unnervingly, as Celia observed, like Boris Johnson, and sent us a baleful stare. We rumbled over the cattle grid to where gravel replaced clay. Past the agricultural barn we went, with hay bales stored one side and loose boxes the other, the latter these days housing classic cars rather than horses, and on towards the arch of the coach house and stable yard where the real equines lived. We purred through the yard, slowing down for the cobbles, and anything that might be tied to a ring and ready to swerve its backside nervously into my path. All the gorgeous creatures my hungry eyes sought, though, were sensibly in the shade, at the back of their stables: only a noble iron-grey had his Roman nose over a door and regarded us with mild interest as we rolled on through and under a corresponding arch. As we emerged, Celia was treated, not only to the best view of the house with its famous John Soane façade creeping with pale pink roses, but crucially, to a panoramic view of the sea, which we drove towards, and which faced the front.

'Oh!' She sat up, duly impressed. Speechless, actually.

The large, rambling old manor sat serene and comfortable, its windows glinting in the sunlight, presiding over a shimmering sweep of pure blue. Out of sight, at the foot of a cliff, which wasn't as steep as it looked and which I knew every inch of how to clamber, lay a pale sandy beach. In a far corner was a small wooden boathouse, inside which Hugo and I had spent many happy hours. All we could see from here, though, was the edge of the garden, which stopped abruptly at the cliff, and was a riot of daisies and cowslips. A more manicured lawn and a formal gravel sweep led to a curving flight of shallow stone steps, worn thin by centuries of feet – not to mention bottoms, for this spot afforded the best view – then double front doors, invitingly open under a splendid fanlight. So many laughs on those steps: so many friends gathered, so many flirtations, so many intense, moonlit conversations. If only they could talk.

'Did you fall in love with the house or with the man?'

I hesitated, remembering the first time I'd come here, on a very different sort of day. It had been the dead of winter, with a frost so hard it made everything sparkle, the windows glittering even more brightly than they did today.

Celia saw my hesitation and laughed. 'Oh, don't worry, Lizzy Bennett gets off on Pemberley, which all the feminist literature professors determinedly overlook. Bugger the wet-shirted Darcy, it's his gaff that clinches it for her.' She gazed out speculatively. 'This is certainly working for me. I say, who's this bucolic character straight out of central casting?'

Celia was prone to saying things like 'I say' which unwittingly betrayed her cultivated right-on persona. I turned. Small, slim and crumpled looking, with a hobbling gait, wearing old-fashioned breeches tied up with binder twine, trying to keep from smiling because she didn't do that sort of thing as a rule, and who, on approach, was actually prettier than you'd think, came the only person I was truly looking forward to seeing. Someone who you'd better think twice about before purring through her stable yard and getting away with it.

'This,' I told her happily, 'is Iris. One of my most favourite people in the world.' I jumped from the car and ran to meet her.

Also by
Catherine Alliott . . .

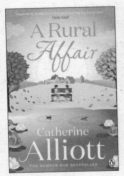

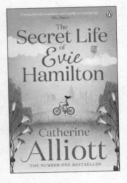

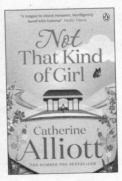